Bonus Book!
For your enjoyment, we've added in
this volume *Beyond Temptation*,
a favorite book by Brenda Jackson!

Selected praise for
New York Times* and *USA TODAY
bestselling author Brenda Jackson

"Brenda Jackson writes romance that sizzles and
characters you fall in love with."
—*New York Times* and *USA TODAY* bestselling author
Lori Foster

"Jackson's trademark ability to weave multiple
characters and side stories together makes shocking
truths all the more exciting."
— *Publishers Weekly*

"There is no getting away from the sex appeal
and charm of Jackson's Westmoreland family."
—*RT Book Reviews* on *Feeling the Heat*

"Jackson's characters are wonderful, strong, colorful
and hot enough to burn the pages."
—*RT Book Reviews* on *Westmoreland's Way*

"The kind of sizzling, heart-tugging story
Brenda Jackson is famous for."
—*RT Book Reviews* on *Spencer's Forbidden Passion*

"This is entertainment at its best."
—*RT Book Reviews* on *Star of His Heart*

Selected Books by Brenda Jackson

Harlequin Desire

*A Wife for a Westmoreland #2077
*The Proposal #2089
*Feeling the Heat #2149
*Texas Wild #2185

Silhouette Desire

*Delaney's Desert Sheikh #1473
*A Little Dare #1533
*Thorn's Challenge #1552
*Stone Cold Surrender #1601
*Riding the Storm #1625
*Jared's Counterfeit Fiancée #1654
*The Chase Is On #1690
*The Durango Affair #1727
*Ian's Ultimate Gamble #1745
*Seduction, Westmoreland Style #1778
*Spencer's Forbidden Passion #1838
*Taming Clint Westmoreland #1850
*Cole's Red-Hot Pursuit #1874
*Quade's Babies #1911
*Tall, Dark...Westmoreland! #1928
*Westmoreland's Way #1975
*Hot Westmoreland Nights #2000
*What a Westmoreland Wants #2035

Kimani Arabesque

†Whispered Promises
†Eternally Yours
†One Special Moment
†Fire and Desire
†Secret Love
†True Love
†Surrender
†Sensual Confessions
†Inseparable

Kimani Romance

**Solid Soul #1
**Night Heat #9
**Beyond Temptation #25
**Risky Pleasures #37
**Irresistible Forces #89
**Intimate Seduction #145
**Hidden Pleasures #189
**A Steele for Christmas #253
**Private Arrangements #269

*The Westmorelands
†Madaris Family Saga
**Steele Family titles

Other titles by this author
are available in ebook format.

BRENDA JACKSON

is a die "heart" romantic who married her childhood sweetheart and still proudly wears the "going steady" ring he gave her when she was fifteen. Because she believes in the power of love, Brenda's stories always have happy endings. In her real-life love story, Brenda and her husband of forty years live in Jacksonville, Florida, and have two sons.

A *New York Times* bestselling author of more than seventy-five romance titles, Brenda is a recent retiree who now divides her time between family, writing and traveling with Gerald. You may write Brenda at P.O. Box 28267, Jacksonville, Florida 32226, by email at WriterBJackson@aol.com or visit her website, www.brendajackson.net.

BRENDA JACKSON

TEXAS WILD
&
BEYOND TEMPTATION

H HARLEQUIN®
entertain, enrich, inspire™

ISBN-13: 978-0-373-83777-9

TEXAS WILD & BEYOND TEMPTATION

Copyright © 2012 by Harlequin Books S.A.

The publisher acknowledges the copyright holder
of the individual works as follows:

TEXAS WILD
Copyright © 2012 by Brenda Streater Jackson

BEYOND TEMPTATION
Copyright © 2007 by Brenda Streater Jackson

Recycling programs
for this product may
not exist in your area.

CONTENTS

TEXAS WILD   7

BEYOND TEMPTATION   247

Dear Reader,

I introduced Rico Claiborne in my seventh Westmoreland novel, *The Chase is On,* as the brother to my heroine, Jessica Claiborne. And you met him again in *A Durango Affair* as the brother of Savannah Claiborne, the heroine in that novel. Your emails began pouring in requesting that I write Rico's story. I put him on my "To Do" list until I thought I had the perfect heroine. Someone who was worthy of his heart.

I found her in Megan Westmoreland.

Texas Wild is Megan and Rico's story as they join forces in search of information about the patriarch of the Denver Westmorelands, Raphel. Their journey takes them from the mountains of Denver to the plains of Texas where the heat they encounter is blazing and wild—and is mainly for each other.

It's time to get to know Rico, up close and personal, in a love story that will leave you breathless and tempt you to get wild.

Happy reading!

Brenda Jackson

TEXAS WILD

* * *

To Gerald Jackson, Sr. My one and only.
My everything. Happy 40th Anniversary!

To my readers who asked for Rico Claiborne's story,
Texas Wild is especially for you!

To my Heavenly Father. How Great Thou Art.

Though your beginning was small,
yet your latter end would increase abundantly.
—*Job* 8:7

THE DENVER WESTMORELAND FAMILY TREE

Raphel and Gemma Westmoreland

Stern Westmoreland (Paula Bailey)

Thomas (Susan)

Adam (Clarisse)

Dillon (Pamela) ①   Micah (Kalina) ⑥   Jason (Bella) ⑤   Riley   Canyon   Stern   Brisbane

Ramsey (Chloe) ②   Zane   Derringer (Lucia) ④   Megan ⑦   Gemma (Callum) ③   Adrian   Aidan   Bailey

⑦ *Texas Wild*

① *Westmoreland's Way*
② *Hot Westmoreland Nights*
③ *What a Westmoreland Wants*

④ *A Wife for a Westmoreland*
⑤ *The Proposal*
⑥ *Feeling the Heat*

ACKNOWLEDGMENTS

To GERALD JACKSON, Sr., my husband, hero and best friend. To my readers who have been waiting patiently for Morgan's story. To my Heavenly Father who gave me the gift to write.

And lead us not into temptation
Matthew 6:13

CHAPTER ONE

"MR. STEELE, YOUR two o'clock appointment has arrived."

Morgan Steele's pulse immediately kicked up a notch with his secretary's announcement. He inhaled deeply and deliberately cleared his mind of everything except the woman who was about to walk into his office. Helena Spears.

"Give me a few minutes, Linda, before sending her in."

"Yes, sir."

After clicking off the line he stood and threw the papers he'd been reading into his briefcase before snapping it shut and inwardly telling himself to relax. Getting Helena to his office had been the first hurdle, and he was determined to make it over the rest. He was smart enough to know that if at first you don't succeed you try again, and today he was a man with a more defined plan.

Putting his briefcase aside he found himself glancing toward the door, his pulse kicking up another notch as he remembered the night—a little more than a year ago—when he had first seen her as she walked into that charity ball wearing a very sexy fuchsia-colored dress. There had been something about her entrance that had momentarily taken his breath away, left him awestruck, mesmerized. And moments later when he had gazed into the warmth of her cinnamon-brown eyes, he had felt it. It had happened just the way he'd known it would once he found her—the perfect woman he had been holding out for all these years.

The only thing that hadn't happened as he'd assumed it would was her acceptance. Lena, as she was known to her family and friends, wasn't seeing things quite his way. She'd tried to explain to him, in a nice way and more than once, that she wasn't interested in a man-woman relationship of any kind. She liked her life just the way it was and had no intentions of wasting her time indulging in a meaningless affair. Nor, she'd gone further on to add, was she interested in a meaningful one, either. She had been there, done that, and she'd learned a valuable lesson and had no intentions of doing a repeat.

All that was well and good but she wasn't dealing with any regular man. At thirty-three he could admit to being arrogant, methodical and unwilling to bend in his pursuit of anything. Once he saw something he wanted and made a decision to have it, he refused to give up until he got it.

And the bottom line was that he wanted Lena.

He had wasted enough time and starting today he intended to use a different approach. He glanced toward the door again when he heard the sound of the knob turning. The moment it opened and his "per-

fect" woman walked in he couldn't help but release
a breath. He felt the sizzle as heat shimmered all
through him. She was wearing a periwinkle-color
business suit and she looked good in it.

"Lena, please come in," he said cordially as his
gaze floated over the rest of her with an analyti-
cal eye. She had just the right amount of makeup
on her strikingly attractive medium brown face,
which placed emphasis on the honey brown curls
that flowed around her shoulders, giving her the appearance of a Queen Latifah look-alike.

She was five feet ten, just the right height for
his six-three stature. Her body was stacked, well
endowed in all the right places, full breasts, wide
child-bearing hips, voluptuous thighs and the most
gorgeous pair of shapely legs he'd ever seen on a
woman. He'd once overheard a conversation she'd
had with his sister-in-law Kylie, who happened to be
her best friend, about what she thought was a weight
problem. As far as he was concerned, she didn't have
one. When he looked at her, what he saw was a full-
figured, thirty-one-year-old attractive and desirable
woman who could start anything and everything inside him to stirring. The woman was temptation at its
finest; however, when it came to her he was prodded
to look beyond temptation and see something a lot
more lucrative and worthwhile. Little did she know
but he intended to open up a whole new world for
the both of them.

"Thank you, Morgan," she said, closing the door

behind her, and breaking into his thoughts. "I'm here for our two o'clock appointment."

From the sound of things she intended to be all business, and that was okay for now. He would give her this time because in the coming weeks he intended to get his. She would find out soon enough that she had just walked into a "Steele cage" and there was no way out. He had failed at plan A, but he had just put plan B into full motion.

LENA PRESSED HER lips firmly together as she looked across the room at the man leaning against his desk. Morgan Steele.

She thought the same thing now that she did that night she'd first met him. He had to be the most gorgeous human male to grace this planet, which prompted her to put her guard up even more. The last thing she needed in her life was a man, especially one like Morgan. She'd learned her lesson a few years ago that when it came to "pretty boys" and "fine as a dime" men, she had to watch her step.

But still…although she tried not to stare but couldn't help herself. She'd been attracted to him from the first. Maybe it was the beautiful coloring of his skin, which reminded her of deep rich chocolate. Or it could have been the long lashes and dark eyes. And heaven forbid if she left out the chiseled jaw, high cheekbones, low-cut black hair and a pair of lips that were too provocative to be attached to any mouth.

The first night they'd met he'd surprised her by

coming on to her and asking her out. She had turned
him down flat. To this day she really didn't know
why he'd bothered since men who looked like him
didn't go for Amazons. They were usually seen with
the slim, willowy, model types. Evidently, once she'd
turned him down he'd seen her as a challenge and
had asked her out several times after that. But each
time she would decline. Finally, she had felt the need
to put an end to whatever game he was playing by
explaining her position on dating to him. She was
too caught up in other things she considered more
important than to be added to another man's list as
his flavor for the month.

As with any potential client she had done her research, which really hadn't been necessary since
Morgan's oldest brother, Chance, had married her
best friend, Kylie, over a year ago. Besides, most
people who'd lived in these parts for a relatively long
period of time knew about those four Steele brothers who ran their family business, the Steele Corporation.

Chance at thirty-seven was CEO. Sebastian
Steele, nicknamed Bas, who had gotten married just
a few weeks ago, was thirty-five and the corporation's problem solver and troubleshooter. Morgan
was thirty-three and headed the research and development department of the company; and Donovan, at
thirty-one, headed the product development division.

Then there were the three female cousins of whom
only one—Vanessa—worked in the company as head
of PR. The other two, Taylor and Cheyenne, had es-

tablished careers outside of the family business but maintained positions on the board of directors.

"May I offer you something to drink, Lena? Springwater, juice, coffee?"

Morgan's question pulled her thoughts back in and she licked her suddenly dry lips and tightened her hand on her briefcase as if it were her block of strength. "No, thanks," she said, moving closer into the room. "And since you're a busy man I'm sure you want us to get right down to business."

"Yes, I prefer that we do since I have another meeting in about an hour."

She nodded, glad they were on one accord. She hadn't known what to expect when he'd set up the appointment. From past encounters she assumed he was a laid-back sort of guy. It was refreshing to know he could be strictly business when the situation called for it.

"Would you like to have a seat so we can get started?" he asked, pushing away from the desk and pulling her thoughts back on track.

"Yes, thanks," she said, forcing the words out from a constricted throat. He was dressed in a business suit that made him look like he belonged on the cover of an issue of *Sexy Man* magazine. She took the seat in front of his desk, and as soon as she sat down she noted once she tilted her head up she had a direct aim to his face, specifically his *let-me-seduce-you* dark eyes.

A sensuous shiver glided down her spine when their eyes met. She cleared her throat, determined to stay on track. "I understand you're interested in purchasing another home," she said to get the conversation going.

"Yes, I am and you come highly recommended."

She couldn't help the smile that curved her lips. "By Kylie?"

He chuckled. "Yes, her too, but I would expect that since she's your best friend. Actually the person who's been singing your praises has been Jocelyn. According to her, you found her and Bas the perfect house."

Lena chuckled. "Finding the right home for Jocelyn was easy. She knew exactly what she wanted."

"Then I should be easy as well since I know exactly what I want, Lena."

There was something about the way Morgan had said the words that had heat flowing hot and heavy through her bloodstream. Was she imagining things or had his voice dropped just a little when he'd made the statement? Deciding she was imagining things she took a deep breath and said, "I need to know your likes and dislikes, and to find those things out there're a series of questions I need to go through to make sure we're on the same page as to what you're looking for in a home." She reached for the briefcase she had placed by her chair, opened it and pulled out a tablet.

"Ready?" she asked, glancing back up at him.

"Yes, ask away," he said, moving around his desk to take the chair behind it.

"Okay. Are you interested in a single-story or a two-story structure?"

"Two-story."

She nodded as she jotted the information down. "Do you anticipate doing a lot of entertaining?"

"Why?"

She glanced up. "Because if you are, you might want to consider a home with a courtyard, a swimming pool or a larger-than-normal living room area."

"Umm, I have a swimming pool at my present home so I'd want to purchase a house with another one. Do you swim, Lena?"

She looked surprised by his question. "Yes."

He nodded. "I'd like another pool and a nice yard. It really doesn't matter how big the living room is as long as the house has a nice-size bedroom. That's where I plan to spend most of my time."

Figures, she thought, jotting the information down. She couldn't help the visual that suddenly flashed through her mind of a sleeping Morgan tangled in silken sheets. "What about the size of the kitchen?"

"What about it?"

She tried not to roll her eyes to the ceiling. "Do you cook a lot? If so, then you might want a home with a large kitchen."

He shrugged. "No, I don't plan on spending a lot of time in the kitchen but my wife might."

She lifted her head from the paper and met his gaze. "Wife?"

"Yes, or perhaps I should say future wife."

"Are congratulations in order?"

"No. But I'm making sure I cover all bases since I don't intend to move again. Whoever becomes the future Mrs. Morgan Steele will be moving into that house with me."

"What if she doesn't like the decor?"

"Then she's free to change it."

Lena nodded. "What about your present home?"

"I want you to sell it."

"All right. Anything other than the swimming pool and large bedroom that you're looking for in the new house? Do you have a preference for carpet or wood floors?"

Again he shrugged. "Doesn't matter to me. Which do you suggest?"

She shrugged her own shoulders. "Either is fine, it's a matter of taste."

"All right, I guess you can show me both."

"That won't be a problem. Now, for your present home, I would need to see it and I prefer that you're there with me when I do."

"Why?"

"So you can point out some things about it that I might overlook, key selling points. We can do a tour and you can tell me things you like most about your house that might hook an interested buyer."

"Okay, you can arrange a date and time with my secretary," he said, trying not to sound too anxious.

"I'm flying out tomorrow on a business trip and won't be back until the end of the week."

"That's fine and I'll get on this right away."

"Thanks, I'd appreciate it."

She stood and glanced over at him. "Any particular time frame you're aiming for to be in your new home?"

"Not particularly. How long do you think it will take?" he asked, coming to his feet as well.

"I don't anticipate it taking long. There are several new subdivisions going up around Charlotte. Is there a certain price range I need to stay in?"

"No. If it's something I want, then I intend to get it."

Another heated sliver passed down her spine with his comment. It seemed he had been looking directly in her eyes when he'd made the statement, but of course she knew she was again imagining things after studying his impassive expression. "All right, then. I'll be in touch when you return. I hope you have a nice trip."

"Thanks."

She gathered her briefcase and headed for the door.

"Lena?"

She glanced back over her shoulder. "Yes?"

"How's your mother?"

Lena couldn't help but smile. No matter when she saw Morgan, he was always kind enough to inquire about her mother. "Mom is fine. Thanks for asking."

"You're welcome."

Lena quickly made it to the door. Without looking back she opened it and stepped out, grateful for her escape. She could handle only so much heat shivering down her spine.

WHEN LENA MADE it to her car she leaned back against the seat, letting her neck relax against the headrest before snapping her seat belt in place. She had been in Morgan's presence less than thirty minutes, but from the way her heart was beating it seemed longer.

There were times when a part of her longed not to be the responsible and sensible person she was. Every once in a while she was tempted to become her Gemini twin, the one who wasn't the good girl; the one who wouldn't hesitate to let her hair down, throw caution to the wind and walk boldly on the wild side. And the first thing she would do is take on a man like Morgan Steele and see if she could hold her own with him. Just the thought of having a one-night stand to feed the sudden, intense hunger she would get whenever she watched a romantic movie, or indulged in those romance novels her secretary would pass on to her, made her breasts tingle.

If she ever became her wannabe mischievous twin, that meant having the courage to trade her sensible four-door sedan in for that two-seater convertible she always wanted—and turning her nighttime fantasies into reality by behaving in such a way that would blow a fuse just thinking about. She didn't want to dwell on all the naughty pleasures she would have.

Lena immediately dismissed the thoughts of her less than sensible twin, knowing she could never do anything like that. Her life was what it was and she couldn't change it. She wasn't the mischievous twin, she was the good one who had responsibilities that took precedence over anything else, including her desire to have Morgan Steele in her bed. Her mother came first.

She was her mother's sole caretaker and had been since her father's death six years ago. Her mother's health began failing her soon after her husband passed, making it hard for her to get around at times. A part of Lena believed it was due more to loneliness than anything else because a lot of her mother's problems were more emotional, especially the bouts of depression.

Her parents had had a rather close marriage and Lena was born after they had already been happily wedded for close to twenty years. A number of miscarriages had convinced her parents they would spend the rest of their lives childless, and Lena had been a big surprise to her forty-three-year-old father and her forty-year-old mother.

Growing up in the Spears household, she had always felt loved and cherished by her parents and she missed her father dearly. For that reason she clearly understood the depth of loss her mother felt and the bouts of occasional depression that had followed. Even now on occasion, Lena would wake up during the night and hear her mother calling out for her father in her sleep, and it always brought tears to Lena's eyes that anyone could have loved someone that deep and strong. It was on those nights after getting her mother settled back down that she would acknowledge the depth of her own loneliness and restlessness and give in to her fantasies of Morgan.

She inhaled deeply as she started her car. She glanced at the clock on the dashboard. In a few hours it would be time to pick her mother up from the adult day care. She went there twice a week for social enrichment and interaction on the recommendation of her mother's social worker. Although it had put a huge dent in her budget, so far it had been a month and Lena hadn't received a call from the day care's director letting her know her mother had begun withdrawing, which usually was a clear sign that she was headed for another bout of depression.

Lena smiled thinking she had an idea as to why. Her mother had been talkative a lot lately when Lena had picked up her, and had told her about Ms. Emily, a newcomer to the day care. It seemed that she and Ms. Emily, who was also a widow in her early seventies, had struck up a friendship and Lena was glad about that. Her mother was someone who didn't warm up to people easily.

And speaking of warming up…she allowed her thoughts to return to Morgan. Everything about him spoke of the dynamics of a man who was used to having his way. Well, unfortunately, she had shown him the few times he'd come on to her that she wasn't putty in any man's hand. The only thing the two of them could ever share was friendship. And after her last serious talk with him about three months ago, he hadn't asked her out again, so she could only assume that he'd finally gotten the message if today was anything to go by. He had acted strictly business.

The last few men she'd fancied herself as possibly having a serious relationship with had painstakingly informed her that as long as she came with extra baggage—namely her elderly mother—no man in his right mind would be interested in marrying her.

She had decided if that was the case, then she would live the rest of her life single and not worry about indulging in a committed relationship because she and Odessa Spears were a package and would remain as such until their dying days.

Deciding she didn't want to spend the rest of the day thinking about the things she would never have, she shifted her thoughts to the things that she could have—namely a big sale if she located Morgan the house he wanted, and if she sold the one he now owned. Pulling off such a feat would pay a hefty commission and she would do her best getting him just what he wanted. And she knew exactly what she would do with the money. She would get her mother involved in even more enrichment programs for senior citizens as well as plan a cruise for the both of them. It had been a while since they'd gone on a vacation together, and it was time that they did.

"YOU'RE LATE, MORGAN. You know I don't like keeping Shari waiting."

Morgan slid into the booth across from his brother

and glanced up into Donovan's annoyed features and rolled his eyes. "Shari today, Kari tomorrow, whatever. Besides, it couldn't be helped. I had an important meeting that I needed to keep."

Morgan glanced around. The Racetrack Café was a popular place in town to grab something to eat and to wet your lips with a drink. Owned by several race car drivers on the NASCAR circuit, it had become one of Donovan's favorite hangouts mainly because his best friend, Bronson Scott, was now one of the drivers on the NASCAR circuit.

Donovan finished off what was left of what he was drinking. "So you did have your meeting with Lena?"

Morgan frowned. "How did you know about our meeting?"

Donovan gave his brother one of his cocky smiles that was known to grate on his nerves before motioning for the waiter to bring him another drink. "To answer your question, I knew something was up with you this morning at the meeting in Chance's office. Most of the time you sat there like you were zoned out. I figured you either had had a rather good night or you were finally putting together a solution to your problem."

They paused in conversation long enough for the waiter to drop Donovan another drink off and to take Morgan's order before Morgan turned narrowed eyes back to his brother. "My problem?"

Donovan chuckled. "Yeah, and don't play dumb.

All of us know how you have the hots for Lena Spears."

The hots didn't come close to covering it, Morgan thought, leaning back in his seat. However, Donovan, who didn't yet know the meaning of one woman for one man, was the last person who needed to know that. "And just who is all of us?"

Donovan grinned. "Me, Chance and Bas, mainly. We're the ones who've been putting up with your bad-ass moods since meeting the woman. Some days you act like it's our fault that she's not interested in you."

Morgan didn't like Donovan's assumptions. "She is interested."

"Could have fooled me. In fact she's doing a good job of fooling a lot of people since she hasn't given you the time of day. How many times has she turned you down for a date, Morgan?"

"None of your damn business." The waiter placed his beer in front of him and it was right on time, Morgan thought, taking a swallow straight from the bottle. It was either that or smashing Donovan's face in.

"Well, you know how I feel about any man running behind a woman. Downright disgusting. It should be the other way around," Donovan said, taking a sip of his drink. "And I understand you're going out of town for a few days to hang out with Cameron in Atlanta. I'm sure sometime during your visit the two of you will have a pity party since he's just as messed up over Vanessa as you are with Lena."

Morgan's features grew dark as he glanced across

the table at Donovan. "Cameron and I are meeting to discuss a business venture we're both interested in and not for any damn pity party." When Donovan merely shrugged Morgan felt the need to add "I hope I'm around when you suffer your first heartbreak."

"Sorry to disappoint you but it won't happen. There isn't that much woman in the world, Morgan. Why settle for just one when the world is filled with so many of them? And now that the Steele Corporation has signed on as one of Bronson's sponsors for NASCAR, and I get to go to many of the races, the pickings are even better. I never knew so many good-looking women were interested in fast cars. Man, if you could only see them. They look just as good with their clothes on as they do with them off. There's this one sista who has a tattoo on her—"

"Hey, spare me the details, Donovan," Morgan said, holding up his hand.

"You don't know what you're missing."

Morgan shook his head. "Trust me, I believe I do."

Donovan leaned back in his chair and rubbed his chin as he studied Morgan. Within a year's time two of his brothers had made it to the altar, and it seemed Morgan was hell-bent on making it three. He liked his sisters-in-law true enough and was happy for his brothers, but his dream girl was one who was no more interested in marriage than he was. Like him the only thing she was interested in was a good time.

"So tell me, Morgan, why did you want to meet here instead of back at the office?"

"Does there have to be a reason?" Morgan asked, putting his bottle down.

Donovan released a long-suffering sigh. "For you, yes. So spill your guts. Get it out."

Morgan glanced away for a moment and when he returned his gaze to Donovan he saw the questions lodged in the darkness of the eyes staring back at him. Knowing he couldn't waste any more time he said, "There are two reasons that I wanted to meet with you. The first is to let you know that I met with Edward Dunlap again."

Donovan nodded and lightly rubbed his chin, regarding his brother intently. "Does that mean you've finally made a decision about running for that city council at-large seat in the fall?" he asked his brother.

He'd known that for years a number of the African American leaders around town wanted Morgan to strongly consider a political career. He had charisma, charm and an ingrained sense of doing what was right. His community service—as well as his public service record—was astonishing and included such notable accomplishments as leading Charlotte's Economic Development and Planning Council.

Another plus was that Morgan had been born and raised in Charlotte. The Steeles were one of the first families to begin a black-owned business that now employed a lot of people and who didn't hesitate to pay their employees a very decent salary.

Another plus Donovan knew Morgan had in his cap was the Steele Corporation's infrastructure. They were a company that believed in being loyal to the people who worked for them. When they had a chance to make a bigger profit by outsourcing a lot of their production department, they had refused since it would have meant putting over five hundred people out of a job.

Yes, there was no doubt in Donovan's mind that if Morgan ever decided to seek a political office he would get it. Some even had him pegged as the man who would eventually become the city's first black mayor.

Only a selected number of individuals were born to be public servants, and he'd always felt that Morgan was one of them. And although Morgan downplayed such, Donovan knew that deep down Morgan did want to become a political candidate mainly because of his ingrained sense of always wanting to help people.

"No. I haven't made a decision, but I am giving it more thought than I did before. Dunlap feels the time is right. He's also afraid if I don't run, Roger Chadwick will, and both you and I know if that happens he will hurt the city more than help it."

Donovan chuckled harshly. "That's an understatement."

"I have to know that I have certain things in place before making my final decision, and one of them involves you," Morgan said.

"Me?"

"Yes. *You.* I'd like you to be my campaign manager if I do decide to run."

Donovan smiled proudly. That meant Morgan

being a candidate was a high likelihood. "Consider it done."

Morgan nodded. "Thanks. Now for the other reason I wanted to meet with you. I met with Lena today because I've decided to sell my house and plan to buy a new one. She'll be handling both transactions for me."

Donovan looked at him and shook his head. "It's your house to do as you please with, but I'm surprised you'd want to sell it. You've always talked about how much you like your home. According to you it was the 'perfect' house."

"It still is, which is why I wanted to meet with you."

Donovan leaned back in his chair. The expression on his face was one indicating he was clearly confused. "Evidently, I'm missing some point here, so maybe you ought to go ahead and tell me what I got to do with you selling your house."

Morgan picked up his beer bottle and took another sip. "Lena mentioned that once I put my house on the market she'd probably begin showing it to a lot of people."

Donovan rolled his eyes toward the ceiling. "Yeah, that's usually how it works."

"That's all well and good," Morgan said, ignoring his brother's sarcasm. "But I don't want anybody to buy it."

"Then why in blazes are you selling it?"

Donovan waited for him to answer and when he saw Morgan wasn't quick with any answers, he couldn't help but laugh when he figured things out. "You're pretty damn desperate to resort to putting your house up for sale just to get on Lena's good side." Donovan's brows shot up. "But you still haven't told me what any of this has to do with me."

Morgan took another pull from his beer bottle. "I want Lena to try to sell it, but in the end I want to feel comfortable knowing the person buying it will take care of it."

"And?"

Morgan sighed. "And I want you to be the one to buy it."

First a grin spread across Donovan's face as he thought Morgan was joking. But after studying his brother's features and seeing Morgan was dead serious, Donovan began shaking his head adamantly. "No can do, man. I don't need a place as large as your house. My condo is just fine."

"But don't you want your space?"

Donovan took another swallow of his drink and said, "I have enough space, thank you very much. I do one woman at a time, so that's all the space I need. Besides, your house is on an acre of land. I don't do yards. I never got along with grass. I don't own a mower and don't plan to buy one. It doesn't bother me to pay those exceedingly high association fees for the golf course in my backyard, although I'm not a golfer. It goes with my image, one I want to keep. Besides, I always thought your place was too big for one person. I still do."

"I need you to buy it, Don."

"Aw, hell, Morgan, why me?"

"Because Chance, Bas and Vanessa already have homes, and Taylor and Cheyenne never stay in one place long enough to own anything but the clothes on their backs. You're my only hope."

"But I don't understand. If you like your house, why are you selling it in the first place? You never did answer that question, although I have an idea."

For a moment Morgan didn't say anything. Then he said, "And your idea is probably right. Selling my house is part of my current plan and that's all you need to know. I'm really hoping things don't get that far, that Lena will realize my present home is the perfect one for us. But just in case things don't go the way I want, I need to have a backup and I want you to be it."

Donovan leaned back in his seat and released a long sigh, the second one in a matter of less than thirty minutes. He studied his brother, the one known to want the perfect everything. Three years ago he had built what he'd touted as the perfect house, and now he was willing to risk losing it for what Morgan saw as the perfect woman. Go figure.

"Is she worth all this, Morgan?" Donovan asked, truly needing to know.

Morgan didn't say anything for a moment. It wasn't that Donovan's question had him thinking, it was just that he didn't know what he could say to make his brother understand. But he believed that although Donovan didn't have a clue how it felt to be undeniably drawn to one woman, one day he would.

But for now the only thing he could do was answer the question as truthfully as he could.

"Yes, Donovan, Lena Spears is definitely worth it."

CHAPTER TWO

AFTER GLANCING AROUND the room for the second time, Lena finally looked over at Morgan. "How can you even think of selling this place? Your home is simply beautiful."

Morgan smiled, pleased with her compliment. Her question was similar to the one Donovan had asked him last week, but of course he couldn't provide her with the same answer. However, it sent a jolt through his stomach that she liked his home. He'd been hoping she would. "I've outgrown the place and would like something bigger, more elegant. Your job is to find me something more perfect than what I already have."

He watched as she scanned the room again. It was just the living room. She hadn't seen the rest of the house, and he couldn't wait until she did. More than one person had offered to buy his home on the spot after seeing it, yet he had never once considered selling...until now, and only as a last resort. A part of him was still holding out that Lena would love it and want to live in it with him. But if she preferred living some place else, then he would gladly move.

"I'd like to know how you can outgrow something

like this," she said, reclaiming his thought. "In my line of business I've been through plenty of homes, but none ever took my breath away from the moment I walked through the front door like this one did. There's no way this place won't sell quickly."

Her last statement was something he didn't want to hear, which was the main reason he'd gotten Donovan involved. "Come on and let me show you the rest of it."

An hour later he and Lena were sitting in his kitchen sipping glasses of iced tea. He tried not to make a big deal that technically this was the first drink they'd shared together alone. They had shared a drink that night at the charity ball, a glass of punch, while standing near the buffet table. And then at Chance and Kylie's wedding they had stood next to each other drinking champagne. The same thing had occurred at Bas and Jocelyn's wedding. But now he had her alone on his turf, and as he sat across from her watching her take slow sips of her tea, he couldn't help noticing how her eyes seemed to take on a darker shade in the March sunlight. Seeing her eye color change did things to his insides. And then there was her scent, a luscious fragrance that nearly had him groaning.

"I know you get tired of hearing me say this, Morgan, but your home is gorgeous," she said, breaking into his thoughts. "I'll be able to find a buyer with no problem, but to be honest with you I'm not sure I'll find a place better for you to live. It's just something about your home, the way you have it decorated, the layout. Even the yard is huge and just take a look at this kitchen." She glanced around. "It's a cook's dream. Any woman would love to lose herself in here. How long have you lived here?"

He pulled his gaze away from her mouth. He'd been watching every word flow from it while thinking of a million things he'd love to do with it, and every one of them was increasing the rate of his pulse. "For about three years now. I bought the land six years ago but didn't get around to building the house until then."

He decided not to go into details that it had taken him three years from the time he had purchased the land to finally approve a design from the architect he'd hired. In his book everything had to be perfect. His brothers would often tease him about always wanting things just right, to the point that it would drive them crazy at times, but he always ignored their taunts. He couldn't help that he was a stickler for how he wanted certain things he deemed important.

"I might as well tell you that Donovan might be interested in buying this place," he said, deciding now was as good a time as any to make that part known. He watched her arched brow rise in surprise.

"He is?"

"Yes, but I don't want you to concentrate on him as a potential buyer just yet. Show it to others, see what they think and how much they're willing to pay before I seriously consider Donovan's offer. I promised him first dibs, but I want to be sure if I do I'm offering him a fair price."

She nodded. "That sounds reasonable," she said, glancing down at her watch.

Morgan noticed the gesture. "Do you have another appointment this afternoon?" he asked, knowing she didn't. She had told him earlier that he was the last person she was scheduled to see that day, other than the lunch she had planned with Kylie around one.

She glanced up and met his eyes. "No, sorry if I appeared distracted for a moment but I was think-ing of my mother. She went on a field trip with her adult day care today and usually I would have heard from them by now letting me know that she didn't fare well. With no phone call I'm hoping that means she had a good time."

He nodded. "Where did they go?"

"The zoo. How was your trip out of town?"

Sensing her need to change the subject he said, "It was great. I had a business meeting with a friend named Cameron Cody. I believe you met him at both Chance's and Bas's weddings."

She nodded as she took another sip of tea. "That's the guy who tried to take over your company at one time, right?"

Morgan chuckled, which he did every time he was reminded of that. "Yes, he's the one. In the end Cam-eron wasn't successful in doing that, but he was in forging a friendship with all of us…at least everyone except Vanessa. She never got over it."

"But you and your brothers did?"

"Yes. We couldn't help but respect a man like Cameron, a self-made millionaire. Although he was determined to add the Steele Corporation to his list of acquisitions, he wasn't ruthless about it. He's a sharp businessman, and the four of us couldn't help but admire him for it. After it was all over we all became good friends."

"I get the feeling Vanessa doesn't care for him much."

Morgan smiled. "No, she doesn't." He decided not to mention that after spending time with Cameron in Atlanta this weekend it seemed they had the same intentions regarding finally taking matters into their own hands to start relentlessly pursuing the women they wanted.

"I'd better be going. I don't want to take up too much more of your time," Lena said, coming to her feet.

It was on the tip of his tongue to try his luck and ask her out again, but he knew like all the other times chances were she would turn him down. Besides, the key to his plan being a success was getting her to assume he was no longer interested in her.

"You're not taking up any of my time unnecessarily. I like this place and want to make sure whoever buys it is worthy."

He stood and then asked, "So what's the next procedure?" He watched as she opened her folder.

"As far as this house goes, it's as good as sold. It has too many strong points for it not to be a quick buy. All the expensive moldings, the marble in the bathrooms and the bathrooms period. They're beautiful and spacious and you're using all the cabinet space to the best advantage. This house is rather large for one person. You're evidently someone who likes his space."

He shrugged. "Not really. I don't mind sharing my space with the right person."

"Well, to answer your question," Lena replied, "what's next is the installation of a lockbox. You don't have a problem with me showing your home when you're not here, do you?"

He wasn't crazy about the idea but knew he couldn't tell her that. "No, I don't have a problem with it."

"Good. I'll try to call before I drop by with anyone."

"That's fine. Do whatever you need to do." He came around the table to stand in front of her. "I'll walk you out since I need to leave myself. I have to drop back by the office to finish up some paperwork and then I'm expected to show up for dinner later at Bas and Jocelyn's place."

Lena smiled as she stood. "I can't help but smile every time I think of how Bas talked Jocelyn in changing their wedding date from June to February."

Morgan grinned. "Chase did the same thing with Kylie. Both Jocelyn and Kylie got cheated out of June weddings because of my eager brothers. I'm glad Jocelyn was able to finalize everything she had to do so she could move from Newton Grove to here permanently. Otherwise, we would have been tempted to ask Bas to take another leave of absence or he would have driven us all nuts."

"They seem so happy."

"They are, and so are Chance and Kylie. Marriage seems to agree with some people."

"Well, yes, I'm sure it does."

He watched how she quickly gathered up her belongings. He got the distinct impression that his closeness was bothering her. "I better get going," she said.

"Okay, I'll see you out."

As he walked her to the door he said, "I'd like weekly updates. Will that be a problem?"

She glanced over at him. "No, that won't be a problem. I'm checking on an area of homes a few miles from here. It's a new subdivision but I don't think the property is more than what you have now. You like a lot of land, don't you?"

"Yes, more yard for my children to play."

He could feel her gaze on him. "You want children?"

"Sure, one day. Don't you?"

"Yes, but…"

He turned to her when they reached the door. "But what?"

"Umm, but nothing. I'll see you later, Morgan," she said, offering him her hand for a business handshake. "And I appreciate you allowing me to handle things for you."

He glanced at her hand before taking it. "Like I said, you come highly recommended. One thing you'll discover about me, Lena, is that I choose my business associates carefully." *As carefully as I choose my lovers,* he decided not to add.

He saw the expression on her face the moment their hands touched. He also felt her response. Although she might wish otherwise, the chemistry between them was still there. He was tempted to lean in and kiss her. Take her mouth the way he'd thought of doing so many times. Once he slipped his tongue between her parted lips, there would be no stopping him. A kiss could be defined as friendly or intimate. Any kiss they shared would definitely be intimate.

The moment he released her hand she turned and he watched as she quickly began strolling down the brick walkway to her car, liking the sway of her hips as she did so. Today she was wearing another powerhouse business suit. This one was a mint green and brought out the rich brown coloring of her skin tone. Something else it brought out was the primal male inside him when he'd gotten close enough to notice she was also wearing a mint-green bra, which made him wonder what else under her clothes was the same color.

He sighed deeply as she pulled back out of his driveway. Part of his plan was to take things slow so she could get to know him, but all he could think about while sitting across from her at that table was speeding things up a bit, saying the hell with slow and taking her into his bedroom and making love to her like there was no tomorrow.

But he knew doing such a thing would only result in a satisfaction of overstimulated hormones and he wanted something a lot more out of a relationship with Lena. So for now the between-the-sheets fantasies had to take a backseat to what was really important, even if the waiting killed him, because everything he was doing now would be all worth it in the end.

LENA LET OUT a deep breath as soon as Morgan's home was no longer in sight. Talk about temptation, she thought, coming to a stop at a traffic light and pursing her lips. Each time her gaze had met his she had been tempted to reach across the table and trace her fingers across those delectable lips of his. That would have given her only a little contentment. What would really have satisfied the woman in her was to have plastered her mouth to his and kissed him the way she often thought of doing.

But that wasn't all. She could vividly recall when he had shown her his bedroom. The moment she had seen the king-size bed with royal-blue satin sheets, an all-consuming need had spread all through her body. And when he had left her side to show how the remote to his window blinds worked, her gaze had devoured him, appreciating how his lean and firm thighs fit his designer trousers and how his broad, muscled shoulders fit the white shirt he wore. And just for a moment, when he had leaned across the bed to brush a piece of lint off the bedspread, she had imagined herself in that bed, tangled in those sheets with him. By the time she had taken a gulp of that ice-cold tea he'd prepared, she had needed it to cool off.

Inwardly she groaned when the traffic light turned green. She had to let go of this obsession since it would lead nowhere. She glanced at her watch again. She and Kylie had their regular lunch date, and today they would plan for Kylie's baby shower.

She smiled thinking that her friend was having another baby after almost fifteen years. But this time the pregnancy would be totally different. Kylie was not that sixteen-year-old who had found herself facing a teenage pregnancy alone after her parents had turned their backs on her. Now she was a woman married to a wonderful man who loved her and who would make her baby a wonderful father.

Lena couldn't help but be happy for her best friend, and inwardly she could admit she was a little envious although such happiness could not have happened to a more deserving person than Kylie. But still, that didn't stop Lena's heart from aching from what she didn't have. Here she was, at thirty-one still the bridesmaid but never the bride, still the godmother but never the mother. And what was so sad was knowing she would never be a bride or a mother.

She inhaled deeply, refusing to give the state of her future any more thought that day.

"WHAT'S THIS I hear about you selling your home, Morgan?"

Morgan lifted a brow. He highly suspected that

Bas had heard the news from Donovan, not that it was a secret.

"Yes, you heard right," he said, accepting the glass of wine his brother was offering him.

"How come?"

Morgan gave a sigh of relief. At least Donovan hadn't told Bas everything. "What do you mean how come?"

"Just what I ask," Bas said, dropping into the lounge chair across from where Morgan sat. "How come? You love that house. As you've told us so many times, it's perfect for you."

Jocelyn was in the kitchen and Morgan could only hope she wasn't privy to their conversation. "Things change."

"Bullshit. Tell that to someone else. Things might change but you don't. You've had this obsession with things being ideal in your life for as long as I can remember. So what's really going on with you, Morgan? What's the real reason you're selling your house? Discovered you're sitting on a gold mine or something?"

"Wished it was that simple," Morgan managed to say finally, studying his glass of wine for a moment before lifting his gaze to Bas's curious one. "Colin Powell once said, and I quote, 'There are no secrets to success. It is the result of preparation, hard work and learning from failure.'"

Bas rolled his eyes. "Will you give it to me straight, Morgan?"

Morgan smiled as he momentarily traced his finger around the rim of his glass. Bas was a trouble-shooter; he looked for problems where there weren't any. Morgan glanced back up and met his brother's gaze. "Okay, Bas, you want me to give it to you straight? Then here goes. Lena Spears."

Morgan watched his brother's expression. For a moment he looked genuinely bewildered. Then slowly, Morgan saw the exact moment he figured things out. For a while there Morgan had gotten worried since Bas wasn't normally a slow man.

"I hope you know what you're doing," Bas said sharply, narrowing his eyes at him.

"Trust me, I do. I want her, Bas."

"Tell me something I don't know, Morgan. That's been evident now for over a year. It's also been evident to everyone but you, it seems, that she doesn't want to be wanted…at least not by you."

"Then it's up to me to convince her otherwise."

"And you'll go so far as to sell your house to do it?"

"Whatever it takes. Wish me luck."

Bas shook his head, smiling. "You need more than luck, brother. You need prayer. I get the distinct impression that Lena likes her life just the way it is."

"I got that impression too, and I wanted to know why such a beautiful woman would not want a man in it."

"Did you ask Kylie?"

"Yes."

"And what did she say?"

"At first she was tight-lipped, like she didn't want

to betray Lena's confidences or something. Then she mumbled something about the men in Lena's past not being able to get past the fact that she and her mother are a package deal."

Bas frowned. "If that's true, then those weren't men, they were assholes who must have been hatched. Who in their right mind would even think about making a person choose between a lover and a parent?"

"How about someone like Dr. Derek Peterson?"

Bas's frown deepened. "He's a good example that what I said is true since everyone knows he's an asshole."

Morgan chuckled. Derek, who'd always taken ego trips even while in high school, was not a favorite of the Steele Brothers since that night a few years ago when he'd tried pulling his aggressive macho ways on Vanessa. Ignoring their advice she had gone out with him. The date had ended rather quickly when she had to resort to kneeing him in the groin when he proved he didn't know the meaning of the word *no*. He never forgave Vanessa for using that technique on him, and to this day was still pissed at the Steele brothers for having taught her how to use it.

"Well, he must not have been the only one for Lena to have developed a complex about it to the point where she thinks the majority of men think that way. I intend to prove otherwise, and certain things can't be rushed. Using her as my Realtor will buy me some time."

He took a sip of his wine, determined to make Bas

understand as he'd done Donovan a few days ago. "I'm serious when I said I want her, Bas. But more importantly," he said, meeting his brother's gaze, "I intend to have her."

"So, Mom, how was the trip to the zoo?"

"It was nice. Mr. Bannister got sick again and Ms. Lilly wanted Mr. Arnold to share his wheelchair but he wouldn't."

Lena nodded. She knew Ms. Lilly was an older woman in her early eighties who had begun showing signs of Alzheimer's last year. On several occasions she had assumed Odessa Spears was her daughter and would try to make her follow her commands. "What about Ms. Emily? How did she do today?" she asked, and glanced over and watched her mother smile.

"Why, Emily did just fine with this being her first trip and all. But she had company. Her granddaughter and great-granddaughter went with us as chaperones. Did I ever tell you that she had six grands and two great-grands?"

Lena's stomach tightened since she knew where this conversation was headed. "Yes, Mama, you told me."

"And Emily agrees with me that it's a shame that I don't even have a grand. She said she can't believe a young woman as pretty as you can't find herself a man."

Lena sighed deeply. There was no way she could tell her mother that men were out there a dime a dozen and she didn't have to "find" one. The problem was hooking up with one who didn't have stipulations that weren't acceptable to her. Lena knew her mother's heart would be crushed if she ever discovered the real reason men didn't come calling and those who did usually stopped real quick, as if in a hurry once they discovered her role in her mother's life.

"Mom, like I told you, my job keeps me busy."

"No job should keep a woman too busy for a man. You're thirty-one. I was married to your father before my twenty-first birthday and we were so happy together. That man was my life. You came along twenty years later and then the both of you became my life. A woman couldn't have been happier. A husband and a child have a way of fulfilling a woman's life."

"I'm sure that's true, Mom, but—"

"And take a look at Kylie. I love Tiffany dearly with her being your godchild and all, but a new baby is nice and it didn't take Kylie long after her marriage to do her duty."

Lena shook her head. *Her duty.* She didn't want to think about what her mother figured her duty was.

"But I don't want to talk about Kylie. You're my daughter and I want to talk about you."

Lena sighed. Her mother hadn't been this talkative in a long time. A part of her was happy about it, but she would be even happier if they discussed another subject. "Mom, we've talked before. They

don't make men like they used to," she said, coming
to a stop at a traffic light.

She glanced over at her mom and met her gaze
when Odessa asked, "Is that what's bothering you?
Are you figuring there isn't a man out there like your
daddy was? Probably not, but it's the woman who
usually makes the marriage and not the man. You
just have to let him think that he does. Why, I can
recall when your father…"

Lena pulled off when the traffic light changed to
green as her mother relived pleasant memories. She
was grateful for the change in subjects, because if
they had stayed on their same conversation path,
there was no way she wouldn't eventually have lost
it. Having lunch with Kylie and seeing how pregnant
she looked made her unconsciously rub her stomach
wishing more than anything a baby could be there.

She cleared her throat in an attempt to keep her
tear ducts from working. For some reason she'd been
in a melancholy mood lately, but she knew it would
eventually pass and she would snap out of it.

Considering everything, she really didn't have
much of a choice.

CHAPTER THREE

LENA GLANCED AROUND when she entered the restaurant. She had been on her way to the Steele Corporation for a meeting with Morgan when she received a call from her secretary saying Morgan wanted to meet with her here instead of his office.

She sighed, feeling tired from a restless night. Her mother had had another outburst for her father and it had taken a while to get her settled back down. It always pained Lena to watch her mother relive her grief. After taking her mother to the day care this morning she had stopped by to visit with Delphine Moore, her mother's social worker.

Delphine had explained that the reason her mother kept having her bouts of grief, even after six years, was that she hadn't yet found anything to fill the void in her life left by her father. God knows it hadn't been for lack of trying on Lena's part. According to both Delphine and Lena's mother's family physician, Odessa's issues, both mentally and physically, stemmed from the same thing. She needed something motivating in her life, something that would give her the will and desire to keep living.

Something like a grandchild.

The conversation she'd had with her mother a few days ago was still firmly embedded in Lena's mind. She knew her mother was lonely and that was understandable. She also knew her mother probably saw her life slowly drifting away without the love of a grandchild to cherish. A part of Lena wished more than anything she could give her mother a granddaughter or grandson to love during her remaining days on earth, but such a thing wasn't possible. Kylie had suggested that she try looking into programs where elderly adults could volunteer to act as surrogate grandparents. Since her mother got around fairly well with minimum help on her good days, that was one idea worth checking out. Lena's heart sank every time she thought of her mother being unhappy.

"May I help you, miss?"

The waiter's question reined Lena's thoughts back to the present. "Yes. I'm to meet Morgan Steele here."

The waiter smiled. "Yes, please follow me. Mr. Steele is waiting."

As she followed the waiter it wasn't long before she was staring into the contours of Morgan's handsome face when he stood for her approach. As usual he was dressed in a tailored suit and looked the epitome of a successful businessman. By the time she reached his table, her heart was jumping crazily in her chest. Although the eyes staring at her were intense, his facial expression was solid, unreadable. But that was all right, she tried assuring herself. If he were to look at her any other way, with even a hint of an open invitation right now, her Gemini twin would be tempted to come out, and heaven forbid if that happened. She had dreamed of Morgan last night, and those dreams were still vivid in her mind. Her body had been flooded with adrenaline of the most sensual kind. In her fantasy he was an expert lover, and she would bet that in reality he would be the same.

By the time she reached his table, her heart was just about ready to explode in her chest. She cleared her throat. "Morgan," she said, automatically reaching her hand out to him.

He took it and for a moment she thought he held it a second longer than necessary. "Lena. Sorry about the change in plans but I'm glad you could meet me here. I appreciate your flexibility."

"No problem," she said, taking her seat with fluid ease. The place Morgan had chosen for lunch was elegant and the furnishings spoke the part. The chairs were soft leather with high-contoured backs for both comfort and style. There was a lit candle in the middle of the table, and it came to her attention for the first time that they were sitting in the back, almost in an alcove that provided a semblance of seclusion and a bit of intimacy—not at all in keeping with what should be a business meeting.

As if he read her thoughts he said, "I had a business meeting here earlier and decided that instead of going back to the office or changing location we could meet here. I hope you don't mind."

She shook her head. "No, I don't mind. It's a nice place."

"Yes, it is."

Morgan knew he couldn't tell her that this was the place he had intended to bring her for their first lunch date, which she never agreed to. And he'd had to do some underhanded maneuverings for her to be with him now. "So, I understand you have information for me," he said.

"Yes. I might have an interested party for your home as well as a place you want to look at. It's located not far in—"

"Well, aren't we a cozy twosome."

A sudden wave of irritation touched Morgan when he glanced up into the face of Cassandra Tisdale, a staunch member of Charlotte's elite social group. She was one of the most self-absorbed women he knew, and to top it off, she was Bas's former fiancée.

The only good thought about that was the word *former*. Bas had broken off the engagement the night of Chance and Kylie's wedding and hadn't given the family a reason why. But it hadn't been that hard to figure things out. Cassandra and Bas were as different as day and night, and a marriage would have made them the odd couple, whereas Bas and Jocelyn were a perfect match.

He slowly came to his feet. "Cassandra, I didn't know you were back." Rumor had it that she left town for an extended trip to her parents' vacation home in the Bahamas a couple of weeks before Bas's wedding because she didn't want to be anywhere near Charlotte when the event took place.

"Oh yes, I returned this week. I had a wonderful time."

Doing nothing, he surmised. Cassandra saw her role in life as to not earn a living but to give parties, entertain and remain a social butterfly. She was wealthy and intended to marry wealthy. Rumor further had it that since her breakup with Bas she had set her sights on Donovan's best friend, Bronson. Luckily Bronson was smart enough to not give Cassandra the time of day.

Everyone also knew she had only latched on to Bas in the first place after Dane Bradford had gotten back with his wife, Sienna. Cassandra had been Dane's girlfriend in high school, but the two had broken up when they'd gone to separate colleges. When they returned to Charlotte she had figured Dane would come rushing back to her. Instead he met and married Vanessa's best friend, Sienna Davis.

Almost two years ago Dane and Sienna began having bad times in their marriage and filed for a divorce. Both Cassandra's family as well as Dane's had hoped with Sienna out of the picture Cassandra could become part of Dane's life again. That didn't happen because Dane and Sienna eventually got back together. Not long after that Cassandra had set her sights on Bas. Eventually, she and Bas had become engaged, but Bas had called off the wedding before a date could be set.

"Glad to hear you had a wonderful time." He glanced over at Lena. "I'm sure you know Lena."

Cassandra's smile didn't quite reach her eyes.

"Yes, I know, Lena," she said, giving Lena only a cursory glance. "I'm really surprised to see the two of you here together in such a cozy setting. I'm disappointed in you, Morgan. I know you can do better."

He heard Lena's sharp intake of breath at the direct insult, and anger, to a degree he didn't think possible, took over him. "Just like I knew Bas could do better, and I was right. I hope you get the chance to meet Jocelyn. She's just what Bas needs, and the Steeles are proud to have her as a member of the family."

When she picked up the water glass, no doubt to throw the contents in his face, he said, "Be careful, Cassandra. Your spiteful claws are showing, and I thought you were too socially cultivated for that." He took his seat, not giving her the courtesy of remaining standing in her presence. "Now if you will excuse me I would like to get back to my lunch guest."

He heard her place the glass back on the table and when he was sure she had walked away, he glanced over at Lena. "I apologize for that."

Lena waved off his apology. "Don't. I've known a long time that I'm not Cassandra's favorite person, ever since I became friends with Sienna. I recommend her to decorate a lot of the houses I sell. So Cassandra's insults don't bother me. She assumed we're here together for something else other than business and she was wrong…as usual."

She leaned closer over the table. "Now, what I was saying before we were interrupted, Morgan, is that I think I've found an interested buyer for your home as well as a place you might like to purchase. I didn't put a contract on your place because of what you told me about Donovan, but I can tell you they are willing to make you a good offer for it."

He nodded, inwardly not caring what kind of offer they made. "Who are they?"

"The Edwardses. He's an executive for Brookshire Industries and his job is transferring him here. Matthew and his wife, Joan, are in their thirties and they have three kids. Meghan is ten, Matt Junior is eight. Then there's Sarah. She's five and is handicapped and confined to a wheelchair, but somehow she can swim with assistance. I think she's the one who liked your pool the best. When she saw it she—"

"You showed them the house already?" he asked in surprise.

Lena raised a brow, wondering what kind of question that was. "Of course I showed them the house. You did give me permission to show your home while you weren't there, didn't you?"

He sighed deeply. "Of course." And being the top-notch Realtor that she was, she wasn't wasting any time doing what she thought he wanted her to do. "What about this place you want me to see?"

She smiled. "I think you're going to like it. In fact I think you're going to like it even better than what you have now, it's just that beautiful."

He lifted a brow. She had piqued his interest if she thought such a thing. "Just where is this place?"

He could see the excitement in her eyes when she said, "It's just minutes from the airport, which will help with your travels, and in some areas it backs up against Lake Wylie, if you're interested in waterfront property."

He nodded. He hadn't been before, but he could be if she was. "So, when can I take a look at it?"

"Whenever you're free."

"Okay, how about today, after lunch?"

Lena blinked. She hadn't expected that. "Lunch?"

"Yes. Since you're here you might as well join me for lunch, unless you've eaten already or have made other plans."

"No, but didn't you eat lunch during your earlier business meeting here?" she inquired curiously.

He lifted impeccably clad shoulders with a negative shake of his head. "No. Anthony and I shared drinks, not a meal. I haven't eaten since breakfast and I need something. If you'd rather we not go check out this place today we can do it at another time. Just call my secretary and see when she'll be able to work you into my calendar again later this week."

Lena didn't like the sound of that. She knew how busy Morgan was and decided she needed to show him the place as soon as she could. "No, it's okay. If today is better for you, then it's fine with me. No, I haven't eaten anything and don't have plans. I can stay and join you for lunch."

He smiled. "Good." He glanced around and called a waiter over to their table.

"Yes, Mr. Steele?"

"Ms. Spears will be joining me for lunch, Ricardo. May we have two menus?"

"Certainly, sir."

When the waiter walked off, Lena said, "I take it that you come here often."

"Yes, I usually hold my business meetings here."

"Oh."

Raising his glass he took a sip of his wine, knowing with those words he had effectively removed any thoughts from Lena's mind that his invitation for her to join him for lunch was anything other than business.

LENA GLANCED OVER at Morgan as he expertly maneuvered his SUV toward their destination, which was a twenty-minute drive from the restaurant. He had suggested saving time by using one vehicle, preferably his. That way she was free to cover the amenities the place had to offer while he did the driving.

In some faraway recess of her mind, she knew it was time to begin going over those things with him, but for some reason she welcomed the quietness between them and wasn't ready for conversation of any kind to intrude. Besides, he seemed to be in his own world, his gaze fixed on the stretch of road in front of him. Nothing played, not even his radio, and she felt a tinge of uneasiness at the thought he could possibly hear her breathing, an erratic sound of wanting and need that she was trying hard to hide. But around him it was nearly impossible.

Even now the scent of him, definitely male, infiltrated her nostrils, sent heat coursing through her blood. In the past she could control her urges and her desires just by turning her mind and thoughts off to them. But since meeting Morgan, she found such a thing difficult, almost impossible, especially when they were in close proximity to each other.

She'd been conscious of a slow, nagging ache in the lower part of her body ever since he had walked her out of the restaurant to his vehicle. By the time she had gotten seated in his truck she'd been almost breathless. And when he had casually bent over her to snap her seat belt in place, it took everything she had to force her Gemini twin back from taunting him by pushing her cleavage forward, showing him as much of her breasts as she could beneath the droopy neckline of her blouse, and go even further by grabbing his tie and pulling him in closer; to have her mouth and tongue ready, willing and wet to meet his and—

"Okay, what you got for me?"

His question snapped her out of her daytime fantasy and she glanced over at him and met his gaze. It was on the tip of her tongue to respond that what she had for him was anything he wanted and it didn't have to be within reason. He had brought the car to a stop at a traffic light and was staring over at her beneath thick, long lashes. That ache in the lower part of her body intensified.

More than ever today she was aware of the absence of her panty hose. Usually, she wore a business suit, but because it was one of those rare warm days in March, she had decided to wear a knee-length melon-striped poplin skirt with a melon-colored pullover droopy-neck tunic sweater that flowed past her waist and a pair of flats.

She reached down by her leg to retrieve her leather portfolio to pull out the papers she needed and said, "Ashton Oaks is one of the premier neighborhoods of the Palisades that contain a limited edition of custom homes within a beautiful gated enclave and is in close proximity to the Palisades Country Club."

Morgan nodded. He was aware of the Palisades because of the magnificent golf course that bordered it. "What's the price range of the homes?" he asked.

"Between seven hundred and two million. The one I'm going to show you falls in between, and I think when you see it you will agree that it's going to exceed your wildest dreams with its custom kitchens, fantasy bathrooms, glorious—"

"Fantasy bathrooms?" Morgan couldn't resist interrupting to ask, while raising a brow.

Lena chuckled. "Yes. You'll know what I mean when you see it. And because over three hundred acres of the land is set aside to preserve nature, there are plenty of hiking and equestrian trails."

"Sounds like a real nice place."

She smiled over at him after closing her folder. "I think you're going to be pleased. It's the ultimate in prestigious living. I really don't think you're going to find anything better."

He brought his SUV to a halt at a stop sign and glanced over at her, appreciating how the fabric of her sweater clung to her full breasts and how the rich coloring of her honey-brown hair fell in lustrous curls past her shoulders. It was his opinion that she had a mouth that was begging to be kissed, and he decided right then and there that she was wrong. He would find something better than the place she was taking him, and that was the place he intended to one day be, which was in her arms, in her bed, inside her body.

"The turnoff is up ahead, Morgan."

Morgan was convinced he wasn't imagining things when he heard that breathless catch in her voice. "All right." He tried putting all his concentration on his driving but found he couldn't. Even now his every breath was filled with the succulent scent of her as it floated through the confines of his vehicle. He decided to get control back before he blew things by pulling the truck to the side of the road and kissing the living daylights out of her.

"You mentioned one of the Edwards children was handicapped. What happened?"

"I didn't want to appear insensitive by asking. I think possibly a birth defect but I'm not sure. But Sarah is the cutest thing, simply adorable. She was ready to get into your pool that day."

Morgan chuckled. "Was she? She sounds like Tiffany the first time she saw it," he said of the niece he'd inherited after his brother's marriage to Kylie. He knew Tiffany was also Lena's godchild. His face formed in a thoughtful expression when he recalled how Chance's son, Marcus, along with Tiffany, had managed to get their parents together. Too bad there was no one out there looking out for him and Lena.

"Turn right at the next corner, please, and stop. I'll get us passage through the gates."

Moments later Morgan brought his car to a stop at the gated entryway, and after Lena had talked to the guard to gain clearance, they were driving through. His breath actually caught at the impossibly beautiful homes he saw showcased, all custom designed and reflecting varying architectural styles. He immediately concluded that this was one extraordinary neighborhood from the lush landscaping to the pristine creeks that ran along the back properties of some.

"Pull into the next driveway on your left."

He did and he had to stop the moment his vehicle pulled into the yard. Before him sat what had to be the most regal and provincial home he'd ever seen. Completely brick, the three-story structure was twice the size of his present home, definitely a lot for one man. But then, he didn't intend to live in it alone. He would have a wife, a number of children and a mother-in-law whom he would gladly welcome with open arms.

"So what do you think?"

He turned to Lena when she asked the question. He smiled. "Umm, I'm curious to know what you think."

He watched as her mouth pursed. "I think this place has your name on it."

He chuckled, deciding not to tell her that if his name was on it, then her name was on it as well.

CHAPTER FOUR

So THIS WAS a fantasy bathroom, Morgan surmised as he studied the huge room that contained a Roman spa with trompe l'oeil walls, the Portuguese cork floors, the romantic recessed lightings, the cornice tile moldings that framed the wall mirror and the chrome fixtures. And then he couldn't omit the stone fireplace, the first he'd ever seen placed in a bathroom where you could soak away a day's worth of stress while enjoying the view of a blazing flame.

The house contained four other bathrooms and they were just as elegant. The walls behind the bathtubs displayed a convergence of ceramic-tile styles against a backdrop of decorative squares and mosaic insets that appeared hand-carved.

But the elegance didn't stop there. The master suite connected to the main house by a glass breezeway with elevator access. There was also an in-law suite on the first floor that was the size of a small apartment. The massive great room with its thirty-foot ceilings and eight-foot-wide brick fireplace added an expressive intricate touch, and the huge kitchen with its granite-top island and ceramic tile floors did more than add a finishing touch. They provided enhancements not normally found in most custom homes, including the one he was living in now.

He turned and leaned against a kitchen counter. Although when he'd made the request he hadn't thought it was possible, Lena had done just what he had asked her to do. She had found a home more perfect than the one he now owned. "I really like this house, Lena," he said quite honestly. "Not only is it a home but it's also a private retreat."

He watched the smile that appeared on her face. "I like it, too, and hoped that you would. I have others to show you but I thought this one was yours."

Morgan shook his head. It definitely was his… and hers. "So what's next?" he asked.

"I prefer you not put a binder on it yet. I feel confident that I can work with the developer to get a few more amenities. I'm not saying he will give us any, but it's worth a try, and I wouldn't be doing my job as your Realtor if I didn't get you the best bang for your buck."

He swallowed and wished she hadn't said the word *bang*. At the moment he would gladly take the best bang for his buck. Even now with her standing across the room he couldn't help but notice her bare legs and would do anything to get up close and personal just to run his hands up her voluptuous thighs. After getting a glimpse of her yellow bra that day he wondered if she always matched her underthings with her outerwear. He would love to investigate, to check things out for himself by going up under her skirt to see just what was beneath it.

She glanced down at her watch. "Oops, I need to leave. I almost forgot I need to pick my mother up a little early today since they're having a meeting at the center. I'll barely have time to make it once you take me back to the restaurant to pick up my car."

"Then I won't. I'll just take you straight to the place to get your mother."

She shook her head. "You don't have to do that, really."

"I'm sure I don't but I don't mind. Besides, I'd like to meet your mother."

She lifted a brow. "Why?"

"Because I've heard a lot about her."

A bemused look touched Lena's features. "You have?"

"Yes."

"From who?"

"Kylie, Tiffany. She wasn't able to make it to Kylie's wedding. I understand she was under the weather."

Lena nodded knowing it was a lot more than that. "It just so happened that Chance and Kylie got married on what would have been my parents' fiftieth wedding anniversary had my father lived. They'd already been married twenty years before I was born."

"Wow, I didn't know that. I'm sure losing your father was hard on her."

Lena nodded. "Yes, it was. They had a rather close relationship, and although he's been gone for six years now, she still has some rough times. The holidays are extremely hard, especially Christmas since it was the day they married. And of course his birthday, which happens to be on the Fourth of July. She goes into a state of depression every year around those days."

Morgan nodded as he thought of his own parents. They would be celebrating their fortieth wedding anniversary in a few years. They, too, had a close relationship and he knew if anything were to happen to either parent, the remaining one would have a difficult time adjusting as well.

At that moment he felt an astounding respect and admiration for Lena. She had technically placed her social life on hold to take care of her mother. He and his brothers had unanimously decided when and if the time came not to place their parents in a nursing home if it was reasonably possible not to do so. Like Lena, they would become their parents' primary caretakers.

When he saw her glance down at her watch again, he said, "Come on. I want to make sure you're there to pick up your mother on time."

It was on the tip of Lena's tongue to tell him that she preferred that he not go. She could just imagine what her mother would think if a man accompanied her to pick her up as it had been over three years since she was actually out on a date. The last guy she'd dated had been Dr. Derek Peterson, who'd had the nerve to tell her that they could pick up their relationship once she put her mother in her own place and stop spending so much time with her. She was glad she hadn't gotten any further with him than the first kiss. After saying what he'd said the man had really turned her stomach.

Once they were back in Morgan's SUV her lips quivered slightly with nerves. Maybe she needed to prepare Morgan in case her mother did something crazy like bring up the subject of grandbabies, her favorite subject lately. "Morgan?"

He glanced over at her as he backed the vehicle out of the driveway. "Yes?"

"My mother. I think I need to prepare you about something so you won't be surprised, in case she brings it up."

"Okay, what is it?"

"She wants grandkids."

"Oh, I see."

Even as he said the words, Lena doubted if he really saw at all and decided to explain. "She's getting older and—"

"Lena, you don't have to explain. I have parents, too, remember. And when it comes to wanting grandkids they're just as bad."

"They are?"

"Yes. For years Marcus was enough for them, but then they started throwing out hints to the four of us again. They felt Chance needed to remarry and Bas, Donovan and I needed to find wives. Now with Bas married and Chance with a new baby on the way, they're satisfied for now, but I'm not counting on it lasting too long. They'll be looking at me and Donovan again in a few years."

A few moments later he asked, "What about you, Lena?"

She lifted a brow. "What about me?"

"I asked you before and you said you wanted kids…but. You never explained what that *but* meant."

Lena recalled that day a couple of weeks ago. She met his gaze when he halted at a stop sign. "*But* means that I would love to have children of my own one day and I would love for my children to know my mother while she's still here with me in good health and a good frame of mind. But since I'm not married and don't see myself getting married in my near or distant future, then it doesn't matter how much I love kids or want them, does it?"

Yes it did. Morgan's jaw tightened and he wished to earth that he could tell her right then and there that it did matter because he was willing to give her as many babies as she wanted. He could provide their child a loving, stable environment that included two parents and grandparents. And he didn't have a problem with Lena being her mother's primary caretaker. They would do it together, share the responsibility. And he would be able to provide all the financial security she'd ever want.

But at the moment he was too deep into his plan of pursuit to tell her that. He would have to show her better than to tell her. In the past men had disappointed her in such a way that it would be hard for Lena to put her complete trust in one again. So he would take his time and continue with his plan to build her trust and belief that he was different. He had to prove that all the other men in her life had been Mr. Wrong but he was her Mr. Right.

When he brought the car to the gate to exit out of the subdivision he smiled and said, "Don't worry. Your mother and I will get along great."

Lena inwardly sighed. That was exactly what she was afraid of. And then when Morgan stopped coming around the way the others had once they realized that her mother was a permanent fixture in her life, she wondered just what her mother was going to think.

"WHO ARE YOU, young man?"

Before Morgan could respond Lena quickly answered as she snapped her mother's seat belt in place. "Mom, this is a client of mine, Morgan Steele. I was out showing him a house and time slipped away. He was kind enough to offer to bring me here to pick you up."

"Oh." Odessa, who was sitting in the front passenger seat, smiled over at Morgan, in the driver's seat. "That was nice of you, Mr. Steele." She then bunched her brows. "I know another Steele. Kylie's husband."

Morgan smiled. "That's Chance, my brother."

The woman's face crinkled into an even wider smile. "So, you're one of those Steele boys."

Morgan chuckled. He hadn't heard him and his brothers referred to that way in a long time. "Yes, ma'am, I am."

"I heard there were four of you."

"Yes, there are."

"Another one got married recently, right?"

"Yes, that was my brother Sebastian."

"You and your other brother are still single?"

"Mom! Please don't make Morgan feel like he's part of an inquisition," Lena said from the backseat as Morgan drove away from the adult day care center.

Odessa glanced over at Morgan. "Sorry about that, son."

He chuckled again. "No harm's been done, Ms. Spears. And to answer your question, yes, my brother Donovan and I are still single."

To avoid her mother asking Morgan any questions about his personal life, Lena quickly asked her how things had gone at the center today. Odessa then went into a lengthy explanation, filling everyone in on the happenings of that day. Lena sat in the backseat thinking most of it was an everyday occurrence, especially the information about Mr. Talbot trying to eat Ms. Meriwether's lunch. But what was different today was that her mother had another set of ears, attentive ears. Lena knew Morgan was just being nice but he was hanging on to her mother's every word; and the more he hung on, the more her mother had to say. She couldn't recall the last time her mother was so chatty with a stranger.

From her position in the backseat Lena watched Morgan. Although he kept his eyes focused on the road, he was still attuned to what her mother was saying and would make occasional comments. Lena finally decided to tune out the conversation and focus on him.

The man had a very sexy mouth. That was one of the first things she had noticed about him the first night they met, which was probably the reason she kept having those fantasies of kissing it. Then there were his hands, the ones that were now gripping the steering wheel. She could just imagine him gripping her thighs in just the same way, while his fingers inched upward toward that heated place and—

"Isn't that wonderful, Lena?"

She blinked, realizing her mother had spoken to her, had asked her a question. "Excuse me, Mom, what did you say? My thoughts were elsewhere."

"I said, isn't it wonderful that Morgan is coming to dinner on Sunday?"

"What!" Lena said, switching her gaze to Morgan and meeting his in the rearview mirror in wild confusion. What was her mother talking about? Morgan was not coming to dinner on Sunday.

"Did I miss something?" she asked, trying to ignore the intensity in the dark eyes staring back at her in the mirror.

"Your mother asked when the last time was that I had homemade chicken and dumplings, and I told her it's been a while. She was kind enough to invite me over on Sunday since she'll be cooking some then."

Lena snatched her gaze from Morgan to stare at the back of her mother's head. "When did you decide to cook?" She couldn't recall the last time her mother had been motivated to go into the kitchen to prepare dinner. Usually Lena did the cooking.

"When Morgan said it's been a while since he'd had chicken and dumplings. I think he should get a taste of mine at least once."

"That's kind of you, Mom, and I'm certain Morgan appreciates the invitation, but I'm sure he has other things to do on Sunday."

"No, I don't."

A surprised brow lifted as Lena met Morgan's gaze in the rearview mirror again. She'd been trying to help him out of what she thought was a situation he hadn't really wanted to be in. "You don't?"

He chuckled. "No, I don't."

"Then it's all settled," Odessa Spears was saying with a smile in her voice. "And I think I'm going to bake a peach cobbler as well. Do you like peach cobbler, Morgan?"

"Yes, ma'am."

"Good."

KYLIE STEELE SMILED, seeing the look of grief on the face of the woman who'd been her best friend since high school. They were having their weekly lunch session at their favorite restaurant. "Come on, Lena. Morgan having dinner at your place can't be that bad."

Lena frowned. "That's what you think. You know that he asked me out a few times and I turned him down, and I had worked so hard making sure he understood there could never be anything between us but friendship. And with him being a client, I've been trying to keep things strictly business between us, and now thanks to Mom he might get the wrong idea and I don't want that."

Kylie took a sip of her apple juice, her eyes meeting Lena's over the rim of her glass. Once she set the glass down on the table she asked, "Okay, Lena. Tell me. What's going on here? What is it that you really want?"

Lena shrugged. "I don't know what you mean."

"No, I think that you do. This is Kylie, remember, the one person who knows you like a book. Pregnancy didn't destroy any of my brain cells. I know the reason you turned Morgan down all those times. You're convinced he's no different than the Derek Petersons of the world."

Lena shook her head. "I never said he was anything like Derek. But then, I have to be fair and objective in dealing with men, Kylie. Taking care of an elderly parent is a huge undertaking, but I do it with pleasure and love because it's *my* mom. I don't see it just as a responsibility, I see it as a way to gladly give back all those things she's given to me over the years."

She took a sip of her wine before continuing. "But I can't expect others to see it that way. Mom is seventy-one and not in the best of health. Morgan's parents are in their late fifties, still alive, and are able to do things together. I'm all Mom has and that's okay. I don't have time to devote to a serious relationship. Being with her takes up most of my time."

"But it doesn't have to be that way, Lena. Your mom is in good health so it's not like she needs a sitter around the clock and—"

"Where would a relationship lead, Kylie? I've never been one to get into casual affairs and maybe that's my downfall. If I could indulge in one, then things would be just great and I wouldn't hurt when the affair ended because I could just brush myself off and start on another. But I can't do that. I get involved with all my emotions."

"You really liked Derek, didn't you?" Kylie asked softly, remembering the man who'd once had the nerve to try and hit on her right in front of Lena. What a jerk!

Emotions, thick and painful, lodged in Lena's throat. "He was a real charmer, I have to admit. I'm just glad I never slept with him. Then him walking away like he did would really have been humiliating. But to answer your question, yes, I really liked him but I didn't love him. I would have begun falling in love with him if I hadn't started seeing his true side. He was just like a spoiled child. He wanted to make me choose between him and my mother and he was too stupid to see there wasn't a choice. But to give me an ultimatum like that showed just what kind of person he was."

"Yes, it did. But let's get back to Morgan for a moment. You can't tell me you don't like him just a little."

Lena couldn't help but smile. "What's there not to like? He's good-looking, has good manners, he's a successful businessman. When I quoted him the price of that house I showed him a couple of days ago, he didn't bat an eye."

"But?"

"But even if I didn't have Mom I still wouldn't get involved with him. I'm way out of my league with him. I can see him with a totally different woman by his side, and I can't risk losing my heart to him. It's as simple as that."

She studied the contents of her glass for a moment, then said, "I didn't tell you that Morgan and I ran into Cassandra Tisdale the day we had our business meeting at that restaurant in town."

Kylie raised a brow. "Cassandra Tisdale? She's back?"

"Yes, and her fangs are sharper than ever. She made a very rude comment about Morgan and me being together."

Kylie frowned. "What kind of comment?"

"Something about how he could do better."

Kylie leaned back in her chair with a look of incredulity on her face. "I can't believe the nerve of that woman," she said, remembering the first time she had come into contact with Cassandra. "For someone who's supposed to be so refined, she can be downright tacky at times."

"Yes, but Morgan put her in her place, but then he should not have. When people see us together they shouldn't see us as a mismatched couple. When a couple walks into the room and heads turn it should be for all the right reasons and not the wrong ones."

"And you see that happening?"

"Possibly. I have no problem with who I am, but I can't honestly think that I'm someone he'd probably consider as his ideal woman."

"Then why do you think he asked you out all those times?"

"Who knows? Maybe out of boredom."

"I don't think you're being fair to Morgan or to yourself." Kylie then leaned forward in her seat and sighed. "Do something for me, Lena."

"What?"

"Stop selling yourself short. When you get home take a look in the mirror. You're a beautiful full-figured African American woman who could walk into any room and put the Cassandra Tisdales of this world to shame, mainly because not only do you have outside beauty, you have inside beauty as well. Don't think a man like Morgan wouldn't know that. And I think you need to think about something."

"What?"

"What if you are Morgan's ideal woman? And what if he's that one man who doesn't care that you're your mother's primary caretaker? Then what?"

A small smile touched the corners of Lena's lips. "Then I'll get the hell out of Dodge quick like and in a hurry."

Kylie lifted a brow. "What does that mean?"

"It means that I would run like hell because I wouldn't know the first thing about handling a man like Morgan…sexually, I mean. I bet his testosterone level is probably close to hitting the Richter scale. I get hot all over at the thought of sleeping with him."

Kylie grinned as her eyes glittered teasingly. "So the thought has crossed your mind?"

A frisson of desire inched its way through Lena's bloodstream at the same moment she knew a heated flush was probably showing in her cheeks. "Yes, more than a few times a week. How about every day?" she said honestly.

Kylie laughed. "Now you know what I was going through after meeting Chance."

Yes, Lena thought. She knew. But she also knew that she and Kylie were different people. Kylie had started out being defiant and determined, but in the end she had given in to Chance's charm. Lena didn't intend to give in to any man's charm again. What Derek and others before him had done had more than pricked her pride. It had made her see things quite clear. And the more she kept her dealings with Morgan on a business level, the better things would be.

CHAPTER FIVE

LENA TRIED TO recall her immunity to any man's charm as she gazed at the two beautiful bouquets of fresh flowers Morgan had just handed her. One for her and the other for her mother.

Finding herself unnerved, she glanced up at him. "Thanks for the flowers, Morgan. Please come in."

She moved aside when he stepped inside. While she closed the door she noticed him glancing around, and when their gazes connected again he said, "You have a nice place."

"Thanks. Please let me take your jacket." The weather had changed and there was a brisk coolness in the air. The warm weather from earlier in the week was gone. In fact the forecasters had predicted the possibility of snow sometime next week.

"Mom's in the kitchen," she said, placing his leather jacket on the rack. "I told her you had arrived, so she should be coming out in a little bit. Can I get you something to drink?"

"No, I'm fine."

Because his brother was married to her best friend, she and Morgan were invited to some of the same functions on occasion, so she had seen him in casual wear before. But there was something about seeing him now, standing tall and handsome in her living room wearing a pair of jeans, a blue pullover sweater and a pair of comfortable-looking sneakers that made her wonder, and not for the first time, why he didn't have a steady girlfriend.

He was definitely one fine specimen of a man, a healthy-looking one at that, which meant he probably had a normal sex drive like most men. And not that she thought he went for the celibacy thing, but since being officially introduced to him at that charity ball over a year ago, she couldn't recall his name linked to any female. Now, with his brother Donovan it was a different story. The fun-loving Donovan Steele had a reputation around town as being a ladies' man.

"If you will excuse me I'm going to find a couple of vases for the flowers. Please make yourself at home."

"All right."

Although she was conscious of the tingly sensations that lit every cell in her body, Lena tried to ignore them as she quickly left the room. When she stepped into the kitchen she saw her mother, bending over the oven with an apron on. Lena had awakened that morning to the smell of fresh peaches cooking and had lain in bed for a while to make sure she was at the right house. Her mother hadn't set foot in the kitchen since they moved in almost five years ago, other than to eat. But her invitation to Morgan had nearly done the impossible.

"Did you get Morgan settled comfortably, dear?"

her mother asked as if she had a pair of eyes in the back of her head.

"Yes, and he brought these for us."

Odessa straightened and turned around. Upon seeing the flowers she smiled. "Now, wasn't that real sweet of him?"

Lena shrugged, knowing that it was but not wanting to give her mother any ideas where Morgan was concerned. "All the Steeles are nice, Mom."

"Yes, and Kylie's blessed to have met Chance. And just to think that Tiffany and Chance's son Marcus got them together."

Lena couldn't help but smile at how the two teenagers had successfully played matchmakers. She glanced over at the stove. "It seems you're serving more than just chicken and dumplings and peach cobbler," she said upon seeing all the pots.

"I decided since that young man hasn't had a good home-cooked meal in a while I would throw in a few more items. I really like him."

To Lena that fact was obvious and she couldn't help wondering why. Her mother had met Derek, Jon and Paul. They'd held conversations with her when they came to pick Lena up for dates, but neither of the three had won her mother over like Morgan to the point to bring her back into the kitchen.

"I'll be back in a second."

Lena watched as her mother left the kitchen to go to the living room and speak to Morgan. A few moments later she could actually hear Morgan's deep voice and her mother laughing about something. She wondered what that was all about, knowing before she left the sanctuary of the kitchen to find out she needed to pull herself together. It seemed Morgan Steele had a way with women, both young and old.

Her mother laughed out again, and then the laughter was followed by the sound of Morgan's voice. Lena paused as she put the flowers in the vase, as her mind, her thoughts and every sensation in her body focused on that voice. It was strong, husky, yet in some ways gentle. But then on the other hand, there was a sensuous quality about it that touched something deep inside her, in the most provocative places. There wasn't a nook, corner or crevice of her body that hadn't at one time or another been affected.

"Lena?"

She snapped out of her thoughts when she heard her mother call out her name. "Yes?" she called back.

"Morgan needs help setting the table."

Lena lifted her brow. Morgan was setting the table? She picked up the vases and walked out of the kitchen. She placed one vase in the middle of the dining room table and the other on a table in the living room. She glanced up and saw the white linen tablecloth in Morgan's hands.

"I guess Ms. Odessa is going to make me work for my supper," he said, smiling.

"At least I'm letting Lena help you," her mother replied, amused as she left them alone to go back into the kitchen.

"I like your mom, Lena. She's fun to be around."

Lena nodded, thinking it strange that none of the

guys she'd brought home to meet her mother had ever made such an observation. "I don't know why Mom felt I needed to help you with this," she said, leading him into the dining room and removing the flowers off the table that she had put there mere minutes ago. "And you should feel honored you get dining room space. Usually our guests just cram with us in the kitchen."

"I wouldn't mind."

Lena glanced up at him, saw the sincerity in his eyes and knew that he would not have minded. That was one thing she had discovered about Morgan. He was so unlike Derek in that he didn't have a conceited bone in his body.

It didn't take them long to spread the linen covering over the table and smooth the center and sides. They worked quietly, not saying anything, and then suddenly they came up short upon realizing they had moved into the same area when they accidentally bumped into each other. His hands reached out, gripped her around the waist to steady her, and her body automatically went into an immobile mode; she felt suspended in space. The hands at her waist felt warm, strong yet gentle.

Breathing deeply, she tilted her head up and looked into his face, met his gaze and nearly got scorched from the deep, hot intensity from his eyes. That look alone overwhelmed her, made her pulse race and her breathing come out forced.

"Sorry," she muttered, quickly taking a step back. "I wasn't watching where I was going."

"No harm done. Neither was I," was Morgan's easy response…which was a lie, he thought. He'd been drawn to her scent like a bee drawn to honey.

"Dinner's ready. I need more hands to bring everything out," Odessa called out from the kitchen.

Thinking it would be best not to bump into her twice since he wouldn't be able to handle it, Morgan used his hand and gestured for her to go ahead of him and he followed her into the kitchen.

MORGAN PUSHED AWAY from the table with a huge smile on his face after finishing off a plate of Odessa's peach cobbler. He licked his lips. "That was the best peach cobbler I've ever eaten," he said. "My mom makes a banana pudding that's to die for, and I can see someone killing for your cobbler as well, not to mention everything else you served today. Dinner was wonderful."

Over the rim of her iced tea glass, Lena watched the smile of pleasure that appeared on her mother's face, and shook her head. Morgan was a real charmer all right.

"I've eaten so much I'm going to have to trek around my neighborhood and walk it off," he added.

"No need to wait until you get home since Lena walks every day after dinner anyway. I'm sure she wouldn't mind the company."

Lena quickly gazed over at her mother, studying the older woman's innocent features. She couldn't help but wonder if her mother had hatched some crazy idea about her and Morgan getting together.

First dinner and now a walk—just the two of them. "I'm sure Morgan has had enough of our company for one day, Mom, and wants to call it a day."

Morgan glanced over at her. "Quite the contrary. I enjoyed both of your company and I'd love going for a walk."

Think! Think! Lena tried unscrambling her mind to come up with a reason she couldn't go walking with him. All through dinner her naughty twin had tried to surface by putting all kinds of thoughts into her head. "It's kind of windy out. It will mess up my hair," she said, saying the first thing that popped into her head, although it sounded rather lame.

"Of course it's windy, Lena. It's March," her mother said, waving off her excuse with her hand.

"And there's a cap in my jacket you can borrow," Morgan tacked on.

Lena sighed. Both her mother and Morgan were looking at her expectantly, as if waiting for her to come up with another excuse. She smiled over at her mother but inwardly narrowed her eyes at Morgan. Why was he going along with Odessa on this? Just wait until they got outside. There was a lot she had to say to him.

"Fine," she said, standing. "Let me change into something more appropriate for walking."

Ten minutes later she returned to find Morgan had helped her mother clear the table. She found them in the kitchen, again sharing another joke. "I'm ready." At the sound of her voice they both turned and smiled, and from the sparkle in her mother's eyes Lena could tell she was in high spirits.

"Here's the cap I was telling you about," Morgan said, moving away from her mother to come stand in front of her. Instinctively, she reached out to take it from him, but instead of handing it to her he placed it on her head. He stepped back and then tipped his head to the side as if to admire his handiwork. "It will work. Looks good on you."

Lena decided she needed to see for herself. She walked a couple of steps out of the kitchen to look into the huge mirror that hung on the dining room wall. He was right. It work would and it looked good…if blue, black and silver were your colors and you supported the Carolina Panthers.

She turned around and saw that Morgan had followed her out of the kitchen and was leaning against the door fame. His muscular shoulders came close to filling the doorway. "You do know I'm not a Carolina native and that I was born and raised in New York. Buffalo in fact," she said, meeting his gaze, and a warm oozy feeling flowed through her bloodstream. That seemed to happen each and every time she looked into his eyes.

He smiled. "Is that a cute way of telling me that you prefer rooting for the Buffalo Bills?"

"Not necessarily. Lucky for you I quickly converted when the Panthers came to town."

"We native Carolinians do appreciate that," he said in a voice that was warm and engaging.

He straightened his stance. "Are you ready for our walk?"

"Yes." *Ready but not looking forward to it,* she thought further.

INSTEAD OF JOGGING or fast walking, they eased into a nice leisurely walk. Neither said anything for a long while, but Morgan was prepared for Lena to have a lot to say. He knew she hadn't liked the way her mother, with his help, had orchestrated this stroll.

Although it was windy, the sun was peeking through the clouds, making it a beautiful day the week before the first day of spring. Not that it mattered in Charlotte. Spring came when spring came. Last year it snowed on the first day of spring. Occasionally, they were visited by the snowstorm the locals called the Beast from the East. Last one had hit a couple of years ago, snowing everyone in the mountains, and surrounding areas, in for a few days.

Deciding they had walked long enough without conversation he decided to start one. "Nice day, isn't it?"

He watched Lena snatch her head around as if she'd forgotten he was there. It was his opinion that she looked downright cute, dressed in a green jogging suit and well-worn sneakers and wearing his cap. "Yes." She then resumed looking straight ahead, up the road, with her mouth shut.

His lips crinkled at the corners. If she thought he was going to let her get away with one-word responses, she had another thought coming. "Tell me in twenty-five words, but not less than ten, just what do you think is nice about it?"

She turned her head slightly, and he knew it was taking a lot of her willpower to keep her features expressionless. He could just imagine what she was thinking. When she didn't say anything he decided to coax her on. "Come on, Lena, you can do it. You're a Realtor so you have to be full of nice, descriptive words. Try it. I double-dare you."

Lena couldn't help the smile that spread across her features. For some strange reason she found Morgan's antics endearing. "Okay, let me tell you what's so nice about it…from a Realtor's viewpoint."

Smiling, he tilted his head downward to hers. "I'm listening."

"Well, there's the scent of spring in the air," she said, dimpling, then breathing in deeply. "That's always nice. Not to mention the brisk breeze that's not too cold. One of the reasons I bought a home in this area was for that lake over there," she said, pointing to the huge body of water that ran through the subdivision.

"I love walking around it, smelling all the dogwoods and seeing them bloom. But then, I need to be honest about something. Spring is nice but I like winter better mainly because I love snow."

He arched a brow, and a smile touched the corners of his lips. "You like snow?"

She returned his smile. "Yes. I love watching the snowflakes fall to the ground and cover everything. I like drinking a mug full of hot chocolate while standing at the window looking at the snow fall and wishing I could just go out there and play in it. At least that wasn't one of the things I had to give up moving from New York. Although I got to see snow more often while living in Buffalo, at least I still get to see it."

She glanced up in the sky and blinked against the sun's brightness and then back at him. "So, how did I do?"

"You went over your word count."

She stopped, tipped her head back and laughed; really laughed. Moments later she stuck her hands in her pockets and continued walking, shaking her head. "I would hate working for you."

He chuckled. "You already do."

Her head shot up and she stared at him with all amusement gone, wondering if he was trying to remind her of their relationship. "Sorry, I forgot."

This time it was Morgan who stopped walking. When she stopped as well, he reached out and lifted her chin with the tip of his finger. "I didn't say that to make you remember."

She shrugged. "That's okay."

Morgan felt the spell that had surrounded them for the past few moments trying to break, but a part of him refused to let it. She had started to relax around him and her mood had been light, almost carefree. He liked that.

"So what made you decide to leave New York to move to North Carolina?" he asked, wanting to get her talking again, as they resumed their walk. And he relaxed.

She didn't say anything for a while, and for a moment he wondered if she was going to answer. Then she said, "My dad. In my senior year of high school his health began failing and the doctors thought a change in climate would help him. So we moved here right after my graduation and I began attending the University of North Carolina. Dad died a month after my graduation from college."

"I'm sorry."

A small smile touched her lips. "So was I. He was a wonderful man and I loved him deeply."

She got quiet for a brief moment and then she continued by saying, "It was really hard for Mama. They had been together so long. There were too many memories in the house where we lived, so we eventually put it up for sale and bought this one. That helped some, but for a while I thought I was going to lose another parent when Mom went into a state of depression from all her grief."

He nodded. "How long did it last?"

She titled her head to look up at him. "Who says it has stopped? She has good days and bad days, and trust me when I say today was one of her good days, and I have to thank you for it. This is the happiest I've seen her in a long time. She actually cooked all of the dinner herself. I can't tell you the last time she went into a kitchen other than to eat or to get a drink of water."

"I can't accept your thanks because I don't know

what I did. Your mother is a nice person and like I told you earlier, I like her. I can't imagine her getting depressed."

"Well, she does. And then there's her obsession with grandchildren. Did she mention anything about that to you?"

He smiled. "It just so happened that she did, briefly today while you were changing clothes and we were clearing the table. But that's okay. Like I said the other day, I think all mothers believe it's their duty to prod their children into parenthood."

Lena stopped walking. "So you think it's a phase that will pass?"

"Maybe. Maybe not. If not, then you might have to do some serious thinking as to what you want as well. And if you want a baby, too, then you're going to have to find a man who'd be more than willing to get you pregnant."

His voice was so low it could almost be defined as a whisper, and his words had sounded too serious. And the eyes staring down at her were more intense than ever.

Lena took a deep breath, inwardly forcing her naughty twin to behave when she felt her fingers itching to reach out and wrap her arms around his neck, bring his mouth down to hers and kiss him in all the ways she'd always dreamed about.

"Maybe we should head back now, Lena."

Morgan's words gave her the strength she needed to regain full control. But for one fleeting moment she felt something had changed, shifted, gotten altered. As they began walking back toward her house she tried not to put too much emphasis on her surprise when he took her hand in his, making her aware of his touch, making her feel a little squeeze in her chest.

Today she would take this, the casual versus professional rapport they were sharing. When they saw each other again it would be business as usual. But today was nice and she planned on making today's pleasantries, as well as Morgan's own special blend of kindness, a very special memory.

CHAPTER SIX

"WE'LL BE ABLE to finish up things once Morgan brings his attention back to the meeting."

Morgan snapped his head up to look into his older brother's intense dark eyes. He glanced around the room and saw that Bas, Donovan and Vanessa were staring at him as well. So okay. He'd been caught daydreaming. No big deal. But with the smirk he saw on Donovan's face he knew that his younger brother would make it a big deal. And Morgan didn't have long to wait.

"In defense of Morgan, he can't help that he has a lot on his mind. The woman of his dreams, his *perfect* woman, still can't seem to notice that he's alive."

"Go to hell, Donovan," Morgan said, glaring over at his youngest brother.

"Okay, you two, knock it off. If you want to go at each other, save it for the next Saturday we're on the court," Chance said.

Morgan nodded. It was a family tradition that he and his three brothers got together every Saturday to play basketball, mainly to get rid of any competitive frustrations they might get from working together. Depending on the depth of their frustrations, the game could get downright mean and ugly. "My pleasure," he said, giving Donovan a look that clearly said...*next time we're on the court, your ass is grass*.

"Who's his perfect woman?" Of course Vanessa had to ask. At twenty-six she was the oldest of the three girl cousins and headed the PR department. It had been challenging for the Steele Brothers to keep an eye out for their younger female cousins while growing up, especially when Vanessa and her best friend from high school, Sienna Davis Bradford, were always getting into trouble.

"Lena Spears is his perfect woman," Donovan was more than happy to say.

A smile touched Vanessa's lips. "Lena Spears? I know her and she's a jewel. We've worked together on several community projects. Now, why doesn't she notice that Morgan is alive?"

"Can we get back to the meeting?" Morgan asked, deciding he didn't want his personal business discussed, especially if everyone had to hear Donovan's take on things.

"You mean you want to get back to the meeting that wasn't holding your attention anyway?" Bas said, rolling his eyes.

When Vanessa laughed, Morgan glared over at her. "Did I happen to mention that I was in Atlanta with Cameron a couple of weekends ago and he asked about you, Van?"

Morgan watched the amusement die on his cousin's face, knowing he'd said something that would shut her up for a while. All it took was the mere mention of Cameron Cody's name. Vanessa couldn't stand the man.

"Okay, knock it off, all of you," Chance said, taking the role as leader. "Let's get back down to business. We have important things to discuss."

An hour later when the meeting ended Morgan was the first to stand and head for the door. "Where's the fire?" Bas called after him.

Morgan smiled as he kept walking. Oddly enough, he felt there was a fire. Every time he thought about Lena a part of him would erupt into a smoldering blaze. It didn't take much effort to recall their walk on Sunday. Even though there had been other people around walking and jogging, there had been something pleasingly intimate about strolling beside Lena, talking to her, listening to her talk. And on those occasions when their arms would occasionally brush, he'd felt a sharp sensation all the way to his toes.

He checked his watch as he stepped onto the elevator. His smile widened. Lena would be receiving a package from him in about an hour and he hoped that she liked her gift.

...IF YOU WANT a baby, too, then you're going to have to find a man who'd be more than willing to get you pregnant....

Morgan's words from yesterday still weighed heavily in Lena's thoughts as she walked into her office. She would even admit that at one time she'd had thoughts of visiting a sperm bank. From a recent article she'd read in a magazine, more and more single professional women who were feeling the ticking of their biological clock were considering just that option. But of course being the ultratraditional person she was, she had dissed the idea. She'd grown up in a home with both a loving father and mother and couldn't see cheating a child out of a chance to have that as well. That reasoning always put her back at square one.

"Good afternoon, Lena."

She smiled over at her secretary as she grabbed the mail off the table and began flipping through it. "And a good afternoon to you, Wendy. Did I get any calls?"

The woman, who was only a few years older, smiled back and said, "Not since the last time you checked earlier, but you did get a package. I put it on your desk."

"Thanks, it's probably those brochures I ordered last week," Lena said, tossing the junk mail in a basket to get shredded while keeping hold of anything she considered important. "I'll be in the back if you need me."

Entering her office, Lena removed her jacket and then took the time to hang it in the closet before taking a seat behind her desk. She eyed the box sitting in the middle of it, immediately thinking it definitely wasn't the brochures she had ordered. It was a beautiful gift box, wrapped in red satin-looking paper with a huge white bow.

She immediately pushed the button for Wendy.

"Yes, Lena?"

"Where did this box come from?"

"It was delivered to you today by a private courier."

Lena lifted a brow as she studied the box. There wasn't a card on the outside. "There's not a card."

"It's probably inside the box. You know, one of those ploys to keep nosy secretaries from reading it. Not that I would do such a thing," Wendy said, chuckling.

"So, you have no idea who sent it?" Lena asked.

"Don't you?" was Wendy's quick response. "It's your box."

Lena shook her head. "I don't have a clue, but there's only one way to find out."

"Wait! You want me to call for the bomb squad?"

"Real cute, Wendy." Lena chuckled as she hung up the phone thinking that her secretary was forever the comic, and Wendy's comment made Lena see just how paranoid she was being about the box.

Deciding she had wasted enough time as it was, she reached out and began opening it, not surprised when Wendy came into the room. "If there's an explosion we blow up together," her faithful secretary said. "But trust me, it's probably safe. The guy who delivered it was too cute to be on the wrong side of the law."

It was on Lena's tongue to say "whatever," but when she removed the tissue paper her heart caught as she pulled out a beautiful handcrafted snow globe. Inside was a miniature replica of Charlotte's skyline, and with a push of a small button, that skyline became covered as snowflakes seemed to drift from the sky over the city. Amazing.

A part of Lena's heart suddenly felt tight in her chest. She knew who had sent the package. Morgan. He had remembered her comments about the snow.

"Umm, it doesn't look like one of those explosive devices, so I guess we're safe," Wendy said, reclaiming her attention but only briefly.

"No, it doesn't and yes, we're safe." A few moments later she said, "Isn't it beautiful?" still in awe of her gift.

"Yes, if you like snow, and we all know that you're one of the few strange ones who do."

Lena chuckled as she looked back at the box and saw there was something else inside. She placed the snow globe on her desk and pulled out another item wrapped in tissue paper. When she had it uncovered she couldn't help but laugh. It was her very own Carolina Panthers cap. She then pulled out the card and it said:

Lena,
I saw the snow globe in a store today and it made me think of you. Hope you like it. And about the cap. I thought you looked so cute in mine that I wanted to get you one of your own. And I truly did enjoy our walk together on Sunday. We must do it again sometime.
Morgan

Emotions Lena wasn't ready for touched her at that moment. She couldn't recall the last time someone saw something in a store—other than an outfit

Kylie might see that she would tell her about saying it would look good on her. But this was different. This was special. And it had come from a man. Definitely no man had ever taken the time to send her a gift such as this, one that reflected something she truly liked.

"Before I get back to work, is there something you want to share with me?"

Lena glanced up. She had forgotten Wendy was still in the room. She pulled herself together and cleared her throat and said, "It's from Morgan Steele."

Her secretary and friend raised a curious brow. "And?"

"And I think it's time you got back to work."

A cute little frown, one that wasn't at all convincing, appeared on Wendy's face. "See if I share my next romance novel with you. From now on you're going to have to buy your own." With her head held high, Wendy then turned and walked out of the office, closing the door behind her.

Lena grinned as she turned her attention back to the snow globe and cap. She then read the note again. She didn't want to acknowledge the warmth she felt. She clenched her hands together trying to think logically and to fight both the tension and the excitement warring within her. A part of her, the woman in her, wanted to feel giddy at the thought that the very handsome Morgan Steele enjoyed the time he had spent with her walking on Sunday and wanted to do so again.

A part of her was too afraid to come out of her protective shell to believe such a thing. It had been that same part of her that had encouraged her to turn down his invitation to go out with him those other times. The way she saw it she had two strikes against her when it came to a man like Morgan. She wasn't the type of woman someone would associate him with dating, and although it appeared he and her mother got along great on Sunday, and he had even gone so far as to say he liked Odessa, she had no reason to believe he would be willing to take on a twosome if things were to get serious between them.

But then, there was her Gemini twin who was right there in her mind taunting with the questions… *But who wants serious? Even if there could never be a forever between you and Morgan, there could be a now. Why not just live each day at a time and take whatever you want?*

Lena knew the answers. She couldn't think that way because she was the sensible one. The one who thought things through before she acted.

Which was what she was driven to do now.

She needed to call and thank Morgan for the gifts. How should she approach that? Should she tell him how much receiving the gifts truly meant to her, or should she hide her true feelings and thank him, making no big deal of it, and move on?

She reached for the phone deciding to let her conscience be her guide. She took a deep breath to pull back in control, making sure it would be her conscience and not that of her naughty twin.

"MR. STEELE, LENA Spears is on the line for you."

Morgan smiled as he tossed the papers he'd been reading aside. "Please put her through, Linda, and hold the rest of my calls."

As soon as his secretary clicked Lena on the line, in a businesslike tone he said, "Morgan Steele."

"Morgan, this is Lena."

The moment he heard her voice, potent desire slid through every part of his body despite his best efforts to stop it from doing so. He inhaled softly and leaned back in his leather chair. "Lena, how are you?"

"I'm fine. I was calling to thank you for my gifts."

"You didn't have to do that."

"Yes, I did. It was very thoughtful of you."

He chuckled softly. "On occasion I try to be a thoughtful person."

"Well, you are. And there's also another reason I called. The developers of the Palisades and I are close to reaching an agreement about those additional amenities I'm pushing for. I've come up with a list and was wondering if you had the time for us to go over them."

He raised a brow. "Now?"

"Yes, now, unless you're busy at the moment."

Morgan looked at his closed briefcase, and then across the room at the golf club resting against the wall where he'd been practicing his swing. He definitely wasn't busy. Besides, it was time he made her an offer she couldn't refuse. Using his skill in the area of research and development, for the past couple of weeks he had been researching just what Lena wanted in her life, and without her knowing it he'd put a plan in place not just to develop those wants but to bring them into the limelight.

For now he needed to continue to stick with his plan, although he was about to sharpen his strategy. "Unfortunately, I'm rather busy at the moment. How about if we got together tomorrow?"

"Okay, when would be a good time for me to drop by your office?"

His office was the last place he intended for them to meet, especially when he presented his proposal to her. "My secretary mentioned earlier that my calendar for tomorrow is full and I'm flying out of town on business Wednesday morning and won't be returning until late Sunday. What about sometime later tomorrow, after my last appointment?"

"How late are we talking about?"

He knew she was asking because she had to pick up her mother from the adult day care center by six. "Let's say around four. You should be able to cover everything in a short while, right?"

"Yes."

"Good. And, Lena?"

"Yes?"

"My last appointment is out of the office on the other side of town. I prefer not driving back into this area if you don't mind. Is there another place where we can meet? What about your office?"

He knew from something she'd said last week that her office officially closed at four, which meant her secretary would have left for the day. Originally, he'd thought of some pretense to get her to his home and speak with her there, but the more he'd thought about, he'd concluded that although he wanted to be completely alone with her, he was willing to do so while on her turf if it would make her feel more comfortable and in control of the situation.

"My office?"

"Yes. Will that be a problem?"

She paused briefly, then said, "No. My office is fine. I'll look for you at four."

"All right. I'll see you then."

When Morgan hung up the phone he smiled broadly. Tomorrow couldn't get there fast enough to suit him.

CHAPTER SEVEN

THE NEXT DAY was the busiest Lena had had in a long time. She was excited over a new sale, but on the other hand, every time she glanced at her watch or clock, butterflies would take off in her stomach to the point where she was about ready to pull her hair out. Just the thought that within hours Morgan would be arriving, invading her space, had her unsettled.

She had tried talking Wendy into working late, but since it was Wednesday, prayer meeting night at church, her friend had refused to stay, saying she needed all the prayers she could get to be blessed with a good man.

As Lena settled back in her chair to go over a new contact she'd acquired, her thoughts drifted to last night. Unlike with the other nights, it hadn't been her mother calling out for her dad that had awakened her. It had been an ache deep within her, gnawing away at her to the point it made her stomach tremble. She had wanted to blame it on nervous energy, but she knew it was more. The inner turmoil and fierce turbulence she'd felt had been a stark reminder of just how empty, unfulfilling and unsatisfying parts of her life were.

She was thirty-one, a relatively healthy young woman, single—a point her mother still reminded her of on occasion. She knew it downright bothered her mother that she didn't have a man in her life.

Maybe her naughty twin was right about some things. If she accepted that her life would remain as it was, then why couldn't she become involved in someone just for sanity's sake? It would be someone who on occasion would take her to dinner or a movie, someone who could be her escort to the different social functions she attended during the year, and someone who would eventually become her exclusive lover.

She tried recalling the last time she'd shared a bed with a man. Had it been over six years ago? Not since the death of her father? Sheesh! No wonder she was having sleepless nights with feelings of emptiness that wouldn't go away. She possessed a healthy sex drive like the next woman, and should she deny herself a relationship with a man just because she never intended to get serious about one?

She sighed deeply and rubbed the back of her neck, wondering if those were the thoughts of her naughty twin or thoughts of her own. For the first time in a long while she was convinced that she and her twin were on the same page. And she knew the reason.

Morgan Steele.

Morgan had a way of making her acutely aware that she was a woman, a living, breathing woman with real needs. Being around him at times unsettled her. All it took was one of his warm smiles, the sound of his deep husky voice or even one of those impersonal glances he could send her way to drum up heat deep inside her. He could look at you with an intensity that took your breath away, strip you of every wall you wanted to erect and pull you to him like metal to a magnet.

And those were the very reasons the thought of being alone with him today was so unnerving.

"I'm out of here, Lena."

Lena glanced up at the doorway and saw her secretary standing there smiling. She then glanced at the clock on her wall. "It's not four o'clock yet."

Wendy chuckled. "I know but I didn't take a lunch and decided to check out early to run by the cleaner's. Do you need anything before I leave?"

Yes, for you to knock some sense into me. Instead she said, "No, I'm fine here. I don't expect Morgan to stay long, so I should be leaving within a few minutes myself."

Wendy nodded. "Okay, then, I'll see you tomorrow."

Lena settled back in her chair and began making a list. She had placed Morgan's file on her desk. First they needed to discuss the amenities for the home he was interested in buying, and then they would go over the potential sale of his home. He would need to make a decision and soon as to whether or not he wanted to sell his house to the Edwardses or his brother Donovan. Then there was the decision of whether he wanted to place a binder on the new house contingent on selling his present one.

When she heard someone in the doorway, assuming it was Wendy, she didn't glance up when she asked, "Forget something?"

"No, I don't think I've forgotten anything."

Lena snatched her head up at the sound of the deep, masculine voice. She sucked in a deep breath at what now filled her vision. There standing in her doorway was Morgan with a sensuous air surrounding him. And he was staring at her with a very opulent look in his eyes. Today he appeared more overpowering than ever, and she met his stare with a leveled gaze while heat rushed through her body.

She released a shaky sigh and slowly stood to her feet. This was supposed to be a business meeting, but at that moment discussing business was the furthest thing from her mind.

HE WANTED HER.

That thought was most prevalent in Morgan's mind as he tried to rein in his control, desires and temptation. Just looking at her did all sorts of things to him. But the last thing he wanted to do was give the impression that the only thing he was interested in was something physical.

He watched her come around her desk as if she were floating on air, moving with sophistication, style and grace. Men who thought there wasn't anything sexy about a full-figured woman needed to take a second look. Here was a woman who was smart, confident and savvy. Combine all those things with a voluptuous figure and what you got was all the woman any man could possibly want.

He took a deep breath thinking that his first rule of seduction was to take control of the situation with authority, from beginning to end. In the past he'd made the mistake of letting Lena decide their future, but not anymore. By the time he left her office today he would have placed his stamp on at least one part of her.

Deciding to take things slow at first, he approached her with an outstretched hand. "Once again I appreciate your flexibility, Lena." From the relieved expression on her face he could tell that his business-like air relaxed her.

"Morgan, I was glad to accommodate you."

One side of his mouth tilted into a deep smile. By the time it was over he would give new meaning to the word *accommodate*. "Shall we get down to business? I'm sure you have other things to do. And how's your mother?"

"She's doing fine."

"That's good. Do you mind if I remove my jacket?"

"No, not at all."

He took off his jacket and hung it on a rack before crossing the room and settling into the chair directly across from Lena's desk. He glanced around, liked the way her office was decorated and liked it even more that she had found a home for the snow globe. It was sitting on top of a bookcase, in eye view.

He also liked the comfortable-looking leather sofa in her office. "Nice sofa."

"Thanks."

"You ever use it?"

She raised a brow. "Use it for what?"

He shrugged. "For anything. The one in my office is mainly there for decoration, but Bas uses the one in his. In fact before he married he used to sleep on it a lot when he would work so late that he couldn't make it home. Of course all that changed after he got married."

She couldn't help but smile. "I would hope so. And to answer your question, my sofa is used a lot like yours, for decoration. I rarely stay late at the office to use it for anything else."

"I see."

When she took the chair behind her desk he didn't waste time asking, "So now, what about those amenities?"

For the next few minutes he listened as she talked, and he watched the movement of her mouth while she did so. She had such luscious lips and the thought of kissing them made his stomach quiver. The woman was temptation standing up, sitting down and he didn't want to imagine how much temptation she would be lying down.

"So there you have it, Morgan. The developers have agreed to everything I asked for but that one thing. They have also agreed to let the contract be contingent on you selling your house within a reasonable period of time."

He nodded. "Sounds like you've been busy looking out for my welfare," he said, leaning slightly forward, pinning her with his gaze.

Lena shivered, feeling the heat of that gaze. As usual he was dressed in a business suit. When he had taken off his jacket her gaze had been drawn to his broad shoulders. No matter what he wore, there was something masculine and virile in every outfit, always relaying a degree of inner strength. "Yes," she finally responded. "And I think the contingency is a good thing."

"Sounds like it is."

"Are you interested?"

Morgan suddenly caught her gaze and held it, and when he did so she suddenly began experiencing a strange sensation in the pit of her stomach. "Yes, I am very much interested," he said, not taking his eyes off her.

It was something in the way he'd made that statement that made her feel that perhaps they weren't talking about the same thing. With all the poise she could muster, she then stood to her feet. "Well, that's all I had to cover with you, Morgan."

He nodded. "There is this business proposition that I'd like to discuss with you, if you have the time."

She smiled as she settled back comfortably in her chair. "You have another house you want me to sell?"

"No, but it is something very important to me, something I've been thinking about for quite some time but kept putting off because there wasn't anyone I'd met that I felt comfortable about approaching to discuss a partnership."

Lena leaned forward. "Not even Cameron Cody? I understand the two of you are good friends and have done business together on several projects."

Morgan cleared his throat, cracked a smile and chuckled. "Trust me, Cameron wouldn't work for this. I need a woman."

He watched her eyes reflect a myriad of questions before she repeated the last part of what he'd said. "A woman?"

"Yes. In order to pull things off successfully, I need a very astute businesswoman, someone with an open mind, who could think outside the box, and who will appreciate a golden opportunity. And I believe that you are just that person."

The charming smile on Morgan's lips almost had Lena agreeing to anything, without knowing exactly what this "business venture" was about. His eyes were hooked on hers, and somehow she felt his keen sense of intelligence as well as his single-minded determination. He had piqued her curiosity and she definitely needed him to elaborate. "Just what type of business proposition are you talking about, Morgan?"

Morgan leaned forward a little, making sure he had her absolute attention. He also wanted to be right there, to gauge her reaction to his words. "I want you to marry me and have my baby."

Dead silence.

Morgan studied her expression as she sat perfectly still. He saw her blink, then witnessed the fine arch-

ing of her brow; and mere seconds later he became
an ardent observer of how her lips trembled slightly
at the corner. His gaze then moved back to her eyes
and saw how they slowly narrowed to sharp slits. Her
expression left no doubt in his mind what he'd just
told her wasn't anything like what she'd expected.

"Excuse me. I must have heard you wrong," she
finally said, not taking her eyes off his.

"No, you heard me right, Lena."

She stared, as if what he'd said didn't make sense
and she was imagining things. Then she spoke as she
straightened up in her chair. "In that case, I need you
to explain why you think I'd be interested in involv-
ing myself in something so preposterous."

He smiled. "Is it really preposterous? Think about
it for a second. It's no different than a couple agreeing to a prenup. Marriages of convenience, or more
simply put, the one I'm interested in, a marriage of
purpose, are not unheard of these days. People are
marrying for a lot of reasons. Not everyone who marries is doing so for love."

Lena heard what he was saying and a part of her
was a little disappointed. She had been the product
of a couple who loved each other dearly, and when
she had met his parents at Kylie's wedding, she had
thought the same thing about them. And if she'd
ever married, it was to have been for love. But then,
she had given up the idea of ever marrying, so her
feelings or lack of feelings were really a moot point.

However, she couldn't understand why Morgan of
all people would settle for a loveless marriage when

his two older brothers had married for love. Chance and Sebastian were so head over heels in love with their wives that it wasn't funny. Was there a reason Morgan intended to fight the same fate?

"All of that may be true, Morgan, but why are you willing to settle for less than love? You're good-looking, a successful businessman and you have a good personality. I think any woman would find you marriage material."

He chuckled. "Thanks, but the question is, would I find them wife material? I have a lot going on in my life. The last thing I need is drama, or getting into a situation I'd be trying to get out of a few weeks after the wedding. And not to put your gender down because there are some in mine that are just as bad, possibly even worse, but there are some women who're conniving, vicious, manipulative and looking to marriage as a way to secure their financial future. I don't have a problem with the latter, but I want that individual to be one of my choosing and not the other way around."

"And you actually see me as that person?"

"Yes. You bring a lot to the table. You're mature in your thinking, you don't have time for games or drama, but more importantly, I think you will make any child a wonderful mother."

She tried not letting his words be the confidence booster that they were. "What makes you think that?"

He shrugged. "I just do. Maybe it's a hidden insight I have, but just from talking to you I know you want a child, and I believe you will do right by one."

Yes, she did want a child, and staring thirty-two in the face wasn't a joke. But still, there was a lot to consider.

"And," he said, interrupting her thoughts. "I think you would make me a good wife."

Now, that got her attention. "Really, Morgan, like I said, there are plenty of women who will—"

"I don't want any of them."

"And you want me to believe that you want me?"

"Yes."

Lena's heart began pounding. She shook her head. This was crazy. What Morgan was proposing was ludicrous.

He leaned forward with his forearms resting on her desk. "Before you turn me down flat, let me tell you what I'll be offering you. First there's financial security, which I know is something that's important to you. Then there's companionship. I like you and you can consider me as a live-in buddy and pal, which is a relationship some married couples don't even have. I have no reason not to think we wouldn't get along. Then there's the baby, which is something I want and so do you. Last but not least is your mother."

Lena's spine stiffened. "What about my mother?"

"I have no problem with her becoming a part of our household. In fact, I more than welcome it. I think Odessa is special and want her to be my child's grandmother as much as I want you as my child's mother."

Lena bit her lip. Of all the selling points he'd presented to her, this was the one that touched her the most and she couldn't help the warm flood of emotions that suddenly flowed through her. No other male in her past had even as much as wanted her mother as part of their lives, let alone wanted to include her in their family fold.

"Lena?"

She met his gaze. "Yes?"

"I know what I'm asking might sound a bit unorthodox, but it's the way I want to do things. I would want us to marry as soon as possible and start working on the baby right away."

Lena's heart lurched, as heat swirled around in her stomach. "Start on the baby right away?"

"Yes, after the wedding of course. And another thing, only the two of us can know our marriage is not the traditional one, which means I want us to share a bed."

The startled look on her face let him know that she hadn't thought about that part of the arrangement. He decided to press on. "Just so you'll know, I'm thinking about going with that last home you showed me because it will be perfect for our family—which includes your mother. It will give her the privacy she needs while at the same time assuring her that she is wanted. It's important to me that she feels that she is a part of our lives and not an outsider."

Lena sighed. Morgan was hitting her at all angles

and using every single argument she would come up with to his advantage. He was right. Financial security was something she craved, and more than anything she did want a child of her own. And her mother being part of her marriage rather than an outcast was more important than anything. But still...

"What if things don't work out?" she asked softly.

Morgan smiled. Now was not the time to tell her that things *would* work out. Once he got her in his bed, made love to her the way he'd dreamt of doing for over a year and lavished her with all the attention and respect she deserved, then she wouldn't want to be anywhere else.

Instead he said, "We can draw up an agreement that we will stay together and make things work for at least twelve months. After that time if you or I feel that marrying was a mistake, we will end the marriage with joint custody of our child."

He watched as Lena inhaled deeply before she said, "I need to think about this."

"Of course. Do you think you can have an answer by the time I return on Sunday? That's five days away."

Lena's chest tightened. She had a lot of thinking to do, and five days wasn't a lot of time. But still, she would have an answer for him. "Yes, I should have a decision for you by then."

"Good." He stood. "I'm on my way to grab something to eat at the Racetrack Café. Would you care to join me?"

Lena shook her head. The last thing she needed

was something to eat. What she needed was time alone to think. "No, but thanks for asking."

"You're welcome." He crossed the room to get his jacket, and she came from around her desk. She decided to ask him the question she'd been pondering since he had arrived. "How did you get in here?"

"Your secretary," he said, slipping into his jacket. "I was walking in when she was leaving."

"Oh."

He smiled. "Was she supposed to hang around and announce me or something?"

"No, I was just surprised when you arrived," she said, walking him to her office door.

He raised a dark brow quizzically. "Had you forgotten about our appointment?"

Hardly. "No, I hadn't forgotten."

Now she stood in front of him at the door, and as usual he appeared overwhelming and his eyes were on her, as if he was studying her for some reason. The intensity of his gaze made her flush. "You're going to St. Louis, right?" she nervously asked.

He nodded. "Yes. You still have that business card I gave you with my cell phone number and e-mail address in case something comes up or if you need to ask me anything about my proposal?"

"Yes, and you still have mine, right?"

"Yes, I still have it."

"Well, don't hesitate to contact me if you want to withdraw your offer of the marriage thing."

He chuckled. "I won't be withdrawing it."

Lena toyed with the button on her jacket thinking he sounded pretty sure of that. "I hope you have a safe flight, Morgan."

"Thanks, and I promise to have an answer for you regarding the sale of my house when I return."

"Okay. Although I've been showing the Edwardses other places, I think they like your house the best."

The smile that tilted his lips widened. "That's good to know. I'll keep that in mind when I make my decision, and I hope you keep it in mind when you make yours."

Lena sighed, trying to ignore the intense stare in Morgan's eyes. She held out her hand. "Goodbye, Morgan. I'll see you in a few days."

He didn't take her outstretched hand. Instead he continued to stare at her, hold her gaze, rattling her already shaken composure. "I want to do things different this time, Lena," he said, his voice low, seductive.

Mesmerized, she dropped her hand to her side. Her palm suddenly felt warm and sweaty. And when he took a step closer to her, an aching need, that throbbing desire that had awakened her last night, was there, clawing at her, and she took a step forward as well.

"I think we can do better than that," he said in a warm, husky tone, which was barely above a whisper, pulling her total concentration back in.

Before she could release her next breath, he lowered his mouth to hers with a quick, clean sweep of his tongue across her lips. He captivated her then and there, snapping her composure and destroying the last hold she had on her control.

She placed her hand on his chest when his mouth closed hungrily, greedily over hers, almost eating her alive and unleashing a degree of passion she didn't know she had. Her naughty twin had passion, yes, but her, no. But this was not her twin who felt the smoldering eruption deep inside her as Morgan's tongue sent her senses reeling from the mastery of his lips.

Nor was it her twin whose moans escaped her lips beneath Morgan's demanding mouth while he grasped her around the waist in a tight hold of possession, bringing her closer to him and making her aware of how masculine and strong his body was.

A part of her was totally stunned at the depth of her need, her passion, her desire, but then another part wasn't. The recesses of her mind taunted that this was Morgan, the man who had invaded her dreams for the past year. Morgan, who practically made her catch her breath every time she saw him. Morgan, the man who wanted to give her the baby she'd always wanted; and Morgan, the man her body was instinctively, unashamedly arching against.

She uttered a low moan of protest when he finally raised his head, and when he pressed her face against his chest she realized the impact the kiss had had on him as well. She heard his heart racing, felt the irregular beats beneath her head and heard the sound of his ragged breathing being forced from his throat. She buried her face deeper into his chest, feeling warm and contented. Moments later she sighed when she felt him rest his chin on the crown on her head.

They stood that way for a while, neither ready to separate, too mesmerized and filled with raw emotions to say anything. Then he reached down and lifted her chin with the tip of his finger, meeting her gaze, and then lowered his mouth to hers again. This kiss was gentler but was filled with a high degree of passion nonetheless.

When he finally released her mouth again, he let out a shaky breath and murmured softly, "I'd better go and please think about my proposal."

Placing one quick kiss to her lips, he turned and then he was gone.

CHAPTER EIGHT

"MORGAN ASKED YOU what!" Kylie asked, staring at Lena disbelievingly.

Lena waited until the waitress had placed her order of French fries on the table and walked away before directing her attention back to Kylie. "I know it sounds crazy but he asked me to marry him and have his baby."

Kylie continued to stare at her, saying nothing, and then she shook her head, smiling as she plucked a fry off Lena's plate. "So you're it."

Lena lifted a confused brow. "I'm what?"

"Morgan's perfect woman."

Lena frowned. "I have no idea what you're talking about."

Kylie scooted in her chair closer to the table so her voice wouldn't carry. At least she scooted as close as her huge stomach would allow. "Everyone in the Steele family knows about Morgan's obsession with finding the perfect woman. Evidently, you've made quite an impression on him."

"Or he's realized there's no such thing as a perfect woman, like there's no perfect man. But that doesn't explain why he wants that person to be me."

Kylie rolled her eyes. "Aw, come on, Lena. Morgan has shown interest in you since that night the two of you met at that charity ball. He asked you out several times but you turned him down."

Lena munched on her fry thinking that yes, he had asked her out, but she really hadn't taken him seriously at first. But when he'd asked a few more times she thought it would be a smart move to break things down to him as to why she wouldn't go out with him. Now he was asking her not only to marry him but also to have his baby.

"So, are you going to do it?"

Kylie's question interrupted her thoughts. She knew of all people, she had to be totally honest with her best friend. "Would I sound like an awful person if I said I was really thinking about the idea? Gosh, Kylie, he's the first man to take Mom into consideration. He actually said he would be proud to have her for his child's grandmother."

"Wow, that's deep, isn't it?"

"Yes, for me it is." Another thing that was deep was the kiss they'd shared. Even now if she were to touch her lips with her fingertips, she was convinced she would still be able to feel the warmth of Morgan's lips there. "But there are other things to consider," she finally said, sighing.

"Like what?"

"Although our union will be a marriage of purpose, as he put it, he still wants us to project a semblance of realness. In other words, he has no qualms about us sharing a bed."

"But you do?"

"Yes. No. Hell, I don't know." The last couple of guys she'd dated—way back when—took that time to cross her mind. They hadn't done anything to light a fire within her, at least not to the degree Morgan had with just a mere kiss. "Trust me, it wouldn't bother me one bit to sleep with Morgan," she finally said. "But what if we start something that neither of us can finish?"

"Meaning?"

"What if things don't work out and he decides I'm not the woman he wants to live with or the right woman for the mother of his child?"

Kylie shrugged. "Knowing Morgan I'm sure he's thought this thing through before approaching you with it. If I were you, the only thing I'd worry about is what decision I'll be giving him in five days."

SHE HADN'T DREAMED today, Lena thought, slipping beneath the covers later that night. She lay on her back and stared up at the ceiling as memories flooded her. It was hard to believe Morgan had actually asked her to marry him and have his baby.

After Morgan had left her office she had hung back, unable to leave as she'd planned to do. Instead she had sat at her desk trying to rationalize what had happened moments earlier, replaying in her mind his every word, every stroke of his tongue in her mouth.

In the end when she'd realized she hadn't been hallucinating, she had called Kylie and asked to meet her at the nearest Burger King after she closed her florist shop that day.

After their talk she had left to pick up her mother from day care, barely remembering what their conversation had been about on the ride home. The only thing she remembered was the one single question that was still floating around in her head.

Why, of all the women he knew, he wanted to marry her?

From the day she had agreed to sell his house and help him locate another one, things had been strictly business between them. Even when he'd had dinner with her and her mother on Sunday he hadn't shown any obvious signs that he was attracted to her.

Or had he?

She had noted the intense looks in his gazes, but he'd always looked at her that way. In the past she had chalked things up as a one-sided attraction that she could never act on…but today, following his lead, she had.

She doubted that she would ever be able to look him in the face and not be reminded of their kiss. Today she had been introduced to another facet of Morgan's unique personality. His passionate side. It would be a side she would be constantly exposed to if they were to marry. Sheesh! For over a year he had been her nightly dream and she wasn't sure she was ready for him to make the jump from being her Mr. Fantasy to taking on the role of her Mr. Reality.

But then, all she had to do was close her eyes to remember the exact moment he'd made his outlandish proposal. *"I want you to marry me and have my baby."* The moment he had said the words, although she hadn't been sure she'd heard him correctly, he had looked at her with that deep, dark gaze of his as a spark of desire had flooded her insides, overheating her senses. And the seductive scent of the cologne he'd been wearing hadn't helped matters.

And later, right before he had left, he had taken the initiative to step closer to her, and she had boldly walked into his arms. And the exact moment their tongues had mingled, zapping her willpower with tenderness, she had known she was a goner. She knew even now that she would probably be whispering his name in her sleep. But that was okay. She didn't know of any other man whose name she'd rather whisper.

And as she closed her eyes to peaceful slumber, it was Morgan's face that occupied her dreams.

MORGAN INHALED A steadying breath as he pushed himself out of bed and sat on the edge of it. The kiss he had shared earlier that day with Lena was still heavily on his mind, in his thoughts, embedded so deep in his memory that he couldn't sleep and was so elemental it made his entire body ache.

The kiss had been everything he had known it would be and more, and she had felt just like he'd figured she would in his arms. Now his senses were incapable of any other thoughts but those of her. At this point if she were to turn down his proposal to marry him and have his baby he didn't know what he would do.

He stood, deciding there wasn't much hope of getting a lot of sleep tonight. His only hope was to try and get some shut-eye on the plane, which he would be catching in a few hours. Throwing on his robe, he made his way down the stairs to get a cup of coffee before going over some paperwork for his meeting with Cameron and Ben Malloy.

Malloy was an entrepreneur with multifaceted interests. A year ago Morgan had approached him and Cameron in regards to what he saw not only as a sound business opportunity but also as a way to give back to his hometown's dying community. His latest venture was to open several shopping malls within urban areas of several handpicked communities around the country.

In recent years there had been an explosion of growth within the suburban areas of various cities, but there seemed to be a constant neglect within the downtown areas—where a number of African Americans lived. Most business owners—although they considered themselves rather astute—failed to recognize or acknowledge the potential growth in urban areas, and as a result, their narrow-mindedness had left the residents, those people living in the neglected areas, with limited access to shopping, adequate housing and entertainment.

Magic Johnson had brought attention to this issue when he opened several theaters within the urban communities across the country. And what Morgan,

Cameron and Ben were poised to do was something similar with the development of a mall in St. Louis. Ben had asked their support and their aid in pouring a substantial amount of money into the project, and after doing a considerable amount of research they had determined it not only would be a worthwhile financial investment, but it would also be a way to help place development in those overlooked areas.

Morgan glanced at the clock when he entered his kitchen. It was three in the morning and he had a flight out at eight. After he'd left Lena he had come home to pack, prepare a quick dinner and savor the memories of his first kiss with the woman of his dreams.

Moments later as he sat at his desk, he absently stirred his coffee while trying to read the report Cameron's secretary had faxed earlier. Instead of concentrating, his mind was stuck on other things, namely Lena. Would she agree to his offer of marriage? He smiled thinking once he had her in his bed there were no limitations to just what he could do and would do.

The die was cast and an indescribable warmth spread through him in knowing that if Lena agreed to become his wife and the mother of his child, he would have her right where he wanted her.

CHAPTER NINE

"How's that Steele boy?"

Lena smiled as she shoved in her briefcase the documents she needed to go over with a potential buyer. Funny, although she knew her mother's usage of the word *boy* was just a term, Lena couldn't visualize Morgan as a boy. She saw the person who had kissed her almost senseless yesterday as being a man in every full sense of the word.

"If you're asking about Morgan, I guess he's fine," she said, trying to keep her voice light, neutral and nonchalant.

"So when will he be coming back?"

Lena lifted her head and met her mother's gaze with an arched brow. "How did you know he was going somewhere?"

"He told me when he called a few days ago," Odessa said, as she sat at the kitchen table and took a sip of her coffee.

Lena, with an incredulous look on her face, shut her briefcase with a click. "Morgan called you?"

"Yes."

"When?"

"I told you it was a few days ago. Monday, I believe."

Lena sighed. "And *when* did he call on Monday?"

"In the afternoon. Before you got home."

Lena leaned against the kitchen counter. "He called to tell you he was leaving town?"

"No. Actually he called to thank me for dinner on Sunday, and then he mentioned he was leaving town." Her mother took another sip of her coffee, then asked, "Why all the questions?"

Lena rolled her eyes heavenward wondering if her mother had forgotten that she was the one who'd brought up Morgan in the first place. She decided to jog her memory. "Mom, you're the one who asked about Morgan. If you had spoken to him this week, then why did you even ask me how he was doing?"

"Because I thought that perhaps you had talked to him since then."

"Yes, I saw him yesterday at my office. You know I'm selling his home and helping him find another." Until she decided how she would handle his proposal she didn't want her mother to get any ideas, so she added, "Our relationship is strictly professional."

"If that's true, then why did he come to dinner?"

Lena sighed. "Because you asked him, and like he told you, he hadn't eaten a home-cooked meal in a long time. No man would have turned that down."

"Maybe, but I think he came for another reason altogether," Odessa said, matter-of-factly.

"And what reason is that?"

Her mother's lips parted into the barest of smiles. "You. That Steele boy likes you. Any fool can see that."

LATER THAT DAY Lena's mind was filled with Morgan's proposition. He would see their marriage as a business venture. Could she do the same? What if she began developing feelings for him and he walked in one day and declared that he wanted out of the marriage? What would she do then?

She was jolted from her thoughts with the ringing of her telephone. She picked it up. "Yes, Wendy?"

"Vanessa Steele is on the line for you."

Lena raised a brow. She and Vanessa had worked together on several community projects around town. Like her own father, Vanessa's father had been the victim of cancer, so it wasn't unusual for them to participate in fund-raising activities to benefit the American Cancer Society. The same thing applied to Chance, whose first wife had died from cancer.

Lena liked Vanessa. She thought she was a person who wasn't just beautiful on the outside but on the inside as well. And unlike some people whose family had a lot of money—namely someone like Cassandra Tisdale—Vanessa Steele didn't have a "better than thou" bone in her body.

"Thanks, Wendy, please put her through."

Lena only had to wait a few moments before the sound of Vanessa's exuberant voice came on the line. "Lena, how are you?"

"I'm fine, Vanessa, and how are you?"

"I'm doing great. I just got a call from the principal at the high school I graduated from requesting that I spearhead this project, and after hearing it, I immediately thought of soliciting your, Jocelyn's and Sienna's help." She chuckled, then added, "Kylie's pregnancy saved her from me pulling her in as well, and we don't have a lot of time to pull this thing together."

Lena's interest was piqued after hearing the excitement in Vanessa's voice. "What sort of project is it?"

"A mini career fair. Only thing is that the head of the school's business department wants it held in a few weeks. If we wait until next month we'll be competing against prom time. Sorry for the late notice but it was something she thought of doing just last night, but I think it's a wonderful idea to showcase local employment opportunities for those who might not be considering college as an option right now."

"I agree, it's a wonderful idea. How can I help?"

"I'm going to need your business to participate by having a booth. It would be nice for the students to see the wonderful opportunities in real estate."

"Do you have a date picked out yet?"

"Yes, the thirtieth of this month. That's a Friday. I've talked to Chance, and to kick things off the Steele Corporation will host a sit-down dinner for all the businesses that will be participating."

"Well, consider me in," Lena said, smiling.

"And consider it done. I'd like to have a meeting this weekend, something informal. How about my place on Saturday evening? Are you available?"

Lena didn't like to commit herself to being somewhere until she made sure her mother would be fine staying alone. So far her mother's condition had improved over the past month or so, and she was taking her medication when she was supposed to, making it easier for her to get around. "Let me get back with you about that meeting on Saturday."

"That's fine. Do you still have my number?"

Lena quickly checked the Rolodex on her desk. "Yes, I still have it."

"Good. I hope to see you if you can make it. If you can't I'll understand and I will call you the early part of next week and go over what was discussed."

"Thanks."

After hanging up the phone, Lena couldn't help but feel good that Vanessa had included her on the committee.

MORGAN ENTERED HIS hotel room after having dinner with Cameron and Ben. Moments later he had set up his laptop on the desk in the room and called home to speak with Chance before going into the bathroom to take a shower.

According to Chance, things were running smoothly back at the office, and Chance was glad to hear that Morgan would be returning home late Friday night instead of Sunday. That meant he would be home for the brothers' weekly basketball game Saturday morning.

After his shower, Morgan sat down at the desk and booted up his computer, immediately checking his e-mail to see if his secretary had sent him the documents he had requested of her earlier. She had, and after downloading all the attachments and reading through most of them, which took almost a full hour, he clicked on his Instant Messages, mainly to see if Donovan was online. His younger brother had a tendency to pick up dates online as well as off.

It appeared Donovan wasn't, but someone else was, he thought, when Lena's screen name popped up. He glanced at the clock radio near the bed. It was almost two in the morning. What was she still doing up?

He remembered her once mentioning that because of her mom, she typically got into bed early. He hoped that whatever reason she was still awake and on her laptop he wouldn't interrupt, because he intended to drop in.

LENA SMILED AS she continued to read the messages her goddaughter, Tiffany, had sent her earlier that day over the computer. Tiffany was excited about the prospect of becoming a big sister to a baby girl or boy, and before going to bed each night she would send Lena information on all the things she planned to do in her new role.

Tiffany had also written to tell her about this guy from school that she simply adored. Although Kylie had lightened up some on Tiffany now that she was sixteen, her best friend was still trying to make sure Tiffany didn't make the same mistakes she had made as a teen, which was understandable. These days

Kylie was handling the situation in a different way, one that would not alienate her daughter. Chance and Kylie, along with Tiffany and Chase's son, Marcus, were one big happy family.

Lena leaned back against the headboard and balanced her laptop on raised knees, remembering what had awakened her at two in the morning. She had had a dream of her and Morgan together, in bed. A shiver ran down her spine at the memory.

In her dream Morgan's kisses had been just as heated as the one in her office. And when he had placed her on the bed, she had watched as his eyes changed from a dark brown to a hot brown as she succumbed to his magnetic pull and sexual appeal. Her breath had become shallow as he slowly removed her clothes, and desire consumed her, sending blood gushing through her veins like water through a fire hose. The eyes that had stared at her while he'd gotten undressed had had her pulse escalating, had made a certain part of her beg for him to take her over the edge. Her tension had mounted when he placed his body over hers, the scent of him sending her senses into overdrive. Her thighs had parted, and mere seconds before he was to enter her she had heard her mother cry out for her father, thus shattering the moment.

Lena sighed, thinking maybe that had been a good thing. She couldn't imagine how things would have been if Morgan had completed the task and made love to her. She was about to log off the computer when an Instant Message popped up on her screen, almost startling her. The message asked *What are you doing up so late?*

She frowned, lifting a brow, pondering the identity of the individual who wanted to know. She was not a person who indulged in Internet chats or instant messages unless it was Kylie or Tiffany, and she knew both of them were in bed asleep now. Her gaze was drawn to the screen name, and her heart almost stopped—*MDSteele*. She immediately sucked in a huge breath upon recognizing the screen name belonged to Morgan Darien Steele.

Ignoring the sensations that shivered up her spine, she nervously typed a response, wanting to make sure it was him.

Morgan?

Yes, it's me.

Satisfied, she then clicked further to answer his question. *Mom woke me. Bad dream. And I couldn't go back to sleep.* She decided not to tell him about his part in her sleepless night. *What about you? Why are you still up?*

Late business meeting and not ready to go to bed, was his typed response. And then *Is your Mom okay?*

Yes, she's fine. And how are things going with your meeting?

All right.

Moments later she typed. *Can I ask you something?*

You can ask me anything.

Why me, Morgan?

He knew what she was asking him and moments

later he typed *Why not you, Lena? You're a very beautiful and desirable woman and I want you.*

She swallowed hard, trying to keep her heart from pounding at his words. She refused to put too much stock into them. She was glad he couldn't hear her low laugh as she typed *Come on, Morgan, be for real. I'm not your type.*

And what do you see as my type?

Lena frowned. If he wanted the truth she would give it to him. *Worldly, highly sophisticated, pencil thin...*

Wrong on all accounts. Is that why you never wanted to go out with me?

She quickly typed a response. *No. I told you the reason. Once burned you learn not to play with fire.*

And you saw me as fire?

Maybe not fire, but definitely someone too hot to handle.

She could tell by the timing that he had paused before sending her his next typed response. *What if I told you that I saw you as someone too hot to handle as well?*

Lena smiled. *Then my response would be that you probably had me mixed up with my twin.*

You have a twin?

I'm a Gemini.

Interesting. What's the difference in the two of you?

I'm not a risk taker. My twin is. She lives for the moment without thinking about her actions. I do just the opposite. She decided to leave off anything about her twin having a tendency to be naughty and wild.

How often does she come out?

Lena rolled her eyes and grinned. Of course as a man Morgan would be interested in knowing that. *She's never actually come out. I've managed to keep her in line.*

What a shame.

Yes, well, that's how it is. And with that said, I'm going to turn in now. I'm finally feeling sleepy.

All right. Pleasant dreams. Good night, Lena.

Good night, Morgan.

MORGAN SMILED WHEN Lena clicked off-line, and moments later he logged off his computer as well. He found it interesting what she'd told him about her so-called twin. Hmm, so there was another side of her, a side she was suppressing, a side where she could become another person, one who wouldn't hesitate to let her hair down.

He would love to meet that Lena Spears.

Now she had him curious and his pulse began racing. Just the thought of a loose Lena had him reaching for one of the chilled bottled waters the housekeeping staff had left in the ice bucket on the desk. He quickly opened it and took a sip, cooling his insides.

He shook his head, remembering when she'd mentioned she hadn't thought she was his type. He definitely had to prove her wrong on that, and while doing so he wanted to prove to her that whether she was the ultraconservative Lena or the not so conservative one, she was the woman he wanted.

OVER BREAKFAST THE next morning Lena thought about her tête-à-tête with Morgan via her laptop. She hated to admit it but she'd actually enjoyed herself. There had been something downright fun about exchanging words with him online rather than by phone or in person. While online he couldn't hear her responses or see her facial expressions. She couldn't believe that she'd actually mentioned her mischievous twin to him. Well, he'd certainly seemed interested in that.

"I'm sorry I woke you last night, Lena."

Lena glanced up when her mother came to the table and sat down. Of all the times her mother had awakened her during the night, this was the first time she had apologized for doing so, and Lena wanted to assure her that there was no need for the apology. "Mom, you don't have to apologize, I understand."

Her mother looked at her with sad eyes. "And what do you understand?"

Lena shrugged. "I understand that you and Dad had a close relationship and that losing him was hard on you, and it still is. I know he was your very best friend and confidant. What the two of you shared was really awesome when you think about it."

Odessa nodded slowly and Lena saw the lone tear that clung to one of her eyelids. "I know you probably think at some point I should let go and move on with my life, Lena, but it's hard. Your father was my life. I feel lonesome without him. I know you're here but it's not the same."

Lena didn't know what to say. One of the main reasons she took her mother to the adult day care center twice a week was so she could be around other senior adults. Deciding to change the subject to a cheerier note, she asked, "So, how's Ms. Emily doing?" She watched a smile appear on her mother's lips.

"Emily is doing fine. I think this is the weekend her grandkids and great-grands are coming over."

Lena swallowed. Now she wished she hadn't brought Ms. Emily up. "Is it?"

"Yes. And I hope some nice young man comes into your life. I want you to share with a man that special love me and your father had. And then more than anything, I wish I could have a little one to cuddle on my knee before the good Lord calls me home."

An ache appeared in Lena's chest as she heard the sadness in her mother's voice. Considering everything, Lena knew that if she was to say yes to Morgan's proposal she would be able to give her mother the one thing she wanted the most.

LATER THAT NIGHT after making sure her mother was settled in for the night, Lena took a shower and then slipped into a pair of silky pajamas Kylie had given her on her last birthday.

She settled in bed with her laptop, deciding to see if Tiffany had sent her a message that day. Today had been hectic, and to keep Morgan off her mind she had thrown herself into her work. She had shown another couple Morgan's house, and the moment she had walked through the door sensations had curled in the pit of her stomach, as if she expected to look up and see him walk down his stairs at any moment.

Unfortunately the couple she'd shown the house to had a three-year-old son who had just finished eating a chocolate bar. Needless to say, a chocolate handprint had gotten on a few of Morgan's doors. The boy's mother had apologized and wiped off those areas, but sometime tomorrow, Lena intended to go to Morgan's place and make sure the woman hadn't missed any spots.

Moments later she chuckled after reading Tiffany's note. The boy she had thought she was interested in a few days ago was no longer the hunk of the week. A new guy at school had caught her eye. Lena shook her head. Her goddaughter was a lot different from Kylie when she'd been that age. At sixteen, Kylie had thought Tiffany's father, Sam Miller, was her entire world. At least she'd thought that until he'd left her alone and pregnant. A part of Lena was glad that Tiffany was not getting serious about any one guy.

Lena tried not to notice that Morgan was also online. Chances were he was aware she was on the computer as well and she couldn't help wondering if he would do as he'd done the night before and engage in online conversation with her. She didn't have long to wonder when Morgan's screen name popped up. But his typed request surprised her.

Lena. I want to chat with your twin tonight.

Do you now? was Lena's typed response as she managed a wry smile, after regaining her composure.

Yes.

Why?

I'd like to get to know her.

Don't think that's a good idea.

Let me be the judge of that. Trust me.

Lena leaned back against her headboard trying to remember the last time she had put her complete trust in a man. When she remembered, her chin firmed as she thought stubbornly, why should she trust Morgan? But then, another part of her wanted to trust him. "I'm a big girl," she murmured softly to herself. "Maybe it's time I act like it."

Smiling, a naughty and wicked shiver sliding down her spine, she began typing. *Okay, I trust you and for the rest of the time you're online, you'll be chatting with my twin.*

Okay. Thanks for trusting me.

Lena nodded. She hadn't expected him to thank her for that.

So, Lena's twin. How are you?

Lena wasn't sure what came over her at that moment. Maybe it was the idea that now she could, even if only for a short while, finally unleash her unruly inner self with a man she'd admitting to trusting. This was her chance to shed her inhibitions, stop being the good girl for a little while and walk on the wild side.

Taking a deep breath and before she could change

her mind she began typing and felt an intense shiver when she sent Morgan her response.

I'm fine, Morgan, but I wish I was there with you.

Morgan was sitting at a large oak desk in his suite when he received Lena's response, and immediately he felt his body transform into hard steel, and inner fire began creeping through his bloodstream. The Lena Spears he knew, even the one he'd kissed the other day, would not have admitted such a thing.

Inhaling deeply he began typing. *And what would you do if you were?*

It didn't take long for her typed response. *I'd try things on you that I've never tried on a man before.*

Feeling hot, he undid the top button of his shirt before typing *Such as?*

Depends on where you are now. You're in your suite, right?

Yes.

In bed?

No. I'm sitting at the desk

That's a good spot. I'd clear off that desk and spread my naked self on top of it.

Mercy! Morgan thought and immediately grabbed a sixteen-ounce bottle of chilled water and practically drained the entire thing just to cool off his heated body. The thought of Lena spread naked across this desk aroused such strong feelings within him that he had to lean back in his chair to place space between him and the desk. Imagining those voluptuous thighs exposed to his view sent a warm flood of anticipated and delicious pleasure racing through him.

Morgan? she typed. *You're still there?*

Barely. But instead of typing that single response, he stroked the keys to ask *And then what you would do?*

Whatever you want. I would become your every woman.

His every woman... Just the thought sent more heat escalating through him. He leaned forward, feeling a heated rush. He tried to remain calm, keep his composure, but it was hard, just like the rest of him.

Before he could type in a response she sent him a question. *And what's your fantasy, Morgan Steele?*

He smiled, not the least ashamed to admit what that was. He typed in his response. *Making love to you all day long and feel you climax beneath me several times. More times than either of us can count.* Then he smiled with a predatory satisfaction when she didn't respond for a while.

You sure about that? was the response she finally sent.

Positive. Now what's your fantasy?

To have you on top of me, making love to you, and I'd be grateful for a half day and at least one climax.

That powerful chemistry that she had failed to acknowledge the first night they'd met was back with a vengeance, stirring every volatile emotion within him. This was the Lena he wanted in his bed, and once he got her there he was going to prove they were one and the same. There weren't two sides of

Lena Spears, and he planned to make sure she realized that.

Don't settle for one climax. Get ready for several, he typed and then added *Your wish will be my every command, Lena Spears. Whatever you want done, I will do...with pleasure.*

There was a pause and then she responded. *I think it's time we ended this conversation before the screens burn out.*

If we must.

We must, and remember, Morgan, tonight you chatted with the twin.

He lifted a challenging brow. The sexual excitement she had aroused in him had gotten to an intense level, had become a momentous force. There was no way he would let her cunningly fall back to being her old self. Even over cyberspace he sensed her emotional withdrawal.

Good night, Morgan.

Good night, Lena.

He waited for her to log off before he did likewise. Then he sagged back against the chair thinking he couldn't return to Charlotte quick enough to suit him.

CHAPTER TEN

THE FOLLOWING DAY Morgan discovered that he had a hard time focusing his attention on anything, even this meeting with Cameron and Ben. By the end of the day business negotiations were behind them, everything had been finalized and it was agreed that they would enter into a partnership for the development of urban real estate, with the objective of fostering economic opportunities in the underserved urban areas around the country.

Ben had caught a flight back to Los Angeles as soon as the meeting was over, and if it hadn't been for the promise Morgan had made to Cameron a few days ago to stick around and play a few rounds of golf, he would have been on the next plane bound for Charlotte. Now with the golfing behind them they both had plans to fly home on Thursday instead of Friday.

After enjoying a scrumptious meal at a very popular soul food restaurant in St. Louis, they decided to have a couple of beers while a jazz band performed.

"So how's Vanessa?"

Morgan lifted his gaze from studying the contents of his glass of beer and glanced across the table at

Cameron. He smiled over at his friend. "She's no different than she was the last time you asked me about her. What can I say? Vanessa is Vanessa."

Cameron took a sip of his own beer, straight from the bottle. "Maybe it's time for me to pay you a visit in Charlotte."

Morgan chuckled. "Yeah, maybe it is. That should really shake things up a bit."

Cameron grinned. "I imagine it would. So how is the sale of your house coming?"

Cameron's questions made Morgan think of Lena, not that he hadn't been thinking about her anyway. "Lena has found several interested buyers, and I actually like the new place she found for me."

Cameron lifted a brow. "But I thought you hiring her as a real estate agent was a cunning ploy to spend time with her."

Morgan smiled. "It started out that way, but this might be one of those situations where I got caught in my own trap."

Cameron chuckled. "That doesn't bother you?"

"No, whatever works I'm for it." Moments later Morgan asked, "Why are we drawn to difficult women?"

Cameron shrugged massive shoulders as he glanced at his watch. "Because we're strong men. Any weaker man would have given up by now. Rejection is something a lot of men don't take very well. But you know that saying about only the strong surviving. I think it has become our slogan. Besides," he said, after another sip of his beer, "it's more than our nature, Morgan. It's our destiny."

Morgan's mouth formed into a determined smile. Cameron had spoken of strength, but Morgan hadn't felt strong after talking with Lena last night. In fact for a long while after their conversation he had sat in the chair behind the desk, too weak in the knees to even move. Never had he gotten so turned on from exchanging words with a woman through cyberspace. And every time he moved around in his hotel room and glanced over at his desk, he could picture a naked Lena spread on it.

He glanced over at Cameron. "So can I expect a visit from you sometime later this month?"

Cameron smiled. "Yes, that's something you can pretty much bank on."

LENA FOUND THAT her emotional side was the pits. She had asked herself a million times upon wakening that morning, how had she done what she did last night? Sheesh! She could blame it on her fictional twin all she wanted, but it was her fingers that had typed in those outlandish words.

What did Morgan think of her? From his typed responses it didn't appear that he'd been put off by her behavior. In fact he seemed to have enjoyed chatting with her naughty twin. She sighed thinking that he was due back in town on Sunday and she was supposed to give him an answer to his proposal. She was no closer to making a decision than she had been the day he'd made it.

She had planned to go by his house that day to clean up any more chocolate handprints left by that little boy, but hadn't had the desire to do so. The last place she needed to go today was the place where Morgan slept, ate, bathed, dressed...

She tossed a file on her desk wondering at what point she would stop fantasizing about the man. Hadn't doing so got her in enough trouble already?

She almost jumped when her intercom sounded. Leaning forward she pushed the button. "Yes, Wendy?"

"Cassandra Tisdale is here to see you."

Lena lifted a brow. Cassandra Tisdale? What would the woman want with her? There was only one way to find out. "Send her in, Wendy."

Lena stood just moments before her office door opened and Cassandra breezed in, bringing all her air of phoniness with her. She decided not to waste any time in asking, "Cassandra, what can I do for you?"

Cassandra smiled brightly. "I think I owe you an apology."

Lena crossed her arms over her chest and eyed the woman skeptically. "Do you?"

"Yes, silly me. When I saw you and Morgan together a couple of weeks ago I jumped to the wrong conclusions when I should have known better. I just heard at lunch that you're selling his home for him. I should have known it was something to do with business and not anything personal."

Lena silently heard what Cassandra was not saying. "And why should you have known that?"

Cassandra smiled affectionately. Lena surmised that it was the same way she would have smiled at a puppy before kicking it. "Because you aren't Morgan's type. In fact I know the perfect woman for him."

Lena leaned her hips against her desk. "Do you?"

"Yes, my cousin Jamie. You probably remember her from the ball that night."

Now it was Lena who smiled. "Oh yes. Isn't that the same cousin you tried pushing off on Chance?"

Cassandra frowned. "Chance disappointed me. I always thought he appreciated the finer things in life."

"He does. That's why he married Kylie. In fact I think he's a man who recognizes top quality when he sees it."

Cassandra's frown deepened. "Well, I wish them the best. But getting back to Morgan."

"And your cousin?"

"Yes. Did you know she was his date at the governor's inaugural ball last year?"

Lena smiled. She had heard it a different way from Kylie. It seemed the young woman was in attendance and had asked Morgan to take her home when she began not feeling well. "And?"

"And I thought he was rather taken with her."

"Really?"

Cassandra smiled. "Yes. Money marries money. What can I say?"

Nothing, Lena thought. The woman had basically said it all. Now it was her time to speak, and what she had to say would definitely burst the woman's bubble. Maybe it was the fact that she was sick and tired of the Cassandras and Jamies of the world who thought good things should happen only to them because they were born with silver spoons in their mouths, or perhaps it was because Cassandra, as usual, had rubbed her the wrong way.

Whatever the reason, Lena had had enough. "I hate to disappoint you and your cousin, but when Morgan returns to town we'll be announcing our engagement."

Cassandra blinked and then burst out laughing. "If you think Morgan is going to marry you, then you are a fool. Everyone knows he wants the perfect woman, and trust me you're far from perfect. Your lack of pedigree, your appearance, your profession. You are definitely not what Morgan Steele needs in a wife, so if he asked you to marry him it had to be during a weak moment when he wasn't thinking rationally. Men marry women they will be proud to be seen with. Although I really don't care for Kylie or that woman Bas married, I have to admit they look decent enough. I can't say the same for you."

Anger tore through Lena and she came close to slapping that smile off Cassandra Tisdale's face, but she wouldn't let the woman know how much her words bothered her. Instead she said, "Thanks for dropping by, Cassandra, and unless you have a house you want me to sell or you're looking to buy one, I really have work to do, so please leave."

"Less than a month."

Lena raised a brow. "Excuse me?"

Cassandra tilted her head back and gave Lena a haughty look. "Jamie has moved here, and like I said, she and Morgan have dated before and if I recall they got rather cozy. I bet that, engaged or not, in less than a month she'll have Morgan and you won't."

And then she turned and breezed out of the office with the same air of phoniness that she'd breezed in with.

"WHAT A WITCH," Jocelyn Steele said, putting down her cup of tea. "I can't believe Bas could have been engaged to marry such a creature."

Jocelyn had joined Kylie and Lena for lunch and Lena told them about Cassandra Tisdale's visit.

"Honestly," Kylie said, sipping her tea. "I think the brothers knew Bas would come to his senses before the wedding. Chance even told me such. And he was right. When we got back from our honeymoon we found out that Bas had broken the engagement."

"Well, I'm glad I'm the woman he chose," Jocelyn said, smiling. She then turned her attention to Lena and smiled. "So, are you and Morgan really getting married?"

Lena wanted to hold her head down in frustration. She hadn't told Morgan of her decision, but she hadn't wasted any time throwing it in Cassandra's face in anger. "I never gave Morgan an answer. I'm supposed to tell him what I've decided when he returns."

"Well, you might as well have told the entire

town," Kylie said, grinning. "I bet it will be spread all over Charlotte by morning. And I hope you don't believe that garbage Cassandra said about her cousin being able to turn Morgan's head in less than a month."

Lena sighed. She had seen Cassandra's cousin and had to admit the woman was a beauty. How would Morgan react if the woman did turn her attention his way?

"Don't think it, Lena."

Lena lifted her head and met Kylie's gaze. "Don't think what?"

"That anything Cassandra said is true. Morgan is not the type of man who would be interested in a woman like Jamie Hollis. I told you what really happened that night at the governor's ball. She claimed a headache and asked Morgan to take her home."

"They've dated before," Jocelyn said.

"But still," Lena said softly, "Jamie Hollis is pretty, she's a socialite, her father is a senator, she comes from money..."

"Evidently none of those things matter to Morgan, Lena. He's made his choice," Kylie interjected. "And as far as I'm concerned you'll be bringing far more to the table, something that Morgan admires. Genuineness. You're not superficial. What people see is what they get. I personally think that's the best quality of all."

LATER THAT NIGHT before getting into bed Lena decided she needed to call Morgan. She preferred that he hear about her conversation with Cassandra from her than from someone else. She braced herself when she began dialing his cell phone.

"Hello."

The greeting was whispered huskily and sent sensuous chills through her body. "Morgan, this is Lena."

"I know."

She raised a brow. "You do? How?"

"Caller ID."

"Oh." She rolled her eyes, calling herself a ninny for not figuring that out.

"How are you doing, Lena?"

She cleared her throat. "I'm fine. What about you?"

"I'm doing okay. How's your mom?"

"She's doing fine. Thanks for asking." Then without missing a beat she said, "Morgan, there's something I need to tell you."

"Yes?"

"About your proposal?"

"What about it?"

"Something happened today that I think you should know about."

"All right, what happened?"

Lena decided to lie back on the bed. "Cassandra Tisdale dropped by my office today and…"

"And what?"

Lena sighed. "She said some things that really rubbed me the wrong way, and before I could catch myself I told her that you and I would be announcing our engagement when you returned to town."

She heard Morgan's chuckle. "I'm sure that shut her up."

Lena shook her head. "Not quite." But Lena had no intention of telling him what else Cassandra had said, especially the part about her cousin Jamie. Instead she added, "I have a feeling it did just the opposite. I bet she's spreading it all around town now and I thought you should know."

"Okay, thanks for telling me."

"You don't sound bothered by it."

"By what?"

Lena stared up at the ceiling. "By what I told her."

"I'm not. I asked you to marry me. You just hadn't given me your answer. Does this mean you'll be accepting the terms of my proposal, Lena?"

She ran a hand over her face. "What do you want, Morgan?"

"You know what I want. I want you. I want you to have my baby. I want us to get married and be best friends. I want your mother to be an integrated part of our lives. I guess you can say I want it all."

Everything but love, she thought, tucking a stray strand of hair behind her ear. In all their conversations he never had mentioned love. She forced that thought from her mind. There were times in life when you couldn't get everything you wanted.

"Well, I'll let you go now. I just wanted you to know," she said softly.

"Okay, we'll talk more about it when I return to Charlotte."

"All right. Good night, Morgan."

"Good night, Lena."

MORGAN DIDN'T RELEASE the phone until he heard the click of Lena's disconnecting the line. Although he was overjoyed that she had decided to accept his proposal, he was curious as to what had driven her to make that decision. He couldn't help wondering exactly what Cassandra had said to her.

Morgan was astute enough to know that there was more to the story than Lena had told him. He knew of only two people who could possibly know. Kylie was one, but when it came to Lena she had a tendency to be tight-lipped. The other person was Donovan. Donovan usually hung around in the right circles, and if there was something amiss he would be the one to know it.

He quickly keyed in Donovan's number, and his brother picked up on the first ring. "Yes?"

"Okay, Donovan, what's going on?"

He heard his brother's chuckle before he said, "You tell me. Rumor has it that you're about to become an engaged man."

Morgan smiled. So word was out already. "Yes, that's right."

"Congratulations. It seems you got the woman you wanted. I'm not going to ask how you managed and maybe it's best if I don't know. But I better tell you the masses are taking bets."

Morgan frowned. "Bets?"

Donovan chuckled again. "Yes. It seems a certain part of Charlotte's elite society group can't imagine you and Lena as a couple. In fact they're taking bets that before it's over you'll come to your senses and marry a woman they feel is more suitable to your breeding."

Morgan's frown deepened. "And who's that supposed to be?"

"Jamie Hollis. It's my understanding Cassandra is certain her cousin can replace Lena. I understand she's even bold enough to tell Lena that."

"Oh, I see." *Now he really did.* So that's what had pushed Lena into action. He shook his head. He would take Lena over Jamie any day. And he intended to do that very thing.

"It appears that all those times you've stated you were looking for the perfect woman, everyone was forming their own opinions as to what you wanted."

Morgan sighed. "Evidently. Seems like I have a lot to straighten out when I return to Charlotte tomorrow."

"I would have to agree. You know Cassandra and her better-than-thou group."

Yes, he did know Cassandra and her group. He would have thought her broken engagement with Bas would keep her quiet for a while. Evidently now that she had returned to town she was trying to take the spotlight off her and place it on someone else.

"And before you come back to town to roll any

heads, I need to remind you of something," Donovan said, breaking into his thoughts.

"What?"

"If you're still thinking about running for public office I wouldn't have my name linked to any negative publicity by stirring up trouble. You know the woman you intend to marry. I wouldn't worry about what is being said."

Morgan frowned. "I will worry about it if it involves Lena," he said roughly. "I won't have people assuming she's competing against Jamie for my attention, because she's not."

"Then show it in other ways. You know what they say about action speaking louder than words. Besides, once it's officially announced that you're engaged to Lena, if Jamie has any class she will bow out of the picture and put an end to this foolishness that Cassandra has started."

Moments later Morgan hung up the phone. All he had to do was show back up in Charlotte and put this foolishness to rest by announcing his engagement. He knew what woman he wanted and it wasn't Jamie Hollis.

CHAPTER ELEVEN

IT OCCURRED TO Lena during lunchtime the following day that she hadn't made a pit stop by Morgan's house to clean up those chocolate smudges.

After talking to him on the phone last night and telling him what to expect when he returned she had immediately felt a sense of relief. But upon waking this morning a lot of doubt now filled her mind. Had she really made the right decision? Had she allowed Cassandra's words to push her into a situation she shouldn't really be in?

Morgan made it seem like a "marriage of purpose" was nothing new, and maybe it wasn't to celebrities, high profilers and those Hollywood types. But she was someone who dealt with reality and she didn't know of any woman in her inner circle who would agree to marry a man and have his baby as part of a business deal. The media would have a field day with that bit of news if they ever got wind of it. And what would his brothers think? His parents? His own friends?

Not knowing what to think herself, Lena brought her car to a stop after pulling into Morgan's driveway. Unsnapping her seat belt she got out and proceeded to check his mailbox before getting the door key from the lockbox. The least she could do was bring in any mail since it seemed the box was overflowing.

Moments later she was walking inside his foyer and closing the door behind her. She smiled as she glanced around, distinctively remembering the first time he'd brought her here for that tour. And each time she had returned to his home she couldn't help but think how massive it was for one person. But then, the one he was thinking of buying was just as huge. And now that she'd decided to accept the terms of his proposal, that meant she and her mother would be sharing with him whatever house he purchased.

There were a number of framed portraits that hung on the walls, detailing the vast extent of his valuable art collection. She thought, and not for the first time, that his house smelled like him, a robust scent of man.

Walking into the living room she placed Morgan's mail on the table in a spot where he would be able to see it when he returned on Sunday. After taking off her jacket and slipping out of her shoes, she noticed a chocolate smudge on the door handle of the French door leading out to the pool and so she walked into the kitchen to get a wet cloth. She hoped and prayed there weren't too many others.

Standing at the kitchen sink she bit back a smile. One of Ms. Emily's daughters had called a couple of nights ago saying she planned to take their mother out to dinner and a movie for her birthday and had invited Odessa along. At first Lena had had mixed emotions about her mother going, but after talking to Cora Jessup and seeing how excited Odessa had gotten with the invitation, she had agreed. Hopefully, this would be the start of some sort of social life for her mother.

"You certainly have a way of brightening up my kitchen."

Lena spun around, holding a hand to her chest, as her gaze connected to Morgan's. And speaking of chest…his was broad, hairy, well defined and at the moment, naked. In fact it was obvious he had just stepped out of the shower. The only thing covering the bottom half of his body was a velour towel and it wasn't all that thick. From the look and shape of things, it was obvious he worked out regularly, which was something she herself had begun doing but not with as much zeal and dedication as some people. But she was determined to get there.

She cleared her throat after her racing heart slowed down a bit. "When did you get back?" she asked, after she was finally able to speak. The fact that he was standing in the middle of the room looking sexy as hell was making her skin feel heated.

He cracked a gorgeous smile. "About an hour ago."

"B-but I talked to you last night. Why didn't you tell me you were coming back today?"

Striding toward her with a smile so hot it could melt butter, he said, "I wanted to surprise you."

Well, he had certainly succeeded in doing that.

She tried averting her gaze from that smile only to have it fall on his chest, and she quickly decided that wasn't good. And if she moved it lower it would hit another spot. Although that area was covered, staring at it wasn't a smart idea, either. Definitely not a decent thing to do, but who could think of decency in the presence of a half-naked man?

When he came to a stop directly in front of her, pinning her between his body and the counter, she forced a smile to her lips and cleared her throat yet again before saying, "So, how was your trip?"

His smile became even sexier when he said, "Mmm, let's talk about my trip later. Right now I'd like the perfect homecoming."

And before she could blink, he leaned forward and captured her lips with his.

The moment Morgan's tongue took control of hers Lena's world turned topsy-turvy and blazing hot all at the same time. This was what spontaneous combustion was all about, she quickly decided. He hadn't given her time to react, to resist, or to think. When he had coaxed her lips apart and seized her tongue, he had been the one to take control. He was a master at what he was doing, and the sensations his skilled lips, tongue and mouth were causing shot straight to areas of her body that hadn't been touched in a long time or ever. He made the last kiss they'd shared in her office seem tame compared to this. Their tongues were mingling, tangling, mating in a private, sensual and heat-blistering dance.

She wanted to wrench her mind back from all

the erratic emotions he was making her feel, all the heated lust invading her body. Instead she was being overtaken by some primal elemental force that sent vibrations of deep need all through her.

The air they were breathing seemed to change and she felt her entire body attune to that change. She heard herself moan. She felt herself surrender, and she felt herself being pulled more and more under the mastery of a Morgan Steele kiss.

Then as if that wasn't enough, his hands moved to her waist, then upward to slip beneath her blouse, unclip her bra and trace hot fingertips to caress her breasts—kneading their softness and then playing, torturing and tantalizing their taut tips. She heard herself whimper when she became entrenched in desire so strong, potent and deliberate she couldn't breathe.

It was then that he broke off the kiss. While trying to force air through their lungs their gazes held, locked, with a need that almost bordered on obsession, and she knew what he wanted. She knew what she wanted as well. Here and now.

She didn't care that they were standing in his kitchen during midday. All that mattered, the only thing that was important, was to finish what they started. Any regrets would come later but not now. Something had taken over, held them in a sensual grip. It was something they couldn't explain, nor did they want to or feel the need to. It was enough that they both felt it. They both wanted it. And they both intended to have it.

Now.

Without uttering a word he reached out and tugged the blouse over her head, then freed the bra completely from her breasts. As he tossed both aside, his hands then moved to her hips and on bended knee he unceremoniously yanked down her skirt, leaving her standing in the middle of his kitchen wearing nothing but a thong.

"Mercy."

Lena heard his growl.

Heat drummed through her when she felt his fingers move slowly up her legs, kneading her flesh while making her body burst into flames. But it seemed it didn't intend to let her burn without him. The next thing she knew was that he was sensually stroking the back of her knee with one hand while tracing his fingertips up her inner thigh with the other. When he reached her thong, his hand slipped beneath the satin barely-there covering and touched her.

She fought the fiery sensations that single touch caused by closing her eyes, throwing her head back and pressing her knees together. She had never felt such intensity, such vulnerability, so possessed with need.

"Lena?"

Deep in the recess of her mind she heard her name. She slowly opened her eyes and looked down and met his gaze, recognizing the look in their dark depths. That look stole her breath, sent even more indescribable sensations shooting through her and made liquid heat, which she could actually feel, pool right smack between her legs where his finger still was located.

"I want you, Lena," he whispered in a husky voice, still holding her gaze. "I want you on the table."

She stared down at him. He was leaning back on his haunches staring back at her. There was a high degree of heat in his eyes, and then suddenly she felt hot all over again. He stood, laced his fingers with hers, positioned her body close to his and turned her slightly and begin inching her backward toward the table. It was then that she noticed his towel had dropped and he was as stark naked as she was.

"I've been fantasizing about you spread out on my desk, but I'm going to make this table work," he whispered huskily into her ear.

They came to a stop when the table was at her back. Morgan remembered how his brothers had joked about him having such a huge table in his kitchen. Now he knew why it was there. It was perfect. His need, his desire and his want for her had built up over a long period. She had become an obsession that nearly bordered on madness.

He wanted to marry her. He wanted her to have his baby. He wanted her to be a part of his life forever.

He *loved* her.

That stark realization ratcheted through him, nearly knocking him off balance. That was the reason why he had come up with those crazy plans, and why, even when Donovan had teased him mercilessly about Lena not giving him the time of day, he hadn't let her rejection deter him one bit from making her his priority.

He knew at that very moment that he had probably fallen in love with her the moment he set eyes on her that night, and he had dreamed about her every night since then. She had fascinated him in a way no other woman had ever done before. He saw a beauty on the outside that he knew radiated from the inside. Her dedication to her mother and those she considered friends was monumental. He admired such a high degree of loyalty and devotion. Her involvement in the various community projects around town that were geared to benefit others was a testimony that she was a person who cared. This was the type of woman he needed in his life, to walk by his side, to be there with him when the going got tough. She didn't know it yet but he had high plans for their future, and they would have a rewarding future together—she might as well bank on it.

He reached down and lifted her bottom and sat her on the edge of the table, then gently scooted her back on it. He stepped back. She was lying flat on her back with her gorgeous legs dangling off the sides, naked and opened for him. Just like he'd imagined in his fantasy.

Morgan inwardly groaned. All that naked flesh only heightened his desire. "You're beautiful, Lena," he whispered and felt the truth of his words all the way to his toes.

He watched as she slid a glance at him, smiled

and said, "You have a way of making me feel sexy, Morgan Steele."

"Because you are sexy. And your sexiness has a way of driving me wild. Pushing me over the edge and making me want to do things I normally don't do," he said truthfully.

He came back to the table, leaned over her and kissed her. Thoroughly. Deeply. And then he was between her spread knees, easing them apart even farther.

The scent of her drove him crazy, made him lose control, made his body even more aroused. He stepped closer, rubbed his hardened shaft against her wet core, teasing it, tantalizing it, provoking it in an enticing way.

"I think this is where I ask if I need to put on a condom," he whispered huskily, as he continued to rub himself against her. "As much as I want to give you my baby, now isn't the time to do it. There are too many number crunchers around here to suit me."

She smiled and slowly shook her head. "I take the pill to regulate my periods, so I'm safe, but if you prefer to—"

"No, I don't prefer. I want to be skin to skin, flesh to flesh with you. I want to know the exact moment I let go and fill you with me, Lena."

He leaned in closer to her ear, letting his warm breath touch her skin underneath when he whispered, "In other words, I want to soak your insides to the point that even next week you'll still know that I came for a visit."

And then he kissed her in a long, drugging kiss that automatically had her eyes closing while the desire within her crested, seeking fulfillment.

"Look at me, Lena," he said in a soft command after pulling back.

She opened her eyes and smiled at him. It was then that she saw that he was on the table with his body straddled over hers. The light shining through his kitchen blinds made him appear as the man he had been—her nighttime fantasy—and into the man he now was, her daytime reality. At that moment she was aware of everything. The way he was staring down at her, the way their breathing was being released in the quiet stillness of the room, the way his shaft was resting between her open legs and the sexual, hot sense they radiated.

He leaned down and placed a light kiss on the tip of her nose and smiled. "I think I'm going to keep this table forever," he said, chuckling softly. And then his expression turned serious and he leaned down and whispered, "Got to have you. Now."

He seemed to rise even higher above her before he sank back down in one fluid motion inside her.

"Oh," she gasped, her sensation one of total fulfillment and extreme gratification, knowing their bodies were connected this way. He moved deeper, going inside her to the hilt, inside her while reaching under her and bracing her voluptuous bottom, holding it tight to the fit of him.

"Does it hurt?" he asked, whispering softly against the thick luxuriousness of her hair.

"No, you feel good," she said, smiling up at him. "Okay, big guy. Show me what you can do." And with the agility of an acrobat, she lifted her legs to lock her ankles in the center of his back.

He grinned down at her. "Remember, you asked for it."

And then he began moving slow at first, easing in and out as if savoring each stroke, liking the feel of his shaft work its way inside her. And then the tempo suddenly changed, and he began pumping fast. Then faster. Relentless with need. Unbelievably detailed with each and every intimate and intense caress.

"More, Morgan. More. Don't stop," she begged.

It was on the tip of Morgan's tongue to tell her that at this point he couldn't stop even if he wanted to. So he continued to pump into her, ignoring the hard feel of her heels in the center of his back with each thrusting motion. He felt her climbing the same ladder of passion that he was climbing, knowing what awaited them at the top was one hell of an orgasm. And when she arched her back, he didn't know how it was possible but he drove deeper into her, hit something and whatever it was had her screaming her release.

He felt it, the tensing of her muscles, the pull, the clenching, and at that moment she became the epitome of everything sensual to him. She was one hell of a woman. His woman.

And then he reached the top with her, clung to everything, felt sensually trapped tight within her inner thighs, wishing he could stay a captive forever. He felt his body explode, shatter, flood her. And he bucked once, twice, a third time, appreciating the sturdiness of the table, grateful it was genuine wood and not glass. He was shattering enough. He didn't need the table to shatter as well.

He threw his head back and growled incoherently. He felt like the wolf claiming his mate and all the innate rights that came with that possession. And as his body began to slow down, he started feeling an inner peace, one he'd never felt before. He could only think of one word for what had just taken place on his kitchen table. Perfect.

He sucked in a deep breath, trying to reclaim a semblance of strength. He gazed down at her and he wanted her again. Just like that. Just like this. But the next time he wanted it in the bedroom, in the bed. This table was of good quality, but it could only take so much.

He leaned down and pressed his mouth gently to hers, not ready to separate from her. Her saw the aftermath of a sexual glaze in her eyes, watched a satisfied smile touch the corners of her lips. Grinning proudly he wanted to beat his fists against his chest. Instead he reached down and cupped her face in his hands. "Tell me," he whispered throatily. "What are you thinking?"

She grinned back at him, still trying to catch her breath. "Are you sure you want to know?"

"Yes."

"Mmm, I was just thinking that you have one hell of an organ, Morgan."

He laughed. He actually laughed and the ripples

from his body went straight through to hers, making them aware they were still joined.

"Besides being a sexy lady, you're also a poet, I see."

She chuckled. "Sometimes. How about this one? *Why waste it when you can taste it?*" And then she was pulling his head down for a kiss that sent an aching need through him. When she released his mouth she smiled up at him, pleased with what she'd done.

"Arrogant woman," he teased gruffly. "You know what I think?" he asked, leaning down and brushing a kiss across her lips.

"No, what?"

"I think we should carry this discussion to the bedroom."

"Think you'll get poetic justice in there?"

"Among other things."

Lena wrapped her arms around him. "I'm curious to find out about those other things."

CHAPTER TWELVE

AND JUST TO think she had convinced herself for six years that she didn't need sex, Lena thought, feeling the heated warmth of Morgan's naked body snuggled so close to hers. His even breathing was an indication that he had drifted off to sleep, but to make sure she didn't go anywhere, his arms were wrapped securely around her waist and one of his legs was thrown over hers.

They were cuddled, spoon position, in his bed after just having another round of mind-blowing lovemaking. Yes, she preferred thinking about what they'd spent doing the better part of the last two hours as making love rather than just having sex. Today he had shown her there was a difference in the two. He had been painstakingly thorough with every detail, passionate with every sensual move and personal and intimate with every word he'd whispered in her ear each and every time he entered her body.

She inhaled deeply, picking up his masculine scent while at the same time feeling an inner peace, one she hadn't felt in a long time—at least not since her father's death. Willie Spears hadn't been just a man. He had been a good father, husband and provider for "his girls," as he had often referred to her and her mother. He had been kindhearted to those he met, strong in his belief in God and a person who was always willing to lend a hand to help others. That was one of the reasons his sickness and subsequent death had taken a toll on both her and her mother.

He had requested only one promise of her, a promise she was living each day to fulfill. "Take care of my Odessa," he'd said in what had been his final hours. "Promise that no matter what, you will take care of her, Lena. She's my most precious gift that I'm leaving to you."

His most precious gift.

How many men thought of the woman they loved, when they had dedicated their lives to for so many years, as their most precious gift? And she'd always wanted to find a man just like that, someone who would think of her that way. A man whose personality, ideals and beliefs so closely mirrored her father's. She'd known that finding such a man wouldn't be easy, and for a time, while in college, she'd thought she would have to settle for less.

She wasn't exactly the type of woman that men eagerly sought out. A pleasing personality always managed to take a backseat to looks and body size. Unfortunately, Cassandra Tisdale had been right that day when she'd said that Lena wasn't Morgan's type. That only made her wonder even more why she was here, in the middle of the day in bed with him after having spent what would go down in her mind as the most memorable two hours she'd ever spent with a man. And an even more demanding question that refused to go away was why, when he could probably have any woman he wanted, he was intent on having her.

There was yet another question lurking deep in her mind. Now that he'd had her did he actually still want her? Did he still want to marry her and give her his baby? Or had she been nothing more than a puzzle he'd wanted to figure out and now that he had…

"What time do you have to pick your mom up today?"

Lena's body tensed and her fingers gripped the bedcovers when she felt Morgan's hot body edge even closer and the leg thrown across hers tighten. She'd thought he was still asleep. It had been so long, she wasn't sure how one behaved afterward. Even now she felt it, that sensual ache between her thighs that begged for more of what he had given her earlier. She felt like a downright greedy hussy, and the sad thing about it was that she could no longer blame her wanton actions on her twin.

"Lena?"

The sound of his voice, a deep, husky, sexy tone, was close to her ear, and her body instantly responded when he licked her earlobe with a hot sweep of his tongue.

"Umm?" That was the only word she could manage between flushed lips and a throat that suddenly felt tight. She felt hot and breathless.

"What time do you have to leave to pick up

Odessa?" he repeated in a husky whisper that made an even deeper throb in the area between her legs.

"I don't," she managed to get out. "One of the ladies at the center who Mom became friends with is having a birthday dinner this evening and she was invited. One of the lady's daughters will be bringing Mom home later tonight. I was told not to expect her before eight."

"And do you have any more appointments scheduled for today?" was his next question.

"No."

"Good."

Before she had an indication of what he was about to do, he quickly eased himself up on his elbows and turned her toward him to stare down at her. And then he did something else she didn't expect, he tossed back the bedspread covering them, exposing their nakedness. But it wasn't his own nudity that held his attention and interest, it was hers.

His gaze left her face and slowly moved down her body, and she could actually feel the heated desire that was emanating from his eyes. She also felt his erection as it got harder and harder, pressed against the backside of her thigh. He didn't say anything, just got his fill looking.

And while he was looking at her, she was looking at him. First she began on his face, zeroing in on his lips and remembering that first kiss in her office, and the one that had started things off today in the kitchen. She still had the taste of him on her tongue.

She then moved her gaze to his throat; saw the

beating of the pulse at the center before moving lower to his shoulders, then his chest. She would have arched her neck to see farther down, but then she felt his hand on her thigh and then he used those same hands to spread her knees apart.

She sighed deeply. She had discovered during the course of the last couple of hours that she had a weakness, which was turning to a raw, primal addiction, whenever Morgan's hands or fingers got close to any areas between her legs.

Like now.

There was this ache that would start right there in the center and move slowly, shivering through all parts of her body. He leaned down toward her mouth and began trailing kisses around her lips and then he pulled back, stared at her lips for a moment and then stuck out his tongue and began nibbling on her as if she was the sweetest chocolate he'd ever tasted.

Simultaneously, his fingers began going to work at her center, and she fought the tide of desire that began overtaking her. He was making her already hot body hotter. He was filling her, making the intense need within her that much greater; and he wasn't far from making her cry out in pleasure. She tried fighting it, and the more she fought it, the more she felt it. His touch was deliberate. It was precise. It was almost too much for her to handle.

"Morgan!"

He had her panting, barely breathing, and when he took his thumb and flicked it over her achy part, right in the juncture of her thighs, she felt her body teeter, right on the edge of an orgasm.

"I want to be inside you again," he whispered, easing his body in place over hers, while at the same time gently scraping his teeth against the dark skin of her shoulder.

"I want to get in and lock down," he said, lifting her hips and cupping her backside.

The only thing she could do was to release a sigh of "Oh." And the moment she did so, he swept his tongue into her mouth at the same time he eased into her body.

She gripped his shoulders. She wrapped her legs around him—not that she thought he was going anywhere. He was working it. Working her. Establishing his own rhythm, thrusting in and out. Then he flung his head back and she felt his thighs tighten, locking down on hers; felt how he clenched her hips higher to the fit of him, to go deeper inside her. She moved with him, followed his beat, his tempo, and closed her eyes thinking that this might be madness but at the moment it was madness at its finest.

It was he who screamed her name, and at that exact moment she felt his body jolt, buck, thrust continuously, almost frantically, into hers. She felt the heat of him, thick and hot, flood her insides. And then she understood what he'd meant when he'd said *lock down*. He was holding her immobile when he continued to slide in and out of her, giving her his own brand of both torture and gratification.

"Morgan!"

Then it happened to her for the umpteenth time that day. Hearing his name he cupped the back of her neck and she opened her eyes and looked at him, stared into his dark eyes, like heated chocolate chips, gazing back at her. And then without saying a word, he lowered his head and covered her mouth with his.

Lena knew at that moment she would go without a man for another six years if she thought the result would be this. Morgan Steele had definitely ended her sexual drought, and he had been well worth the wait.

And that was the last thought that crossed her mind when another orgasm hit and her body began exploding all over again.

A SHORT WHILE later, Morgan switched their positions to make things more comfortable for a sleeping Lena. He smiled. His perfect woman had actually fallen asleep, but that was fine. He was inside her, locked down, locked in tight and he didn't intend to go anywhere. Their legs were tangled, making them fixed in place, their bodies bolted, almost making true the words "joined at the hips." But they weren't joined at the hip. They were joined at the organs, sexual organs.

He smiled, remembering her compliment of that particular organ of his. This woman was so amazing that he couldn't think straight. All he had to do was close his eyes to remember the past several hours. He'd wanted a special homecoming but had gotten a whole lot more.

The moment he had kissed her in his kitchen he had felt it. Her response had been spontaneous, hot. And the way she had yielded to him sparked every desire within his body that could be named, arousing passions he had kept well under control for years and stirring such volatile emotions within him, he couldn't do anything but succumb to the powerful chemistry that had gripped him.

Just the thought that once they were married he would have a right to this, a chance to share a bed with her every night, had him getting hard all over again. But he had to admit what he felt was something a lot more than just physical.

He *loved* her.

LENA SLOWLY OPENED her eyes and glanced around the room. When she saw it was almost dark outside she jerked up in bed and glanced over at the clock. It wasn't quite six yet.

She eased back down, released a long, ragged breath. She was alone, and for a moment that was a good thing. She needed to get her thoughts together. She closed her eyes again, and it didn't take much to remember what she and Morgan had been doing for the majority of the afternoon. She felt sore between her legs like you wouldn't believe. But that wasn't all. Her mouth felt sore as well and she couldn't help wondering if it was swollen. But each time she thought about Morgan's kisses, deep, intense, and the way he would explore her mouth, plundering it, stealing her breath away and mating almost nonstop with her tongue, she wondered just what kind of vitamins he was on.

Her nipples felt taut with her just thinking about how she responded to him, greedily taking what he was offering and then falling into peaceful sleep afterward. And when she would wake after her catnap he would be there, wide awake, with dark eyes staring down at her, focused, intent, hungry. His breathing would get shallow and she would automatically melt in a pool of succulent desire.

She heard a sound downstairs and knew that now was the perfect time to get up, get dressed and get out. The last thing she needed was for him to walk into the room while she was still in bed. If nothing else, she had discovered that when it came to Morgan Steele, she had little, if no, resistance left.

Slipping out of bed she began putting on her clothes. When she had awakened that morning she'd been a little confused, and now she was more confused than ever about just what was happening between her and Morgan.

MORGAN PULLED HIMSELF out of the pool after taking one last lap around it. Never in his life had he felt so rejuvenated, so bursting with energy…and so filled with love.

Now he fully understood how Chance and Bas felt. He clearly comprehended those possessive stares they would give their wives, and realized why on those days they would rush home from the office or show up late from lunch with twisted ties around their necks and silly grins on their faces.

He now had a firm handle on what emotions his two older brothers were dealing with. Hell, the only reason he had finally left Lena asleep to come downstairs for a swim was that, had he been in bed when she'd awakened, he would have been tempted to make love to her again.

Tempted, hell! He would have made love to her just as sure as there was a Charlotte sky overhead.

He began drying off with the huge towel, knowing that he and Lena needed to talk. They needed to announce their intentions to marry to their families and to anyone else who wanted to listen. He was ready to go to the tallest building and begin shouting.

"I'm leaving now, Morgan."

He turned and saw her standing in the doorway that separated his family room from his patio. Seeing her standing there, looking as sexy as sexy could get, and remembering what they had shared most of the afternoon sent a shiver of deep desire combined with hot excitement through him.

He tossed aside the towel and began walking toward her. When he got within three feet of her he noticed the apprehension in her eyes, the uncertainty, and he wondered, how could she not know, not sense how he felt at that moment? But then he had to admit they hadn't had a normal relationship. He had been a man with a plan, first using business and then ultimate pleasure to seduce her, win her over. But he had a feeling he hadn't completely won her over. She was having doubts, and from the look in her eyes, lots of them.

He could get on bended knee and tell her to hell with that business proposal. He wanted to marry her because he loved her. But would she believe him? He doubted it. Lena was a woman who would need more action than words, and that's just what he would give her. By the time she walked down the aisle to him, there would be no doubt in her mind just how deep his emotions were for her.

Instead of saying anything when he reached her, he took hold of her hand and gently pulled her closer to him. Then he leaned down and gently touched his lips to hers. He pulled back, cupped her jaw and intently studied her lips. She definitely looked like a woman who'd been well kissed all afternoon.

"What are you going to tell Odessa if she asks what happened to your lips?"

Lena's shoulders shrugged, but he saw the mocking challenge in her gaze and immediately sensed some sort of withdrawal taking place. It was a withdrawal he refused to have.

"I don't know. Got any suggestions?"

He returned that look by cocking a challenging eyebrow. "You can always tell her the truth, Lena. That we got carried away today and—"

"I don't think so."

He smiled. "I figured as much. I guess you can claim you got swollen lips from sipping too long on a soda bottle."

She lifted her own brow. "Can that happen?"

He chuckled. "It happened to Donovan once, or so he claims."

She rolled her eyes. "Well, if she asks I guess that's one excuse I could try." She then glanced at her watch. "I need to go, Morgan."

"Okay, and we need to talk. Will Odessa be at the day care again tomorrow?"

"No, she'll be at home all day watching her soaps."

He nodded. "Will you have dinner with me tomorrow? We can make it early. You and I need to talk."

She inhaled deeply. Yes, they did. "Okay, what time?"

"How about four? Is that time good for you?"

"Yes, that time is fine." She turned to leave and remembered he was still holding her hand.

"Hey, not so fast," he said, looking into her eyes. Then slowly he lowered his head and kissed her, gently and deeply.

Before releasing her he whispered into her ear, "And get on your computer tonight. Around ten. I want to talk to your twin."

Sensations rushed through Lena's body as she remembered their last conversation and how they had come close to playing out that fantasy in his kitchen. But still, she wasn't certain exchanging sexual banter in cyberspace again was a good idea. "I might be busy."

"If you're not, then pop into my space."

She nodded and quickly turned and left.

CHAPTER THIRTEEN

ODESSA HAD BEEN so chatty about how her day and evening had gone that if she'd noticed anything odd about Lena's lips she hadn't said anything. Despite her initial concern, by the time she had gotten home, taken a shower and eaten a salad for dinner, Lena was too keyed up to worry about how her mouth looked. Her main concern was her future.

Morgan had left her with the impression that the business deal between them was still in place, but she needed to know for certain, which is why she had readily accepted his invitation to dinner.

After getting her mother settled for the night she had slipped into a nightgown and gone into her room to read some real estate literature she'd received in the mail. She tried ignoring her laptop that was sitting on the desk in her room. And she tried not to notice the time. It was after nine. Close to nine-thirty.

Moments later she glanced at the clock again. It was ten. She sighed and glanced over at her laptop. Should she or shouldn't she? Hadn't she gotten into enough trouble with Morgan today? Okay, she would admit that after the type of afternoon she'd had it would only be natural to want to spend time talking to him again. But why not by phone instead of cyberspace?

She quickly knew the answer to that one. She and Morgan had crossed the lines of professionalism on their laptops in a way that they could never retract. And although she had claimed it was her twin being naughty and not her, her behavior this afternoon had proven differently. And on top of that, there was something relaxing and comforting, as well as daring, in having a private, intimate and provocative conversation with someone you knew, yet didn't really know at the same time.

Deciding to stop fighting the impulse, she tossed the magazine aside and got out of bed and reached for her laptop. Taking a deep breath she quickly logged on. It was almost ten minutes after the hour. Had he checked to see if she'd logged on and when he found out she hadn't had already logged off? She inhaled deeply again, knowing there was only one way to find out.

She signed on with her Internet server and sighed in relief when his name was still there. Leaning back against the headboard she settled into a comfortable position and waited. She didn't have long for action when Morgan clicked on, invading her space.

Lena?

She clicked a response. *Yes, I'm here.*

Thanks for dropping by.

And then their fun time began.

Morgan asked the first question. *What's your favorite sport?*

Lena chuckled. That would be a quick response and she typed it in. *I really don't have one.*

Umm, have you ever played Sex by Design?

She lifted a brow and her fingers went to work. *No. How is it played?*

Easy. All you need is one woman and one man.

She shook her head, grinning as she clicked a response. *Good. I don't go for that kinky stuff.*

Neither do I.

Good to know. So, how do you play it?

You think of a word, the first one that comes to your mind, and the other person has to come up with some sort of sexual story about it.

Lena frowned. *That's a lot of typing.*

Abbreviations are accepted.

Okay.

I'll let you go first and you give me a word.

She paused a moment to think hard. She glanced around the room and smiled when she saw something on her dresser and decided not to make things easy for him. *Cotton balls.*

Cotton balls?

Yes.

There was a long pause and then he began typing. *Picture this. You and me together, naked in bed. Like we were this afternoon.*

Heat shivered through her bloodstream. *Okay I got the picture.*

And I take a bunch of those little cotton balls and strategically place them to cover your front. You know, that particular area between your legs. They

*will fit you like a perfect triangle. Then I use my
mouth to remove them, one by one. The object is not
to let one fall. Each time I remove one I get to lick
the area where it had been.*

Lena swallowed. Her mouth suddenly felt dry,
tight, and her nipples felt hard against her nightgown.
She couldn't help but type and ask. *What happens
when they're all gone?*

*Then I get to taste the entire area; nibble and lick
as much as I want. Then I get to use my mouth and
place them back and start the game all over again.
So what do you think?*

When visions of him doing that engulfed her
mind, what Lena really thought was that they had
to be nuts to be having this sort of conversation, especially when the most prolific and exquisite sensations flowed through her body. *I think we've said
enough for tonight.*

Chicken. Where's your twin?

Some place safe. Good night, Morgan.

Good night, Lena.

MORGAN WAS STANDING at the window the next day
thinking about his and Lena's cyberspace chat of the
night before when his secretary's voice on the intercom intruded into this thoughts.

"Yes, Linda, what is it?"

"Edward Dunlap is here to see you."

Morgan raised a brow before saying, "Please send
him in."

A few minutes later Edward walked in. He was

in his late fifties, the same age as Morgan's father. In fact, his father and the man had been business associates for years before Edward had chosen a life of politics. He had been elected as Charlotte's first African American councilman and remained in that office for years. From there he had become a state representative and was now eying a position in Congress. In recent years he had appointed himself as Morgan's mentor, determined to see him enter the political arena.

"Edward, this is a surprise," Morgan said, crossing the room to shake the older man's hand.

"Yes, and I hate to come unannounced but this meeting is important. Word has it that Roger Chadwick will be holding a press conference in a few hours to announce his candidacy. So you know what this means?"

Morgan leaned back against his desk. Yes, he knew what that meant. If he was going to announce his own intentions to run for that same seat, now was the time to finally make up his mind. "Yes, I know what it means, Edward, but there is someone I need to discuss this with."

Edward nodded. "And that brings me to another reason I'm here. There's a rumor floating around about you."

Morgan lifted a brow. "What rumor?"

"That you're thinking of getting married."

Morgan couldn't help the smile that touched his lips. "That's no rumor. I am getting married."

"I think we need to discuss that, Morgan."

"Discuss what?"

"Your choice of a wife."

Morgan cast him a glance that nearly bordered on anger. "Excuse me?"

"I said your choice of a wife. I understand you're thinking about marrying Lena Spears, which comes as a surprise because I wasn't aware you were serious about anyone."

Morgan frowned, wondering if the man assumed he had to know everything about his business, personal or otherwise. "Yes, I've asked Lena to marry me."

"I'm sure you know family name, style and connections are everything."

"To some people."

Edward shook his head. "Don't kid yourself. You're a Steele about to run for office. You don't need to consider marrying any woman who won't be an asset to your career. Lena Spears is a nice woman, but she won't do as a wife for you. Now, take Senator Hollis's daughter. I understand she's—"

"No, you take Senator Hollis's daughter," Morgan said, after having heard enough. "For God's sake, Edward, this is the twenty-first century. Lena won't be the one running for office, I will. And who I decide to marry is really no one's business."

"Don't make the mistake of thinking it's not, Morgan. I met with a few people earlier today and the rumor of your possible engagement came up. They asked that I come and meet with you to discuss it."

Morgan straightened his stance, getting angrier

by the minute. "In that case, tell them you have met with me and discussed it. And that my response is that in my opinion Lena Spears has more style and beauty in her little finger than most women have in their entire body. I'm marrying her and if the masses don't like it, then I'll run without their support."

"You won't win."

Morgan chuckled. "I might not get their vote, but if they feel the way they do about the woman I intend to marry, then I don't want their vote. They only represent a small population of Charlotte's society. I refuse to believe that the majority of the people in this town is that narrowed-minded and shallow. Good day, Edward."

Edward stared at him and shook his head for a moment before turning and walking out the door.

"FOR PETE'S SAKE, calm down, Morgan."

Chance, Bas and Donovan watched as an angry Morgan paced back and forth around his office. As soon as Edward had left, Morgan had summoned his brothers. After he'd told them about Edward's visit and what had been said, they had gotten just as angry as Morgan. But not quite.

"I can't believe Dunlap actually said that to you," Donovan said, shaking his head as he sat in one of the chairs in the room. "I can see him saying that to me since he never liked me anyway."

Bas rolled his eyes. "Might be from that time he caught you *almost* making out with his youngest daughter in a parked car right in front of his house."

"Hey, she asked for it," Donovan said in defense. "What was I supposed to do?"

Chance shook his head. "Turning her down might have been the decent thing to do," he said sarcastically. "But let's get back to the issue of Morgan and Lena."

Morgan stopped his pacing and met Chance's gaze. "There's no issue. Who the hell do they think they are, deciding what woman is appropriate for me?" he asked angrily. "It's nobody's business who I marry."

"Damn right it's not, now let's go kick some asses," was Bas's quick reply.

Now it was Chance who rolled his eyes. Everyone in Charlotte knew that of all the Steeles, Bas had always been the hothead, the one ready to not only start trouble but put an end to it as well. He'd always been known as the not-so-sterling Steele, a reputation he'd garnered proudly until he turned twenty-one, dropped out of college and had to face the real world…and a man by the name of Jim Mason—Jocelyn's father.

"Just think how that sounds, Bas. Fighting never solves anything. What we need to do is to put our heads together. Whether you want to admit it or not, Morgan, you're going to need Edward and his group's support."

"Then I don't want it, and in that case I won't run."

Chance shook his head. "Think hard on that before making a decision. Have you discussed any of this with Lena?"

"No."

"Don't you think you should? Especially if the two of you are getting married, which is a mystery within itself. Two weeks ago she wasn't giving you the time of day," Chance said, eying his brother curiously. "What happened?"

Morgan stared at his brothers, and since he wanted to make sure they understood the depth of his feelings for Lena he said, "Love happened. I fell for her that night of the charity ball. I just thought I wanted her. But it's more. I love her."

Chance and Bas slowly nodded, indicating they understood. They had been there, done that and were still doing it. However, it was Donovan who was looking at him with what amounted to pity in his eyes.

"Okay, then," Chance said, smiling, as if satisfied with what he'd been told. "I suggest you talk things over with Lena. I probably won't go so far as to tell her about Edward's visit, but I think she at least deserves to know you're thinking about running for a political office."

Morgan nodded, knowing Chance was right. He and Lena had a dinner date later that day. He would tell her of his decision then.

LENA GLANCED AROUND. She was lucky that although she'd arrived at the restaurant early, there had been a table reserved for her.

McIntosh Steak House and Seafood was a popular restaurant in town. Simple and elegant it catered to businesspeople with money, the power brokers of Charlotte. The interior spoke of old money with its plush carpeting, the rich-looking furnishing and the expensive art collections of oil paintings on the walls. Service was always magnificent, the food always tasty. Sometimes people traveled for miles just to dine here.

The waiter had already brought her one glass of wine and had come to see if she wanted another when she glanced up and saw Cassandra Tisdale and a couple of women she recognized as being in the woman's inner circle, including her cousin Jamie. She immediately got cold chills.

She hoped they would pass by the table and not see her as they were leaving the restaurant, but it seemed that was one layer of hope that wouldn't be granted.

"Well, if it isn't the woman who thinks she's going to be the future Mrs. Morgan Steele."

Lena glanced up, smiling. She refused to let Cassandra's snide comment rattle her. "Hi, Cassandra, Debra, Karen and Jamie. I see the four of you are leaving."

"Yes, we are," Debra Kendall said, almost apologetically. And not for the umpteenth time Lena had to inwardly question why someone as nice as Debra would hang around with someone like Cassandra. Maybe she believed that sooner or later her kindness would rub off on Cassandra.

"So, what do you think of Morgan running for

office?" Karen Smith asked, after looking at Cassandra and getting her cue.

"Excuse me?" Lena asked.

Cassandra smiled. "Oh, didn't you know? Now that Chadwick has announced he's running for office, speculation is high that Morgan will, too. He's very well thought of in this town."

Lena didn't say anything. She was still recovering from Karen's comment about the possibility of Morgan being a political candidate.

"Of course it's not definite whether Morgan is even interested," Debra said, as if to smooth things over.

"But if he does," Cassandra said, grinning, "he's going to need a woman who will complement him. Someone well groomed with a good name, a sense of fashion, style and grace, and a pedigree. Wouldn't you agree, Lena?"

Before Lena could say anything, it was Jamie who spoke, smiling sweetly. "And I'm sure if you care anything for Morgan as well as recognize what an asset he would be in this community in politics, then you'd agree that all of us need to give him all the support he needs and the chance to win. I understand entering politics has been his lifelong dream. If you really care for him, you wouldn't take that dream away. In fact you would work hard to make it become a reality."

Then three of the women walked off. Debra, however, remained behind long enough to at least say goodbye.

The cold chills Lena had gotten earlier were there in full force. Why hadn't Morgan mentioned he was thinking about entering politics? Did he just assume she would want to be a politician's wife? Well, she didn't. She was a person who liked her life the way it was. She and her mother lived a quiet and peaceful existence, and she had no intention of being thrust out into the limelight.

Besides, how much did Morgan know about her? Oh, he'd learned a lot about her this afternoon and probably from the two chats they'd had, but that had all been sexual. What did Morgan really know about her? Nothing. If he did, he would know that she and politics didn't mix because she was too opinionated when it came to certain issues and she didn't know how to remain quiet when it involved a subject she was passionate about.

She thought about what Cassandra and her group said as well as what they didn't say. The people she hung out with, as well as those her parents hung out with, had a lot of influence and power. They would back Morgan fully if he had what they perceived as the right kind of wife by his side. But she knew they wouldn't use any of that to help get him elected if he was intent on marrying her.

Her father had once told her there was more to be an elected official than working on balancing the budget, attending meetings and making speeches. There was a matter of respect and Morgan had it, from a lot of people; but it seemed he ran the risk of losing it because of her, mainly because she was not a fit.

She paused and sat quietly for a moment, and when she felt a tear slide from her eye to wet her cheek, she knew why. At some point during their business relationship, those sexy chats and their romp between the sheets yesterday, she had fallen in love with Morgan. And she had fallen hard. So hard that she knew what she had to do. She could only think of one other time she'd actually felt noble in her life. The first had been at thirteen when she'd actually saved Paula Brewster's baby sister from drowning in the community pool, and the other time was now.

To help Morgan retain his regal public image and give him all the support he needed to pursue what evidently was his lifelong dream, she knew what she had to do. Summoning the waiter over to the table she said, "Please bring me my check, and when Mr. Steele arrives let him know something came up and I had to leave."

CHAPTER FOURTEEN

NOT READY TO go home yet, Lena returned to her office. She had placed a quick call to her mother to make sure she was okay and had eaten dinner. After Odessa had assured her that she was fine and not to worry about her, Lena decided to stay and work late at the office.

Wendy had already left for the day and the office was quiet. Although Lena tried concentrating on the listing of new homes she had in front of her, she found her focus wasn't what it should be. One part of her was absorbed with anger for a certain group of people—those who thought they were influential enough to dictate how people should live their lives and with whom. Then another part of her knew that bowing out was the best thing. It had nothing to do with pride, confidence or self-esteem but everything to do with making a sacrifice for the man she loved. Under any other circumstances, she and Morgan might have had a chance to make their "marriage of purpose" work, but now entering into such an agreement with him would serve no purpose. He needed a different type of woman to be by his side and have his baby, and that woman wasn't her.

She glanced up when the phone on her desk began to ring. She picked it up. "Yes?"

"It's Morgan."

Lena's throat suddenly felt tight. She swallowed past the lump before saying, "Yes, Morgan?"

"I'm outside at your office door. Let me in."

When she heard the click she pulled the phone away from her ear and stared at it a few moments before hanging it up. The last person she wanted to see right now was Morgan. She rubbed the bridge of her nose and slumped back in her chair. If he had given her time, she would have told him to go away because she couldn't see him now.

Not bothering to slip back into her shoes she stood and headed down the hallway toward the door. She could clearly see Morgan through the glass front. As usual, he was dressed immaculately like the businessman he was. He was wearing a navy blue suit, a light blue shirt and a printed tie that coordinated perfectly.

She turned off the alarm and unlocked the door and then stepped back as he entered and watched as he raised a brow and searched her face. "Are you okay?"

She wondered if he'd found out about her conversation with Cassandra and her nasty-girl squad but then figured that he couldn't have. "Yes, I'm fine. Why wouldn't I be?"

He crossed his arms over his chest and stared at her. "You tell me. We had a dinner date and when I arrived one of the waiters said you had been there but left, and that you'd left a message that something had come up and you had to leave. Of course the first thought that crossed my mind was that something had happened to Odessa. I tried calling you at home and she picked up. When I asked for you she said you were at the office working late. So what was the big emergency, Lena?"

If only he knew. But at the moment she didn't plan on telling him anything. "There was no big emergency, Morgan. I figured there were some things I could be doing here and figured our talk could wait. No biggie."

He continued to stare at her and then gestured to the hallway leading to her office. "Do what you were doing before I got here while I bring everything in."

She arched a brow. "Everything like what?"

"Dinner."

"Dinner?"

"Yes, dinner," he replied. "Have you eaten?"

"No, but I didn't expect you to bring me anything."

"No, what I expected was to have dinner with you at McIntosh's. So I got takeouts."

Her brows arched a little higher. "*McIntosh* doesn't do takeouts."

"They do if you know the right people."

At the moment that wasn't what she needed to hear. She threw up her hands. "Yes, you're right," she all but snapped. "It's all about connections, isn't it?"

He frowned. "What do you mean by that?"

"Nothing," she said and quickly turned away from

him. After taking a deep breath she turned back toward him. "I'm just not in a good mood at the moment."

He nodded as if he understood when he honestly didn't have a clue, she thought. "Look, I have a tray table around here somewhere. I'll go dig it out." And then she walked off, leaving him standing there.

BY THE TIME Lena had located the tray table, Morgan had brought in all the bags of food, and a delicious scent filled her office. If she wasn't hungry before, she was certainly hungry now. She also noticed that Morgan had brought in his briefcase.

"Need help with anything?" he asked.

She glanced over in his direction. He had removed his jacket and looked rather comfortable in her office. "No, I don't need help. Thanks for asking."

"No problem."

She continued what she was doing as she drew in a deep breath. She and Morgan were virtually acting like strangers and not like the two people who had mated like rabbits yesterday. A part of her wished she could remove what happened yesterday from her mind. And then there was the chat they'd had online last night. How can you move from a high level of intimacy to a lower one that was basically nonintimate?

"Now that does it. I set you up over here," she said, after placing a tray table near the sofa. "And I'll just use my desk."

She met his gaze, and the smile that touched his lips let her know he'd caught on to what she'd done.

She had deliberately placed him away to the other side of the room. "Any reason I can't share your desk with you?" he asked, with eyes that glinted with mischief.

She shrugged as she moved toward her desk. "I thought you'd want more room."

"What I really want, Lena, is more of you."

She quickly turned back toward him and paused to take a deep, calming breath. His words hadn't been what she'd expected. And the impact they had on her was unnerving. The sexual excitement, desire and longing that she'd tried not to think about were now hitting her in the face. She felt her heart as it began to race and her stomach began fluttering.

Before she could say anything he said, "But I'll behave and stay on this side of the room...for now."

She glared at him and started to say something, but then changed her mind and crossed the room to her desk.

ONCE LENA HAD settled in at her desk and begun eating, the mischief that had been in Morgan's eyes a few moments ago was replaced with concern. Something was going on with Lena and he couldn't help wondering what. Had she heard anything about the possibility of him going into politics? Even if she had, why would that have driven her to cancel their dinner date and leave the restaurant before he had arrived?

And from the moment he had walked into her office, he had sensed her withdrawal. She was definitely not acting like the woman who had shared his bed for almost four hours yesterday. He didn't know what was bothering her, but he was determined to find out, and whatever it was, he intended to remove it from between them.

He settled on the sofa and placed the tray table in front of him and unloaded the bag with his food. He glanced over at her. She was eating, not saying anything, so he decided to break the silence. "I dropped by your house and left your mom something to eat as well."

He watched as she quickly lifted her head and a surprised look was on her face. "You did?"

"Yes. She said she'd already eaten but would save it as leftovers for tomorrow."

Lena nodded. "Thanks. That was thoughtful of you, Morgan."

"You're welcome." He watched as she took another sip of the iced tea that had been included with her dinner. When her lips touched the edge of the cup his stomach clenched, as he remembered how his lips had devoured hers yesterday, which then reminded him of something else.

"Did your mom ask why your lips were bruised when she saw you last night?"

Lena lifted her head and their gazes connected. "No, she didn't ask," she responded softly. "Why?"

"Just curious." And what he didn't add was that asking her about it would make her remember, just in case she had forgotten.

"Everything tastes good, Morgan. Thanks again for thinking of me."

"I always think of you, Lena."

Heat. Awesome heat, vibrant heat flowed all through Lena. It wasn't what he'd said but rather how he'd said it. And she wondered if this was a game he was playing with her. And had yesterday been a game as well? She inhaled deeply. No matter what, she refused to let Morgan get next to her until he was totally up front with her. Then she would be up front with him and let him know their deal was off. She was not the woman he needed to move his career forward.

For the next few moments they continued to eat in silence, sharing little or no conversation. But each time she would glance over at him, he would be watching her with an intensity that made it almost impossible to chew her food. He could generate so much heat within her from just a look, and she could feel even more heat radiating from the depths of his eyes each time he looked at her.

So she tried not to look over at him, but she still felt it. The chemistry, the attraction and the desire that wouldn't go away no matter how hard she was fighting it.

"Would you like some dessert?"

She raised her head and met his gaze. "What?"

He smiled. "Dessert. I think they put everything in my bag. I bought slices of chocolate cake."

"No, thanks. I'm full. I'll just save it for tomorrow."

He nodded and then stood. "Okay. I'll start discarding the trash. Do you have a Dumpster nearby?"

"Yes. It's out back."

She watched as he began putting everything back in the bags. He had rolled his sleeves up and she couldn't help but notice all the hair on his arms. But then, she'd noticed yesterday just what a hairy man he was. He had hair all over—his chest, his thighs and even that thick thatch where his manhood rested.

"You're through?"

She looked at him. He was standing in front of her desk. "Excuse me?"

He chuckled. "I asked if you were through. All the food is gone off your plate, but you're still sitting there, holding your fork like you're going to take another bite where there's nothing left."

"Oh," she said and immediately dropped the fork down on her plate. "Sorry, I was just thinking about something."

"No problem. I've been sitting over there thinking about some things as well."

She lifted a brow. "You have?"

"Yes. It seems my mind has been busy a lot lately."

She nodded. His mind wasn't the only thing that had been busy a lot. He had used his mouth and hands yesterday with a skill that was absolutely astounding.

"I'm taking the trash out. I'll be back in a second."

"All right." It was only when he left the room that she finally let out a deep sigh. She couldn't help wondering what was next. Would he be leav-

ing when he returned or would he be staying? And
if he stayed what did he intend to do?

HE DIDN'T LEAVE, nor did it seem he intended to. When
he returned she had deliberately placed work on her
desk to look busy. He had merely crossed the room,
folded up the tray table and then sat down with his
briefcase. She started to ask what he was doing but it
had been obvious. He'd evidently brought work with
him to do and intended doing his while she did hers.

For the next half hour or so, the only sounds that
could be heard in the room was their breathing and
papers shuffling. But there was something comforting, relaxing and intimate about them sharing space
that wasn't cyberspace.

He finished working on whatever papers he had
long before she did and stood, stretching his muscles
before walking over to the window. Her office was
located in one of those minimalls that faced a busy
street. When Morgan opened one of the blinds, she
saw that the parking area was pretty well lit and already the floodlights had come on and it wasn't even
six o'clock yet.

She knew Morgan was standing there, studying
the casual surroundings out the window. She, however, was studying him. Her gaze flowed across the
contours of his back that was covered with his dress
shirt, remembering how she had placed love bites on
that back yesterday. At the time she'd thought they
were merely nibbles, but now, considering how she
felt about him, she knew they'd been love bites.

And then there were his slacks, the way they fit his thighs and hips, and the way he had his hands shoved into his pockets showed just what a fine tush he had. She decided she had read enough and placed her papers aside. More memories of yesterday filled her mind, and suddenly that ache between her thighs returned. On top of that, her body began humming with awareness, and it became charged as if certain parts of her had lives of their own.

She tried fighting the feelings. What she and Morgan needed to do was to talk. He needed to tell her about his decision to get into politics, and she needed to explain to him why it wouldn't work between them. The last thing she should be doing was sitting there ogling him and inhaling his scent, remembering his taste and the very feel of him buried deep within her.

Hard Steele.

She blinked when he suddenly turned and caught her staring. The depths of the dark eyes gazing back at her caused a hot flame to burst to life within her. If nothing else they had proven yesterday that when it came to the sexual chemistry between them they had a tendency to act on it, regardless of the time or the place.

And she had a feeling tonight would be one of those times.

She could feel it. It was there in the air again, transmitting between them like hot lava. It was like a heated mist, surrounding them in a sexual haze. Instinctively she pushed back her chair and stood.

No matter if they were on the verge of going separate ways, there was no way she could let tonight end without feeling the hardness of him embedded within her one last time.

Through eyes filled with desire she watched as he closed the blinds and pulled his shirt from within his pants and began unbuttoning it. When he had completely removed it and tossed it aside, her body responded. This was the naked chest that had rubbed against her bare breasts yesterday. The chest she had covered with more kisses than she could count.

She walked from around her desk but stayed a good distance from him. "I feel hot," she said, her voice breathy and husky in a way it could get only around him.

"Then let me cool you off," was his reply.

"Cool me off or make me hotter?"

He only shook his head and smiled before saying, "I'll let you be the judge."

Emboldened by the same force that had overtaken her yesterday, she began removing her blouse while he watched her. His gaze was intense, intimate and hot. After tossing her blouse aside she unsnapped her bra. Her breasts poured out before she could get the bra off completely and she felt a sheen of perspiration forming between the twin globes.

She shimmied out of her skirt and when she stood in front of him wearing a thong, this one black lace and covering less of her femininity than the one she'd worn yesterday, he suddenly made a sound. She heard the low growl that radiated from deep within his throat. It was then that he moved away from the window to return to the sofa and sat down and continued to hold her gaze. And then in a deep, husky, desire-laden voice, he said, "Come here, Lena."

On legs that could barely hold her, she slowly crossed the room to him, locked with a gaze that was so intense it nearly took her breath away. When she came to a stop between his widened thighs, he leaned forward, almost bringing him face-to-face with her womanly core.

His face was so close she could feel his breath through the thin wispy material. And then she felt something else, the wetness of his tongue as he snaked it out and began licking the lace. She remembered their chat the night before, and suddenly she felt so weak she had to reach out and grab hold of his shoulders to keep from falling.

Then he was pushing her a few steps back so that he could ease down on his knees in front of her.

"I need to taste you, Lena," he whispered in a husky voice, still holding her gaze.

His words torched the flame within her, suddenly made her crazy with desire. She watched his breathing quicken, his eyes darken just mere seconds before he lowered his head and began kissing and licking his way upward, toward her inner thigh.

"Open your legs for me, baby," he requested softly and it was then she realized she still had them pressed together. The moment she opened them he slowly peeled the thong down her legs, leaving her completely bare for his view.

His finger that was lodged between her legs moved and she inhaled a sharp breath. "You're awfully wet, baby," he whispered huskily. "And I can't imagine letting all that deliciousness go to waste."

And before she could draw her next breath he was kissing and licking his way up her inner thigh again. The moment she felt his hot breath within inches of her womanly core, she dug her hands in his shoulders, bracing for the onslaught, and when it happened, when his tongue invaded her, both torturing and satisfying the ache between her legs, she almost lost consciousness. But he wouldn't let her. The sensations that tore into her were too sharp and keen. Too electrifying to do anything other than to enjoy the moment.

So she held on as he relentlessly devoured her, tonguing and sucking, as sensations shot all the way through her bloodstream. She felt the explosion and tried pushing him away before it happened, but his hand was firm, possessively cupping her hips steady, locked to his mouth as his tongue continued to pound into her over and over.

"Morgan!"

She heard herself making moaning sounds at the same exact time she felt her stomach constrict. And she began experiencing sensations that swept through her that were so strong, so totally out of her control that they had her screaming. It was like nothing she'd ever felt before. Her body began vibrating between her thighs and she found herself pushing hard against his hot mouth instead of pulling away from it.

It took some doing but the sensations began ebbing and her body was slowly being pulled back into dimension. There was a heartbeat of silence and then she heard Morgan say huskily, "Get ready, baby. We've barely got started yet."

CHAPTER FIFTEEN

LENA GLANCED ACROSS the room at the man who was putting back on his clothes while she put back on hers. "We never got around to talking," she said, forcing herself to speak calmly.

There hadn't been anything remotely calm about what she and Morgan had shared for the past hour. Even now she knew they weren't through with each other. It was bad enough they couldn't get dressed without looking at each other, but there was this surge of nonstop desire that kept flowing through her.

"I know. Do you need to call your mother and check on her?"

She knew why he was asking. She should have been gone hours ago. It was almost eight. She couldn't recall the last time she stayed away from home that late in the evening. "That's not a bad idea." She then tossed aside the blouse she was about to put on and walked over to her desk to call home, not missing the glint of heated desire she saw in the depths of his dark eyes.

Moments later she hung up the phone, shaking

her head and chuckling. "What's so funny?" Morgan asked.

"Mom was on the other line with Ms. Emily and rushed me off."

"That's her friend from the day care, right?"

"Yes. Sounds like the two of them are having one whale of a conversation. Usually Mom is in bed by nine, but she said they would be chatting for a while tonight."

"Sounds like she's found a good friend."

Lena nodded. "Yes, it seems that way. I'm glad she's finally coming around, but she's been depressed for so long that…"

"That what?"

"Although I always wanted her to come out of it, a part of me wondered if she ever would."

Morgan nodded. He then crossed the room to stand in front of her and cupped her chin, gently lifting it so their eyes could meet. "And?"

She arched a brow. "And what?"

"And how do you feel about that?"

Sometimes she felt he could read her like a book. "Of course a part of me is happy, Morgan, but then, I've gotten used to being there for her, taking care of her, and having her to need me."

He smiled. "And you'll always do that—be there for her, take care of her—and she will continue to need you."

As if he knew she needed a hug he pulled her into his arms and rested his chin on the top of her head. "But I know how you feel. I felt that way when Chance got married again."

Lena pulled back and met his gaze. "You did?"

"Yes. I would never tell Chance but Bas, Donovan and I have always looked up to him. He seemed to always make the right decisions when it concerned not only the company but us as well. My father was a strict disciplinarian. He was a good man, but strict. He and Bas butted heads more times than I care to remember, and when Bas dropped out of college and had no contact with the family for almost a year, he did maintain contact with Chance."

Lena nodded. "But why did it bother you when Chance married?"

Morgan smiled. He knew she was asking mainly because Chance had married her best friend. "It bothered me because since Cyndi's death, he hadn't really shown any real interest in a woman until Kylie. I thought she would come and disrupt our little family circle."

"But she didn't," Lena said defensively to the point it made Morgan chuckle.

"No, she didn't. In fact I think she's the best thing for Chance and Marcus, as well as for us. And now with Bas married and Jocelyn getting ready to manage one of Cameron's construction companies here, it seems the Steele brothers are getting married one by one, although the jury is still out on Donovan, and will be for a while. He claims he's having too much fun to settle down."

Lena inhaled a deep breath knowing whether by

accident or intentionally, Morgan had given her the
opening she needed for them to start talking about
their issues. "Morgan?"

"Yes?"

"Why didn't you tell me you were thinking of
running for public office?"

For a few moments he didn't say anything, and
then he released her and took a step back as if he
needed full control of his mind and body to respond
to her question. "I hadn't really made a decision. Before I had merely thought about it."

She nodded. "And now?"

"And now I have made a decision and will officially announce my candidacy next week."

She inhaled deeply. "When were you planning
to tell me?"

"This afternoon at dinner. And then tonight,
which is why I came over here. But I kind of got
distracted."

They both had. She moved across the room to
stand at the window. Opening the blinds she looked
out. Like him she needed full control of her mind
and body. After several moments she turned toward
him. "I hope you know this changes everything and
I can no longer agree to your business proposal."

Immediately, she felt his inner tension. "One has
nothing to do with the other, Lena."

She shook her head. "Yes, it does. I'm not cut out
to be a political wife."

"I think you are."

"You need someone else by your side, Morgan. Someone who would complement you and—"

He crossed the room. "What the hell are you saying?" he asked angrily. "Don't you think I'm old enough to know what I want and need?"

"Yes, but when you had made that decision things were different. Then all you needed was a woman who would have your baby. Now you need a…"

"Trophy wife?" he asked in a tone of voice filled with even more anger.

She sighed deeply. "Yes, if you want to refer to it as such."

"So me wanting you as the mother of my child means nothing?"

"It did before but not now." Lena felt a tightening around her heart when she added, "Don't you see what I'm trying to do?"

"Honestly, no, I don't. Mainly because I know what I want and who I want, and let me tell you something else, Lena. I refuse for you or anyone else to decide my future for me." He crossed the room to the coatrack and got his jacket and slipped it on. "Come on, I'll walk you out."

Lena knew he was angry but she didn't know what else she could say or do to make him see reason. Why couldn't he understand that things needed to be back on a professional level between them?

When they reached her car, he asked before opening the door, "So what was tonight about, Lena?"

"I don't know what you mean."

"Yes, you do. Why did you let me make love to

you tonight if you knew things would be over between us?"

When she didn't say anything he shook his head, understanding completely. "So it was one of those kinds of nights."

She raised her head and met his gaze. "What kind of nights?"

"Nothing but sex, pure sex and nothing but sex."

She cringed. His words had made it sound so dirty. "Why are you giving me a hard time about my decision, Morgan? I would think you would be overjoyed."

He stared at her before moving aside and opening the car door for her. "Yes, you would think that and you know what, Lena? I'm going to announce my candidacy without you or anyone else beside me."

When she got inside the car, she watched as he walked over to his own, and instead of getting in he stood there, staring at her. She held back the tears that threatened to fall. Why couldn't he see that everything she was doing was because she loved him?

"LET ME GET this straight," Kylie said, glaring at her best friend. "You actually told Morgan you couldn't marry him because he's decided to run for public office?"

Lena was glad they were the only two in the house. They were in the kitchen. She was sitting at the kitchen table when Kylie stood at the counter folding laundry.

Chance was out playing the usual Saturday morning basketball game with his brothers; Marcus and his latest girlfriend had left earlier for the mall, and Tiffany had gone to spend the weekend with her grandparents.

"Calm down, Kylie. I wouldn't want Chance to blame me if you went into labor early. And yes, I told him I couldn't marry him. It would not have been a real marriage anyway."

Kylie tossed the items she was about to fold back in the laundry basket and came and sat across the table from Lena. "And just what do you mean it would not have been a real marriage?"

Lena sighed. She knew that Kylie would be upset because she had held all the facts of her pending engagement to Morgan from her. "First promise that you won't get mad."

Kylie rolled her eyes. "I won't promise you anything because I'm already mad. I can't believe you let Cassandra Tisdale and her band of Merry Hussies get to you."

"They didn't get to me."

"Sounds to me like they did. So let's get back on track. What do you mean that your marriage to Morgan would not have been real?"

Lena didn't say anything for a long time. Then she said, "Morgan and I entered into a business agreement."

Kylie lifted an arched brow. "What kind of business agreement?"

"I was to marry him and have his baby."

"What!"

"You heard me. He asked me to marry him just to have his baby."

Kylie stared at her for a long moment. And then she did the one thing Lena hadn't expected. She burst out laughing.

And she continued laughing to the point where Lena began getting slightly irritated. Personally, she didn't see anything funny, she thought, leaning back in her chair and crossing her arms over her chest and glaring across the table at Kylie. "Excuse me, I hate to interrupt, especially when I've evidently brought so much amusement into your life this morning, but can you please explain to me what the hell is so funny?"

Kylie stopped laughing, slightly. She then got up and went to the kitchen counter and grabbed a paper towel to dab at her eyes and said, "I'm so sorry, Lena, but Morgan pulled one over on you."

Lena's glare deepened. "Meaning?"

Kylie dabbed at her eyes some more and chuckled a few times before saying, "Meaning, he would have told you anything to get you married to him."

Lena inhaled deeply, still not knowing just what Kylie meant. "Kylie, I'm going to count to ten, and if you don't get that rump of yours back in this chair and tell me what you're talking about, then you will be going into labor early."

Kylie saw the threatening look in her eyes and knew her best friend meant business. "All right, all right," she said, coming back to sit down at the table.

"Now talk."

Kylie raised her eyes to the ceiling. "You're so smart I'm surprised you hadn't figured things out, Lena. Think," she said, reaching across the table and tapping a finger against what at the moment she considered her best friend's thick skull. "For months Morgan has been after you. He asked you out several times."

She glared at Kylie. "So? I'm sure he's asked several women out. Big deal."

"No, Lena. For Morgan it wasn't just a big deal. I think it almost became an obsession."

Lena frowned. "An obsession?"

"Yes. Not to the point that he would have resorted to stalking you or anything like that," Kylie said, grinning. "But he was determined to get you."

Lena considered Kylie's words for a moment, then asked softly, "In bed?"

Kylie immediately knew where Lena's thoughts were going and reached out and captured her hand. "No, Lena. I think it was more serious than that."

Lena's frown deepened. "What's more serious than a man going after a woman for the sole intent of getting her in his bed? And you knew about this and didn't tell me?"

Kylie shrugged. "I knew what Chance was telling me, which wasn't much, but enough to figure out what was going on. The reason I didn't tell you is that my husband asked me not to. He felt sooner or later sexual chemistry would do the both of you in. The brothers knew how bad Morgan wanted you, so they figured out why he'd hired you to sell his house and buy another."

Lena's eyes widened in startled shock. "Are you saying the reason Morgan hired me as a Realtor was that he wanted to sleep with me?"

Kylie rolled her eyes. "No, that's not what I'm saying, and will you please be quiet for a moment so I can give you my take on things?"

When Lena reluctantly nodded, she said, "My take on things is this. For Morgan it was more than having you in his bed. I honestly think he was quite taken with you, Lena, and he concocted this plan to get you right where he wanted you, as a permanent part of his life. Remember that day at lunch I told you about his belief about his *perfect* woman? In his mind you're it and he would have done anything for you to become a part of his life like he wanted to become a part of yours. But first he had to prove himself to you, let you see that he's not like those guys you dated before."

Lena bit her bottom lip. A part of her couldn't buy what Kylie was saying. Mainly because she couldn't see herself as any man's perfect anything. "I think you're wrong, Kylie."

"And I think I'm right, Lena. If all Morgan wanted was to sleep with you, once he'd done that he wouldn't have come back, and I know the two of you have slept together."

Lena leaned forward. "And how do you know that?"

Kylie smiled. "The same way you knew that

Chance and I had slept together without me having said one word. I was celibate for over fifteen years and I know you haven't been with anyone since your dad died. Although I hadn't seen you in the past couple of days when I talked to you a couple of days ago you sounded funny."

Lena leaned back in the chair and lifted a brow. "Funny how?"

"Like you were tired, exhausted, sexually fulfilled. And when I talked to your mom yesterday and she happened to mentioned the fact that you had swollen lips, I thought that—"

Lena straightened in her chair. "Mom told you that?"

Kylie couldn't help but giggle. "Yes, you know mothers don't miss anything. They see everything. Trust me, although she might not have said anything, she noticed."

Lena nodded. "So what did you tell her?"

Kylie smiled. "I told her it must have been a soda bottle. I heard Donovan give that excuse to Chance once."

Lena inhaled deeply. "Okay, Morgan and I did sleep together, once."

Kylie lifted a brow, then reached out and touched a mark on Lena's upper arm. "Once? This sure looks like a recent passion mark to me."

Lena rolled her eyes. "Okay, more than once. So he got what he wanted."

Kylie shook her head. "I'm sorry you think that way. You know what your problem is, Lena?"

"No, what do you think my problem is, Kylie?" she asked sarcastically.

"I've known you all my life and you've always felt you've had to complete against skinny females. Why can't you believe and accept that there are some men who don't give a damn about a woman's weight? They see beyond all that and see what's in her heart. Why can't you believe Morgan is one of those men? To him, you are his perfect woman. You and not Jamie Hollis or any other slim woman who wants to catch his eye. But until you believe in your own beauty, both inside and outside, what he sees doesn't really matter."

DONOVAN GLARED AT his two oldest brothers. "I refuse to play another game until the two of you calm Morgan down. What the hell is his problem?"

Bas smiled as he grabbed the ball from Chance. Morgan had called time-out for a bathroom break and they were using the time while he was gone to discuss him. "If I recall, you pissed him off that day when he was daydreaming in the meeting. You should have figured then there would be hell to pay. Stop whining and take it like a man."

"No, it's more than just that particular day," Chance said, concerned. "He's been playing pretty rough with all of us. I wonder what's going on."

"Whatever it is, I bet it has something to do with Lena," Donovan said.

Bas rolled his eyes. "What else is new?"

"Hey, look at who just walked in," Chance said.

Both Bas and Donovan squinted their eyes against the gym's bright lights. "Isn't that Jamie Hollis and your ex, Bas?" Donovan asked.

Bas frowned. "You make her sound like she used to be my wife," he said of the woman with Jamie, Cassandra Tisdale. "I wonder what the hell the two of them are doing here."

Donovan grinned. "Oh, I know the answer to that one. Jamie is after Morgan. In fact there are bets going around that she's going to be the one he eventually marries instead of Lena."

Chance shook his head. "Does Morgan know that?"

"Yes, I told him. I also told him that I'd heard that Cassandra had even boasted about it to Lena," Donovan said.

"No wonder Lena dumped him," Bas said, frowning.

"Lena didn't dump me," Morgan said angrily, approaching his brothers from behind. "Ready to play another game?" He then glanced up into the bleachers, recognized the two women and frowned. "What the hell are they doing here?"

Bas turned to his brother and grinned. "Evidently, they came to see you get your ass kicked all over the basketball court today."

A few hours later Morgan was back at his place soaking in a hot tub of water. He and his brothers had played some pretty rough games today, but then he'd need the brutal workout to work out his frustrations. Now he could settle down and think.

He shook his head at the audacity of Cassandra and Jamie. They had tried their best to get him to agree to meet them some place for drinks and to play a game of tennis. He leaned back in the water thinking he wasn't stupid. He had seen that same look in Jamie Hollis's eyes that he'd seen in other women on a manhunt. She was a woman with a plan just like he had been a man with a plan. A plan that had backfired on him.

He wondered if Lena had figured things out yet and if she had, did she even care? Well, hell, he cared and if she thought he had given up on her she had another thought coming.

He got out of the tub and began drying off. Something Bas had said earlier piqued his interest. Evidently Lena was a part of Vanessa's latest community project, and there would be a meeting at her house sometime this evening. There was no reason for him not to stop by and give his regards to the ladies.

VANESSA STEELE ROLLED her eyes at the man standing on her doorstep. "What are you doing here, Morgan?"

He smiled. "Do I need a reason to visit one of my favorite cousins?"

She frowned. "No, but it does seem odd since you haven't been over here since Christmas."

He chuckled. "Only because the last time I dropped by you told me not to come back."

Her frown deepened. "I told you not to come back if you had to bring Cameron Cody with you. That man is not welcome in my home."

Morgan shook his head. "Wasn't it just last Sunday that Pastor Givens spoke about forgiveness?"

She lifted an arched brow. "I'm surprised you remembered the sermon since you, Donovan and Bas usually fall asleep during service. It's a sin and a shame."

"No need to get ugly about it." He shoved away from the wall. "So, are you going to invite me in or not?"

Vanessa stared at him as if she was considering his question, and then she moved aside. "Only because Dane's going to drop Sienna off and he might hang around if you're here."

Morgan entered the house and glanced around, heard feminine voices coming from the back and smiled when he heard one in particular. He then turned to Vanessa and asked, "Why does Dane have to drive Sienna over here?"

Vanessa couldn't stop the smile that spread across her lips. "Because they're driving to Memphis right after the meeting to spend the weekend." She leaned closer and whispered, "Sienna has some special news for Dane."

Morgan nodded. From the way Vanessa had said it, he had an idea just what that news was. He then thought of Lena and the day she would tell him some special news. But first he knew he had to win her over. First he had to get the wife, and then the baby.

"WELL, LADIES, LOOK who just showed up," Vanessa said to the three women in her kitchen.

Everyone turned and stared at Morgan, but it was Lena who held his gaze the longest. "Hello, everyone. I just decided to pay Vanessa a visit, so don't mind me," he said.

Jocelyn, who was still trying to get to know her husband's family, smiled over at him and said, "It's good seeing you, Morgan."

"Same here, Jocelyn." He then glanced over at Kylie. "And how are you, Kylie, besides pregnant?"

She made a face at him before saying, "Fine and counting. One more month to go and I'm free."

He nodded. He then crossed the room to Lena. She was standing alone near the sink. Remembering their last conversation he wasn't sure how her attitude would be toward him. "Hello, Lena."

"Morgan."

"How's your mother?"

"She's doing fine. Thanks for asking."

He nodded. "I told Vanessa I would make myself useful while I'm here. I'll be outside trimming her hedges if you need me for anything."

She lifted a brow. "If I need you for anything?"

He smiled. "Yes."

Lena stared at him, remembering what Kylie had told her just that morning. The only reason Morgan had hired her to sell his house was that he had wanted her, although she and Kylie had a difference of opinion of just what the word *want* actually meant.

"I'm glad you came here today since I was going to seek you out tomorrow."

She watched the smile spread to his eyes. "You were?"

"Yes. There's something I needed to tell you, and if you have time, since the meeting hasn't started yet, maybe I can do it now."

His smile widened. "Sure. Let's go into Vanessa's study for privacy."

Lena nodded and then glanced around the room at the other ladies, not surprised to find them staring at her and Morgan. Evidently there weren't too many secrets in the Steele family. Had all of them known of his obsession to have her in his bed? "If you'll excuse me for a moment, I need to speak with Morgan about something."

She followed Morgan to Vanessa's study, and the moment the door was closed, she inhaled deeply, feeling angry and frustrated.

He leaned back on Vanessa's desk and smiled at her. "So, what did you want to talk to me about?"

She crossed the room, trying to hold back her anger and the hurt she felt. "It has come to my attention that you hired me as your real estate agent for an indecent reason and I just want you to know that effective today, I quit."

Then without saying anything else, she turned and walked out of the room.

CHAPTER SIXTEEN

ON MONDAY MORNING Morgan was standing at the window in his office thinking about what Lena had told him on Saturday. Since the meeting had started he hadn't gotten a chance to talk to her after that because as soon as the meeting was over she'd left.

But then, what exactly could he have said? He couldn't deny that he'd had ulterior motives for hiring her as a Realtor. But she was wrong about any of it being indecent.

He was in love with her, but he knew he would have a hard time convincing her of that now. He had talked to Kylie yesterday and she had convinced him that the best thing to do was to just give Lena time to come around. Well, he didn't want to give her time. He wanted and needed her like he needed his next breath.

His secretary's voice on the intercom intruded into his thoughts.

"Yes, Linda?"

"There's a Ms. Jamie Hollis here to see you. She doesn't have an appointment but indicated she's Senator Hollis's daughter."

Morgan rolled his eyes. Like he gave a flip, and he

was ready to tell Linda to advise the senator's daughter he was too busy to see her. But then he decided what the hell? He needed to set Jamie straight once and for all. "All right, Linda, please send her in."

A few minutes later Jamie walked in with her expensive perfume almost choking him. She was dressed in an outfit that probably cost a pretty penny, and she looked the epitome of a wealthy, sophisticated, aristocratic lady. He had to admit she was an attractive woman, but he was able to see beyond that beauty to someone he wouldn't be attached to even for a billion dollars. "Jamie," he said, with a forced smile, crossing the room to give her a formal handshake. "What can I do for you?"

She smiled up at him as she took the seat he offered. "The question, Morgan, is what I can do for you. I'd like to make you an offer I don't think you'll be able to refuse."

He lifted a brow and leaned back on his desk. "Really, and what is it?"

"A partnership between us."

He inwardly shuddered, wondering if that's how he'd sounded that day he had offered Lena a business deal between them. If so, then he regretted every word he'd spoken. "What kind of a partnership?"

"Marriage. I'll be thirty this time next year, and Daddy thinks it's time I do something."

Morgan crossed his arms over his chest. "Does he?"

"Yes. And I was bred and groomed to be a politician's wife, someone who's going places. And I want to become a mother one day, with a nanny of course."

She shifted in the chair, and her smile widened and excitement shone in her eyes as she continued. "Everyone sees you as a top contender for Charlotte's first black mayor in a few years, and who knows where that will lead? I could see you as the governor, even president one day. And I intend to be your First Lady all the way."

Like hell you will. He cleared his throat. Evidently she had erroneously thought things through. "I appreciate your offer, Jamie, but I thought you knew."

"Knew what?"

"I've asked someone else to marry me. In fact we'll be announcing our engagement sometime this week."

The spark in her eyes was replaced with a furious dart. "Really? Who?"

"Lena Spears."

She blinked and then he watched a smile touch her lips before she waved her well-manicured, neatly polished hand in the air like his words had held no significant meaning. "Really? Morgan, Lena is not the woman you need, I am. In fact after our little talk last week with Lena, Cassandra and I were sure we had convinced her that if she cared anything for you she would get out of the picture."

He straightened. "Excuse me?"

"I said we had a talk with Lena last week. We happened to run into her at McIntosh's. She's a very sensible woman who I believes loves you, but we made it quite clear that she wasn't the woman for you. For a man of your caliber, you need a woman who possesses style, grace, pedigree, wealth and connections."

Morgan shook his head. "Let me get this straight. You actually said those things to Lena?"

She smiled. "Of course. Someone needed to be honest and up front with her. And since the two of you hadn't announced an engagement this weekend, I assumed she took our advice."

Morgan nodded. *She had.* No wonder she had given him that garbage that night in her office about not being the appropriate woman for him. He walked over to the chair Jamie was sitting in and leaned over, placing his hands on the arms and pinning her in. Anger, the likes he'd never known before, flowed through him.

"Listen, Jamie, and listen well," he said through gritted teeth. "There will never be a business partnership of any kind between us. When I marry, I will marry for love, and the woman I marry will be Lena Spears. And I will be marrying her for all the right reasons, and if I ever hear of you or anyone else spouting anything to her about not being good enough for me and my political future, you will have to deal with me. Do you understand?"

"Are you threatening me, Morgan?"

"No, I'm telling it like it is, and if you ever come back I will get on television and tell everyone about why it was necessary for you to take that trip to London for six months last year."

She blinked. "What are you talking about?"

"You figure it out. But like you, I do have connections and mine talk and have all the proof we need. It would be an embarrassment not only for your father but also for the Tisdale family, who think so highly of their family name."

He'd said enough. Cameron, who made it a point to keep tabs on people who could either be a menace or someone useful to him in the future, had picked up wind of the senator's daughter's pregnancy and how she'd gone to London to give the child up for adoption. He had found it interesting and had passed the information on to Morgan earlier that year.

He stepped back, more than certain she was ready to leave his office and wouldn't be coming back any time soon. Before she walked out the door he said, "And if I were you I would try and find a way to convince Cassandra to keep her mouth shut, too. There's a lot she doesn't want taken out of her closet as well."

He walked back to the window and didn't even look around when he heard the door slam shut.

AFTER LUNCH MORGAN placed a call to a friend from college who happened to be the top anchorwoman at the city's leading television station. When Gail Winston came on the line he said, "All right, Gail, I promised you first dibs when I decided to run for office."

He laughed and placed the phone away from his ear when he heard her scream. "Yes, I'd like to announce it on your show Friday morning, but there's a catch."

He knew that would grab her attention. "Listen up. This is how I want you to handle things."

GAIL WINSTON SMILED into the camera. It was Friday morning and in a few seconds another segment of her local morning talk show would begin. When the producer gave her cue, she began.

"First, I want to thank our next guests who have joined forces with our local high schools to present a career fair that will be held next week. We have with us today Vanessa Steele, PR representative for the Steele Corporation. Lena Spears, a local Realtor from our area. And Jocelyn Steele, who will be the general manager of Cody Construction here in town. And it's my understanding Cody Construction will be establishing apprenticeship training in the areas of bricklaying, air-conditioning and plumbing this fall for individuals who are interested in those occupations."

Putting an even bigger smile on her face, Gail said, "Good morning, ladies."

"Good morning," the three women said simultaneously.

And for the next ten minutes, under the direction of Gail's intense questions, they talked to the television audience about the importance of the students in the area coming out and taking part in such a worthwhile event.

After a commercial break, Gail came back on the

air with the three ladies still sitting with her onstage in guest seats. "The reason I asked these ladies to remain is that two of them are members of the Steele family. And it just so happens that we have a surprise guest for everyone today. For years it's been speculated that sooner or later one of this city's favorite sons would enter politics, and today history is in the making. I have as our special guest someone most of you know because of his involvement in so many community affairs. Let's give a warm welcome to Morgan Steele, director of research and development for the Steele Corporation."

The audience applauded when Morgan walked out onstage and took the extra guest seat, which just happened to be beside Lena. Lena's heart almost stopped when he walked out. Impeccably dressed in a dark suit, white shirt and red tie, he looked like a movie celebrity rather than a businessman and easily took the breath away of any female seeing him.

She tried to focus her gaze on the monitor and not on him, for fear of another heartbreak. She loved him, and wooing her had been nothing more than a game to him.

Morgan settled into his seat. He hoped like hell this plan worked and had felt confident that it would, but now he wasn't all that sure, especially with the tension he could feel radiating from Lena.

Gail took control and pulled in his attention.

"Morgan has been a guest on my show before to promote numerous community causes, but this time he's here for another reason, right, Morgan?"

He smiled into the camera. "Right, Gail. Today I want to officially announce my candidacy for the council-at-large seat here in Charlotte. However, there is one condition."

Gail leaned forward and smiled. "And what condition is that?" she dutifully asked.

"I am a single man and there are a group of people who believe it's important that I have a good woman by my side, and I agree. What I don't agree with is the theory that I should choose a woman because the public thinks she and I will do well together politically as a team."

The camera angled in on him, and the intensity in his features couldn't be missed as he continued. "The woman I will marry is a woman I trust, a woman I know will have my back no matter what, and a woman I know is capable of being everything I could ever want in a wife. She is also a woman I love. I don't care if some people out there think she's not what they want for me. She is the woman I want for myself."

He paused for a second, then said, "So many times when people are involved in politics, they marry for all the wrong reasons. They form a partnership instead of a real marriage, and that's not what I want for myself. I could not understand the importance of the family and marriage dynamics if I didn't have a real marriage of my own. I want to marry for love and nothing else."

Anyone listening to what Morgan had said, whether a romantic or not, had to have felt the deep emotions he'd just conveyed in his words. Even Gail dabbed at her eyes.

"So, have you asked this young lady to marry you yet?" Gail couldn't help asking since she knew her audience would want to know.

"Yes, but at the time I asked her for the wrong reason. Now I want to ask her for the right one. I want her to know how much I truly do love her and that more than anything I want her to be my wife and the mother of my children. And whether I win this election bid doesn't matter as long as I have her by my side and in my life."

Gail dabbed at her eyes again. "Do you think she's out there watching the show and knows what you're saying?"

"It's even better than that," he said, smiling. "The woman I love just happens to be here onstage with us." Then before anyone could blink, Morgan got out of his chair and on his knees in front of Lena, while pulling a small white velvet box out of his pants pocket.

The cameras moved in closer, determined to capture the entire thing on film. Morgan took Lena's hand in his and gazed up into her eyes and took a deep breath. "Lena, if there is anything such as love at first sight, then it happened to me the night of the American Cancer Society's annual ball, when you walked into that ballroom. I can remember in full detail the dress you were wearing that night because you were such a vision of beauty in it that it took my breath away. And I knew from that night on I had to make you mine.

"And I'm here before you, on bended knee, wanting to do that. I love you and I believe you love me, too. Otherwise you would not have cared what became of my future. But what you don't know is that I truly don't have a future without you. You are the essence of my very being. You are the woman I want to see when I wake up in the morning, and the last face I want to see before going to sleep at night. You are the only woman I want and need in my life. You are my perfect woman. You are my everything."

His smile wavered just a little when he saw all her tears. He hoped they weren't tears of sadness but tears of joy. He opened the ring box and held the ring in his hand. "And will you make me the happiest man on earth, sweetheart, by agreeing to marry me? Will you marry me, Lena, and have my babies, to stick beside me for better or worse, richer or poorer, sickness and in health, until death do us part?"

Tears continued to stream down Lena's face. The man she loved more than anything was proclaiming his love for her for all to hear. It was only when everything in the studio got quiet, except for the sounds of more than a few sniffles, that she realized that everyone, especially Morgan, was waiting on her answer.

She leaned forward and cupped his face in her hand. Meeting his gaze she said, loud and clear, "And I love you, too, Morgan, and yes, I will marry you and have your babies. And you will make me an extremely happy woman as well."

Morgan slid the ring on Lena's hand, and of course the cameraman had to slide his camera over for the ultimate shot for the television audience.

"Can you believe the size of that rock?" Gail exclaimed to everyone as the monitor continued to zero in on Lena's hand.

"Well, folks, this is certainly a first. I don't know of any other morning show where someone can officially announce their candidacy and do a marriage proposal in the same ten-minute segment."

Everyone heard her words, but most people were staring at Morgan when he stood to his feet and pulled Lena into his arms for one whopper of a kiss.

Gail smiled brightly, knowing her ratings would soar. "Well, there you have it, folks. A man who puts love before any political career he might be seeking certainly will definitely get my vote. And remember you saw it live right here."

LENA SMILED TREMENDOUSLY as she glanced around the room. "Are you sure this is the house you want, Morgan? Your other home was—"

"My other home. I want to start somewhere new with you and Odessa. I knew when you showed this house to me that day that it would be perfect for us and our family."

She nodded happily as she walked into his outstretched arms. "What about your other home? Does Donovan still want it?"

Morgan threw his head back and chuckled. "Honey, Donovan never wanted my house. I talked him into buying it as part of my plan to get you."

Lena shook her head. "And you were that desperate?"

"Yes, for you I was that desperate. Plan A failed badly, but I was determined to make plan B a success. I hit a few bumps along the way but in the end I got you just where I want you, in my arms."

She cocked her head back and looked at him. "And not your bed."

He grinned. "Yes, there, too."

Lena moved closer and placed her head on her fiancé's chest. Today had to be the happiest day of her life. "Thanks for making sure Mom and everyone at the adult day care center was able to see this morning's show. She was so proud."

Morgan smiled. "And I'm glad. She's a part of our family and I never want her to forget it."

Lena leaned back in his arms to look up at him. Tears shone in her eyes. "Thanks. That means a lot to me."

"I know it, sweetheart. And because it means a lot to you it means a lot to me as well. And you know the question everyone will be asking. When is our wedding date?"

Lena sighed. "I always wanted a June wedding, but so did Kylie and Jocelyn and they never got one."

Morgan smiled. "Only because my impatient brothers couldn't wait. Luckily for you, June is only three months away. It might kill me but I'll wait."

She leaned back and kissed his chin. "Thanks, Morgan. You are a wonderful man."

He chuckled. "Yeah, and don't you ever forget it. And I have a wonderful idea."

"What?"

"Let's christen our new home right now."

Lena grinned. She had an idea just how he wanted that particular ceremony done. "But it doesn't have any furniture."

"You think not? Then come with me."

Morgan took Lena's hand and led her up the stairs and toward the master suite that connected to the main house by a glass breezeway and elevator access. "Now close your eyes," he said.

Lena did as he demanded and felt him tug her along. Moments later he said, "You can open them now."

She gasped after opening her eyes. The master suite was completely furnished. She glanced around, not believing the beauty and the workmanship of the furniture. "But how? Who?"

Morgan grinned as he drew her to him again. "I left the decorating up to Sienna. We've always considered her the Steeles' personal interior decorator. And Reese Singleton, Jocelyn's brother-in-law, built the furniture by hand. I commissioned him to start building it last summer when I went to Newton Grove, and he, Bas, Donovan and I went on a fishing trip together one weekend. I'd seen his work and knew I wanted him to design our bedroom furniture. I didn't know at the time just how I was going to get you to become a permanent part of my life, but I intended to do whatever I had to do to succeed."

Lena laughed as she glanced around at the beautiful furniture and decorating. He even had decorative blinds up to the windows. Everything was simply elegant. "But who gave you permission to put furniture in here? You haven't purchased this place yet."

Morgan shook his head, grinning. "Technically I have. When my Realtor quit on me last weekend," he said with a teasing glint in his eyes, "I decided I had to do what I needed to do. I used the company's attorney to close the deal, but with the understanding that my Realtor would still get the commission."

Lena shook her head. Morgan had basically thought of everything. "And I guess it was your idea for Mom to be invited over to Chance and Kylie's place for the night, right?"

He laughed. "Right."

Lena looked up at the ceiling. "What am I going to do with you, Morgan Steele?"

"Love me. Marry me and have my babies?" He leaned forward and captured her lips with his. The moment his tongue touched hers she felt fire light up inside her. And then the seduction began.

Lena had discovered that Morgan was skilled at whatever he did. And when it came to multitasking, he was at the top of the list. He began stroking her back, grinding the lower part of his body against her spread thighs, rubbing his chest against the taut tips of her breasts, while kissing her senseless. She closed her eyes and moaned like a woman in dire need of her man.

All she could think about and all she wanted to focus on were being in that bed with him, him making love to her, and having him inside her. He pulled back and whispered in her ear, "Undress for me, baby."

She smiled, liking the idea of stripping for him. She took a step back to slide the blouse over her head and skimmed the skirt she was wearing down her hips, leaving her clad only in a royal-blue thong. She placed her hands on her hips and smiled at him. "So, what do you think?"

He returned her smile. "I'd rather show you than tell you."

Quickly, he begin removing all of his clothes with a wicked grin plastered to his face. In no time at all he was standing in front of her, completely naked, but he saw she had one remaining piece left on. Her thong.

His smile widened as he got down on his knees in front of her. "I see you save the best for last."

She balanced her hands on his shoulders while he slowly slid the thin wispy material down her legs. And just like she'd known he would do, once it was removed he leaned forward and attached his mouth to her womanly core, giving her one hell of a tongue-lashing kiss there. She had to grip his shoulders to keep her balance, and when an orgasm hit her she screamed his name.

Moments later he stood, smiled and took her hand

in his. "That was just an appetizer. Come on, sweetheart, let's christen our bed."

Morgan's groin tightened as he watched Lena ease her naked body into the huge bed. *Perfect,* he thought, easing onto the bed behind her, like a lion stalking his prey. And then he had her in his arms, kissing her deeply, with all the love in his heart.

Lena gazed up at him when he positioned his body over hers, and she knew this would be a moment she would remember for the rest of her life. Today on television he had asked her to marry him, and now in the beautiful home he had purchased for her he was about to make her his in the most elemental way.

"I love you, Morgan," she whispered.

He smiled down at her. "And I love you, too. For always."

And then he eased his body into hers, closed his eyes and locked in place for a moment to absorb the intensity of the moment and to thank God for sending such a beautiful woman into his life. He then opened his eyes at the same time his body began to move. Sexual need combined with every deep emotion he possessed took over, and he established a rhythm that immediately sent all kinds of shudders racing through him.

"Lena!"

He was hit by the strongest force that could ever take down a man and literally bring him to his knees. The force of love. And he lifted her hips as another orgasm hit, and when he felt her body shattering as well he screamed out her name yet again.

And he knew what the two of them were sharing went beyond temptation. It went beyond anything he knew. And it would set the stage for the wonderful love they would always share. Together.

EPILOGUE

A beautiful day in June

"YOU MAY KISS your bride, Morgan."

Those were the very words Morgan had been waiting for, although he felt it had taken Reverend Givens long enough to say them. As far as he was concerned this had to have been the longest wedding ceremony on record. But as he glanced down at the beautiful woman in front of him, he knew it had been well worth it and more.

He pulled her into his arms and captured her lips in his, making another promise; one only the two of them understood. Today would begin the rest of their lives together and tonight they intended to start work on their dynasty. She had gone off the Pill months ago and tonight he would start another mission.

He pulled back when he felt a jab to his ribs and knew it had to have been Bas. Evidently the kiss had lasted longer than some people felt it should have. He smiled down into Lena's beautiful smiling face. "I love you, Mrs. Steele."

She smiled back up at him with tears shining in her eyes. "And I love you, Mr. Steele."

They turned to their audience, all five hundred of their guests, and smiled as the pastor announced proudly, "I now present to everyone, Morgan and Lena Steele."

Morgan shot a glance over at Cameron, who had served as one of his groomsmen. He then looked at his cousin Vanessa, who didn't look like a happy camper. He chuckled. He would give Cameron at least until the end of the summer to finally win his stubborn cousin over.

But Morgan knew he himself had other things to worry about. Making his wife happy, making a baby, and starting his campaign at full force. He had a lot to accomplish.

But of course like always, he was a man with a plan.

* * * * *

BEYOND TEMPTATION

To Gerald Jackson, Sr.,
my husband, hero and best friend.

To my readers who have been waiting patiently
for Morgan's story.

To my Heavenly Father,
who gave me the gift to write.

And lead us not into temptation…
—*Matthew* 6:13

PROLOGUE

A beautiful June day

"OMG, WHO'S THE latecomer to the wedding?"

"Don't know, but I'm glad he made it to the reception."

"Look at that body."

"Look at that walk."

"He should come with a warning sign that says Extremely Hot."

Several ladies in the wedding party whispered among themselves, and all eyes were trained on the tall, ultrahandsome man who'd approached the group of Westmoreland male cousins across the room. The reception for Micah Westmoreland's wedding to Kalina Daniels was in full swing on the grounds of Micah Manor, but every female in attendance was looking at one particular male.

The man who'd just arrived.

"For crying out loud, will someone please tell me who he is?" Vickie Morrow, a good friend of Kalina's, pleaded in a low voice. She looked over at Megan Westmoreland. "Most of the good-looking men here are related to you in some way, so tell us. Is he another Westmoreland cousin?"

Megan was checking out the man just as thoroughly as all the other women were. "No, he's no kin of mine. I've never seen him before," she said. She hadn't seen the full view yet, either, just his profile, but even that was impressive—he had handsome features, a deep tan and silky straight hair that brushed against the collar of his suit. He was both well dressed and good-looking.

"Yes, he definitely is one fine specimen of a man and is probably some Hollywood friend of my cousins, since he seems to know them."

"Well, I want to be around when the introductions are made," Marla Ford, another friend of Kalina's, leaned over and whispered in Megan's ear. "Make that happen."

Megan laughed. "I'll see what I can do."

"Hey, don't look now, ladies, but he's turned this way and is looking over here," Marla said. "In fact, Megan, your brother Zane is pointing out one of us to him…and I hope it's me." Seconds later, Marla said in a disappointed voice, "It's *you,* Megan."

Marla had to be mistaken. Why would Zane point her out to that man?

"Yeah, look how the hottie is checking you out," Vickie whispered to Megan. "It's like the rest of us don't even exist. *Lordy, I do declare.* I wish some man would look at me that way."

Megan met the stranger's gaze. Everyone was right. He was concentrated solely on her. And the

moment their eyes connected, something happened.
It was as if heat transmitted from his look was burn-
ing her skin, flaming her blood, scorching her all
over. She'd never felt anything so powerful in her
life.

Instant attraction.

Her heart pounded like crazy, and she shivered
as everything and everyone around her seemed to
fade into the background…everything except for the
sound of the soft music from the orchestra that pulled
her and this stranger into a cocoon. It was as if no
one existed but the two of them.

Her hand, which was holding a glass of wine,
suddenly felt moist, and something fired up within
her that had never been lit before. Desire. As potent
as it could get. How could a stranger affect her this
way? For the first time in her adult life, at the age
of twenty-seven, Megan knew what it meant to be
attracted to someone in a way that affected all her
vital signs.

And, as an anesthesiologist, she knew all about
the workings of the human body. But up until now
she'd never given much thought to her own body or
how it would react to a man. At least, not to how it
would react to this particular man…whomever he
was. She found her own reaction as interesting as
she found it disconcerting.

"That guy's hot for you, Megan."

Vickie's words reminded Megan that she had an
audience. Breaking eye contact with the stranger, she

glanced over at Vickie, swallowing deeply. "No, he's not. He doesn't know me, and I don't know him."

"Doesn't matter who knows who. What just happened between you two is called instant sexual attraction. I felt it. We all did. You would have to be dead not to have felt it. That was some kind of heat emitting between the two of you just now."

Megan drew in a deep breath when the other women around her nodded and agreed with what Vickie had said. She glanced back over at the stranger. He was still staring and held her gaze until her cousin Riley tapped him on the shoulder to claim his attention. And when Savannah and Jessica, who were married to Megan's cousins Durango and Chase, respectively, walked up to him, she saw how his face split in a smile before he pulled both women into his arms for a huge hug.

That's when it hit her just who the stranger was. He was Jessica and Savannah's brother, the private investigator who lived in Philadelphia, Rico Claiborne. The man Megan had hired a few months ago to probe into her great-grandfather's past.

Rico Claiborne was glad to see his sisters, but the woman Zane had pointed out to him, the same one who had hired him over the phone a few months ago, was still holding his attention, although he was pretending otherwise.

Dr. Megan Westmoreland.

She had gone back to talking to her friends, not looking his way. That was fine for now since he needed to get his bearings. What in the hell had that been all about? What had made him concentrate solely on her as if all those other women standing with her didn't exist? There was something about her that made her stand out, even before Zane had told him the one in the pastel pink was his sister Megan.

The woman was hot, and when she had looked at him, every cell in his body had responded to that look. It wasn't one of those I'm-interested-in-you-too kind of looks. It was one of those looks that questioned the power of what was going on between them. It was quite obvious she was just as confused as he was. Never had he reacted so fiercely to a woman before. And the fact that she was the one who had hired him to research Raphel Westmoreland made things even more complicated.

That had been two months ago. He'd agreed to take the case, but had explained he couldn't begin until he'd wrapped up the other cases he was working on. She'd understood. Today, he'd figured he could kill two birds with one stone. He'd attend Micah's wedding and finally get to meet Micah's cousin Megan. But he hadn't counted on feeling such a strong attraction to her, one that still had heat thrumming all through him.

His sisters' husbands, as well as the newlyweds, walked up to join him. And as Rico listened to the conversations swirling around him, he couldn't help but steal glances over at Megan. He should have known it would be just a matter of time before one of his sisters noticed where his attention had strayed.

"You've met Megan, right? I know she hired you to investigate Raphel's history," Savannah said with a curious gleam in her eyes. He knew that look. If given the chance she would stick that pretty nose of hers where it didn't belong.

"No, Megan and I haven't officially met, although we've talked on the phone a number of times," he said, grabbing a drink off the tray of a passing waiter. He needed it to cool off. Megan Westmoreland was so freaking hot he could feel his toes beginning to burn. "But I know which one she is. Zane pointed her out to me a few minutes ago," he added, hoping that would appease his sister's curiosity.

He saw it didn't when she smiled and said, "Then let me introduce you."

Rico took a quick sip of his drink. He started to tell Savannah that he would rather be introduced to Megan later, but then decided he might as well get it over with. "All right."

As his sister led him over to where the group of women stood, all staring at him with interest in their eyes, his gaze was locked on just one. And he knew she felt the strong attraction flowing between them as much as he did. There was no way she could not.

It was a good thing they wouldn't be working together closely. His job was just to make sure she received periodic updates on how the investigation was going, which was simple enough.

Yes, he decided, as he got closer to her, with the way his entire body was reacting to her, the more distance he put between himself and Megan the better.

CHAPTER ONE

Three months later

"DR. WESTMORELAND, THERE'S someone here to see you."

Megan Westmoreland's brow arched as she glanced at her watch. She was due in surgery in an hour and had hoped to grab a sandwich and a drink from the deli downstairs before then. "Who is it, Grace?" she asked, speaking into the intercom system on her desk. Grace Elsberry was a student in the college's work-study program and worked part-time as an administrative assistant for the anesthesiology department at the University of Colorado Hospital.

"He's hot. A Brad Cooper look-alike with a dark tan," Grace whispered into the phone.

Megan's breath caught and warm sensations oozed through her bloodstream. She had an idea who her visitor was and braced herself for Grace to confirm her suspicions. "Says his name is Rico Claiborne." Lowering her voice even more, Grace added, "But I prefer calling him Mr. Yummy...if you know what I mean."

Yes, she knew exactly what Grace meant. The

man was so incredibly handsome he should be arrested for being a menace to society. "Please send Mr. Claiborne in."

"Send him in? Are you kidding? I will take the pleasure of *escorting* him into your office, Dr. Westmoreland."

Megan shook her head. She couldn't remember the last time Grace had taken the time to escort anyone into her office. The door opened, and Grace, wearing the biggest of grins, escorted Rico Claiborne in. He moved with a masculine grace that exerted power, strength and confidence, and he looked like a model, even while wearing jeans and a pullover sweater.

Megan moved from behind her desk to properly greet him. Rico was tall, probably a good six-four, with dark brown hair and a gorgeous pair of hazel eyes. They had talked on the phone a number of times, but they had only met once, three months ago, at her cousin Micah's wedding. He had made such an impact on her feminine senses that she'd found it hard to stop thinking about him ever since. Now that he had completed that case he'd been working on, hopefully he was ready to start work on hers.

"Rico, good seeing you again," Megan said, smiling, extending her hand to him. Grace was right, he did look like Brad Cooper, and his interracial features made his skin tone appear as if he'd gotten the perfect tan.

"Good seeing you again as well, Megan," he said, taking her hand in his.

The warm sensation Megan had felt earlier intensified with the touch of his hand on hers, but she fought to ignore it. "So, what brings you to Denver?"

He placed his hands in the pockets of his jeans. "I arrived this morning to appear in court on a case I handled last year, and figured since I was here I'd give you an update. I actually started work on your case a few weeks ago. I don't like just dropping in like this, but I tried calling you when I first got to town and couldn't reach you on your cell phone."

"She was in surgery all morning."

They both turned to note Grace was still in the room. She stood in the doorway smiling, eyeing Rico up and down with a look of pure female appreciation on her face. Megan wouldn't have been surprised if Grace started licking her lips.

"Thanks, and that will be all Grace," Megan said.

Grace actually looked disappointed. "You sure?"

"Yes, I'm positive. I'll call you if I need you," Megan said, forcing back a grin.

"Oh, all right."

It was only when Grace had closed the door behind her that Megan glanced back at Rico to find him staring at her. A shiver of nervousness slithered down her spine. She shouldn't feel uncomfortable around him. But she had discovered upon meeting Rico that she had a strong attraction to him, something she'd never had for a man before. For the past three months, out of sight had meant out of mind where he was concerned—on her good days. But with him standing in the middle of her office she was forced to remember why she'd been so taken with him at her cousin's wedding.

The man was hot.

"Would you like to take a seat? This sounds important," she said, returning to the chair behind her desk, eager to hear what he had to say and just as anxious to downplay the emotional reaction he was causing.

A few years ago, her family had learned that her great-grandfather, Raphel Stern Westmoreland, who they'd assumed was an only child, had actually had a twin brother, Reginald Scott Westmoreland. It all started when an older man living in Atlanta by the name of James Westmoreland—a grandson of Reginald—began genealogy research on his family. His research revealed a connection to the Westmorelands living in Denver—her family. Once that information had been uncovered, her family had begun to wonder what else they didn't know about their ancestor.

They had discovered that Raphel, at twenty-two, had become the black sheep of the family after running off with the preacher's wife, never to be heard from again. He had passed through various states, including Texas, Wyoming, Kansas and Nebraska, before settling down in Colorado. It was found that he had taken up with a number of women along the way. Everyone was curious about what happened to those women, since it appeared he had been married to each one of them at some point. If that was true, there were possibly even more Westmorelands out there that Megan and her family didn't know about.

That was why her oldest cousin, Dillon, had taken it upon himself to investigate her great-grandfather's other wives.

Dillon's investigation had led him to Gamble, Wyoming, where he'd not only met his future wife, but he'd also found out the first two women connected with Raphel hadn't been the man's wives, but were women he had helped out in some way. Since that first investigation, Dillon had married and was the father of one child, with another on the way. With a growing family, he was too busy to chase information about Raphel's third and fourth wives. Megan had decided to resume the search, which was the reason she had hired Rico, who had, of course, come highly recommended by her brothers and cousins.

Megan watched Rico take a seat, thinking the man was way too sexy for words. She was used to being surrounded by good-looking men. Case in point, her five brothers and slew of cousins were all gorgeous. But there was something about Rico that pulled at her in a way she found most troublesome.

"I think it's important, and it's the first break I've had," he responded. "I was finally able to find something on Clarice Riggins."

A glimmer of hope spread through Megan. Clarice was rumored to have been her great-grandfather's third wife. Megan leaned forward in her chair. "How? Where?"

"I was able to trace what I've pieced together to a small town in Texas, on the other side of Austin, called Forbes."

"Forbes, Texas?"

"Yes. I plan to leave Thursday morning. I had thought of leaving later today, after this meeting, but your brothers and cousins talked me out of it. They want me to hang out with them for a couple of days."

Megan wasn't surprised. Although the Westmorelands were mostly divided among four states—Colorado, Georgia, Montana and Texas—the males in the family usually got together often, either to go hunting, check on the various mutual business interests or just for a poker game getaway. Since Rico was the brother-in-law to two of her cousins, he often joined those trips.

"So you haven't been able to find out anything about her?" she asked.

"No, not yet, but I did discover something interesting."

Megan lifted a brow. "What?"

"It's recorded that she gave birth to a child. We can't say whether the baby was male or female, but it was a live birth."

Megan couldn't stop the flow of excitement that seeped into her veins. If Clarice had given birth, that could mean more Westmoreland cousins out there somewhere. Anyone living in Denver knew how important family was to the Westmorelands.

"That could be big. Really major," she said, thinking. "Have you mentioned it to anyone else?"

He shook his head, smiling. "No, you're the one who hired me, so anything I discover I bring to you first."

She nodded. "Don't say anything just yet. I don't want to get anyone's hopes up. You can say you're going to Texas on a lead, but nothing else for now."

Presently, there were fifteen Denver Westmorelands. Twelve males and three females. Megan's parents, as well as her aunt and uncle, had been killed in a plane crash years ago, leaving Dillon and her oldest brother, Ramsey, in charge. It hadn't been easy, but now all of the Westmorelands were self-supporting individuals. All of them had graduated from college except for the two youngest—Bane and Bailey. Bane was in the U.S. Navy, and Bailey, who'd fought the idea of any education past high school, was now in college with less than a year to go to get her degree.

There had never been any doubt in Megan's mind that she would go to college to become an anesthesiologist. She loved her job. She had known this was the career she wanted ever since she'd had her tonsils removed at six and had met the nice man who put her to sleep. He had come by to check on her after the surgery. He'd visited with her, ate ice cream with her and told her all about his job. At the time, she couldn't even pronounce it, but she'd known that was her calling.

Yet everyone needed a break from their job every once in a while, and she was getting burned out. Budget cuts required doing more with less, and she'd known for a while that it was time she went somewhere to chill. Bailey had left that morning for Charlotte to visit their cousin Quade, his wife Cheyenne and their triplets. Megan had been tempted to go with her, since she had a lot of vacation time that she rarely used. She also thought about going to Montana, where other Westmorelands lived. One nice thing about having a large family so spread out was that you always had somewhere to go.

Suddenly, a thought popped into Megan's head, and she glanced over at Rico again to find him staring at her. Their gazes held for a moment longer than necessary before she broke eye contact and looked down at the calendar on her desk while releasing a slow breath. For some reason she had a feeling he was on the verge of finding out something major. She wanted to be there when he did. More than anything she wanted to be present when he found out about Clarice's child. If she was in Denver while he was in Texas, she would go nuts waiting for him to contact her with any information he discovered. Once she'd gotten her thoughts and plans together, she glanced back up at him.

"You're leaving for Texas in two days, right?"

He lifted a brow. "Yes. That's my plan."

Megan leaned back in her chair. "I've just made a decision about something."

"About what?"

Megan smiled. "I've decided to go with you."

RICO FIGURED THERE were a lot of things in life he didn't know. But the one thing he did know was that there was no way Megan Westmoreland was going anywhere with him. Being alone with her in this office was bad enough. The thought of them sitting together on a plane or in a car was too close for comfort. It was arousing him just thinking about it.

He was attracted to her big-time and had been from the moment he'd seen her at Micah's wedding. He had arrived late because of a case he'd been handling and had shown up at the reception just moments before the bride and groom were to leave for their honeymoon. Megan had hired him a month earlier, even though they'd never met in person. Because of that, the first thing Rico did when he arrived at the reception was to ask Zane to point her out.

The moment his and Megan's gazes locked he had felt desire rush through him to a degree that had never happened before. It had shocked the hell out of him. His gaze had moved over her, taking in every single thing he saw, every inch of what he'd liked. And he'd liked it all. Way too much. From the abundance of dark curls on her head to the creamy smoothness of her mahogany skin, from the shapely body in a bridesmaid gown to the pair of silver stilettos on her feet. She had looked totally beautiful.

At the age of thirty-six, he'd figured he was way too old to be *that* attracted to any woman. After all, he'd dated quite a few women in his day. And by just looking at Megan, he could tell she was young, that she hadn't turned thirty yet. But her age hadn't stopped him from staring and staring and staring... until one of her cousins had reclaimed his attention. But still, he had thought about her more than he should have since then.

"Well, with that settled, I'll notify my superiors so

they can find a replacement for me while I'm gone," she said, breaking into his thoughts. "There are only a few surgeries scheduled for tomorrow, and I figure we'll be back in a week or so."

Evidently she thought that since he hadn't said anything, he was okay with the idea of her accompanying him to Texas. Boy, was she wrong. "Sorry, Megan, there's no way I'll let you come with me. I have a rule about working alone."

He could tell by the mutinous expression on her face that he was in for a fight. That didn't bother him. He had two younger sisters to deal with so he knew well how to handle a stubborn female.

"Surely you can break that rule this one time."

He shook his head. "Sorry, I can't."

She crossed her arms over her chest. "Other than the fact that you prefer working alone, give me another reason I can't go with you."

He crossed his arms over his own chest. "I don't need another reason. Like I said, I work alone." He did have a reason, but he wouldn't be sharing it with her. All he had to do was recall what had almost happened the last time he'd worked a case with a woman.

"Why are you being difficult?"

"Why are you?" he countered.

"I'm not," she said, throwing her head back and gritting out her words. "This is my great-grandfather we're talking about."

"I'm fully aware of who he was. You and I talked extensively before I agreed to take on this case, and

I recall telling you that I would get you the information you wanted…doing things my way."

He watched as she began nibbling on her bottom lip. Okay, so now she was remembering. Good. For some reason, he couldn't stop looking into her eyes, meeting her fiery gaze head on, thinking her eyes resembled two beautiful dark orbs.

"As the client, I demand that you take me," she said, sharply interrupting his thoughts.

He narrowed his gaze. "You can demand all you want, but you're not going to Texas with me."

"And why not?"

"I've told you my reasons, now can we move on to something else, please?"

She stood up. "No, we can't move on to something else."

He stood, as well. "Now you're acting like a spoiled child."

Megan's jaw dropped. "A spoiled child? I've never acted like a spoiled child in my entire life. And as for going to Texas, I will be going since there's no reason that I shouldn't."

He didn't say anything for a moment. "Okay, there is another reason I won't take you with me. One that you'd do well to consider," he said in a calm, barely controlled tone. She had pushed him, and he didn't like being pushed.

"Fine, let's hear it," she snapped furiously.

He placed his hands in the pockets of his jeans, stood with his legs braced apart and leveled his gaze on her when he spoke in a deep, husky voice. "I want you, Megan. Bad. And if you go anywhere with me, I'm going to have you."

He then turned and walked out of her office.

Shocked, Megan dropped back down in her chair. "Gracious!"

THREE SURGERIES LATER, back in her office, Megan paced the floor. Although Rico's parting statement had taken her by surprise, she was still furious. Typical man. Why did they think everything began and ended in the bedroom? So, he was attracted to her. Big deal. Little did he know, but she was attracted to him as well, and she had no qualms about going to Texas with him. For crying out loud, hadn't he ever heard of self-control?

She was sister to Zane and Derringer and cousin to Riley and Canyon—three were womanizers to the core. And before marrying Lucia, Derringer had all but worn his penis on his sleeve and Zane, Lord help him, wore his anywhere there was a free spot on his body. She couldn't count the number of times she'd unexpectedly shown up at Zane's place at the wrong time or how many pairs of panties she'd discovered left behind at Riley's. And wasn't it just yesterday she'd seen a woman leave Canyon's place before dawn?

Besides that, Rico Claiborne honestly thought all he had to do was decide he wanted her and he would have her? Wouldn't she have some kind of say-so in the matter? Evidently he didn't think so, which meant he really didn't know whom he was dealing with. The doctors at the hospital, who thought she was cold and incapable of being seduced, called her "Iceberg Megan."

So, okay, Rico had thawed her out a little when she'd seen him at the wedding three months ago. And she would admit he'd made her heart flutter upon seeing him today. But he was definitely under a false assumption if he thought all he had to do was snap his fingers, strut that sexy walk and she would automatically fall into any bed with him.

She scowled. The more she thought about it, the madder she got. He should know from all the conversations they'd shared over the phone that this investigation was important to her. Family was everything to her, and if there were other Westmorelands out there, she wanted to know about them. She wanted to be in the thick of things when he uncovered the truth as to where those Westmorelands were and how quickly they could be reached.

Megan moved to the window and looked out. September clouds were settling in, and the forecasters had predicted the first snowfall of the year by the end of the week. But that was fine since she had no intention of being here in Denver when the snow started. Ignoring what Rico had said about her not going to Texas with him, she had cleared her calendar for not only the rest of the week, but also for the next month. She had the vacation time, and if she didn't use it by the end of the year she would end up losing it anyway.

First, she would go to Texas. And then, before re-

turning to work, she would take off for Australia and
spend time with her sister Gemma and her family.
Megan enjoyed international travel and recalled the
first time she'd left the country to visit her cousin
Delaney in the Middle East. That had been quite an
enjoyable experience.

But remembering the trip to visit her cousin
couldn't keep her thoughts from shifting back to
Rico, and she felt an unwelcoming jolt of desire as
she recalled him standing in her office, right in this
very spot, and saying what he'd said, without as
much as blinking an eye.

If he, for one minute, thought he had the ability to
tell her what to do, he had another thought coming.
If he was *that* attracted to her then he needed to put
a cap on it. They were adults and would act accord-
ingly. The mere thought that once alone they would
tear each other's clothes off in some sort of heated
lust was total rubbish. Although she was attracted to
him, she knew how to handle herself. It *was* going
to be hard to keep her hands to herself.

But no matter what, she would.

"You sure I'm not putting you out, Riley? I can certainly get a room at the hotel in town."

"I won't hear of it," Riley Westmoreland said,
smiling. "Hell, you're practically family."

Rico threw his luggage on the bed, thinking he
certainly hadn't felt like family earlier when he'd
been alone with Megan. He still couldn't get over
her wanting to go to Texas with him. Surely she had

felt the sexual tension that seemed to surround them whenever they were within a few feet of each other.

"So how are things going with that investigation you're doing for Megan?" Riley asked, breaking into Rico's thoughts.

"Fine. In fact, I'm on my way to Texas to poke around a new lead."

Riley's brow lifted. "Really? Does Megan know yet?"

"Yes. I met with her at the hospital earlier today."

Riley chuckled. "I bet she was happy about that. We're all interested in uncovering the truth about Poppa Raphel, but I honestly think Megan is obsessed with it and has been ever since Dillon and Pam shared those journals with her. Now that Dillon has made Megan the keeper of the journals she is determined to uncover everything. She's convinced we have more relatives out there somewhere."

Rico had read those journals and had found them quite interesting. The journals, written by Raphel himself, had documented his early life after splitting from his family.

"And it's dinner tonight over at the big house. Pam called earlier to make sure I brought you. I hope you're up for it. You know how testy pregnant women can get at times."

Rico chuckled. Yes, he knew. In fact, he had noted the number of pregnant women in the Westmoreland family. Enough to look like there was some sort of epidemic. In addition to Pam, Derringer's wife, Lucia, was expecting and so was Micah's wife, Kalina. There were a number of Atlanta Westmorelands expecting babies, as well.

Case in point, his own sisters. Jessica was pregnant again, and Savannah had given birth to her second child earlier that year. They were both happily married, and he was happy for them. Even his mother had decided to make another go of marriage, which had surprised him after what she'd gone through with his father. But he liked Brad Richman, and Rico knew Brad truly loved his mother.

"Well, I'll let you unpack. We'll leave for Dillon's place in about an hour. I hope you're hungry because there will be plenty of food. The women are cooking, and we just show up hungry and ready to eat," Riley said, laughing.

A half hour later Rico had unpacked all the items he needed. Everything else would remain in his luggage since he would be leaving for Texas the day after tomorrow. Sighing, he rubbed a hand down his face, noting his stubble-roughened jaw. Before he went out anywhere, he definitely needed to shave. And yes, he was hungry since he hadn't eaten since that morning, but dinner at Dillon's meant most of the Denver Westmorelands who were in town would be there. That included Megan. Damn. He wasn't all that sure he was ready to see her again. He was known as a cool and in-control kind of guy. But those elements of his personality took a flying leap around Megan Westmoreland.

Why did he like the way she said his name? To pronounce it was simple enough, but there was something about the way she said it, in a sultry tone that soothed and aroused.

Getting aroused was the last thing he needed to think about. It had been way too long since he'd had bedroom time with a woman. So he was in far worse shape than he'd realized. Seeing Megan today hadn't helped matters. The woman was way too beautiful for her own good.

Grabbing his shaving bag off the bed, Rico went into the guest bath that was conveniently connected to his room. Moments later, after lathering his face with shaving cream, he stared into the mirror as he slowly swiped a razor across his face. The familiar actions allowed his mind to wander, right back to Megan.

The first thing he'd noticed when he'd walked into her office was that she'd cut her hair. She still had a lot of curls, but instead of flowing to her shoulders, her hair crowned her face like a cap. He liked the style on her. It gave her a sexier look…not that she needed it.

He could just imagine being wheeled into surgery only to discover she would be the doctor to administer the drug to knock you out. Counting backward while lying flat on your back and staring up into her face would guarantee plenty of hot dreams during whatever surgery you were having.

He jolted when he nicked himself. Damn. He needed to concentrate on shaving and rid his mind of Megan. At least he didn't have to worry about that foolishness of hers, about wanting to go with him to Texas. He felt certain, with the way her eyes had nearly popped out of the sockets and her jaw had dropped after what he'd said, that she had changed her mind.

He hadn't wanted to be so blatantly honest with her, but it couldn't be helped. Like he told her, he preferred working alone. The last time he had taken a woman with him on a case had almost cost him his life. He remembered it like it was yesterday. An FBI sting operation and his female partner had ended up being more hindrance than help. The woman blatantly refused to follow orders.

Granted, there was no real danger involved with Megan's case per se. In fact, the only danger he could think of was keeping his hands to himself where Megan was concerned. That was a risk he couldn't afford. And he had felt the need to be blunt and spell it out to her. Now that he had, he was convinced they had an understanding.

He would go to Texas, delve into whatever he could discover about Clarice Riggins and bring his report back to her. Megan was paying him a pretty hefty fee for his services, and he intended to deliver. But he would have to admit that her great-grandfather had covered his tracks well, which made Rico wonder what all the old man had gotten into during his younger days. It didn't matter, because Rico intended to uncover it all. And like he'd told Megan, Clarice Riggins had given birth, but there was nothing to indicate that she and Raphel had married. It had been a stroke of luck that he'd found anything at all on Clarice, since there had been various spellings of the woman's name.

He was walking out of the bathroom when his cell phone rang, and he pulled it off the clip. He checked and saw it was a New York number. He had several associates there and couldn't help wondering which one was calling.

"This is Rico."

There was a slight pause and then… "Hello, son. This is your father."

Rico flinched, drew in a sharp breath and fought for control of his anger, which had come quick…as soon as he'd recognized the voice. "You must have the wrong number because I don't have a father."

Without giving the man a chance to say anything else, he clicked off the phone. As far as he was concerned, Jeff Claiborne could go to hell. Why on earth would the man be calling Rico after all this time? What had it been? Eighteen years? Rico had been happy with his father being out of sight and out of mind.

To be quite honest, he wished he could wash the man's memory away completely. He could never forget the lives that man had damaged by his selfishness. No, Jeff Claiborne had no reason to call him. No reason at all.

CHAPTER TWO

MEGAN TRIED TO downplay her nervousness as she continued to cut up the bell pepper and celery for the potato salad. According to Pam, Rico had been invited to dinner and would probably arrive any minute.

"Has Rico found anything out yet?"

Megan glanced over at her cousin-in-law. She liked Pam and thought she was perfect for Dillon. The two women were alone for now. Chloe and Bella had gone to check on the babies, and Lucia, who was in the dining room, was putting icing on the cake.

"Yes, there's a lead in Texas he'll follow up on when he leaves here," Megan said. She didn't want to mention anything about Clarice. The last thing she wanted to do was get anyone's hopes up.

"How exciting," Pam said as she fried the chicken, turning pieces over in the huge skillet every so often. "I'm sure you're happy about that."

Megan would be a lot happier if Rico would let her go to Texas with him, but, in a way, she had solved that problem and couldn't wait to see the expression on his face when he found out how. Chances were, he thought he'd had the last word.

She sighed, knowing if she lived to be a hundred years old she wouldn't be able to figure out men. Whenever they wanted a woman they assumed a woman would just naturally want them in return. How crazy was that bit of logic?

There was so much Megan didn't know when it came to men, although she had lived most of her life surrounded by them. Oh, she knew some things, but this man-woman stuff—when it came to wants and desires—just went over her head. Until she'd met Rico, there hadn't been a man who'd made her give him a second look. Of course, Idris Elba didn't count.

She lifted her gaze from the vegetables to look over at Pam. Megan knew Pam and Dillon had a pretty good marriage, a real close one. Pam, Chloe, Lucia and Bella were the older sisters she'd never had, and, at the moment, she needed some advice.

"Pam?"

"Hmm?"

"How would you react if a man told you he wanted you?"

Pam glanced her way and smiled. "It depends on who the man is. Had your brother told me that, I would have kicked my fiancé to the curb a lot sooner. The first thing I thought when I saw Dillon was that he was hot."

That was the same thing Megan had thought when she'd seen Rico. "So you would not have gotten upset had he said he wanted you?"

"Again, it depends on who the man is. If it's a man I had the hots for, then no, I wouldn't have gotten upset. Why would I have? That would mean we were of the same accord and could move on to the next phase."

Megan raised a brow. "The next phase?"

"Yes, the I-want-to-get-to-know-you-better phase." Pam looked over at her. "So tell me. Was this a hypothetical question or is there a man out there who told you he wants you?"

Megan nervously nibbled on her bottom lip. She must have taken too long to answer because Pam grinned and said, "I guess I got my answer."

Pam took the last of the chicken out of the skillet, turned off the stove and joined Megan at the table. "Like I said, Megan, the question you should ask yourself is…if he's someone you want, too. Forget about what he wants for the moment. The question is what do *you* want?"

Megan sighed. Rico was definitely a looker, a man any woman would want. But what did she really know about him, other than that he was Jessica and Savannah's older brother, and they thought the world of him?

"He doesn't want to mix business with pleasure, not that I would have, mind you. Besides, I never told him that I wanted him."

"Most women don't tell a man. What they do is send out vibes. Men can pick up on vibes real quick, and depending on what those vibes are, a man might take them as a signal."

Megan looked perplexed. "I don't think I sent out anything."

Pam laughed. "I hate to say this, but Jillian can probably size a man up better than you can. Your brothers and cousins sheltered you too much from the harsh realities of life." Jillian was Pam's sister, who was a sophomore in college.

Megan shook her head. "It's not that they sheltered me, I just never met anyone I was interested in."

"Until now?"

Megan lifted her chin. "I'm really not interested in him, but I want us to work closer together, and he doesn't…because he wants me."

"Well, I'm sure there will be times at the hospital when the two of you will have no choice but to work together."

Pam thought the person they were discussing was another doctor. Megan wondered what Pam's reaction would be if she found out the person they were talking about was one of her dinner guests.

Megan heard loud male voices and recognized all of them. One stood out, the sound a deep, husky timbre she'd come to know.

Rico had arrived.

RICO PAUSED IN his conversation with Dillon and Ramsey when Megan walked into the room to place a huge bowl on the dining room table. She called out to him. "Hello, Rico."

"Megan."

If his gaze was full of male appreciation, it couldn't be helped. She had changed out of the scrubs he'd seen her in earlier and into a cute V-neck blue pullover sweater and a pair of hip-hugging jeans. She looked both comfortable and beautiful. She had spoken, which was a good indication that he hadn't offended her by what he'd told her. He was a firm believer that the truth never hurt, but he'd known more than one occasion when it had pissed people off.

"So, you're on your way to Texas, I hear." Dillon Westmoreland's question penetrated Rico's thoughts.

He looked at Dillon and saw the man's questioning gaze and knew he'd been caught ogling Megan. Rico's throat suddenly felt dry, and he took a sip of his wine before answering. "Yes. I might have a new lead. Don't want to say what it is just yet, until I'm certain it is one."

Dillon nodded. "I understand, trust me. When I took that time off to track down information on Raphel, it was like putting together pieces of a very complicated puzzle. But that woman," he said, inclining his head toward Pam when she entered the room, "made it all worthwhile."

Rico glanced over to where Pam was talking to Megan. He could see how Pam could have made Dillon feel that way. She was a beautiful woman. Rico had heard the story from his sisters, about how Dillon had met Pam while in Wyoming searching for leads on his great-grandfather's history. Pam had been engaged to marry a man who Dillon had exposed as nothing more than a lying, manipulating, arrogant SOB.

Rico couldn't help keeping his eye on Megan as her brother Ramsey and her cousins Dillon and Riley carried on conversations around him. Thoughts of her had haunted him ever since they'd met back in June. Even now, he lay awake with thoughts of her on his mind. How could one woman make such an impression on him, he would never know. But like he told her, he wanted her, so it was best that they keep their distance, considering his relationship with the Westmoreland family.

"So when are you leaving, Rico?"

He turned to meet Ramsey Westmoreland's inquisitive gaze. The man was sharp and, like Dillon, had probably caught Rico eyeing Megan. The hand holding Rico's wineglass tensed. He liked all the Westmorelands and appreciated how the guys included him in a number of their all-male get-togethers. The last thing he wanted was to lose their friendship because he couldn't keep his eyes off their sister and cousin.

"I'm leaving on Thursday. Why do you ask?"

Ramsey shrugged. "Just curious."

Rico couldn't shake the feeling that the man was more than just curious. He frowned and stared down at his drink. It was either that or risk the wrath of one of the Westmorelands if he continued to stare at Megan, who was busy setting the table.

Dillon spoke up and intruded into Rico's thoughts when he said, "Pam just gave me the nod that dinner is ready."

Everyone moved in the direction of the dining room. Rico turned to follow the others, but Ramsey touched his arm. "Wait for a minute."

Rico nodded. He wondered why Ramsey had detained him. Had Megan gone running to her brother and reported what Rico had said to her earlier? Or was Ramsey about to call him out on the carpet for the interest in Megan that he couldn't hide? In either of those scenarios, how could he explain his intense desire for Megan when he didn't understand it himself? He'd wanted women before, but never with this intensity.

When the two of them were left alone, Ramsey turned to him and Rico braced himself for whatever the man had to say. Rico was older brother to two sisters of his own so he knew how protective brothers could be. He hadn't liked either Chase or Durango in the beginning only because he'd known something was going on between them and his sisters.

Ramsey was silent for a moment, doing nothing more than slowly sipping his wine, so Rico decided to speak up. "Was there something you wanted to discuss with me, Ramsey?" There were a couple of years' difference in their ages, but at the moment Rico felt like it was a hell of a lot more than that.

"Yes," Ramsey replied. "It's about Megan."

Rico met Ramsey's gaze. "What about her?"

"Just a warning."

Rico tensed. "I think I know what you're going to say."

Ramsey shook his head, chuckling. "No. I don't think that you do."

Rico was confused at Ramsey's amusement. Hell,

maybe he didn't know after all. "Then how about telling me. What's the warning regarding Megan?"

Ramsey took another sip of his drink and said, "She's strong-willed. She has self-control of steel and when she sets her mind to do something, she does it, often without thinking it through. And…if you tell her no, you might as well have said yes."

Rico was silent for a moment and then asked, "Is there a reason you're telling me this?"

Ramsey's mouth curved into a smile. "Yes, and you'll find out that reason soon enough. Now come on, they won't start dinner without us."

MEGAN TRIED DROWNING out all the conversation going on around her. As usual, whenever the Westmorelands got together, they had a lot to talk about.

She was grateful Pam hadn't figured out the identity of the man they'd been discussing and seated them beside each other. Instead, Rico was sitting at the other end of the table, across from Ramsey and next to Riley. If she had to look at him, it would be quite obvious she was doing so.

Riley said something and everyone chuckled. That gave her an excuse to look down the table. Rico was leaning back against the chair and holding a half-filled glass of wine in his hand, smiling at whatever the joke was about. Why did he have to look so darn irresistible when he smiled?

He must have felt her staring because he shifted his gaze to meet hers. For a moment she forgot to breathe. The intensity of his penetrating stare almost made her lips tremble. Something gripped her stomach in a tight squeeze and sent stirrings all through her nerve endings.

At that moment, one thought resonated through her mind. The same one Pam had reiterated earlier. *It doesn't matter if he wants you. The main question is whether or not you want him.*

Megan immediately broke eye contact and breathed in slowly, taking a sip of her wine. She fought to get her mind back on track and regain the senses she'd almost lost just now. She could control this. She had to. Desire and lust were things she didn't have time for. The only reason she wanted to go to Texas with Rico was to be there when he discovered the truth about Raphel.

Thinking it was time to make her announcement, she picked up her spoon and tapped it lightly against her glass, but loud enough to get everyone's attention. When all eyes swung her way she smiled and said, "I have an announcement to make. Most of you know I rarely take vacation time, but today I asked for an entire month off, starting tomorrow."

Surprised gazes stared back at her…except one. She saw a look of suspicion in Rico's eyes and noted the way his jaw tightened.

"What's wrong? You're missing Bailey already and plan to follow her to North Carolina?" her cousin Stern asked, grinning.

Megan returned his grin and shook her head. "Although I miss Bailey, I'm not going to North Carolina."

"Let me guess. You're either going to visit Gemma in Australia or Delaney in Tehran," Chloe said, smiling.

Again Megan shook her head. "Those are on my to-do list for later, but not now," she said.

When others joined in, trying to guess where she was headed, she held up her hand. "Please, it's not that big of a deal."

"It's a big deal if you're taking time off. You like working."

"I don't like working, but I like the job I do. There is a difference. And to appease everyone's curiosity, I talked to Clint and Alyssa today, and I'm visiting them in Texas for a while."

"Texas?"

She glanced down the table at Riley, which allowed her to look at Rico again, as well. He was staring at her, and it didn't take a rocket scientist to see he wasn't pleased with her announcement. Too bad, too glad. She couldn't force him to take her to Texas, but she could certainly go there on her own. "Yes, Riley, I'm going to Texas."

"When are you leaving?" her brother Zane asked. "I need to, ah, get that box from you before you leave."

She nodded, seeing the tense expression in Zane's features. She wondered about the reason for it. She was very much aware that he had a lock box in her hall closet. Although she'd been tempted, she'd never satisfied her curiosity by toying with the lock and looking inside. "That will be fine, Zane. I'm not leaving until Friday."

She took another quick glance at Rico before resuming dinner. He hadn't said anything, and it was just as well. There really wasn't anything he could say. Although they would end up in the same state and within mere miles from each other, they would not be together.

Since he didn't want her to accompany him, she would do a little investigating on her own.

CHAPTER THREE

THE NEXT MORNING Rico was still furious.

Now he knew what Ramsey's warning had been about. The little minx was going to Texas, pretty damn close to where he would be. He would have confronted her last night, but he'd been too upset to do so. Now here he was—at breakfast time—and instead of joining Zane, Riley, Canyon and Stern at one of the local cafés that boasted hotcakes to die for, he was parked outside Megan's home so he could try and talk some sense into her.

Did she not know what red-hot desire was about? Did she not understand how it was when a man really wanted a woman to the point where self-control took a backseat to longing and urges? Did she not comprehend there was temptation even when she tried acting cool and indifferent?

Just being around her last night had been hard enough, and now she was placing herself in a position where they would be around each other in Texas without any family members as buffers. Oh, he knew the story she was telling her family, that she would be visiting Clint in Austin. Chances were, she would—for a minute. He was friends with Clint and

Alyssa and had planned to visit them as well, during
the same time she planned to be there. Since Forbes
wasn't that far from Austin, Clint had offered Rico
the use of one of their cabins on the Golden Glade
Ranch as his headquarters, if needed.

But now Megan had interfered with his plans.
She couldn't convince Rico that she didn't have ulterior motives and that she didn't intend to show up
in Forbes. She intended to do some snooping, with or
without him. So what the hell was she paying him for
if she was going to do things her way? He got out of
the car and glanced around, seeing her SUV parked
at the side of her house. She had a real nice spread,
and she'd kept most of it in its natural state. In the
background, you could see rolling hills and meadows, mountains and the Whisper Creek Canyon. It
was a beautiful view. And there was a lake named
after her grandmother Gemma. Gemma Lake was
huge and, according to Riley, the fish were biting all
the time. If Megan hadn't been throwing him for a
loop, Rico would have loved to find a fishing pole
while he was here to see if the man's claim was true.

Megan's home was smaller than those owned by
her brothers and male cousins. Their homes were two
or three stories, but hers was a single story, modest
in size, but eye-catching just the same. It reminded
him of a vacation cabin with its cedar frame, wraparound porch and oversize windows. It had been built
in the perfect location to take advantage of both lake
and canyon.

He'd heard the story of how the main house and

the three hundred acres on which it sat had been willed to Dillon, since he was the oldest cousin. The remaining Denver Westmorelands got a hundred acres each once they reached their twenty-fifth birthdays. They had come up with pet names for their particular spreads. There was Ramsey's Web, Derringer's Dungeon, Zane's Hideout and Gemma's Gem. Now, he was here at Megan's Meadows.

According to Riley, Megan's property was prime land, perfect for grazing. She had agreed to let a portion of her land be used by Ramsey for the raising of his sheep, and the other by Zane and Derringer for their horse training business.

If Riley suspected anything because of all the questions Rico had asked last night about Megan, he didn't let on. And it could have been that the man was too preoccupied to notice, since Riley had his little black book in front of him, checking off the numbers of women he intended to call.

It was early, and Rico wondered if Megan was up yet. He would find out soon enough. Regardless, he intended to have his say. She could pretend she hadn't recognized the strong attraction between them, that sexual chemistry that kept him awake at night, but he wasn't buying it. However, just in case she didn't have a clue, he intended to tell her. Again. There was no need for her to go to Texas, and to pretend she was going just to visit relatives was a crock.

The weather was cold. Tightening his leather jacket around him, he moved quickly, walking up onto the porch. Knocking on the door loudly, he waited a minute and then knocked again. When there was no answer, he was about to turn around, thinking that perhaps she'd gone up to the main house for breakfast, when suddenly the door was snatched open. His jaw almost dropped. The only thing he could say when he saw her, standing there wearing the cutest baby-doll gown, was *wow*.

MEGAN STARED AT Rico, surprised to see him. "What are you doing here?"

He leaned in the doorway. "I came to talk to you. And what are you doing coming to the door without first asking who it is?"

She rolled her eyes. "I thought you were one of my brothers. Usually they are the only ones who drop by without notice."

"Is that why you came to the door dressed like that?"

"Yes, what do you want to talk to me about? You're letting cold air in."

"Your trip to Texas."

Megan stared at him, her lips tight. "Fine," she said, taking a step back. "Come in and excuse me while I grab my robe."

He watched her walk away, thinking the woman looked pretty damn good in a nightgown. Her shapely backside filled it out quite nicely and showed what a gorgeous pair of legs she had.

Thinking that the last thing he needed to be thinking about was her legs, he removed his jacket and placed it on the coatrack by the door before moving into the living room. He glanced around. Her house was nice and cozy. Rustic. Quaint. The interior walls, as well as the ceiling and floors, were cedar like the outside. The furniture was nice, appropriate for the setting and comfortable-looking. From where he stood, he could see an eat-in kitchen surrounded by floor-to-ceiling windows where you could dine and enjoy a view of the mountains and lake. He could even see the pier at her brother Micah's place that led to the lake and where the sailboat docked.

"Before we start talking about anything, I need my coffee."

Rico turned when she came back into the room, moving past him and heading toward the kitchen. He nodded, understanding. For him, it was basically the same, which was why he had drunk two cups already. "Fine. Take your time," he said. "I'm not going anywhere because I know what you're doing."

She didn't respond until she had the coffeemaker going. Then she turned and leaned back against a counter to ask, "And just what am I doing?"

"You're going to Texas for a reason."

"Yes, and I explained why. I need a break from work."

"Why Texas?"

She lifted her chin. "Why not Texas? It's a great state, and I haven't been there in a while. I missed that ball Clint, Cole and Casey do every year for their uncle. It will be good to see them, especially since Alyssa is expecting again."

"But that's not why you're going to Texas and you

know it, Megan. Can you look me in the eyes and say you don't plan to set one foot in Forbes?"

She tilted her head to look at him. "No. I can't say that because I do."

"Why?"

Megan wondered how she could get him to understand. "Why not? These are my relatives."

"You are paying me to handle this investigation," he countered.

She tried not to notice how he filled the entrance to her kitchen. It suddenly looked small, as if there was barely any space. "Yes, and I asked to go to Forbes with you. It's important for me to be there when you find out if I have more relatives, but you have this stupid rule about working alone."

"Dammit, Megan, when you hired me you never told me you would get involved."

She crossed her arms over her chest. "I hadn't planned on getting involved. However, knowing I might have more kin out there changes everything. Why can't you understand that?"

Rico ran a frustrated hand down his face. In a way, he did. He would never forget that summer day when his mother had brought a fifteen-year-old girl into their home and introduced her as Jessica—their sister. Savannah had been sixteen, and he had been nineteen, a sophomore in college. It hadn't mattered to him that he hadn't known about Jessica before that time. Just the announcement that he had another sister had kicked his brotherly instincts into gear.

"I do understand, Megan," he said in a calm

voice. "But still, there are things that I need to handle. Things I need to check out before anyone else can become involved."

She lifted a brow. "Things like what?"

Rico drew in a deep breath. Maybe he should have leveled with her yesterday, but there were things that had come up in his report on Raphel that he needed to confirm were fact or fiction. So far, everything negative about Raphel had turned out not to be true in Dillon's investigation. Rico wanted his final report to be as factual as possible, and he needed to do more research of the town's records.

She poured a cup of coffee for herself and one for him, as well. "What's wrong, Rico? Is there something you're not telling me?"

He saw the worry in her eyes as he accepted his coffee. "Look, this is my investigation. I told you that I was able to track down information on Clarice and the fact that she might have given birth to a child. That's all I know for now, Megan. Anything else is hearsay."

"Hearsay like what?"

"I'd rather not say."

After taking a sip of coffee, she said, "You're being evasive."

He narrowed his gaze. "I'm being thorough. If you want to go to Texas to visit Clint and Alyssa, then fine. But what I *don't* need is you turning up where you don't need to be."

"Where I don't need to be?" she growled.

"Yes. I have a job to do, and I won't be able to do it with you close by. I won't be able to concentrate."

"Men!" Megan said, stiffening her spine. "Do you all think it's all about you? I have brothers and male cousins, plenty of them. I know how you operate. You want one woman one day and another woman the next. Get over it already. Please."

Rico just stared at her. "And you think it's that simple?"

"*Yesss*. I'm Zane and Derringer's sister, Riley, Canyon and Stern's cousin. I see them. I watch them. I know their M.O. Derringer has been taken out of the mix by marrying Lucia, thank goodness. But the rest of them, and now the twins…oh, my God…are following in their footsteps.

"You see. You want. You do. But not me. *You*, Rico Claiborne, assume just because you want me that you're going to get me. What was your warning? If we go somewhere together alone, that you're going to *have* me. Who are you supposed to be? Don't I have a say-so in this matter? What if I told you that I *don't* want you?"

Rico just stared at her. "Then I would say you're lying to yourself. You want me. You might not realize it, but you want me. I see it every time you look at me. Damn, Megan, admit there's a strong attraction between us."

She rolled her eyes. "Okay, I find you attractive. But I find a lot of men attractive. No big deal."

"And are you sending out the same vibes to them

that you're sending to me?" he asked in a deep, husky voice.

Megan recalled that Pam had said something about vibes. Was she sending them out to him without realizing she was doing so? No, she couldn't be. Because right now she wasn't feeling desire for him, she was feeling anger at him for standing there and making such an outlandish claim.

But still, she would have to admit that her heart was pounding furiously in her chest, and parts of her were quivering inside. So, could he be right about those vibes? Naw, she refused to believe it. Like she'd told him, she'd seen men in operation. Zane probably had a long list of women he wanted who he imagined were sending out vibes.

From the first, Rico had come across as a man who knew how to control any given situation, which was why she figured he was the perfect person for the job she'd hired him to do. So what was his problem now? If he did want her, then surely the man could control his urges.

"Look, I assure you, I can handle myself, and I can handle you, Rico," she said. "All of my senses are intact, and you can be certain lust won't make me lose control. And nothing you or any man can say or do will place me in a position where I will lose my self-control." The men who thought so didn't call her "Iceberg Megan" for nothing.

"You don't think so?" Rico challenged her. "You aren't made of stone. You have feelings. I can tell that you're a very passionate woman, so consider your words carefully."

She chuckled as if what he'd said was a joke. "Passionate? Me?"

"Yes, you. When I first looked at you at the wedding reception and our gazes connected, the air between us was bristling with so much sexual energy I'm sure others felt it," he said silkily. "Are you going to stand there and claim you didn't feel it?"

Megan gazed down into her coffee and erased her smile. Oh, she remembered that day. Yes, she'd felt it. It had been like a surge of sexual, electrical currents that had consumed the space between them. It had happened again, too, every time she saw him looking at her. Until now, she'd assumed she had imagined it, but his words confirmed he had felt the connection, as well.

After that night at the wedding, she'd gone to bed thinking about him and had thought of him several nights after that. What she'd felt had bothered her, and she had talked to Gemma about it. Some of the things her married sister had shared with her she hadn't wanted to hear, mainly because Megan was a firm believer in self-control. Everybody had it, and everybody could manage it. Regardless of how attracted she was to Rico, she had self-control down pat. Hers was unshakable.

She'd had to learn self-control from the day she was told she would never see her parents again. She would never forget how Dillon and Ramsey had sat her down at the age of twelve and told her that not only her parents, but also her aunt and uncle, whom she'd adored, had been killed in a plane crash.

Dillon and Ramsey had assured her that they would keep the family together and take care of everyone, although the youngest—Bane and Bailey—were both under nine at the time. On that day, Ramsey had asked her to stay strong and in control. As the oldest girl in the Denver Westmoreland family, they had depended on her to help Gemma and Bailey through their grief. That didn't mean she'd needed to put her own grief aside, but it had meant that in spite of her grief, she'd had to be strong for the others. And she had. When the younger ones would come to her crying, she was the one who would comfort them, regardless of the circumstances or her emotions.

The ability to become emotionally detached, to stay in control, was how she'd known being an anesthesiologist was her calling. She went into surgery knowing some patients wouldn't make it through. Although she assured the patient of her skill in putting them to sleep, she never promised they would pull through. That decision was out of her hands. Some of the surgeons had lost patients and, in a way, she felt she'd lost them, as well. But no matter what, she remained in control.

Drawing in a deep breath, she eyed Rico. "You might have a problem with control, but I don't. I admit I find you desirable, but I can regulate my emotions. I can turn them on and off when I need to, Rico. Don't worry that I'll lose control one day and jump your bones, because it won't happen. There's not that much desire in the world."

Rico shook his head. "You honestly believe that, don't you?"

She placed her coffee cup on the counter. "Honestly believe what?"

"That you can control a desire as intense as ours."

"Yes, why wouldn't I?"

"I agree that certain desires can be controlled, Megan. But I'm trying to tell you, what you refuse to acknowledge or accept—desire as intense as ours can't always be controlled. What we have isn't normal."

She bunched her forehead. "Not normal? That's preposterous."

Rico knew then that she really didn't have a clue. This was no act. He could stand here until he was blue in the face and she still wouldn't understand. "What I'm trying to say, Megan," he said slowly, trying not to let frustration get the best of him, "is that I feel a degree of desire for you that I've never felt for any woman before."

She crossed her arms over her chest and glared at him. "Should I get excited or feel flattered about it?"

He gritted his teeth. "Look, Megan…"

"No, *you* look, Rico," she said, crossing the room to stand in front of him. "I don't know what to tell you. Honestly, I don't. I admitted that I'm attracted to you, as well. Okay, I'll admit it again. But on that same note, I'm also telling you I won't lose control over it. For crying out loud, there're more important things in life than sexual attraction, desire and passion. It's not about all of that."

"Isn't it?" He paused a moment, trying to keep his vexation in check. And it wasn't helping matters that she was there, standing right in front of him, with a stubborn expression on her face and looking as beautiful as any woman could. And he picked up her scent, which made him fight to keep a grip on his lust. The woman was driving him mad in so many ways.

"Let me ask you something, Megan," he said in a voice he was fighting to keep calm. "When was the last time you were with a man you desired?"

Rico's question surprised Megan, and she didn't say anything. Hell, she'd never been with a man she truly desired because she'd never been with a man period. She had dated guys in high school, college, and even doctors at the hospital. Unfortunately, they'd all had one thing in common. They had reminded her too much of her player-card-toting brothers and cousins, even hitting on her using some of the same lines she'd heard her family use. And a few bold ones had even had the nerve to issue ultimatums. She had retaliated by dropping those men like hot potatoes, just to show she really didn't give a royal damn. They said she was cold and couldn't be thawed and that's when they'd started calling her Iceberg Megan. Didn't bother her any because none of those men had gotten beyond the first boring kiss. She was who she was and no man—coming or going—would change it.

"I'm waiting on an answer," Rico said, interrupting her thoughts.

She gazed up at him and frowned. "Wait on. I don't intend to give you an answer because it's none of your business."

He nodded. "All right. You claim you can control the passion between us, right?"

"Yes."

"Then I want to see how you control this."

The next thing Megan knew, Rico had reached out, pulled her into his embrace and swooped his mouth down onto hers.

DESIRE THAT HAD been lingering on the edges was now producing talons that were digging deep into Megan's skin and sending heated lust all through her veins—and making her act totally out of control. He parted her lips with his tongue and instead of immediately going after her tongue, he rolled the tip around, as if on a tasting expedition. Then he gradually tasted more of it until he had captured it all. And when she became greedy, he pulled back and gave her just the tip again. Then they played the tongue game over and over again.

She felt something stir within her that had never stirred before while kissing a man. But then no man had ever kissed her like this. Or played mouth games with her this way.

He was electrifying her cells, muddling her brain as even more desire skittered up her spine. She tried steadying her emotions, regaining control when she felt heat flooding between her thighs, but she couldn't help but release a staggering moan.

Instead of unlocking their mouths, he intensified the kiss, as his tongue, holding hers in a dominant grip, began exploring every part of her mouth with strokes so sensual her stomach began doing somersaults. She felt her senses tossed in a number of wild spins, and surprised herself when she wrapped her arms around his neck and began running her fingers through the softness of his hair, absently curling a strand around her finger.

She could taste the hunger in his kiss, the passion and the desire. Her emotions were smoldering, and blocking every single thought from her already chaotic mind. The man was lapping up her mouth, and each stroke was getting hotter and hotter, filling her with emotions she had pushed aside for years. Was he ever going to let go of her mouth? Apparently no time soon.

This kiss was making her want to do things she'd never done before. Touch a man, run her hands all over him, check out that huge erection pressing against her belly.

She felt his hands rest on her backside, urging her closer to his front. And she shifted her hips to accommodate what he wanted. She felt the nipples of her breasts harden and knew her robe was no barrier against the heat coming from his body.

No telling how long they would have stood in the middle of her kitchen engaged in one hell of a feverish kiss if his cell phone hadn't gone off. They broke apart, and she drew in a much needed breath and watched him get his phone out of the back pocket of his jeans.

She took note of the angry look on his face while he talked and heard him say to the caller, "I don't want you calling me." He then clicked off the line without giving the person a chance to respond.

She tensed at the thought that the person he'd just given the brush-off was a woman. Megan lifted her chin. "Maybe you should have taken that call."

He glanced over at her while stuffing his phone back into the pocket of his jeans. She watched as his hazel eyes became a frosty green. "I will never take *that* call."

She released a slow, steady breath, feeling his anger as if it were a personal thing. She was glad it wasn't directed at her. She wondered what the woman had done to deserve such animosity from him. At the moment, Megan didn't care because she had her own problems. Rico Claiborne had made her lose control. He had kissed her, and she had kissed him back.

And rather enjoyed it.

Dread had her belly quaking and her throat tightening when she realized she wasn't an iceberg after all. Rico had effectively thawed her.

She drew in a deep breath, furious with herself for letting things get out of hand when she'd boasted and bragged about the control she had. All it had taken was one blazing kiss to make a liar out of her. It was a fluke, it had to be. He had caught her off guard.

She didn't enjoy kissing him as much as she wanted to think she did.

Then why was she licking her lips and liking the taste he'd left behind? She glanced over and saw he'd been watching her and was following the movement of her tongue. Her fingers knotted into a fist at her side, and she narrowed her gaze. "I think you need to leave."

"No problem, now that I've proven my point. You're as passionate as you are beautiful, Megan. Nothing's changed. I still want you, and now that I've gotten a taste, I want you even more. So take my warning, don't come to Texas."

A part of Megan knew that if she was smart, she would take his warning. But the stubborn part of her refused to do so. "I'm going to Texas, Rico."

He didn't say anything for a long moment, just stood there and held her gaze. Finally, he said, "Then I guess I'll be seeing you at some point while you're there. Don't say I didn't warn you."

Rico strode away and, before opening the door to leave, he grabbed his jacket off the coatrack. He turned, smiled at her, winked and then opened the door and walked out.

Megan took a deep breath to calm her racing heart. She had a feeling that her life, as she'd always known it, would never, ever be the same. Heaven help her, she had tasted passion and already she was craving more.

CHAPTER FOUR

UPON ARRIVING AT Megan's place early Friday morning, Ramsey glanced down at the two overpacked traveling bags that sat in the middle of her living room. "Hey, you're planning on coming back, aren't you?" he asked, chuckling.

Megan smiled and tapped a finger to her chin. "Umm, I guess I will eventually. And those bags aren't *that* bad."

"They aren't? I bet I'll strain my back carrying them out to the truck. And how much you want to bet they're both overweight and you'll pay plenty when you check them in at the airport."

"Probably, but that's fine. A lot of it is baby stuff I bought for Alyssa. She's having a girl and you know how I like buying all that frilly stuff." He would know since his two-year-old daughter, Susan, had been the first female born to the Denver Westmorelands since Bailey. Megan simply adored her niece and would miss her while away in Texas.

She looked up at Ramsey, her oldest brother, the one she most admired along with her cousin Dillon. "Ram?"

He looked over at her after taking a sip of the coffee she'd handed him as soon he had walked through the door. "Yes?"

"I was a good kid while growing up, wasn't I? I didn't give you and Dillon any trouble, right?"

He grinned, reached out and pulled one of her curls. "No, sport, you didn't give us any trouble. You were easier to handle than Bailey, the twins and Bane. But everyone was easier than those four."

He paused a moment and added, "And unlike a lot of men with sisters, I never once had to worry about guys getting their way with the three of you. You, Gemma and Bail did a good job of keeping the men in line yourselves. If a guy became a nuisance, you three would make them haul ass the other way. Dillon and I got a chuckle out of it, each and every time. Especially you. I think you enjoyed giving the guys a hard time."

She playfully jabbed him in the ribs. "I did not."

He laughed. "Could have fooled us." He grabbed her close for a brotherly hug. "At one time we thought you were sweet on Charlie Bristol when you were a senior in high school. We knew for a fact he was sweet on you. But according to Riley, he was too scared to ask you out."

Megan smiled over at him as she led him to the kitchen. She remembered Charlie Bristol. He used to spend the summers with one of his aunts who lived nearby. "He was nice, and cute."

"But you wouldn't give him the time of day," he said, sitting down at the table.

Ramsey was right, she hadn't. She recalled having a crush on Charlie for a quick second but she'd been too busy helping out with Gemma and Bailey to think about boys.

"I'm going to miss you, sport," Ramsey said, breaking into her thoughts.

Megan smiled over at him as she joined him at the table. "And I'm going to miss you, as well. Other than being with Gemma during the time she was giving birth to CJ, and visiting Delaney those two weeks in Tehran, this is the first real vacation I've taken, and the longest. I'll be away from the hospital for a full month."

"How will they make it without you?" Ramsey teased.

"I'm sure they'll find a way." Even while attending college, she had stayed pretty close to home, not wanting to go too far away. For some reason, she'd felt she was needed. But then, she'd also felt helpless during Bailey's years of defiance. She had tried talking to her baby sister, but it hadn't done any good. She'd known that Bailey's, the twins' and Bane's acts of rebellion were their way of handling the grief of losing their parents. But still, at the time, she'd wished she could do more.

"Ram, can I ask you something?"

He chuckled. "Another question?" He faked a look of pain before saying, "Okay, I guess one more wouldn't hurt."

"Do you think having control of your emotions is a bad thing?" She swallowed tightly as she waited for his answer.

He smiled at her. "Having too much self-control isn't healthy, and it can lead to stress. Everyone needs to know how to let loose, release steam and let their hair down every once in a while."

Megan nodded. Releasing steam wasn't what she was dealing with. Letting go of a buildup of sexual energy was the problem. And that kiss the other day hadn't helped matters any.

She hadn't seen Rico since then, and she knew he'd already left for Texas. She'd been able to get that much out of Riley when he'd dropped by yesterday. "So it's okay to…"

"Get a little wild every once in a while?" He chuckled. "Yes, I think it is, as long as you're not hurting anyone."

He paused a second and then asked, "You're planning to enjoy yourself while you're in Texas, right?"

"Yes. But as you know, it won't be all fun, Ram." Ramsey and Dillon were the only ones she'd told the real reason why she was going to Texas. They also knew she had asked Rico to take her with him, and he'd refused. Of course, she hadn't told them what he'd told her as the reason behind his refusal. She'd only told them Rico claimed he preferred working alone and didn't need her help in the investigation. Neither Dillon nor Ramsey had given their opinions about anything, because she hadn't asked for them. The "don't ask—don't tell" rule was one Dillon and Ramsey implemented for the Westmorelands who were independent adults.

"You can do me a favor, though, sport," he said in a serious tone.

She lifted an eyebrow. "What?"

"Don't be too hard on Rico for not wanting to take you along. You're paying him to do a job, and he wants to do it."

Megan rolled her eyes. "And he will. But I want to be there. I could help."

"Evidently he doesn't want your help."

Yes, but he does want something else, Megan thought. She could just imagine what her brother would think if he knew the real reason Rico didn't want her in Texas. But then, Ramsey was so laidback it probably wouldn't faze him. He'd known for years how Callum had felt about Gemma. But he'd also known his sisters could handle their business without any interference from their big brother unless it became absolutely necessary.

"But what if there are other Westmorelands somewhere?" she implored. "I told you what Rico said about Clarice having a baby."

"Then Rico will find out information and give it to you to bring to us, Megan. Let him do his job. And another thing."

"Yes?"

"Rico is a good guy. I like him. So do the rest of the Westmorelands. I judge a man by a lot of things and one is how he treats his family. He evidently is doing something right because Jessica and Savannah think the world of their brother."

Megan leaned back in her chair and frowned. "Is there a reason you're telling me that?"

Ramsey was silent for a moment as he stared at her. Then a slow smile touched his lips. "I'll let you figure that one out, Megan."

She nodded and returned his smile. "Fair enough. And about that self-control we were discussing earlier?"

"Yes, what about it?" he asked.

"It *is* essential at times," she said.

"I agree, it is. At times."

"But I'm finding out I might not have as much as I thought. That's not a bad thing, right, Ram?"

Ramsey chuckled. "No, sport, it's just a part of being human."

RICO HAD JUST finished eating his dinner at one of the restaurants in Forbes when his cell phone vibrated. Standing, he pulled it out of his back pocket. "This is Rico."

"Our father called me."

Rico tensed when he heard Savannah's voice. He sat back down and leaned back in his chair. "He called me as well, but I didn't give him a chance to say anything," he said, trying to keep his anger in check.

"Same here. I wonder what he wants, and I hope he doesn't try contacting Jessica. How long has it been now? Close to eighteen years?"

"Just about. I couldn't reach Jessica today, but I did talk to Chase. He said Jess hadn't mentioned anything about getting a call from Jeff Claiborne, and I think if she had, she would have told him," said Rico.

"Well, I don't want him upsetting her. She's pregnant."

"And you have a lot on your hands with a new baby," he reminded her.

"Yes, but I can handle the likes of Jeff regardless. But, I'm not sure Jessica can, though. It wasn't our mother who committed suicide because of him."

"I agree."

"Where are you?" Savannah asked him.

"Forbes, Texas. Nice town."

"Are you on a work assignment?"

"Yes, for Megan," he replied, taking a sip of his beer.

"Is she there with you?"

Rico's eyebrows shot up. "No. Should she be?"

"Just asking. Well, I'll be talking with—"

"Savannah?" he said in that particular tone when he knew she was up to something. "Why would you think Megan was here with me? I don't work that way."

"Yes, but I know the two of you are attracted to each other."

He took another sip of his beer. "Are we?"

"Yes. I noticed at Micah's wedding. I think everyone did."

"Did they?"

"Yes, Rico, and you're being evasive."

He laughed. "And you're being nosy. Where's Durango?" he asked, changing the subject.

"Outside giving Sarah her riding lessons."

"Tell him I said hello and give my niece a hug."

"I will…and, Rico?"

"Yes?"

"I like Megan. Jess does, too."

Rico didn't say anything for a long moment. He took another sip of his beer as he remembered the kiss they'd shared a couple of days ago. "Good to hear because I like her, too. Now, goodbye."

He clicked off the phone before his sister could grill him. Glancing around the restaurant, he saw it had gotten crowded. The hotel had recommended this place, and he was glad they had. They had served good Southern food, the tastiest. But nothing he ate, no matter how spicy, could eradicate Megan's taste from his tongue. And personally, he had no problem with that because what he'd said to Savannah was true. He liked Megan. A capricious smile touched his lips. Probably, too damn much.

He was about to signal the waitress for his check when his phone rang. He hoped it wasn't Savannah calling back being nosy. He sighed in relief when he saw it was Martin Felder, a friend who'd once worked with the FBI years ago but was now doing freelance detective work. He was an ace when it came to internet research. "Sorry, I meant to call you earlier, Rico, but I needed to sing Anna to sleep."

Rico nodded, understanding. Martin had become a single father last year when his wife, Marcia, had died from pancreatic cancer. He had pretty much taken early retirement from the Bureau to work from home. He had been the one to discover information about Clarice's pregnancy.

"No problem, and I can't tell you enough about what a great job you're doing with Anna."

"Thanks, Rico. I needed to hear that. She celebrated her third birthday last week, and I wished Marcia could have been here to see what a beautiful little girl we made together. She looks more and more like her mom every day."

Martin paused a minute and then said, "I was on the internet earlier today and picked up this story of a woman celebrating her one-hundredth birthday in Forbes. They were saying how sharp her memory was for someone her age."

"What's her name?" Rico asked, sitting up straight in his chair.

"Fanny Banks. She's someone you might want to talk to while in town to see if she remembers anything about Clarice Riggins. I'll send the info over to you."

"That's a good idea. Thanks." Rico hung up the phone and signaled for the waitress.

A few moments later, back in his rental car, he was reviewing the information Martin had sent to his iPhone. The woman's family was giving her a birthday party tomorrow so the earliest he would be able to talk to her would be Saturday.

His thoughts shifted to Megan and the look in her eyes when she'd tried explaining why it was so important for her to be there when he found out information on Raphel. Maybe he *was* being hard-nosed about not letting her help him. And he had given her fair warning about how much he wanted her. They'd kissed, and if she hadn't realized the intensity of their attraction before, that kiss should have cinched it and definitely opened her eyes.

It had definitely opened his, but that's not all it had done. If he'd thought he wanted her before then he was doubly certain of it now. He hadn't slept worth a damn since that kiss and sometimes he could swear her scent was in the air even when she wasn't around. He had this intense physical desire for her that he just couldn't kick. Now he had begun to crave her and that wasn't good. But it was something he just couldn't help. The woman was a full-blown addiction to his libido.

He put his phone away, thinking Megan should have arrived at Clint's place by now. It was too late to make a trip to Austin tonight, but he'd head that way early tomorrow…unless he could talk himself out of it overnight.

And he doubted that would happen.

CHAPTER FIVE

"I CAN'T EAT a single thing more," Megan said, as she looked at all the food Alyssa had placed on the table for breakfast. It wouldn't be so bad if she hadn't arrived yesterday at dinnertime to a whopping spread by Chester, Clint's cook, housekeeper and all-around ranch hand.

Megan had met Chester the last time she'd been here, and every meal she'd eaten was to die for. But like she'd said, she couldn't eat a single thing more and would need to do some physical activities to burn off the calories.

Clint chuckled as helped his wife up from the table. Alyssa said the doctor claimed she wasn't having twins but Megan wasn't too sure.

"Is there anything you need me to do?" she asked Alyssa when Clint had gotten her settled in her favorite recliner in the living room.

Alyssa waved off Megan's offer. "I'm fine. Clint is doing great with Cain," she said of her three-year-old son, who was the spitting image of his father. "And Aunt Claudine will arrive this weekend."

"How long do you think your aunt will visit this

time?" Megan asked as she took the love seat across from Alyssa.

"If I have anything to do with it, she won't be leaving," Chester hollered out as he cleared off the kitchen table.

Megan glanced over at Clint, and Alyssa only laughed. Then Clint said, "Chester is sweet on Aunt Claudine, but hasn't convinced her to stay here and not return to Waco."

"But I think he might have worn her down," Alyssa said, whispering so Chester wouldn't hear. "She mentioned she's decided to put her house up for sale. She told me not to tell Chester because she wants to surprise him."

Megan couldn't help but smile. She thought Chester and Alyssa's aunt Claudine, both in their sixties, would make a nice couple. She bet it was simply wonderful finding love at that age. It would be grand to do so at any age…if you were looking for it or interested in getting it. She wasn't.

"If it's okay, I'd like to go riding around the Golden Glade, especially the south ridge. I love it there."

Clint smiled. "Most people do." He looked lovingly at Alyssa. "We've discovered it's one of our most favorite places on the ranch."

Megan watched as Alyssa exchanged another loving look with Clint. She knew the two were sharing a private moment that involved the south ridge in some way. They made a beautiful couple, she thought. Like all the other Westmoreland males, Clint was

too handsome for his own good, and Alyssa, who
was even more beautiful while pregnant, was his
perfect mate.

Seeing the love radiating between the couple—
the same she'd witnessed between her cousins and
their wives, as well as between her brothers and their
wives—made a warm feeling flow through Megan.
It was one she'd never felt before. She drew in a deep
breath, thinking that feeling such a thing was out-
right foolish, but she couldn't deny what she'd felt
just now.

As if remembering Megan was in the room, Clint
turned to her, smiled and said, "Just let Marty know
that you want to go riding, and he'll have one of the
men prepare a horse for you."

"Thanks." Megan decided it was best to give Clint
and Alyssa some alone time. Cain was taking a nap,
and Megan could make herself scarce real fast. "I'll
change into something comfortable for riding."

After saying she would see them later, she quickly
headed toward the guest room.

ONE PART OF Rico's mind was putting up one hell of
an argument as to why he shouldn't be driving to
Austin for Megan. Too bad the other part refused
to listen. Right now, the only thing that particular
part of his brain understood was his erection throbbing something fierce behind the zipper of his pants.
Okay, he knew it shouldn't be just a sexual thing. He
shouldn't be allowing all this lust to be eating away

at him, practically nipping at his balls, but hell, he couldn't help it. He wanted her. Plain and simple.

Although there was really nothing plain and simple about it, anticipation made him drive faster than he should. *Slow down, Claiborne. Are you willing to get a speeding ticket just because you want to see her again?*

Yes.

He drew in a sharp breath, not understanding it. So he continued driving and when he finally saw Austin's city-limits marker, he felt a strong dose of adrenaline rush through his veins. It didn't matter that he still had a good twenty minutes to go before reaching the Golden Glade Ranch. Nor did it matter that Megan would be surprised to see him, and even more surprised that he would be taking her back with him to Forbes to be there when he talked to Fanny Banks.

But he would explain that taking her to meet Fanny would be all he'd let her do. He would return Megan to the Golden Glade while he finished up with the investigation. Nothing had changed on that front. Like he'd told her, he preferred working alone.

He checked the clock on the car's dashboard. Breakfast would be over by the time he reached the ranch. Alyssa might be resting, and if Clint wasn't around then he was probably out riding the range.

Rico glanced up at the sky. Clear, blue, and the sun was shining. It was a beautiful day in late September, and he planned to enjoy it. He pressed down on the accelerator. Although he probably didn't need to be in a hurry, he was in one anyway.

A short while later he released a sigh of anticipation when he saw the marker to the Golden Glade Ranch. Smiling, he made a turn down the long, winding driveway toward the huge ranch house.

MEGAN WAS CONVINCED that the south-ridge pasture of the Golden Glade was the most beautiful land she'd ever seen. The Westmorelands owned beautiful property back in Denver, but this here was just too magnificent for words.

She dismounted her horse and, after tying him to a hitching post, she gazed down in the valley where it seemed as though thousands upon thousands of wild horses were running free.

The triplets, Clint, Cole and Casey, had lived on this land with their uncle Sid while growing up. Sid Roberts had been a legend in his day. First as a rodeo star and then later as a renowned horse trainer. Megan even remembered studying about him in school. In their uncle's memory, the triplets had dedicated over three thousand acres of this land along the south ridge as a reserve. Hundreds of wild horses were saved from slaughter by being shipped here from Nevada. Some were left to roam free for the rest of their days, and others were shipped either to Montana, where Casey had followed in her uncle's footsteps as a horse trainer, or to Denver, where some of her cousins and brothers were partners in the operation.

Megan could recall when Zane, Derringer and Jason had decided to join the partnership that included Clint, their cousin Durango, Casey and her husband, McKinnon. All of the Westmorelands involved in the partnership loved horses and were experts in handling them.

Megan glanced across the way and saw a cabin nestled among the trees. She knew it hadn't been here the last time she'd visited. She smiled, thinking it was probably a lovers' hideaway for Clint and Alyssa and was probably the reason for the secretive smile they'd shared this morning.

Going back to the horse, she unhooked a blanket she'd brought and the backpack that contained a book to read and a Ziploc bag filled with the fruit Chester had packed. It didn't take long to find the perfect spot to spread the blanket on the ground and stretch out. She looked up at the sky, thinking it was a gorgeous day and it was nice to be out in it. She enjoyed her job at the hospital, but there was nothing like being out under the wide-open sky.

She had finished one chapter of the suspense thriller that her cousin Stone Westmoreland, aka Rock Mason, had written. She was so engrossed in the book that it was a while before she heard the sound of another horse approaching. Thinking it was probably Clint or one of the ranch hands coming to check on her, to make sure she was okay, she'd gotten to her feet by the time a horse and rider came around the bend.

Suddenly she felt it—heat sizzling down her

spine, fire stirring in her stomach. Her heart began thumping hard in her chest. She'd known that she would eventually run in to Rico, but she'd thought it would be when she made an appearance in Forbes. He had been so adamant about her not coming to Texas with him that she'd figured she would have to be the one to seek him out and not the other way around.

Her breasts began tingling, and she could feel her nipples harden against her cotton shirt when he brought his horse to a stop beside hers. Nothing, she thought, was more of a turn-on than seeing a man, especially this particular man, dismount from his horse…with such masculine ease and virile precision, and she wondered if he slid between a woman's legs the same way.

She could feel her cheeks redden with such brazen thoughts, and her throat tightened when he began walking toward her. Since it seemed he didn't have anything to say, she figured she would acknowledge his presence. "Rico."

He tilted his hat to her. She thought he looked good in his jeans, chambray shirt and the Stetson. "Megan."

She drew in a deep breath as he moved toward her. His advance was just as lethal, just as stealthy, as a hunter who'd cornered his prey. "Do you know why I'm here?" he asked her in a deep, husky voice.

Megan she shook her head. "No. You said you wanted to work alone."

He smiled, and she could tell it didn't quite reach

his eyes. "But you're here, which means you didn't intend on letting me do that."

She lifted her chin. "Just pretend I'm not here, and when you see me in Forbes, you can pretend I'm not there."

"Not possible," he said throatily, coming to a stop in front of her. Up close, she could see smoldering desire in the depths of his eyes. That should have jarred some sense into her, but it didn't. Instead it had just the opposite effect.

Megan tilted her head back to look up at him and what she saw almost took her breath away again— hazel eyes that were roaming all over her, as if they were savoring her. There was no way she could miss the hunger that flared in their depths, making her breath come out in quick gulps.

"I think I need to get back to the ranch," she said.

A sexy smile touched his lips. "What's the rush?"

There was so much heat staring at her that she knew any minute she was bound to go up in flames. "I asked why you're here, Rico."

Instead of answering, he reached out and gently cradled her face between his hands and brought his mouth so close to hers that she couldn't keep her lips from quivering. "My answer is simple, Megan. I came for you."

He paused a moment and then added, "I haven't been able to forget that kiss and how our tongues tangled while I became enmeshed in your taste. Nothing has changed other than I think you've become an addiction, and I want you more than before."

And then he lowered his mouth to hers.

He knew the instant she began to lose control because she started kissing him back with a degree of hunger and intimacy that astounded him.

He wrapped his arms around her waist while they stood there, letting their tongues tangle in a way that was sending all kinds of sensual pulses through his veins. This is what had kept him up nights, had made him drive almost like a madman through several cities to get here. He had known this would be what awaited him. Never had a single kiss ignited so much sexual pressure within him, made him feel as if he was ready to explode at any moment.

She shifted her body closer, settling as intimately as a woman still wearing clothes could get, at the juncture of his legs. The moment she felt his hard erection pressing against her, she shifted her stance to cradle his engorged shaft between her thighs.

If he didn't slow her down, he would be hauling her off to that blanket she'd spread on the ground. Thoughts of making love to her here, in such a beautiful spot and under such a stunning blue sky, were going through his mind. But he knew she wasn't ready for that. She especially wasn't ready to take it to the level he wanted to take it.

His thoughts were interrupted when he felt her hand touch the sides of his belt, trying to ease his shirt out of his pants. She wanted to touch some skin, and he had no problems letting her do so. He shifted again, a deliberate move on his part to give her better access to what she wanted, although what she wanted to do was way too dangerous to his peace of mind. It wouldn't take much to push him over the edge.

When he felt her tugging at his shirt, pulling it out of his jeans, he deepened the kiss, plunging his tongue farther into her mouth and then flicking it around with masterful strokes. He wasn't a man who took advantage of women, but then he was never one who took them too seriously, either, even while maintaining a level of respect for any female he was involved with.

But with Megan that respect went up more than a notch. She was a Westmoreland. So were his sisters. That was definitely a game changer. Although he wanted Megan and intended to have her, he needed to be careful how he handled her. He had to do things decently and in the right order. As much as he could.

But doing anything decently and in the right order was not on his mind as he continued to kiss her, as his tongue explored inside her mouth with a hunger that had his erection throbbing.

And when she inched her hand beneath his shirt to touch his skin, he snatched his mouth from hers to draw in a deep breath. He held her gaze, staring down at her as the silence between them extended. Her touch had nearly scorched him it had been so hot. He hadn't been prepared for it. Nor had he expected such a reaction to it.

He might have reeled in his senses and moved away from her if she hadn't swiped her tongue across her lips. That movement was his downfall, and he felt fire roaring through his veins. He leaned in closer and began licking her mouth from corner to corner. And when she let out a breathless moan, he slid his tongue back inside to savor her some more.

Their tongues tangled and dueled and he held on to her, needing the taste as intense desire tore through him. He knew he had to end the kiss or it could go on forever. And when her hips began moving against him, rotating against his huge arousal, he knew where things might lead if he didn't end the kiss here and now.

He slowly pulled back and let out a breath as his gaze seized her moistened lips. He watched the eyes staring back at him darken to a degree that would have grown hair on his chest, if he didn't have any already.

"Rico?"

Heat was still simmering in his veins, and it didn't help him calm down when she said his name like that. "Yes?"

"You did it again."

He lifted a brow. "What did I do?"

"You kissed me."

He couldn't help but smile. "Yes, and you kissed me back."

She nodded and didn't deny it. "We're going to have to come to some kind of understanding. About what we can or cannot do when we're alone."

His smile deepened. *That would be interesting.* "Okay, you make out that list, and we can discuss it."

She tilted her head back to look at him. "I'm serious."

"So am I, and make sure it's a pretty detailed list because if something's not on there, I'll be tempted to try it."

When she didn't say anything, he chuckled and told her she was being too serious. "You'll feel better after getting dinner. You missed lunch."

She shook her head as he led her over to the horses. "I wasn't hungry."

He licked his mouth, smiled and said, "Mmm, baby, you could have fooled mc."

CHAPTER SIX

ONCE THEY HAD gotten back to the ranch and dismounted, Rico told the ranch hand who'd come to handle the horses not to bother, that he would take care of them.

"You're from Philadelphia, but you act as if you've been around horses all your life," she said, watching him remove the saddles from the animals' backs.

He smiled over at her across the back of the horse she'd been riding. "In a way, I have. My maternal grandparents own horses, and they made sure Savannah and I took riding lessons and that we knew how to care for one."

She nodded. "What about Jessica?"

He didn't say anything for a minute and then said, "Jessica, Savannah and I share the same father. We didn't know about Jess until I was in college."

"Oh." Megan didn't know the full story, but it was obvious from Rico and Savannah's interracial features that the three siblings shared the same father and not the same mother. She had met Rico and Savannah's mother at one of Jessica's baby showers and thought she was beautiful as well as kind. But then Megan had seen the interaction between the three siblings and could tell their relationship was a close one.

"You, Jessica and Savannah are close, I can tell. It's also obvious the three of you get along well."

He smiled. "Yes, we do, especially since I'm no longer trying to boss them around. Now I gladly leave them in the hands of Chase and Durango and have to admit your cousins seem to be doing a good job of keeping my sisters happy."

Megan would have to agree. But then she would say that all the Westmorelands had selected mates that complemented them, and they all seemed so happy together, so well connected. Even Gemma and Callum. She had visited her sister around the time Gemma's baby was due to be born and Megan had easily felt the love radiating between Gemma and her husband. And Megan knew Callum Junior, or CJ as everyone called him, was an extension of that love.

"We'll be leaving first thing in the morning, Megan."

She glanced back over at Rico, remembering what he'd said when he'd first arrived. He had come for her. "And just where are we supposed to be going?"

She couldn't help noticing how a beam of light that was shining in through the open barn door was hitting him at an angle that seemed to highlight his entire body. And as weird as it sounded, it seemed like there was a halo over his head. She knew it was a figment of her imagination because the man was no angel.

"I'm taking you back to Forbes with me," he said,

leading both horses to their stalls. "You did say you wanted to be included when I uncover information about Clarice."

She felt a sudden tingling of excitement in her stomach. Her face lit up. "Yes," she said, following him. "You found out something?"

"Nothing more than what I told you before. However, my man who's doing internet research came across a recent news article. There's a woman living in Forbes who'll be celebrating her one-hundredth birthday today. And she's lived in the same house for more than seventy of those years. Her address just happens to be within ten miles of the last known address we have for Clarice. We're hoping she might remember her."

Megan nodded. "But the key word is *remember*. How well do you think a one-hundred-year-old person will be able to remember?"

Rico smiled. "According to the article, she credits home remedies for her good health. I understand she still has a sharp memory."

"Then I can't wait for us to talk to her."

Rico closed the gate behind the horses and turned to face her. "Although I'm taking you along, Megan, I'm still the one handling this investigation."

"Of course," she said, looking away, trying her best not to get rattled by his insistence on being in charge. But upon remembering what Ramsey had said about letting Rico do his job without any interference from her, she decided not to make a big deal of it. The important thing was that Rico was including her.

He began walking toward the ranch house, and she fell in step beside him. "What made you change your mind about including me?" she asked as she tilted her head up.

He looked over at her. "You would have shown up in Forbes eventually, and I decided I'm going to like having you around."

Megan stopped walking and frowned up at him. "It's not going to be that kind of party, Rico."

She watched how his lips curved in a smile so sensuous that she had to remind herself to breathe. Her gaze was drawn to the muscular expanse of his chest and how the shirt looked covering it. She bet he would look even better shirtless.

Her frown deepened. She should not be thinking about Rico without a shirt. It was bad enough that she had shared two heated kisses with him.

"What kind of party do you think I'm having, Megan?"

She crossed her arms over her chest. "I don't know, you tell me."

He chuckled. "That's easy because I'm not having a party. You'll get your own hotel room, and I'll have mine. I said I wanted you. I also said eventually I'd have you if you came with me. But I'll let you decide when."

"It won't happen. Just because we shared two enjoyable kisses and—"

"So you did enjoy them, huh?"

She wished she could swipe that smirk off his face. She shrugged. "They were okay."

He threw his head back and laughed. "Just okay? Then I guess I better improve my technique the next time."

She nibbled on her bottom lip, thinking if he got any better she would be in big trouble.

"Don't do that."

She raised a brow. "Don't do what?"

"Nibble on your lip that way. Or else I'm tempted to improve my technique right here and now."

Megan swallowed, and as she stood there and stared up at him, she was reminded of how his kisses could send electrical currents racing through her with just a flick of his tongue.

"I like it when you do that."

"Do what?"

"Blush. I guess guys didn't ever talk to you that way, telling you what they wanted to do to you."

She figured she might as well be honest with him. "No."

"Then may I make a suggestion, Megan?"

She liked hearing the sound of her name from his lips. "What?"

"Get used to it."

RICO SAT ON a bar stool in the kitchen while talking to Clint. However, he was keeping Megan in his peripheral vision. When they'd gotten back to the house, Clint had been eager to show Rico a beauty of a new stallion he was about to send to his sister Casey to train, and Alyssa wanted to show Megan how she'd finished decorating the baby's room that morning.

Cain was awake, and, like most three-year-olds, he wanted to be the life of the party and hold everyone's attention. He was doing so without any problems. He spoke well for a child his age and was already riding a horse like a pro.

Rico had admired the time Clint had spent with his son and could see the bond between them. He thought about all the times he had wished his father could have been home more and hadn't been. Luckily, his grandfather had been there to fill the void when his father had been living a double life.

Megan had gone upstairs to take a nap, and by the time he'd seen her again it had been time for dinner. She had showered and changed, and the moment she had come down the stairs it had taken everything he had to keep from staring at her. She was dressed in a printed flowing skirt and a blouse that showed what a nice pair of shoulders she had. He thought she looked refreshed and simply breathtaking. And his reaction upon seeing her reminded him of how it had been the first time he'd seen her, that day three months ago.

"Rico?" Clint said, snapping his fingers in front of his face.

Rico blinked. "Sorry. My mind wandered there for a minute."

"Evidently," Clint said, grinning. "How about if we go outside where we can talk without your mind wandering so much?"

Rico chuckled, knowing Clint knew full well where his concentration had been. "Fine," he said, grabbing his beer off the counter.

Moments later, while sitting in rocking chairs on the wraparound porch, Clint had brought Rico up to date on the horse breeding and training business. Several of the horses would be running in the Kentucky Derby and Preakness in the coming year.

"So how are things going with the investigation?" Clint asked when there was a lull in conversation. "Megan mentioned to Alyssa something about an old lady in Forbes who might have known Clarice."

"Yes, I'm making plans to interview her in a few days, and Megan wants to be there when I do." Rico spent the next few minutes telling Clint what the news article had said about the woman.

"Well, I hope things work out," Clint said. "I know how it is when you discover you have family you never knew about, and I guess Megan is feeling the same way. If it hadn't been for my mother's deathbed confession, Cole, Casey and I would not have known that our father was alive. Even now, I regret the years I missed by not knowing."

Clint stood and stretched. "Well, I'm off to bed now. Will you and Megan at least stay for breakfast before taking off tomorrow?"

Rico stood, as well. "Yes. Nothing like getting on the road with a full stomach, and I'm sure Chester is going to make certain we have that."

Clint chuckled. "Yes, I'm certain, as well. Good night."

By the time they went back into the house, it was quiet and dark, which meant Alyssa and Megan had gone to bed. Rico hadn't been aware that he and Clint had talked for so long. It was close to midnight.

Clint's ranch house was huge. What Rico liked most about it was that it had four wings jutting off from the living room—north, south, east and west. He noted that he and Megan had been given their own private wing—the west wing—and he couldn't help wondering if that had been intentional.

He slowed his pace when he walked past the guest room Megan was using. The door was closed but he could see light filtering out from the bottom, which meant she was still up. He stopped and started to knock and then decided against it. It was late, and he had no reason to want to seek her out at this hour.

"Of course I can think of several reasons," he muttered, smiling as he entered the guest room he was using. He wasn't feeling tired or sleepy so he decided to work awhile on his laptop.

Rico wasn't sure how long he had been sitting at the desk, going through several online sites, piecing together more information about Fanny Banks, when he heard the opening and closing of the door across the hall, in the room Megan was using. He figured she had gotten up to get a cup of milk or tea. But when moments passed and he didn't hear her return to her room, he decided to find out where she'd gone and what she was doing.

Deciding not to turn on any lights, he walked down the hall in darkness. When he reached the liv-

ing room, he glanced around before heading for the
kitchen. There, he found her standing in the dark
and looking out the window. From the moonlight
coming in through the glass, he could tell she was
wearing a bathrobe.

Deciding he didn't want to startle her, he made
his presence known. "Couldn't you sleep?"

She swung around. "What are you doing up?"

He leaned in the doorway with his shoulder
propped against a wall. "I was basically asking you
the same thing."

She paused a moment and didn't say anything
and then said, "I tried sleeping but couldn't. I kept
thinking about my dad."

His brows furrowed. "Your dad?"

"Yes. This Saturday would have been his birthday. And I'm proud to say I was a daddy's girl," she
said, smiling.

"Were you?"

She grinned. "Yes. Big-time. I remember our last
conversation. It was right before he and Mom got
ready to leave for the airport. As usual, the plan
was for Mrs. Jones to stay at the house and keep us
until my parents returned. He asked that I make sure
to help take care of Gemma, Bailey and the twins.
Ramsey was away at college, Zane was about to leave
for college and Derringer was in high school. I was
twelve."

She moved away from the window to sit at the
table. "The only thing was, they never returned, and

I didn't do a good job of taking care of Bailey and the twins. Gemma was no problem."

Rico nodded. Since getting to know the Denver Westmorelands, he had heard the stories about what bad-asses Bailey, the twins and Bane were. And each time he heard those stories, his respect and admiration for Dillon and Ramsey went up a notch. He knew it could not have been easy to keep the family together the way they had. "I hope you're not blaming yourself for all that stupid stuff they did back then."

She shook her head. "No, but a part of me wishes I could have done more to help Ramsey with the younger ones."

Rico moved to join her at the table, figuring the best thing to do was to keep the conversation going. Otherwise, he would be tempted to pull her out of that chair and kiss her again. Electricity had begun popping the moment their gazes had connected. "You were only twelve, and you did what you could, I'm sure," he said, responding to what she'd said. "Everybody did. But people grieve in different ways. I couldn't imagine losing a parent that young."

"It wasn't easy."

"I bet, and then to lose an aunt and uncle at the same time. I have to admire all of you for being strong during that time, considering what all of you were going through."

"Yes, but think of how much easier it would have been had we known the Atlanta, Montana and Texas Westmorelands back then. There would have been others, and Dillon and Ramsey wouldn't have had to do it alone. Oh, they would have still fought to keep us together, but they would have had some kind of support system. You know what they say…it takes a village to raise a child."

Yes, he'd heard that.

"That's one of the reasons family is important to me, Rico. You never know when you will need the closeness and support a family gives to each other." Silence lingered between them for a minute and then she asked, "What about you? Were you close to your parents…your father…while growing up?"

He didn't say anything for a while. Instead, he got up and walked over to the refrigerator. To answer her question, he needed a beer. He opened the refrigerator and glanced over his shoulder. "I'm having a beer. Want one?"

"No, but I'll take a soda."

He nodded and grabbed a soda and a beer out of the refrigerator and then closed the door. Returning to the table, he turned the chair around and straddled it. "Yes. Although my father traveled a lot as a salesman, we were close, and I thought the world of him."

He popped the top on his beer, took a huge swig and then added, "But that was before I found out what a two-bit, lying con artist he was. He was married to my mother, who was living in Philly, while he was involved with another woman out in California, stringing both of them along and lying through his teeth. Making promises he knew he couldn't keep."

Rico took another swig of his beer. "Jessica's

grandfather found out Jeff Claiborne was an imposter and told Jessica's mother and my mother. Hurt and humiliated that she'd given fifteen years to a man who'd lied to her, Jessica's mother committed suicide. My mother filed for a divorce. I was in my first year of college. He came to see me, tried to make me think it was all Mom's fault and said, as males, he and I needed to stick together, and that Mom wouldn't divorce him if I put in a good word for him."

Rico stared into his beer bottle, remembering that time, but more importantly, remembering that day. He glanced back at her. "That day he stopped being my hero and the man I admired most. It was bad enough that he'd done wrong and wouldn't admit to it, but to involve me and try to pit me against Mom was unacceptable."

Rico took another swig of his beer. A long one this time. He rarely talked about that time in his life. Most people who knew his family knew the story, and chances were that Megan knew it already since she was friends with both of his sisters.

She reached out and took his hand in hers, and he felt a deep stirring in his groin as they stared at each other, while the air surrounding them became charged with a sexual current that sent sparks of desire through his body. He knew she felt it, as well.

"I know that must have been a bad time for you, but that just goes to show how a bad situation can turn into a good one. That's what happened for you, Savannah and Jessica once the three of you found out about each other, right?"

Yes, that part of the situation had turned out well, because he couldn't imagine not having Jessica and Savannah in his life. But still, whenever he thought of how Jessica had lost her mother, he would get angry all over again. Yet he said, "Yes, you're right."

She smiled and released his hand. "I've been known to be right a few times."

For some reason, he felt at ease with her, more at ease than he'd felt with any other woman. Why they were sitting here in the dark he wasn't sure. In addition to the sexual current in the room, there was also a degree of intimacy to this conversation that was ramping up his libido, reminding him of how long it had been since he'd slept with a woman. And when she had reached out and touched his hand that hadn't helped matters.

He studied her while she sipped on her soda. Even with the sliver of light shining through the window from the outside, he could see the smooth skin of her face, a beautiful shade of mocha.

She glanced over at him, caught him staring, and he felt thrumming need escalate all through him. He'd kissed her twice now and could kiss her a dozen more times and be just as satisfied. But at some point he would want more. He intended to get more. She had been warned, and she hadn't heeded his warning. The attraction between them was too great.

He wouldn't make love to her here. But they would make love, that was a given.

However, he *would* take another kiss. One that would let her know what was to come.

She stood. "I think I'll go back to bed and try to sleep. You did say we were leaving early, right?" she asked, walking over to the garbage with her soda can.

"Yes, right after breakfast." He didn't say anything but his gaze couldn't help latching on to her backside. Even with her bathrobe on, he could tell her behind was a shapely one. He'd admired it in jeans earlier that day.

On impulse, he asked, "Do you want to go for a ride?"

She turned around. "A ride?"

"Yes. It's a beautiful night outside."

A frown tugged at her brow. "A ride where?"

"The south ridge. There's a full moon, and the last time I went there at night with Clint while rounding up horses under a full moon, the view of the canyon was breathtaking."

"And you want us to saddle horses and—"

"No," he chuckled. "We'll take my truck."

She stared at him like he couldn't be thinking clearly. "Do you know what time it is?"

He nodded slowly as he held her gaze. "Yes, a time when everyone else is sleeping, and we're probably the only two people still awake."

She tilted her head and her gaze narrowed. "Why do you want me to take a ride with you at this hour, Rico?"

He decided to be honest. "Because I want to take you someplace where I can kiss you all over."

CHAPTER SEVEN

THE LOWER PART of Megan's stomach quivered, and she released a slow breath. What he was asking her, and pretty darn blatantly, was to go riding with him to the south ridge where they could park and make out. They were too old for that sort of thing, weren't they? Evidently he didn't think so, and he was a lot older than she was.

And what had he said about kissing her all over? Did he truly know what he was asking of her? She needed to be sure. "Do you know what you're asking me when you ask me to go riding with you?"

A smile that was so sexy it could be patented touched his lips. "Yeah."

Well, she had gotten her answer. He had kissed her twice, and now wanted to move to the next level. What had she really expected from a man who'd told her he wanted her and intended to have her? In that case, she had news for him: two kisses didn't mean a thing. She had let her guard down and released a little of her emotional control, but that didn't mean she would release any more. Whenever he kissed her, she couldn't think straight, and she considered doing things that weren't like her.

She stood there and watched his hazel eyes travel all over her, roaming up and down. When his gaze moved upward and snagged hers, the very air between them crackled with an electrical charge that had certain parts of her tingling.

"Are you afraid of me, Megan?" he asked softly.

Their gazes held for one searing moment. No, she wasn't afraid of him per se, but she was afraid of the things he had the ability to make her feel, afraid of the desires he could stir in her, afraid of how she could lose control around him. How could she make him understand that being in control was a part of her that she wasn't ready to let go of yet?

She shook her head. "No, I'm not afraid of you, Rico. But you say things and do things I'm not used to. You once insinuated that my brothers and cousins might have sheltered me from the realities of life, and I didn't agree with you. I still don't, but I will say that I, of my own choosing, decided not to take part in a lot of things other girls were probably into. I like being my own person and not following the crowd."

He nodded, and she could tell he was trying to follow her so she wasn't surprised when he asked, "And?"

"And I've never gone parking with a guy before." There, she'd said it. Now he knew what he was up against. But when she saw the unmistakable look of deep hunger in his eyes, her heart began pounding, fast and furious.

Then he asked, "Are you saying no guy has ever taken you to lover's lane?"

Why did his question have to sound so seductive, and why did she feel like her nerve endings were being scorched? "Yes, that's what I'm saying, and it was my decision and not theirs."

He smiled. "I can believe that."

"I saw it as a waste of time." She broke eye contact with him to look at his feet. They were bare. She'd seen men's feet before, plenty of times. With as many cousins and brothers as she had she couldn't miss seeing them. But Rico's were different. They were beautiful but manly.

"Did you?"

She glanced back up at him. "Yes, it was a waste of time because I wasn't into that sort of thing."

"You weren't?"

She shook her head. "No. I'm too in control of my emotions."

"Yet you let go a little when we kissed," he reminded her.

And she wished she hadn't. "Yes, but I can't do that too often."

He got up from the table, and she swallowed deeply while watching him cross the floor and walk over to her on those beautiful but manly bare feet. He came to a stop in front of her, reached out and took her hand. She immediately felt that same sexual charge she'd felt when she'd taken his hand earlier.

"Yet you did let go with me."

Yes, and that's what worried her. Why with him and only him? Why not with Dr. Thad Miller, Dr. Otis Wells or any of the other doctors who'd been trying for years to engage her in serious—or not so serious—affairs?

"Megan?"

"Yes?"

"Would you believe me if I were to say I would never intentionally hurt you?"

"Yes." She could believe that.

"And would it help matters if I let you set the pace?" he asked huskily in a voice that stirred things inside of her.

"What do you mean?"

"You stay in control, and I'll only do what you allow me to do and nothing more."

She suddenly felt a bit disoriented. What he evidently didn't quite yet understand was that he was a threat to her self-imposed control. But then, hadn't Ramsey said that she should let loose, be wild, release steam and let her hair down every once in a while? But did that necessarily mean being reckless?

"Megan?"

She stared up at him, studying his well-defined features. Handsome, masculine. Refined. Strong. Controlled. But was he really controlled? His features were solid, unmovable. The idea that perhaps he shared something in common with her was a lot to think about. In the meantime...

Taking a ride with him couldn't hurt anything. She couldn't sleep, and perhaps getting out and letting the wind hit her face would do her some good. He did say he would let her be in control, and she believed him. Although he had a tendency to speak his mind, he didn't come across as the type of man who would force himself on any woman. Besides, he knew her brothers and cousins, and was friends with them. His sisters were married to Westmorelands, and he wouldn't dare do anything to jeopardize those relationships.

"Okay, I'll go riding with you, Rico. Give me a minute to change clothes."

RICO SMILED THE moment he and Megan stepped outside. He hadn't lied. It was a beautiful night. He'd always said if he ever relocated from Philadelphia, he would consider moving to Texas. It wasn't too hot and it wasn't too cold, most of the time. He had fallen in love with the Lone Star state that first time he'd gone hunting and fishing with his grandfather. His grandparents had never approved of his mother's marriage, but that hadn't stopped them from forging a relationship with their grandchildren.

"There's a full moon tonight," Megan said when he opened the SUV's door for her.

"Yes, and you know what they say about a full moon, don't you?"

She rolled her eyes. "If you're trying to scare me, please don't. I've been known to watch scary movies and then be too afraid to stay at my own place. I've crashed over at Ramsey's or Dillon's at times because I was afraid to go home."

He wanted to tell her that if she got scared tonight, she could knock on his bedroom door and join him there at any time, but he bit back the words.

"Well, then I won't scare you," he said, grinning as he leaned over to buckle her seat belt. She had changed into a pretty dress that buttoned up the front. There were a lot of buttons, and his fingers itched to tackle every last one of them.

And he thought she smelled good. Something sweet and sensual with an allure that had him wanting to do more than buckle her seat belt. He pulled back. "Is that too tight?"

"No, it's fine."

He heard the throatiness in her voice and wondered if she was trying to downplay the very thing he was trying to highlight. "All right." He closed the door and then moved around the front of the truck to get in the driver's side.

"If it wasn't for that full moon it would be pitch-black out here."

He smiled. "Yes, you won't be able to see much, but what I'm going to show you is beautiful. That's why Clint had that cabin built near there. It's a stunning view of the canyon at night, and whenever there's a full moon the glow reflects off certain boulders, which makes the canyon appear to light up."

"I can't wait to see it."

And I can't wait to taste you again, he thought, as he kept his hand firmly on the steering wheel or else he'd be tempted to reach across, lift the hem of her dress and stroke her thigh. When it came to women, his manners were usually impeccable. However, around Megan he was tempted to touch, feel and savor.

He glanced over at her when he steered the truck around a bend. She was gnawing on her bottom lip, which meant she was nervous. This was a good time to get her talking, about anything. So he decided to let the conversation be about work. Hers.

"So you think they can do without you for thirty days?"

She glanced over at him and smiled. "That's the same thing Ramsey asked. No one is irreplaceable, you know."

"What about all those doctors who're pining for you?"

She rolled her eyes. "Evidently you didn't believe me when I said I don't date much. Maybe I shouldn't tell you this, but they call me Iceberg Megan behind my back."

He jerked his eyes from the road to glance over at her. "Really?"

"Yes."

"Does it bother you?"

"Not really. They prefer a willing woman in their beds, and I'm not willing and their beds are the last places I'd want to be. I don't hesitate to let them know it."

"Ouch."

"Whatever," she said, waving her hand in the air. "I don't intend to get in any man's bed anytime soon."

He wondered if she was issuing a warning, and he decided to stay away from that topic. "Why did you decide to become an anesthesiologist?"

She leaned back in the seat, getting comfortable. He liked that. "When I got my tonsils out, this man came around to talk to me, saying he would be the one putting me to sleep. He told me all about the wonderful dreams I would have."

"And did you?"

She looked confused. "Did I what?"

"Have wonderful dreams?"

"Yes, if you consider dreaming about a promised trip to Disney World a wonderful dream."

He started to chuckle and then he felt the rumble in his stomach when he laughed. She was priceless. Wonderful company. Fun to have around. "Did you get that trip to Disney World?"

"Yes!" she said with excitement in her voice. "It was the best ever, and the first of many trips our family took together. There was the time…"

He continued driving, paying attention to both the rugged roads and to her. He liked the sound of her voice, and he noticed that more than anything else, she liked talking about her family. She had adored her parents, her uncle and aunt. And she thought the world of her brothers, cousins and sisters. There were already a lot of Westmorelands. Yet she was hoping there were still more.

His mother had been an only child, and he hadn't known anything about his father's family. Jeff Claiborne had claimed he didn't have any. Now Rico wondered if that had been a lie like everything else.

She gasped. He glanced over at her and followed

her gaze through the windshield to look up at the sky. He brought the truck to a stop. "What?"

"A shooting star. I saw it."

"Did you?"

She nodded and continued to stare up at the sky. "Yes."

He shifted his gaze to stare back at her. "Hurry and make a wish."

She closed her eyes. A few minutes later she re-opened them and smiled over at him. "Done."

He turned the key in the ignition to start the truck back up. "I'm glad."

"Thanks for taking the time to let me do that. Most men would have thought it was silly and not even suggested a wish."

He grinned. "I'm not like most men."

"I'm beginning to see that, Mr. Claiborne."

He smiled as he kept driving, deciding not to tell her that if the truth be known, she hadn't seen anything yet.

CHAPTER EIGHT

"I THINK THIS is a good spot," Rico said, bringing the car to a stop.

Megan glanced around, not sure just what it was a good spot for, but decided not to ask. She looked over at him and watched as he unbuckled his seat belt and eased his seat back to accommodate his long legs. She decided to do the same—not that her legs were as long as his, mind you. He was probably six foot four to her five foot five.

When she felt his gaze on her, she suddenly felt heated. She rolled down her window and breathed in the deep scent of bluebonnets, poppies and, of all things, wild pumpkin. But there was another scent she couldn't ignore. The scent of man. Namely, the man sitting in the truck with her.

"Lean toward the dash and look out of the windshield."

Slowly, she shifted in her seat and did as he instructed. She leaned forward and looked down and what she saw almost took her breath away. The canyon appeared lit, and she could still see horses moving around. Herds of them. Beautiful stallions with their bands of mares. Since she and Rico were high up and had the help of moonlight, she saw a portion of the lake.

"So what do you think of this place, Megan?"

She glanced over at him. "It's beautiful. Quiet." *And secluded,* she thought, realizing just how alone they were.

"It didn't take you long to change clothes," he said.

She chuckled. "A habit you inherit when you have impatient brothers. Zane drove me, Gemma and Bailey to school every day when he was around. And when he wasn't, the duty fell on Derringer."

Rico seemed to be listening so she kept on talking, telling him bits and pieces about her family, fun times she'd encountered while growing up. She knew they were killing time and figured he was trying to make sure she was comfortable and not nervous with him. He wanted her to be at ease. For what, she wasn't sure, although he'd told her what he wanted to do and she'd come anyway. They had kissed twice so she knew what to expect, but he'd also said he would let her stay in control of the situation.

"You're hot?"

She figured he was asking because she'd rolled down the window. "I was, but the air is cooler outside than I thought," she said, rolling it back up. She took a deep, steadying breath and leaned forward again, trying to downplay the sexual energy seeping through her bones. He hadn't said much. He'd mainly let her talk and listened to what she'd said. But as she stared down at the canyon again she felt his presence in an intense way.

"Megan?"

Her pulse jumped when he said her name. With a deliberate slowness, she glanced over at him. "Yes?"

"I want you over here, closer to me."

She swallowed and then took note that she was sort of hugging the door. The truck had bench seats, and there was a lot of unused space separating them. Another body could sit between them comfortably. "I thought you'd want your space."

"I don't. What I want is you."

It was what he said as well as how he'd said it that sent all kinds of sensations oozing through her. His voice had a deep, drugging timbre that made her feel as if her skin were being caressed.

Without saying anything, she slid across the seat toward him, and he curved his arms across the back of the seat. "A little closer won't hurt," he said huskily.

She glanced up at him. "If I get any closer, I'll end up in your lap."

"That's the idea."

Megan's brows furrowed. He wanted her in his lap? He had to be joking, right? She studied his gaze and saw he was dead serious. Her stomach quivered as they stared at each other. The intensity in the hazel eyes that held her within their scope flooded her with all kinds of feelings, and she was breathless again.

"Do you recall the first time we kissed, Megan?"

She nodded. "Yes." How on earth could she forget it?

"Afterward, I lay awake at night remembering how it had been."

She was surprised a man would do that. She thought since kisses came by the dozen, they didn't remember one from the next. "You did?"

"Yes. You tasted good."

She swallowed and felt her bottom lips began to tremble. "Did I?"

He reached out and traced a fingertip across her trembling lips. "Yes. And do you know what else I remembered?"

"No, what?"

"How your body felt pressed against mine, even with clothes on. And of course that made me think of you without any clothes on."

Desire filtered through her body. If he was saying these things to weaken her, break down her defenses, corrode her self-control, it was working. "Do you say this to all the girls?" she asked—a part of her wanted to know. Needed to know.

He frowned. "No. And in a way, that's what bothers me."

She knew she shouldn't ask but couldn't stop herself from doing so. "Bothers you how?"

He hesitated for a moment, broke eye contact with her to look straight ahead, out the window. Slowly, methodically, he returned his gaze back to her. "I usually don't let women get next to me. But for some reason I'm allowing you to be the exception."

He didn't sound too happy about it, either, she concluded. But then, wasn't she doing the same thing? She had let him kiss her twice, where most men hadn't made it as far as the first. And then she was here at two in the morning, sitting in a parked truck with him in Texas. If that wasn't wild, she didn't know what was.

"You have such warm lips."

He could say some of the most overwhelming words...or maybe to her they were overwhelming because no other man had said them to her before. "Thanks."

"You don't have to thank me for compliments. Everything I say is true. I will never lie to you, Megan."

For some reason, she believed him. But if she wasn't supposed to thank him, what was she supposed to say? She tilted her head back to look at him and wished she hadn't. The intense look in his gaze had deepened, and she felt a stirring inside of her, making her want things she'd never had before.

He must have seen something in her eyes, because he whispered, "Come here." And then he lifted her into his arms, twisted his body to stretch his legs out on the seat and sat her in his lap. Immediately, she felt the thick, hard erection outlined against his zipper and pressed into her backside. That set off a barrage of sensations escalating through her, but nothing was as intense as the sensual strokes she felt at the juncture of her thighs.

And then, before she could take her next breath, he leaned down and captured her lips in his.

RICO WASN'T SURE just what there was about Megan that made him want to do this over and over again— mate his mouth with hers in a way that was sending him over the edge, creating more memories that would keep him awake at night. All he knew was that he needed to taste her again like he needed to breathe.

In the most primal way, blood was surging through his veins and desire was slamming through him, scorching his senses and filling him with needs that only she could satisfy. He couldn't help but feel his erection pressing against her and wishing he could be skin-to-skin with her, but he knew this wasn't the time or the place. But kissing her here, now, was essential.

His tongue continued to explore her mouth with an intensity that had her trembling in his arms. But he wouldn't let up. It couldn't be helped. There was something between them that he couldn't explain. It was wild and, for him, unprecedented. First there had been that instant attraction, then the crackling of sexual chemistry. Then, later, after their first kiss, that greedy addiction that had him in a parked truck, kissing her senseless at two in the morning.

He slowly released her mouth to stare down at her and saw the glazed look in her eyes. Then he slowly began unbuttoning her shirt dress. The first sign of her bra had him drawing in a deep breath of air—which only pulled her scent into his nostrils, a sensuous blend of jasmine and lavender.

Her bra had a front clasp and as soon as his fingers released it, her breasts sprang free. Seeing them made him throb. As he stared down at them, he saw the nipples harden before his eyes, making hunger take over his senses. Releasing a guttural moan, he leaned down and swooped a nipple between his lips and began sucking on it. Earnestly.

Megan gasped at the contact of his wet mouth on her breast, but then, when the sucking motion of his mouth made her sex clench, she threw her head back and moaned. His tongue was doing the same things to her breasts that it had done inside her mouth, and she wasn't sure she could take it. The strokes were so keen and strong, she could actually feel them between her legs.

She reached out and grabbed at his shoulder and when she couldn't get a firm grip there, she went for his hair, wrapping some of the silky strands around her finger as his mouth continued to work her breasts, sending exquisite sensations ramming through her.

But what really pushed her over the edge was when his hand slid underneath her dress to touch her thigh. No man had ever placed his hand underneath her dress. Such a thing could get one killed. If not by her, then surely by her brothers. But her brothers weren't here. She was a grown woman.

And when Rico slid his hands higher, touching her in places she'd never been touched, his fingertips making their way to her center, she shamelessly lifted her hips and shifted her legs wider to give him better access. Where was her self-control? It had taken a freaking hike the moment he had touched his mouth to hers.

Then he was kissing her mouth again, but she was

fully aware of his hand easing up her thigh, easing inside the crotch of her panties to touch her.

She almost shot out of his lap at the contact, but he held her tight and continued kissing her as his fingers stroked her, inching toward her pulsating core.

He broke off the kiss and whispered, "You feel good here. Hot. Wet. I like my fingers here, touching you this way."

She bit down on her lips to keep from saying that she liked his fingers touching her that way, as well. Whether intentional or not, he was tormenting her, driving her over the edge with every stroke. She was feeling light-headed, sensually intoxicated. He was inciting her to lose control, and she couldn't resist. The really sad thing was that a part of her didn't want to resist.

"And do you know what's better than touching you here?" he asked.

She couldn't imagine. Already she had been reduced to a trembling mess as he continued to stroke her. She gripped his hair tighter and hoped she wasn't causing him any pain. "No, I can't imagine," she whispered, struggling to get the words out. Forcing anything from her lungs was complicated at the moment.

"Then let me show you, baby."

Her mind had been so focused on his term of endearment that she hadn't realized he had quickly shifted their bodies so her head was away from him, closer to the passenger door. The next thing she knew he had pushed the rest of her dress aside, eased off her panties and lifted her hips to place her thighs over his shoulders.

He met her gaze once, but it was enough for her to see the smoldering heat in his eyes just seconds before he lowered his head between her legs. Shock made her realize what he was about to do, and she called out his name. "Rico!"

But the sound was lost and became irrelevant the moment his mouth touched her core and his tongue slid between the folds. And when he began stroking her, tasting her, she couldn't help but cry out his name again. "Rico."

He didn't let up as firm hands held her hips steady and a determined mouth licked her like she was a meal he just had to have. She continued to moan as blood gushed through her veins. His mouth was devouring her, driving her over the edge, kicking what self-control remained right out the window. The raw hunger he was exhibiting was sending her senses scurrying in all directions. She closed her eyes as moan after moan after moan tore from her lips. The feelings were intense. Their magnitude was resplendent and stunning. Pleasure coiled within her then slowly spread open as desire sharpened its claws on her. Making her feel things she had never felt before. Sensations she hadn't known were possible. And the feel of his stubble-roughened jaw on her skin wasn't helping her regain control.

"Rico," she whispered. "I—I need…" She couldn't finish her thought because she didn't have a clue what she needed. She'd never been with a man like this before, and neither had Gemma before Callum. All her sister had told Megan was that it was something well worth the wait. But if this was the prologue, the wait just might kill her.

And then he did something, she wasn't sure what, with his tongue. Some kind of wiggly formation followed by a fierce jab that allowed his mouth to actually lock down on her.

Sensations blasted through her, and she flung back her head and let out a high-pitched scream. But he wouldn't let go. He continued to taste and savor her as if she was not only his flavor of the day, but also his flavor of all time. She pushed the foolish thought from her mind as she continued to be bombarded with feelings that were ripping her apart.

She gasped for breath before screaming again when her entire body spiraled into another orgasm. She whimpered through it and held tight to his hair as she clutched his shoulders. He kept his mouth locked on her until the very last moan had flowed from her lips. She collapsed back on the car seat, feeling totally drained.

Only then did he pull back, adjusting their bodies to bring her up to him. He tightened his hold when she collapsed weakly against his chest. Then he lowered his head and kissed her, their lips locked together intensely. At that moment, she was craving this contact, this closeness, this very intimate connection. Moments later, when he released her mouth, he pulled her closer to him, tucking her head beneath his jaw, and whispered, "This is only the beginning, baby. Only the beginning."

CHAPTER NINE

THE NEXT MORNING, Rico and Megan left the Golden Glade Ranch after breakfast to head out to Forbes. He had been driving now for a little more than a half hour and his GPS indicated they had less than a hundred miles to go. He glanced up at the skies, saw the gray clouds and was certain it would rain before they reached their destination.

Rico then glanced over at Megan and saw she was still sleeping soundly and had been since he'd hit the interstate. Good. He had a feeling she hadn't gotten much sleep last night.

She had pretty much remained quiet on the drive back to the ranch from the south ridge, and once there, she quickly said good-night and rushed off to her room, closing the door behind her. And then this morning at breakfast, she hadn't been very talkative. Several times he had caught her barely able to keep her eyes open. If Clint and Alyssa had found her drowsiness strange, neither had commented on it.

Rico remembered every single thing about last night, and, if truth be told, he hadn't thought of much of anything else since. Megan Westmoreland had more passion in her little finger than most women had in their entire bodies. And just the thought that no other man had tempted her to release all that passion was simply mind-boggling to him.

Ramsey had warned him that she was strong-willed. However, even the most strong-willed person couldn't fight a well-orchestrated seduction. But then, being overcome with passion wasn't a surrender. He saw it as her acceptance that nothing was wrong with enjoying her healthy sexuality.

I like being my own person and not following the crowd. Those were the words she had spoken last night. He remembered them and had both admired and respected her for taking that stance. His sisters had basically been the same and had handled their own business. Even when Savannah had gotten pregnant by Durango, she had been prepared to go at it alone had he not wanted to claim the child as his. And knowing his sister, marriage had not been on her mind when she'd gone out to Montana to tell Durango he was going to be a father. Thanks to Jeff Claiborne, a bad taste had been left in Savannah's mouth where marriage was concerned. That same bad taste had been left in Rico's, as well.

But Savannah had married Durango and was happy and so were Jess and Chase. Rico was happy for them, and with them married off, he had turned his time and attention to other things. His investigation business mainly. And now, he thought, glancing over at Megan again, to her. She was the first woman in years who had garnered any real attention from him.

What he'd told her last night was true. What they'd started was just the beginning. She hadn't responded to what he'd said one way or the other, but he hadn't really expected her to. He had been tempted to ask if she'd wanted to talk about last night but she had dozed off before he could do so.

But before he had a conversation with her about anything, it would be wise to have one with himself. When it came to her, he was still in a quandary as to why he was as attracted to her as he was. What was there about her that he wanted to claim?

He would let her sleep, and when she woke up, they would talk.

THE SOUND OF rain and thunder woke Megan. She first glanced out the windshield and saw how hard it was raining, before looking over at Rico as he maneuvered the truck through the downpour. His concentration was on his driving, and she decided to allow her concentration to be on him.

Her gaze moved to the hands that gripped the steering wheel. They were big and strong. Masculine hands. Even down to his fingertips. They were hands that had touched her in places no other man would have dared. But he had. And what had happened as a result still had certain parts of her body tingling.

She started to shift in her seat but then decided to stay put. She wasn't ready for him to know she was awake. She needed time to think. To ponder. To pull herself together. She was still a little rattled from last night when she had literally come unglued. Ramsey had said that everyone needed to let loose and let her hair down every once in a while, and she had definitely taken her brother's suggestion.

She didn't have any regrets, as much as she wished she did. The experience had been simply amazing. With Rico's hands, mouth and tongue, she had felt things she had never felt before. He had deliberately pushed her over the edge, given her pleasure in a way she'd never received it before and wouldn't again.

This is only the beginning.

He had said that. She remembered his words clearly. She hadn't quite recovered from the barrage of pleasurable sensations that had overtaken her, not once but twice, when he had whispered that very statement to her. Even now she couldn't believe she had let him do all those things to her, touch her all over, touch her in all those places.

He'd said he would let her stay in control, but she had forgotten all about control from the first moment he had kissed her. Instead, her thoughts had been on something else altogether. Like taking every single thing he was giving, with a greed and a hunger that astounded her.

"You're awake."

She blinked and moved her gaze from his hands to his face. He'd shaven, but she could clearly remember the feel of his unshaven jaw between her legs. She felt a tingling sensation in that very spot. Maybe, on second thought, she should forget it.

She pulled up in her seat and stared straight ahead. "Yes, I'm awake."

Before she realized what he was doing, he had pulled the car over to the shoulder of the road, unleashed his seat belt and leaned over. His mouth took hers in a deep, languid and provocative kiss that whooshed the very air from her lungs. It was way too passionate and too roastingly raw to be a morning kiss, one taken on the side of the road amidst rush-hour traffic. But he was doing so, boldly, and with a deliberate ease that stirred everything within her. She was reminded of last night and how easily she had succumbed to the passion he'd stirred, the lust he had provoked.

He released her mouth, but not before one final swipe of his tongue from corner to corner. Her nipples hardened in response and pressed tightly against her blouse. Her mouth suddenly felt hot. Taken. Devoured.

"Hello, Megan," he said, against her lips.

"Hello." If this was how he would wake her up after a nap, then she would be tempted to doze off on him anytime.

"Did you get a good nap?"

"Yes, if you want to call it that."

He chuckled and straightened in his seat and resnapped his seat belt. "I would. You've been sleeping for over an hour."

She glanced back at him. "An hour?"

"Yes, I stopped for gas, and you slept through it."

She stretched her shoulders. "I was tired."

"I understand."

Yes, he would, she thought, refusing to look over

at him as he moved back into traffic. She licked her lips and could still taste him there. Her senses felt short-circuited. Overwhelmed. She had been fore-warned, but she hadn't taken heed.

"You feel like talking?"

Suddenly her senses were on full alert. She did look at him then. "What about?"

"Last night."

She didn't say anything. Was that the protocol with a man and a woman? To use the morning after to discuss the night before? She didn't know. "Is that how things are done?"

He lifted a brow. "What things?"

"The morning-after party where you rehash things. Say what you regret, what you wished never happened, and make promises it won't happen again."

She saw the crinkling of a smile touch the cor-ners of his lips. "Not on my watch. Besides, I told you it will happen again. Last night was just the be-ginning."

"And do I have a say in the matter?"

"Yes." He glanced over at her. "All you have to say is that you don't want my hands on you, and I'll keep them to myself. I've never forced myself on any woman, Megan."

She could believe that. In fact, she could very well imagine women forcing themselves on him. She began nibbling at her bottom lip. She wished it could be that simple, just tell him to keep his hands to himself, but the truth of the matter was…she liked his hands on her. And she had thoroughly enjoyed his mouth and tongue on her, as well. Maybe a little too much.

Looking over at him, she said, "And if I *don't* tell you to keep your hands to yourself?"

"Then the outcome is inevitable," he said quietly, with a calmness that stirred her insides. She knew he meant it. From the beginning, he had given her fair warning. "Okay, let's talk," she said softly.

He pulled to the side of the road again, which had her wondering if they would ever reach their destination. He unfastened his seat belt and turned to her. "It's like this, Megan. I want you. I've made no secret of that. The degree of my attraction to you is one that I can't figure out. Not that I find the thought annoying, just confusing, because I've never been attracted to a woman to this magnitude before."

Welcome to the club, she thought. She hadn't ever been this attracted to a man before, either.

"This should be a business trip, one to find the answers about your family's history. Now that you're here, it has turned into more."

She lifted a brow. "What has it turned into now?"

"A fact-finding mission regarding us. Maybe constantly being around you will help me understand why you've gotten so deeply under my skin."

Megan's heart beat wildly in her chest. He wanted to explore the reason why they were so intensely attracted to each other? Did there need to be any other reason than that he was man and she was woman? With his looks, any woman in her right mind would be attracted to him, no matter the age. He had certainly done a number on Grace, without even trying. But Megan had been around good-looking men before and hadn't reacted the way she had with him.

"I won't crowd you, and when we get to Forbes you will have your own hotel room if you want."

He paused a moment and then added, "I'm not going to assume anything in this relationship, Megan. But you best believe I plan to seduce the hell out of you. I'm not like those other guys who never made it to first base. I plan on getting in the game and hitting a home run."

You are definitely in the game already, Rico Claiborne. She broke eye contact with him to gaze out the window. If nothing else, last night should have solidified the knowledge that her resistance was at an all-time low around him. Her self-control had taken a direct hit, and since he was on a fact-finding mission, maybe she needed to be on one, as well. Why was she willing to let him go further than any man had before?

"If you think I'm going to sit here and say I regret anything about last night, then you don't have anything to worry about, Rico."

He lifted a brow. "I don't?"

"No."

She wouldn't tell him that he had opened her eyes about a few things. That didn't mean she regretted not engaging in any sort of sexual activity before, because she didn't. What it meant was that there was a reason Rico was the man who'd given her her first orgasm. She just didn't know what that reason was yet, which was why she wanted to find out. She needed to know why he and he alone had been able to make her act in a way no other man before him had been capable of making her act.

"So we have an understanding?" he asked.

"Sort of."

He raised a brow. "Sort of?" He started the ignition and rejoined traffic again. It had stopped raining, and the sun was peeking out from beneath the clouds.

"Yes, there's still a lot about you that I don't know."

He nodded. "Okay, then ask away. Anything you want."

"Anything?"

A corner of his mouth eased into a smile. "Yes, anything, as long I don't think it's private and privileged information."

"That's fair." She considered the best way to ask her first question, then decided to just come out with it. "Have you ever been in love?"

He chuckled softly. "Not since Mrs. Tolbert."

"Mrs. Tolbert?"

"Yes, my third-grade teacher."

"You've got to be kidding me."

He glanced over at her and laughed at her surprised expression. "Kidding you about what? Being in love with Mrs. Tolbert or that she was my third-grade teacher?"

"Neither. You want me to believe that other than Mrs. Tolbert, no other woman has interested you?"

"I didn't say that. I'm a man, so women interest me. You asked if I've ever been in love, and I told you yes, with Mrs. Tolbert. Why are you questioning my answer?"

"No reason. So you're like Zane and Riley," she said.

"Maybe you need to explain that."

"Zane and Riley like women. Both claim they have never been in love and neither wants their names associated with the word."

"Then I'm not like Zane and Riley in that respect. Like I said, women interest me. I am a man with certain needs on occasion. However, falling in love doesn't scare me and it's not out of the realm of possibility. But I haven't been in a serious relationship since college."

She was tempted to ask him about that phone call he'd refused to take at her place the other day. Apparently, some woman was serious even if he wasn't. "But you have been in a serious relationship before?"

"Yes."

Her brow arched. "But you weren't in love?"

"No."

"Then why were you in the relationship?"

He didn't say anything for a minute. "My maternal grandparents are from old money and thought that as their grandson the woman I marry should be connected to old money, as well. They introduced me to Roselyn. We dated during my first year of college.

She was nice, at least I thought she was, until she tried making me choose between her and Jessica."

Megan's eyes widened. "Your sister?"

"Yes. Roselyn said she could accept me as being interracial since it wasn't quite as obvious, but there was no way she could accept Jessica as my sister."

Megan felt her anger boiling. "Boy, she had some nerve."

"Yes, she did. I had just met Jessica for the first time a month before and she felt that since Jessica and I didn't have a bond yet, she could make such an ultimatum. But she failed to realize something."

"What?"

"Jessica was my sister, whether Roselyn liked it or not, and I was not going to turn my back on Jessica or deny her just because Roselyn had a problem with it. So I broke things off."

Good for you, Megan thought. "How did your grandparents feel about you ending things?"

"They weren't happy about it, at least until I told them why. They weren't willing to make the same mistake twice. They were pretty damn vocal against my mother marrying my father, and they almost lost her when Mom stopped speaking to them for nearly two years. There was no way they would risk losing me with that same foolishness."

"You're close to your grandparents?"

"Yes, very close."

"And your father? I take it the two of you are no longer close."

She saw how his jaw tightened and knew the answer before he spoke a single word. "That's right. What he did was unforgivable, and neither Jess, Savannah or I have seen him in almost eighteen years."

"That's sad."

"Yes, it is," he said quietly.

Megan wondered if the separation had been his father's decision or his but decided not to pry. However, there was another question—a very pressing one—that she needed answered right away. "Uh, do you plan to stop again anytime soon?" She recalled he'd said he had stopped for gas while she was asleep. Now she was awake, and she had needs to take care of.

He chuckled. "You have to go to the little girl's room, do you?"

She grinned. "Yes, you can say that."

"No problem, I'll get off at the next exit."

"Thanks."

He smiled over at her, and she immediately felt her pulse thud and the area between her thighs clench. The man was too irresistible, too darn sexy, for his own good. Maybe she should have taken heed of his warning and not come to Texas. She had a feeling things were going to get pretty darn wild now that they were alone together. Real wild.

CHAPTER TEN

RICO STOPPED IN front of Megan and handed her the key. "This is for your room. Mine is right next door if you need me for anything. No matter how late it is, just knock on the connecting door. Anytime you want."

She grinned at his not-so-subtle, seductive-assin hint as she took the key from him. "Thanks, I'll keep that in mind."

She glanced around. Forbes, Texas, wasn't what she'd imagined. It was really a nice place. Upon arriving to town, Rico had taken her to one of the restaurants for lunch. It was owned by a Mexican family. In fact, most of the townspeople were Mexican, descended from the settlers who had founded the town back in the early 1800s. She had been tempted to throw Raphel's name out there to see if any of them had ever heard of him but had decided not to. She had promised Rico she would let him handle the investigation, and she intended to keep her word.

"You can rest up while I make a few calls. I want to contact Fanny Banks's family to see if we can visit in a day or so."

"That would be nice," she said as they stepped on the elevator together. The lady at the front desk had told them the original interior of the hotel had caught fire ten years ago and had been rebuilt, which was why everything inside was pretty modern, including the elevator. From the outside, it looked like a historical hotel.

They were the only ones on the elevator, and Rico stood against the panel wall and stared over at her. "Hey, come over here for a minute."

She swallowed, and her nipples pressed hard against her shirt. "Why?"

"Come over here and find out."

He looked good standing over there, and the slow, lazy smile curving his mouth had her feeling hot all over. "Come here, Megan. I promise I won't bite."

She wasn't worried about him taking a bite out of her, but there were other things he could do that were just as lethal and they both knew it. She decided two could play his game. "No, you come over here."

"No problem."

When he made a move toward her, she retreated and stopped when her back touched the wall. "I was just kidding."

"But I kid you not," he said, reaching her and caging her with hands braced against the wall on either side of her. "Open up for me."

"B-but, what if this elevator stops to let more people on? We'll be on our floor any minute."

He reached out and pushed the elevator stop button. "Now we won't." Then he leaned in and plied her mouth with a deep and possessively passionate kiss.

She did as he'd asked. She opened up for him, letting him slide his tongue inside her mouth. He settled the middle of himself against her, in a way that let her feel his solid erection right in the juncture of her thighs. The sensations that swamped her were unreal, and she returned his kiss with just as much hunger as he was showing.

Then, just as quickly as he'd begun, he pulled his mouth away. Drawing in a deep breath, she angled her head back to gaze up at him. "What was that for?"

"No reason other than I want you."

"You told me. Several times," she murmured, trying to get her heart to stop racing and her body to cease tingling. She glanced up at him—the elevator wasn't that big and he was filling it, looking tall, dark and handsome as ever. He was looking her up and down, letting his gaze stroke over her as if it wouldn't take much to strip her naked then and there.

"And I intend to tell you several more times. I plan to keep reminding you every chance I get."

"Why?" Was it some power game he wanted to play? She was certain he had figured out that her experience with men was limited. She had all but told him it was, so what was he trying to prove? Was this just one of the ways he intended to carry out his fact-finding mission? If that was the case, then she might have to come up with a few techniques of her own.

He pushed the button to restart the elevator, and

she couldn't help wondering just where her self-control was when she needed it.

RICO ENTERED HIS hotel room alone and tossed his keys on the desk. Never before had he mixed business with pleasure, but he was doing so now without much thought. He shook his head. No, that wasn't true, because he was giving it a lot of thought. And still none of it made much sense.

He was about to pull off his jacket when his phone rang. He pulled his cell out of his jeans pocket and frowned when he recognized the number. Jeff Claiborne. Couldn't the man understand plain English? He started to let the call go to voice mail but impulsively decided not to.

Rico clicked on the phone. "What part of *do not call me back* did you not understand?"

"I need your help, Ricardo."

Rico gritted his teeth. "My help? The last thing you'll get from me is my help."

"But if I don't get it, I could die. They've threatened to kill me."

Rico heard the desperation in his father's voice. "Who are they?"

"A guy I owe a gambling debt. Morris Cotton."

Rico released an expletive. His grandfather had told Rico a few years ago that he'd heard Jeff Claiborne was into some pretty shady stuff. "Sounds like you have a problem. And I give a damn, why? And please don't say because you're my father."

There was a pause. "Because I'm a human being who needs help."

Rico tilted his head back and stared up at the ceiling. "You say you're in trouble? Your life is threatened?"

"Yes."

"Then go to the police."

"Don't you understand? I can't go to the police. They will kill me unless…"

"Unless what?"

"I come up with one hundred thousand dollars."

Rico's blood boiled with rage. "And you thought you could call the son and daughter you hadn't talked to in close to eighteen years to bail you out? Trust me, there's no love lost here."

"You can't say I wasn't a good father!"

"You honestly think that I can't? You were an imposter, living two lives, and in the end an innocent woman took her life because of you."

"I didn't force her to take those pills."

Rico couldn't believe that even after all this time his father was still making excuses and refusing to take ownership of his actions. "Let me say this once again. You won't get a penny out of me, Jessica or Savannah. We don't owe you a penny. You need money, work for it."

"Work? How am I supposed to work for that much money?"

"You used to be a salesman, so I'm sure you'll think of something."

"I'll call your mother. I heard she remarried, and the man is loaded. Maybe she—"

"I wouldn't advise you to do that," Rico interrupted to warn him. "She's not the woman you made a fool of years ago."

"She was my only wife."

"Yes, but what about Jessica's mother and the lies you told to her? What about how she ended her life because of you?"

There was a pause and then… "I loved them both."

Not for the first time, Rico thought his father was truly pitiful. "No, you were greedy as hell and used them both. They were good women, and they suffered because of you."

There was another pause. "Think about helping me, Ricardo."

"There's nothing to think about. Don't call me back." Rico clicked off the phone and released a deep breath. He then called a friend who happened to be a high-ranking detective in the NYPD.

"Stuart Dunn."

"Stuart, this is Rico. I want you to check out something for me."

A short while later Rico had showered and re-dressed, putting on khakis instead of jeans and a Western-style shirt he had picked up during his first day in Forbes. He knew one surefire way to get information from shop owners was to be a buying customer. Most of the people he'd talked to in town had been too young to remember Clarice. But he had

gone over to the *Forbes Daily Times* to do a little research, since the town hadn't yet digitally archived
their oldest records.

Unfortunately, the day he'd gone to the paper's office, he'd been told he would have to get the permission of the paper's owner before he could view any
documents from the year he wanted. He'd found that
odd, but hadn't put up an argument. His mind had
been too centered on heading to Austin to get Megan.

Now that he had her—and right next door—he
could think of a number of things he wanted to do
with her, and, as far as he was concerned, every one
of them was fair game. But would acting on those
things be a smart move? After all, she was cousin-
in-law to his sisters. But he *had* warned her, not once
but several times. However, just to clear his mind
of any guilt, he would try rattling her to the point
where she might decide to leave. He would give her
one last chance.

And if that didn't work, he would have no regrets, no guilty conscience and no being a nice, keep-
your-hands-to-yourself kind of guy. He would look
forward to putting his hands—his mouth, tongue,
whatever he desired—all over her. And he desired
plenty. He would mix work with pleasure in a way
it had never been done before.

Suddenly, his nostrils flared as he picked up her
scent. Seconds later, there was a knock at his hotel
room door. Amazing that he had actually smelled her
through that hard oak. He'd discovered that Megan
had an incredible scent that was exclusively hers.

He crossed the room and opened the door. There she was, looking so beautiful he felt the reaction in his groin. She had showered and changed clothes, as well. Now she was wearing a pair of jeans and a pullover sweater. She looked spectacular.

"I'm ready to go snooping."

He lifted a brow. "Snooping?"

"Yes, I'm anxious to find out about Raphel, and you mentioned you were going back to the town's newspaper office."

Yes, he had said that in way of conversation during their drive. He figured they had needed to switch their topic back to business or else he would have been tempted to pull to the side of the road and tear away at her mouth again.

"I'm ready," he said, stepping out into the hall and closing his hotel room door behind him. "I thought you would be taking a nap while I checked out things myself."

"I'm too excited to rest. Besides, I slept a lot in the car. Now I'm raring to go."

He saw she was. Her eyes were bright, and he could see excitement written all over her face. "Just keep in mind that this is my investigation. If I come across something I think is of interest I might mention it or I might not."

She frowned up at him as they made their way toward the elevator. "Why wouldn't you share anything you find with me?"

Yes, why wouldn't he? There was still that article Martin Felder had come across. Rico had been barely able to read it from the scan Martin had found on the internet, but what he'd read had made Rico come to Forbes himself to check out things.

"That's just the way I work, Megan. Take it or leave it. I don't have to explain the way I operate to you as long as the results are what you paid me to get."

"I know, but—"

"No buts." He stopped walking, causing her to stop, as well. He placed a stern look on his face. "We either do things my way or you can stay here until I get back." He could tell by the fire that lit her eyes at that moment that he'd succeeded in rattling her.

She crossed her arms over her chest and tilted her head back to glare up at him. "Fine, but your final report better be good."

He bent slowly and brushed a kiss across her lips. "Haven't you figured out yet that everything about me is good?" he whispered huskily.

"Arrogant ass."

He chuckled as he continued brushing kisses across her lips. "Hmm, I like it when you have a foul mouth."

She angrily pushed him away. "I think I'll take the stairs."

He smiled. "And I think I'll take you. Later."

She stormed off toward the door that led to the stairwell. He stared after her. "You're really going to take the stairs?"

"Watch me." She threw the words over her shoulder.

"I am watching you, and I'm rather enjoying the sight of that cute backside of yours right now."

She turned and stalked back over to him. The indignant look on her face indicated he might have pushed her too far. She came to a stop right in front of him and placed her hands on her hips. "You think you're the only one who can do this?"

He intentionally looked innocent. "Do what?"

"Annoy the hell out of someone. Trust me, Rico. You don't want to be around me when I am truly annoyed."

He had a feeling that he really wouldn't. "Why are you getting annoyed about anything? I meant what I said about making love to you later."

She looked up at the ceiling and slowly counted to ten before returning her gaze back to him. "And you think that decision is all yours to make?"

"No, it will be ours. By the time I finish with you, you'll want it as much as I do. I guarantee it."

She shook her head, held up her hand and looked as if she was about to say something that would probably blister his ears. But she seemed to think better of wasting her time doing so, because she tightened her lips together and slowly backed up as if she was trying to retain her control. "I'll meet you downstairs." She'd all but snarled out the words.

He watched her leave, taking the stairs.

Rico rubbed his hand over his jaw. Megan had had a particular look in her eyes that set him on edge. She had every reason to be ticked off with him since he had intentionally pushed her buttons. And now he had a feeling she would make him pay.

THE NERVE OF the man, Megan thought as she took the stairs down to the lobby. When she had decided to take this route she had forgotten that they were on the eighth floor. If she needed to blow off steam, this was certainly one way to do it.

Rico had deliberately been a jerk, and he had never acted that way before. If she didn't know better she would think it had been intentional. Her eyes narrowed suspiciously, and she suddenly slowed her pace. Had it been intentional? Did he assume that if he was rude to her she would pack up and go running back to Denver?

Well, if that's what he thought, she had news for him. It wouldn't happen. Now that she was here in Forbes, she intended to stay, and he would find out that two could play his game.

Not surprisingly, he was waiting for her in the lobby when she finally made it down. Deciding to have it out with him, here and now, she walked over and stared up at him. "I'm ready to take you on, Rico Claiborne."

He smiled. "Think you can?"

"I'm going to try." She continued to hold his gaze, refusing to back down. She felt the hot, explosive chemistry igniting between them and knew he felt it, too.

"I don't think you know what you're asking for, Megan."

Oh, she knew, and if the other night was a sample, she was ready to let loose and let her hair down again. "Trust me, I know."

His smile was replaced with a frown. "Fine. Let's go."

They were on their way out the revolving doors when his cell phone rang. They stopped and he checked his caller ID, hoping it wasn't Jeff Claiborne again, and answered it quickly when he saw it was Fanny Banks's granddaughter returning his call. Moments later, after ending the call, he said to Megan, "Change in plans. We'll go to the newspaper office later. That was Dorothy Banks, and her grandmother can see us now."

CHAPTER ELEVEN

"YES, MAY I help you?"

"Yes, I'm Rico Claiborne and this is Megan West-moreland. You were expecting us."

The woman, who appeared to be in her early fifties, smiled. "Yes, I'm Dorothy Banks, the one you spoke to on the phone. Please come in."

Rico stepped aside to let Megan enter before him and followed her over the threshold, admiring the huge home. "Nice place you have here."

If the house wasn't a historical landmark of some sort then it should be. He figured it had to have been built in the early 1900s. The huge two-story Victorian sat on what appeared to be ten acres of land. The structure of the house included two huge columns, a wraparound porch with spindles, and leaded glass windows. More windows than he thought it needed, but if you were a person who liked seeing what was happening outside, then it would definitely work. The inside was just as impressive. The house seemed to have retained the original hardwood floors and inside walls. The furniture seemed to have been selected to complement the original era of the house.

Because of all the windows, the room had a lot of light from the afternoon sunshine.

"You mentioned something about Ms. Westmoreland being a descendant of Raphel Westmoreland?" the woman asked.

"Yes. I'm helping her trace her family roots, and in our research, the name Clarice Riggins came up. The research indicated she was a close friend of Raphel. Since Ms. Banks was living in the area at the time, around the early nineteen hundreds, we thought that maybe we could question her to see if she recalls anyone by that name."

Dorothy smiled. "Well, I can tell you that, and the answer is yes. Clarice Riggins and my grandmother were childhood friends. Although Clarice died way before I was born, I remember Gramma Fanny speaking of her from time to time when she would share fond memories with us."

Megan had reached out and touched his hand. Rico could tell she had gotten excited at the thought that the Bankses knew something about Clarice.

"But my grandmother is the one you should talk to," Dorothy added.

"We would love to," Megan said excitedly. "Are you sure we won't be disturbing her?"

The woman stood and waved her hand. "I'm positive. My grandmother likes talking about the past." She chuckled. "I've heard most of it more times than I can count. I think she would really appreciate a new set of ears. Excuse me while I go get her. She's sitting on the back porch. The highlight of her day is watching the sun go down."

"And you're sure we won't be disrupting her day?" Megan asked.

"I'm positive. Although I've heard the name Clarice, I don't recall hearing the name of Raphel Westmoreland before. Gramma Fanny will have to tell you if she has."

Megan turned enthusiastic eyes to Rico. "We might be finding out something at last."

"Possibly. But don't get your hopes up, okay?"

"Okay." She glanced around. "This is a nice place. Big and spacious. I bet it's the family home and has been around since the early nineteen hundreds."

"Those were my thoughts."

"It reminds me of our family home and—"

Megan stopped talking when Dorothy returned, walking with an older woman using a cane. Both Megan and Rico stood. Fanny Banks was old, but she didn't look a year past eighty. To think the woman had just celebrated her one-hundredth birthday was amazing.

Introductions were made. Megan thought she might have been mistaken, but she swore she'd seen a hint of distress in Fanny's gaze. Why? In an attempt to assure the woman, Megan took her hand and gently tightened her hold and said, "It's an honor to meet you. Happy belated birthday. I can't believe you're a hundred. You are beautiful, Mrs. Banks."

Happiness beamed in Fanny Banks's eyes. "Thank

you. I understand you have questions for me. And call me Ms. Fanny. Mrs. Banks makes me feel old."

"All right," Megan said, laughing at the teasing. She looked over at Rico and knew he would do a better job of explaining things than she would. The last thing she wanted was for him to think she was trying to take over his job.

They continued to stand until Dorothy got Ms. Fanny settled into an old rocking chair. Understandably, she moved at a slow pace.

"Okay, now what do you want to ask me about Clarice?" Ms. Fanny asked in a quiet tone.

"The person we really want information about is Raphel Westmoreland, who we believe was an acquaintance of Clarice's."

Megan saw that sudden flash of distress again, which let her know she hadn't imagined it earlier. Ms. Fanny nodded slowly as she looked over at Megan. "And Raphel Westmoreland was your grandfather?"

Megan shook her head. "No, he was my great-grandfather, and a few years ago we discovered he had a twin brother we hadn't known anything about."

She then told Ms. Fanny about the Denver Westmorelands and how they had lost Raphel's only two grandsons and their wives in a plane crash, leaving fifteen of them without parents. She then told Fanny how, a few years ago, they discovered Raphel had a twin named Reginald, and how they had begun a quest to determine if there were more Westmorelands they didn't know about, which had brought them here.

Ms. Fanny looked down at her feeble hands as if studying them…or trying to make up her mind about something. She then lifted her gaze and zeroed in on Megan with her old eyes. She then said, "I'm so sorry to find out about your loss. That must have been a difficult time for everyone."

She then looked down at her hands again. Moments later, she looked up and glanced back and forth between Rico and Megan. "The two of you are forcing me to break a promise I made several years ago, but I think you deserve to know the truth."

Nervous tension flowed through Megan. She glanced over at Rico, who gazed back at her before he turned his attention back to Ms. Fanny and asked, "And what truth is that?"

The woman looked over at her granddaughter, who only nodded for her to continue. She then looked at Megan. "The man your family knew as Raphel Westmoreland was an imposter. The real Raphel Westmoreland died in a fire."

Megan gasped. "No." And then she turned and collapsed in Rico's arms.

"MEGAN," RICO WHISPERED softly as he stroked the side of her face with his fingertips. She'd fainted, and poor Ms. Fanny had become nervous that she'd done the wrong thing, while her granddaughter had rushed off to get a warm facecloth, which he was using to try to bring Megan back around.

He watched as she slowly opened her eyes and looked at him. He recognized what he saw in her gaze. A mixture of fear and confusion. "She's wrong, Rico. She has to be. There's no way my great-grand-father was not who he said he was."

Rico was tempted to ask why was she so certain but didn't want to upset her any more than she already was. "Then come on, sit up so we can listen to her tell the rest of it and see, shall we?"

Megan nodded and pulled herself up to find she was still on the sofa. There was no doubt in her mind that both Ms. Fanny and Dorothy had heard what she'd just said. Manners prompted her to apologize. "I'm sorry, but what you said, Ms. Fanny, is over-whelming. My great-grandfather died before I was born so I never knew him, but all those who knew him said he was a good and honest person."

Ms. Fanny nodded. "I didn't say that he wasn't, dear. What I said is that he wasn't the real Raphel."

Tightening his hand on Megan's, Rico asked, "If he wasn't Raphel, then who was he?"

Ms. Fanny met Rico's gaze. "An ex-convict by the name of Stephen Mitchelson."

"An ex-convict!" Megan exclaimed, louder than she'd intended to.

"Yes."

Megan was confused. "B-but how? Why?"

It took Ms. Fanny a while before she answered then she said, "It's a long story."

"We have time to listen," Rico said, glancing over at Megan. He was beginning to worry about her.

Finding out upsetting news like this was one of the reasons he hadn't wanted her here, yet he had gone and brought her anyway.

"According to Clarice, she met Raphel when she was visiting an aunt in Wyoming. He was a drifter moving from place to place. She told him about her home here and told him if he ever needed steady work to come here and her father would hire him to work on their ranch."

She paused a moment and then said, "While in Wyoming, she met another drifter who was an ex-con by the name of Stephen Mitchelson. She and Stephen became involved, and she became pregnant. But she knew her family would never accept him, and she thought she would never see him again."

Ms. Fanny took a sip of water from the glass her granddaughter handed her. "Only the man who showed up later, here in Texas, wasn't Raphel but Stephen. He told her Raphel had died in a fire. To get a fresh start, he was going to take Raphel's identity and start a new life elsewhere. And she let him go, without even telling him she was pregnant with his child. She loved him that much. She wanted to give him a new beginning."

Ms. Fanny was quiet for a moment. "I was there the day she made that decision. I was there when he drove away and never looked back. I was also there when she gave birth to their child. Alone."

The room was silent and then Megan spoke softly. "What happened to her and the baby?"

"She left here by train to go stay with extended

family in Virginia. Her father couldn't accept she had a baby out of wedlock. But she never made it to her destination. The train she was riding on derailed, killing her and the baby."

"My God," Megan said, covering her hands with her face. "How awful," she said. A woman who had given up so much had suffered such a tragic ending.

She drew in a deep breath and wondered how on earth she was going to return home to Denver and tell her family that they weren't Westmorelands after all.

SEVERAL HOURS LATER, back in his hotel room, Rico sat on the love seat and watched as Megan paced the floor. After leaving the Bankses' house, they had gone to the local newspaper office, and the newspaper articles they'd read hadn't helped matters, nor had their visit to the courthouse. The newspapers had verified the train wreck and that Clarice and her child had been killed. There was also a mention of the fire in Wyoming and that several men had been burned beyond recognition.

There were a lot of unanswered questions zigzagging through Rico's mind but he pushed them aside to concentrate on Megan. At the moment, she was his main concern. He leaned forward and rested his arms on his thighs. "If you're trying to walk a hole in the floor, you're doing a good job of it."

She stopped, and when he saw the sheen of tears in her eyes, he was out of his seat in a flash. He was unsure of what he would say, but he knew he had to say something. "Hey, none of that," he whispered quietly, pulling her into his arms. "We're going to figure this out, Megan."

She shook her head and pushed away from him. "This is all my fault. In my eagerness to find out everything about Raphel, I may have caused the family more harm than good. You heard Fanny Banks. The man everyone thought was Raphel was some ex-convict named Stephen Mitchelson. What am I going home to say? We're not really Westmorelands, we're Mitchelsons?"

He could tell by the sound of her voice she was really torn up over what Fanny Banks had said. "But there might be more to what she said, Megan."

"But Fanny Banks was there, Rico," she countered. "I always said there was a lot about my great-grandfather that we didn't know. He went to his grave without telling anyone anything about having a twin brother or if he had family somewhere. Now I know why. He probably didn't know any of Raphel's history. He could never claim anyone. I don't know how the fourth woman named Isabelle fits in, but I do know Raphel—Stephen— finally settled down with my great-grandmother Gemma. From the diary she left behind, the one that Dillon let me read, I know they had a good marriage, and she always said he was a kind-hearted man. He certainly didn't sound like the kind who would have been an ex-con. The only thing I ever heard about Raphel was that he was a kind, loving and honorable man."

"That still might be the case, Megan."

As if she hadn't heard him, she said, "I have to face the possibility that the man my father and uncle idolized, the man they thought was the best grandfather in the entire world, was nothing but a convict who wasn't Raphel Westmoreland and—"

"Shh, Megan," he whispered, breaking in and pulling her closer into his arms. "Until we find out everything, I don't want you getting upset or thinking the worst. We'll go to the courthouse tomorrow and dig around some more."

Sighing deeply, she pulled away from him, swiped at more tears and tilted her head back to look up at him. "I need to be alone for a while so I'm going to my room. Thanks for the shoulder to cry on."

Rico shoved his hands into the pockets of his khakis. "What about dinner?"

"I'm not hungry. I'll order room service later."

"You sure?"

She shrugged. "Right now, Rico, I'm not sure about anything. That's why I need to take a shower and relax."

He nodded. "Are you going to call Dillon or Ramsey and tell them the latest developments?"

She shook her head. "Not yet. It's something I wouldn't be able to tell them over the phone anyway." She headed for the door. "Good night. I'll see you in the morning."

"Try to get some sleep," he called out to her. She nodded but kept walking and didn't look back. She opened the connecting door and then closed it behind her.

Rico rubbed his hand down his face, feeling frustration and anger all rolled into one. He glanced at his watch and pulled his cell phone out of his back pocket. A few moments later a voice came on the line. "Hello."

"This is Rico. A few things came up that I want you to check out." He spent the next twenty minutes bringing Martin up to date on what they'd found out from Fanny Banks.

"And you're actually questioning the honesty of a one-hundred-year-old woman?"

"Yes."

Martin moaned. "Ah, man, she's one hundred."

"I know."

"All right. In that case, I'll get on it right away. If the man was an imposter then I'll find out," Martin said. "But we are looking back during a time when people took on new identities all the time."

That's the last thing Rico wanted to hear.

After hanging up the phone he stared across the room at the door separating him from Megan. Deciding to do something with his time, before he opened the connecting door, he grabbed his jacket and left to get something to eat.

AN HOUR LATER, Megan had showered, slipped into a pair of pajamas and was lounging across her bed when she heard the sound of Rico returning next door. When she'd knocked on the connecting door earlier and hadn't gotten a response, she figured he had gone to get something to eat. She had ordered

room service and had wanted to know if he wanted
to share since the hotel had brought her plenty.

Now she felt fed and relaxed and more in control of her emotions. And what she appreciated more
than anything was that when she had needed him the
most, Rico had been there. Even while in the base-
ment of the newspaper office, going through micro-
film of old newspapers and toiling over all those
books to locate the information they wanted, he had
been there, ready to give her a shoulder to cry on if
she needed one. And when she had needed one, after
everything had gotten too emotional for her, she'd
taken him up on his offer.

He had been in his room for no more than ten minutes when she heard a soft knock on the connecting
door. "Come in."

He slowly opened the door, and when he appeared
in her room the force of his presence was so powerful she had to snatch her gaze away from his and
train it back on the television screen.

"I was letting you know I had returned," he said.

"I heard you moving around," she said, her fingers tightening around the remote.

"You've had dinner?" he asked her.

From out of the corner of her eye, she could see
him leaning in the doorway, nearly filling it completely. "Yes, and it was good."

"What did you have?"

"A grilled chicken salad. It was huge." *Just like
you,* she thought and immediately felt the blush
spread into her features.

"Why are you blushing?"

Did the man not miss anything? "No reason."

"Then why aren't you looking at me?"

Yes, why wasn't she looking at him? Forcing herself to look away from the television, she slid her eyes over to his and immediately their gazes clung. That was the moment she knew why it had been so easy to let her guard down around him, why it had been so effortless to lose her control and why, even now, she was filled with a deep longing and the kind of desire a woman had for the man she loved.

She had fallen in love with Rico.

A part of her trembled inside with that admission. She hadn't known something like this could happen this way, so quickly, completely and deeply. He had gotten to her in ways no other man had. Around him she had let go of her control and had been willing to let emotions flow. Her love hadn't allowed her to hold anything back. And when she had needed his strength, he'd given it. Unselfishly. He had an honorable and loyal spirit that had touched her in ways she'd never been touched before. Yes, she loved him, with every part of her being.

She sucked in a deep breath because she also knew that what she saw in his eyes was nothing more than pent-up sexual energy that needed to be released. And as she continued to watch him, his lips curved into a smile.

Now it was her time to ask all the questions. "Why are you smiling?"

"I don't think you want to know," he said, doing

away with his Eastern accent and replacing it with a deep Texas drawl.

"Trust me, I do." Tonight she needed to think about something other than her grandfather's guilt or innocence, something other than how, in trying to find out about him, she might have exposed her family to the risk of losing everything.

"Since you really want to know," he said, straightening his stance and slowly coming toward her. "I was thinking of all the things I'd just love to do to you."

His words made her nipples harden into peaks, and she felt them press hard against her pajama top. "Why just think about it, Rico?"

He stopped at the edge of the bed. "Don't tempt me, Megan."

She tilted her head to gaze up at him. "And don't tempt me, Rico."

"What do you know about temptation?"

She became caught up by the deep, sensuous look in his eyes. In one instant, she felt the need to look away, and then, in another instant, she felt the need to be the object of his stare. She decided to answer him the best way she knew how. "I know it's something I've just recently been introduced to," she said, remembering the first time she'd felt this powerful attraction, at Micah's wedding.

"And I know just how strong it was the first time I saw you. Something new for me. Then I remember our first kiss, and how the temptation to explore more was the reason I hadn't wanted it to end," she whispered softly.

"But I really discovered what temptation was the night you used your mouth on me," she said, not believing they were having this sort of conversation or that she was actually saying these things. "I've never known that kind of pleasure before, or the kind of satisfaction I experienced when you were finished, and it tempted me to do some things to you, to touch you and taste you."

She saw the darkening of his eyes, and the very air became heated, sensuously so. He reached out, extending his hand to hers, and she took it. He gently pulled her up off the bed. The feel of the hard, masculine body pressed against hers, especially the outline of his arousal through his khakis, made her shiver with desire. When his hand began roaming all over her, she drew in a deep breath.

"I want to make love to you, Megan," he said, lowering his head to whisper in her ear. "I've never wanted a woman as much as I want you."

For some reason she believed him. Maybe it was because she wanted to believe. Or it could be that she wanted the feeling of being in his arms. The feeling of him inside her while making love. She wanted to be the woman who could satisfy him as much as he could satisfy her.

He tilted her chin up so their gazes could meet again. She was getting caught up in every sexy thing about him, even his chin, which looked like it needed a shave, and his hair, which seemed to have grown an inch and touched his shoulders. And then he leaned down and captured her mouth in one long, drugging kiss. Pleasure shot to all parts of her body, and her nerve endings were bombarded with all sorts of sensations while he feasted on her mouth like it was the last morsel he would ever taste.

At that moment, she knew what she wanted. She wanted to lose control in a way she'd never lost it before. She wanted to get downright wild with it.

She pulled back from the kiss and immediately went for his shirt, nearly tearing off the buttons in her haste. "Easy, baby. What are you doing?"

"I need to touch you," she said softly.

"Then here, let me help," he said, easing his shirt from his shoulders. A breathless moan slipped from her throat. The man was so perfectly made she could feel her womb convulsing, clinching with a need she was beginning to understand.

Her hand went to his belt buckle and within seconds she had slid it out of the loops to toss it on the floor. On instinct, she practically licked her lips as she eased down his zipper. Never had she been this bold with a man, never this brazen. But something was driving her to touch him, to taste him, the same way he had done to her last night.

All she could register in her mind was that this scenario was one she had played out several times in her dreams. The only thing was, all the other times she would wake up. But this was reality at its best.

"Let me help you with this, as well," he whispered.

And then she watched as he eased his jeans and briefs down his legs and revealed an engorged erection. He was huge, and on instinct, her hand reached out and her fingers curled around the head. She heard how his breathing changed. How he was forcing air into his lungs.

When she began moving her fingers, getting to know this part of him, she felt rippling muscles on every inch of him. The thick length of his aroused shaft filled her hand and then some. This was definitely a fine work of art. Perfect in every way. Thick. Hard. With large veins running along the side.

"Do you have what you want?" he asked in a deep, husky tone.

"Almost." And that was the last word she spoke before easing down to her knees and taking him into her mouth.

A BREATHLESS GROAN escaped from between Rico's lips. He gripped the curls on Megan's head and threw his head back as her mouth did a number on him. He felt his muscles rippling as her tongue tortured him in ways he didn't know were possible. Her head, resting against his belly, shifted each time her mouth moved and sent pleasurable quivers all through him.

He felt his brain shutting down as she licked him from one end to the other, but before it did, he had to know something. "Who taught you this?"

The words were wrenched from his throat, and he had to breathe hard. She paused a moment to look up at him. "I'll tell you later."

She then returned to what she was doing, killing him softly and thoroughly. What was she trying to do? Lick him dry and swallow him whole? Damn, it felt like it. Every lick of her tongue was causing him to inhale, and every long powerful suck was forcing him to exhale. Over and over again. He felt on the edge of exploding, but forced himself not to. He wanted it to be just like in his dreams. He wanted to spill inside of her.

"Megan." He gently tugged on a section of her hair, while backing up to pull out of her mouth.

And before she could say anything, he had whipped her from her knees and placed her on the bed, while removing her pajama top and bottoms in the process. He wanted her, and he wanted her now.

Picking up his jeans off the floor, he retrieved a condom packet from his wallet and didn't waste any time while putting it on. He glanced at her, saw her watching and saw how her gaze roamed over his entire body. "Got another question for you, Megan, and you can't put off the answer until later. I need to know now."

She shifted her gaze from below his waist up to face. "All right. What's your question?"

"How is your energy level?"

She lifted a brow. "My energy level?"

"Yes."

"Why do you want to know?"

"Because," he said, slowly moving toward the bed. "I plan to make love to you all night."

CHAPTER TWELVE

ALL NIGHT?

Before Megan had time to digest Rico's proc-
lamation, he had crawled on the bed with her and
proceeded to pull her into his arms and seize her
mouth. They needed to talk. There were other things
he needed to know besides her energy level; things
she wanted to tell him. She wanted to share with him
what was in her heart but considering what they were
sharing was only temporary, it wouldn't be a good
idea. The last thing she wanted was for him to feel
guilty about not reciprocating her feelings. And then
there was the issue of her virginity. He didn't have a
clue right now, but pretty soon he would, she thought
as he slid his tongue between her lips.

His skin, pressed next to hers, felt warm, intoxi-
cating, and he was kissing her with a passion and
greed that surpassed anything she'd ever known.
There was no time for talking. Just time to absorb
this, take it all in and enjoy. A shiver ran through her
when he released her mouth and lowered his head to
aim for her breasts, sucking a nipple.

He really thought they could survive an all-
nighter? she asked herself. No way. And when he

reached down to slide his fingers between her legs and stroked her there, she moaned out his name. "Rico."

He paid her no mind, but continued to let his mouth lick her hardened nipple, while his hand massaged her clit, arousing her to the point where jolts of pleasure were running through her body.

She knew from his earlier question that he assumed she was experienced with this sort of thing. Little did he know she was as green as a cucumber. Again she thought, he needed to be told, but not now. Instead, she reached out to grip his shoulders as his fingers circled inside of her, teasing her mercilessly and spreading her scent in the air.

Then he leaned up, leaving her breasts. Grabbing a lock of her hair with his free hand, he tugged, pulling her face to his and kissing her hard on the mouth, sending her passion skyrocketing while shock waves of pleasure rammed through her.

He pulled his mouth from hers and whispered against her moist lips. "You're ready for me now. You're so wet I can't wait any longer," he said, nibbling on her earlobe and running his tongue around the rim of her ear, so close that she could feel his hot breath.

He moved to slide between her legs and straddle her thighs, looked down at her and whispered, "I'm going to make it good for you, baby. The best you've ever had."

She opened her mouth to tell him not only would it be the best, but that it would also be the first she

ever had when his tongue again slid between her lips.
That's when she felt him pressing hard against her,
trying to make an entry into her.

"You're tight, baby. Relax," he whispered against
her cheek as he reached down and grabbed his penis,
guiding it into her. He let the head stroke back and
forth along her folds. She started moaning and
couldn't stop. "There, you're letting go. Now I can
get inside you," he whispered huskily.

"It's not going to be easy," she whispered back.

He glanced down at her. "Why do you say that?"
he asked as he continued to stroke her gently, sliding back and forth through her wetness.

Megan knew he deserved an answer. "I'm tight
down there for a reason, Rico."

"What reason is that?"

"Because I've never made love with a man before."

His hand went still. "Are you saying—"

"Yes, that's what I'm saying. But I've never
wanted any man before." *Never loved one before
you,* she wanted to say, but didn't. "Don't let that stop
you from making love to me tonight, Rico."

He leaned in and gently kissed her lips. "Nothing
can stop me from making love to you, sweetheart. I
couldn't stop making love to you tonight even if my
life depended on it."

And then he was kissing her again, this time with
a furor that had her trembling. Using his knees, he
spread her legs wider, and she felt the soft fabric
against her skin when he grabbed a pillow to ease

under her backside. He pulled back from the kiss. "I wish I could tell you it's not going to hurt. But…"

"Don't worry about it. Just do it."

He looked down at her. "Just do it?"

"Yes, and please do it now. I can't wait any longer. I've waited twenty-seven years for this, Rico." *And for you.*

She looked dead center into his eyes. She felt the head of him right there at her mound. He reached out and gently stroked the side of her face and whispered, "I want to be looking at you when I go inside of you."

Their gazes locked. She felt the pressure of him entering her and then he grabbed her hips, whispered for her to hold on and pushed deeper with a powerful thrust.

"Rico!" she cried out, but he was there, lowering his head and taking her mouth while he pushed even farther inside her, not stopping until he was buried deep. And then, as if on instinct, her inner muscles began clenching him hard.

He threw his head back and released a guttural moan. "What are you doing to me?"

He would ask her that. "I don't know. It just feels right" was the only reply she could give him. In response, he kissed her again while his lower body began moving. Slowly at first, as if giving her body time to adjust. And then he changed the rhythm, while leaning down to suck on her tongue.

Megan thought she was going to go out of her mind. Never had she thought, assumed, believed—until now. He was moving at a vigorous pace, and she cried out, not in pain but in sensations so pleasurable they made her respond out loud.

Her insides quivered, and she went after his tongue with speed and hunger. She cried out, screamed, just like she'd done that night at the south ridge. That only made him thrust harder and penetrate deeper. Then they both ignited in one hell of an explosion that sent sparks flying all through her body, and especially to the area where their bodies were joined.

He shook, she shook and the bed shook almost off the hinges as he continued to pound into her… making her first time a time she would always remember. It seemed as if it took forever for them to come down off their orgasmic high. When they did, he shifted his weight off hers and pulled her to him.

"We'll rest up a bit," he said silkily. "How do you feel?"

She knew her eyes were filled with wonderment at what they'd done. "I feel good." And she meant it.

Her heart was beating fast, and her pulse was off the charts. She had totally and completely lost control. But all that was fine because she had gotten the one thing she'd wanted. A piece of Rico Claiborne.

RICO PULLED HER closer to him, tucked her body into the curve of his while he stroked a finger across her cheek. He'd only left the bed to dispose of the condom and get another. Now he was back and needed the feel of her in his arms. She had slept for a while, but now she was awake and he had questions.

"I think it's time to tell me how someone who

can work their mouth on a man the way you do has managed to remain a virgin. I can think of one possibility, but I want to hear it from you."

She smiled up at him. "What? That I prefer oral sex to the real thing?" She shook her head. "That's not it, and just to set the record straight, I've never gone down on a man until you."

He leaned back and lifted a brow. "Are you saying that—"

"Yes. What I did to you tonight was another first for me."

He chuckled. "Hell, you could have fooled me."

Excitement danced in her eyes. "Really? I was that good?"

"Yeah," he said, running a finger across her cheek again. "Baby, you were that good. So, if I was your first, how did you know what to do?"

She snuggled closer to him. "I was snooping over at Zane's place one day, looking for a pair of shoes I figured I'd left there, and came across this box under his bed. I was curious enough to look inside and discovered a bunch of DVDs marked with *X*s. So of course I had to see what was on them."

Rico chuckled again. "Is that the box he mentioned he would get from you after dinner the other night?"

She smiled. "No, that's another box altogether, a lock box. So he would know if I had tampered with it. Those videos were in a shoe box, and to this day I've never told Zane about it. I was only seventeen at the time, but I found watching them pretty darn fascinating. I was curious about how a woman could give a man pleasure that way, with her mouth."

"But not curious enough to try it on anyone until now?"

There was amusement in his voice, but to her it wasn't amusing, not even a little bit, because what he'd said was true. She hadn't had any desire to try it out on any other man but him. "Yes."

"I'm glad. I'm also surprised you've never been curious enough to sleep with anyone."

"I couldn't see myself sharing a bed with a man just for the sake of curiosity. Had I been in a serious relationship things might have been different, but most of my life has been filled with either going to school or working. I never had time for serious relationships. And the few times that a man wanted to make it serious, I just wasn't feeling it."

But she hadn't had a problem feeling him. She had wanted him. Had wanted to taste him the way he had tasted her. Had wanted to put her mouth on him the same way he'd put his on her. And she didn't regret doing so.

But nothing had prepared her for when he had shed his pants and briefs and shown his body to her. He was so magnificently made, with a masculine torso and rippling muscles. What had captured her attention more than anything else was the engorged erection he had revealed. Seeing it had aroused her senses and escalated her desires.

But for her, last night had been about more than just sex. She loved him. She wasn't certain just how she felt being in a one-sided love affair, but she wouldn't worry about it for now. She had let her hair down and was enjoying the situation tremendously. She had been in control of her emotions for so long, and she'd thought that was the best way to be, but now she was seeing a more positive side of being out of control. She knew what it felt like to be filled with a need that only one man could take care of. She knew how it felt to be wild.

And she wanted to experience more of it.

She pulled away from Rico and shifted her body to straddle his.

"Hey, what do you think you're doing?" he asked, trying to pull her back into his arms.

She shook her head. "Taking care of this," she whispered. "You said I can have control so I'm claiming ownership. You also told me you wanted me, and you told me what would happen if we were together. It did happen, and now I want to show you how much I want you."

"But you're sore."

She chuckled. "And I'll probably be sore for a long time. You aren't a small man, you know. But I can handle it, and I can handle you. I want to handle you, Rico, so let me."

He held her gaze, and the heat radiating between them filled the room with desire. His hands lifted and stroked her face, touched her lips that had covered his shaft, and she understood the degree of hunger reflected in his eyes. There was no fighting the intense passion they seemed to generate. No fighting it, and no excusing it.

"Then you are going to handle it, baby. You are the only woman who can," she heard him whisper.

Pleased by what he said, she lowered her head, and he snagged her mouth by nibbling at her lips, stroking them with his tongue. She gripped his shoulders, and his erection stood straight up, aimed right for her womanly core like it had a mind of its own and knew what it wanted.

The need to play around with his mouth drove her to allow his tongue inside her lips. And then she toyed with his tongue, sucked on it and explored every aspect of his mouth. The way his hand was digging into her scalp made her tongue lash out even more, and she felt him tremble beneath her. The thought that she could make him feel this way, give him this much pleasure, sent her blood rushing through her veins.

She eased the lower part of her body down but deliberately did it in a way that had his penis under her and not inside of her. Then she moved her thighs to grind herself against his pubic bone.

"Oh, hell." The words rushed from his lips, and she closed her eyes, liking the feel of giving him such an intimate massage. Moving back and forth, around in circular motions, christening his flesh with her feminine essence.

"I need you now, Megan. I can't take any more." His voice was filled with torment. Deciding to put him out of his misery, she leaned up and positioned her body so he could slide inside of her.

Megan shuddered when she felt the head of his shaft pierce through her wetness, pushing all the way until it could go no more. She held his gaze as she began to ride him. She'd always heard that she was good at riding a horse, and she figured riding a man couldn't be much different. So she rode him. Easing lower then easing back up, she repeated the steps until they became a sensual cycle. She heard his growl of pleasure, and the sound drove her to ride him hard.

Grabbing her hips, he lifted his own off the bed to push deeper inside of her. "Aw, hell, you feel so damn good, Megan." His shaft got even larger inside of her, burying deeper.

His words triggered a need within her, a need that was followed by satisfaction when her body exploded. She screamed and continued coming apart until she felt his body explode, as well. Pleasure was ripping through her, making it hard to breathe. He was rock-solid, engorged, even after releasing inside of her. He wouldn't go down. It was as if he wasn't through with her yet.

He shifted their bodies, pulling her beneath him with her back to him. "Let me get inside you this way, baby. I want to ride you from behind."

Pulling in as much energy as she could, she eased up on all fours, and no sooner had she done so than she felt the head of his erection slide into her. And then he began moving, slowly at first, taking long, leisurely strokes. Each one sent bristles of pleasure brushing over her. But then he increased the rhythm and made the strokes deeper, harder, a lot more provocative as he rode her from the back. She moved her hips against him, felt his stomach on the cheeks of her backside while his hand caressed her breasts.

She glanced over her shoulder, their gazes connected, and she saw the heated look in his eyes. It fueled even more desire within her, making her moan and groan his name aloud.

"Rico."

"That sounds good, baby. Now I want to hear you say 'Ricardo.'"

As spasms of pleasure ripped through her, she whispered in a low, sultry voice. "Ricardo."

Hearing her say his birth name made something savage inside of Rico snap. He grabbed her hips as unadulterated pleasure rammed through him, making him ride her harder, his testicles beating against her backside. The sound of flesh against flesh echoed loudly through the room and mingled with their moans and groans.

And then it happened. The moment he felt her inner muscles clamp down on him, felt her come all over him, he exploded. He wouldn't be surprised if the damn condom didn't break from the load. But, at that moment, the only thing he wanted to do was fill her with his essence. Only her. No other woman.

He continued to shudder, locked tight inside of her. He threw his head back and let out a fierce, primal growl. The same sound a male animal made when he found his true mate. As pleasure continued to rip through him, he knew, without a shadow of a doubt, that he had found his.

He lowered his head and slipped his tongue inside her mouth, needing the connection as waves of pleasure continued to pound into him. It seemed to take forever before the last spasm left his body. But he couldn't move. Didn't want to. He just wanted to lie there and stay intimately connected to her.

But he knew being on all fours probably wasn't a comfortable position for her, so he eased their bodies down in a way that spooned his body against hers but kept him locked inside of her. He needed this moment of just lying with her, being inside of her while holding her in his arms.

She was so damn perfect. What they'd just shared had been so out-of-this-world right. He felt fulfilled in a way he had never felt before, in a way he hadn't thought he was capable of feeling.

"Anything else you think I ought to know?" he asked, wrapping his arms around her, liking the feel of her snuggled tightly to him.

"There is this thing about you using a condom."

"Mmm, what about it?"

"You can make it optional if you want. I take birth control injections, to stay regulated, so I'm good."

He had news for her. She was better than good. "Thanks for telling me."

"And I'm healthy so I'm safe that way, as well," she added.

"So am I," he assured her softly, gently rubbing her stomach, liking the knowledge that the next time they made love they could be skin-to-skin.

"Rico."

He looked down at her. She had tilted her head back to see him.

"Yes?"

"I like letting go with you. I like getting wild."

He lowered his head to brush a kiss across her lips. "And I like letting go and getting wild with you, too."

And he meant it in a way he wasn't ready to explain quite yet. Right now, he wanted to do the job she had hired him to do. He hadn't accepted everything Ms. Fanny and her daughter had said, although the newspapers and those documents somewhat supported their claims, especially the details of the fire and the train wreck. There was still a gut feeling that just wouldn't go away.

Something wasn't adding up, but he couldn't pinpoint what it was. He had been too concerned about the impact of their words on Megan to take the time to dissect everything. He hadn't been on top of his A-game, which is one of the reasons he hadn't wanted her here. He tended to focus more on her than on what he was supposed to be doing.

But now, as he replayed everything that had transpired over the past fourteen hours in his mind, a lot of questions were beginning to form. In the morning, he would talk to Megan over breakfast. Right now, he just wanted to hold her in his arms for a while, catch a little sleep and then make love to her again.

If he had thought he was addicted to her before, he knew he was even more so now.

CHAPTER THIRTEEN

"I THINK FANNY Banks's story isn't true."

Megan peered across the breakfast table at Rico. It took a few seconds for his words to fully sink in. "You do?"

"Yes. Someone is trying to hide something."

Serious doubt appeared in her gaze. "I don't know, Rico. What could they be trying to hide? Besides, we saw the articles in the newspapers, which substantiated what she said."

"Did they?"

Megan placed her fork down and leaned back in her chair. "Look, I admit I was upset by what I learned, and I wish more than anything that Fanny Banks might have gotten her information wrong or that at one hundred years old she couldn't possibly remember anything. But her memory is still sharp."

"Too sharp."

Megan leaned forward, wondering why he suddenly had a doubtful attitude. "Okay, why the change of heart? You seemed ready to accept what she said."

"Yes, I was too ready. I was too quick to believe it because, like you, I thought it made sense, especially after reading those newspaper articles. But last night while you slept, I lay there and put things together in my mind and there's one thing that you and I can't deny that we didn't give much thought to."

She lifted a brow. "And what is that?"

"It's no coincidence that the Westmorelands of Atlanta and the Denver Westmorelands favor. And I don't mean a little bit. If you put them in a room with a hundred other people and asked someone to pick out family members, I'd bet ninety-eight percent of all the Westmorelands in the room would get grouped together."

Megan opened her mouth to say something and then decided there was nothing she could say because he was right. The first time the two groups had gotten together, and Dare Westmoreland—one of the Atlanta Westmorelands who was a sheriff in the metro area—had walked into the room, every member of the Denver Westmorelands' jaws had dropped. He and Dillon favored so much it was uncanny.

"And that level of similarity in looks can only come from the same genes," Rico added. "If push comes to shove, I'll have DNA testing done."

She picked up her fork. "You still haven't given me a reason for Ms. Banks to make up such a story."

Rico tossed down his napkin. "I don't have a reason, Megan, just a gut feeling."

He reached across the table and took her hand in his. "I saw yesterday that what she said took a toll on you and that became my main concern. I got caught up in your hurt and pain. I felt it, and I didn't want that for you."

She understood what he meant. Last night, making love to him had been an eye opener. She had felt connected to him in a way she'd never been connected to a man. She was in tune to her emotions and a part of her felt in tune to his, as well. Their time together had been so special that even now the memories gave her pause. "If your theory is true, how do we prove it?" she asked him.

"We don't. We visit them again and ask questions we didn't ask yesterday when our minds were too numb to do so."

He gently tightened his hold on her hand. "I need you to trust me on this. Will you do that?"

She nodded. "Yes, I will trust you."

AFTER MAKING A call to the Banks ladies after breakfast, they discovered they would have to put their visit on hold for a while. Dorothy Banks's daughter advised them that her mother and great-grandmother weren't at home and had gone on a day trip to Brownwood and wouldn't be returning until that evening.

So Rico and Megan went back to their hotel. The moment they walked into the room he gently grabbed her wrist and tugged her to him. "You okay? How is the soreness?"

He found it odd to ask her that since he'd never asked a woman that question before. But then he couldn't recall ever being any woman's first.

She rested her palms on his chest and smiled up at him. "My body is fine. Remember, I do own a horse that I ride every day, and I think that might have helped some." She paused and then asked, "What about you?"

He raised a brow. "Me?"

"Yes," she said, smiling. "I rode you pretty darn hard."

Yes, she had. The memory of her doing so made his erection thicken against her. "Yes, but making love with you was amazing," he said, already feeling the air crackling with sexual energy. "Simply incredible. I enjoyed it tremendously."

Her smile widened, as if she was pleased. "Did you?"

"Yes. I can't really put it into words."

She leaned closer and ran the tip of her tongue alongside his lips. Tempting him. Seducing him, slowly and deliberately. "Then show me, Rico. Show me how much you enjoyed it. Let's get wild again."

He was already moving into action, tugging off his shirt and bending down to remove his shoes and socks. She wanted wild, he would give her wild. Texas wild. Following his lead, she began stripping off her clothes. He lowered his jeans and briefs while watching her ease her own jeans down her thighs. He discovered last night that she wore the cutest panties. Colorful. Sexy. No thongs or bikinis. They were hip-huggers, and she had the shapely hips for them. They looked great on her. Even better off her.

He stood there totally nude while she eased her panties down. She was about to toss them aside when he said, "Give them to me."

She lifted a brow as she tossed them over to him.

He caught them with one hand and then raised them to his nose. He inhaled her womanly scent. His erection throbbed and his mouth watered, making him groan. He tossed her panties aside and looked at her, watching her nipples harden before his eyes.

He lowered his gaze to her sex. She kept things simple, natural. Some men liked bikini or Brazilian, but he preferred natural. She was beautiful there, her womanly core covered with dark curls.

His tongue felt thick in his mouth, and he knew where he wanted it to be. He moved across the room and dropped to his knees in front of her. Grabbing her thighs he rested his head against her stomach and inhaled before he began kissing around her belly button and along her inner and outer thighs. He tasted her skin, licking it all over and branding it as his. And then he came face-to-face with the core of her and saw her glistening folds. With the tip of his tongue, he began lapping her up.

She grabbed hold of his shoulders, dug her fingernails into the blades, but he didn't feel any pain. He felt only pleasure as he continued to feast on her. Savoring every inch of her.

"Rico."

He heard her whimper his name, but instead of letting up, he penetrated her with his tongue, tightened his hold on her hips and consumed her.

He liked having his tongue in her sex, tasting her honeyed juices, sucking her and pushing her into the kind of pleasure only he had ever given her. Only him.

"Rico!"

She called out his name a little more forcefully this time, and he knew why. She removed her hands from his shoulders to dig into his hair as she released another high-pitched scream that almost shook the room. If hotel security came to investigate, it would be all her fault.

Moments later, she finished off her orgasm with an intense moan and would have collapsed to the floor had he not been holding her thighs. He stood. "That was just an appetizer, baby. Now for the meal."

Picking her up in his arms he carried her to the bedroom, but instead of placing her on the bed, he grabbed one of the pillows and moved toward the huge chair. He sat and positioned her in his lap, facing him. Easing up he placed the pillows under his knees.

"Now, this is going to work nicely. You want wild, I'm about to give you wild," he whispered, adjusting her body so that she was straddling him with her legs raised all the way to his shoulders. He lifted her hips just enough so he could ease into her, liking the feel of being skin-to-skin with her. The wetness that welcomed him as he eased inside made him throb even more, and he knew he must be leaking already, mingling with her wetness.

"You feel so good," he said in a guttural tone. They were almost on eye level, and he saw the deep desire in the depths of her gaze. She moved, gyrating her hips in his lap. Her movement caused him to moan, and then he began moving, setting the rhythm, rocking in place, grasping her hips tightly to receive his upward thrusts. And she met his demands, tilting her hips and pushing forward to meet him.

He could feel heat building between them, sensations overtaking them so intensely that he rocked harder, faster. His thrusts were longer, deeper, even more intense as they worked the chair and each other.

He knew the moment she came. He felt it gush all around him, triggering his own orgasm. He shuddered uncontrollably, as his body did one hell of a blast inside of her. She stared into his face and the look in her eyes told him she had felt his hot release shooting inside of her. And he knew that was another new experience for her. The thought was arousing, and he could only groan raggedly. "Oh, baby, I love coming inside of you. It feels so good."

"You feel good," she countered. And then she was kissing him with a passion that was like nothing he'd ever experienced before. No woman had ever put this much into her kiss. It was raw, but there was something else, something he couldn't define at the moment. It was more than just tongues tangling and mating aggressively. There were emotions beneath their actions. He felt them in every part of his body.

He would have given it further thought if she hadn't moved her mouth away to scream out another orgasm. As she sobbed his name, he felt his body explode again, as well. He cried out her name over and over as he came, increasing the rocking of the chair until he was convinced it would collapse beneath them.

But it didn't. It held up. Probably better than they did, he thought, as they fought for air and the power to breathe again. Megan's head fell to his chest and he rubbed her back gently. Passion had his vision so blurred he could barely see. But he could feel, and what he was feeling went beyond satisfying his lust for her. It was much deeper than that. With her naked body connected so tightly to his, he knew why they had been so in tune with each other from the first. He understood why the attraction had been so powerful that he hadn't been able to sleep a single night since without dreaming of her.

He loved her.

There was no other way to explain what he was feeling, no other way to explain why spending the rest of his life without her was something he couldn't do. He pulled in a deep breath before kissing her shoulder blades. When he felt her shiver, his erection began hardening inside of her all over again.

She felt it and lifted her head to stare at him with languid eyes, raising both brows. "You're kidding, right? You've just got to be."

He smiled and combed his hands through the thick curls on her head. "You said you wanted wild," he murmured softly.

She smiled and wrapped her hands around his neck, touching her own legs, which were still on his shoulders. "I did say that, didn't I?" she purred, beginning to rotate her hips in his lap.

He eased out of the chair with their bodies still locked together. "Yes, and now I'm going to take you against the wall."

"HEY, YOU AWAKE over there?" Rico asked when he came to a traffic light. He glanced across the truck seat at Megan. She lifted her head and sighed. Never had she felt so satiated in her life. For a minute, she'd thought he would have to carry her out of the hotel room and down to the truck.

They had made love a couple more times after the chair episode. First against the wall like he'd said, and then later, after their nap, they'd made out in the shower. Both times had indeed been wild, and such rewarding experiences. Now she was bone-tired. She knew she would have to perk up before they got to the Bankses' place.

"I'm awake, but barely."

"You wanted it wild," he reminded her.

She smiled drowsily. "Yes, and you definitely know how to deliver."

He chuckled. "Thanks. And that's Texas wild. Wait until I make love to you in Denver and show you Colorado wild."

She wondered if he realized what he'd insinuated. It sounded pretty much like he had every intention of continuing their affair. And since he didn't live in Denver did that mean he planned to come visit her at some point for pleasure rather than business?

Before she could ask him about what he'd said, his cell phone rang. After he checked the ID, Megan heard him let out a low curse. "I thought I told you not to call me."

"You didn't say you would sic the cops on me," Jeffery Claiborne accused.

"I didn't sic the cops on you. I wanted to check out your story. I have, and you lied. You need money for other things, and I'm not buying." He then clicked off the phone.

Megan had listened to the conversation. That was the second time he'd received a similar phone call in her presence. The thought that he was still connected to some woman in some way, even if he didn't want to be bothered, annoyed her. She tried pushing it from her mind and discovered she couldn't. A believer in speaking her mind, she said, "Evidently someone didn't understand your rule about not getting serious."

He glanced over at her. His gaze penetrated hers. "What are you talking about?"

"That call. That's the second time she's called while I was with you."

"She?"

"Yes, I assume it's a female," she said, knowing she really didn't have any right to assume anything.

He said nothing for a minute and then, "No, that wasn't a female. That was the man who used to be my father."

She turned around in her seat. "Your father?" she asked, confirming what he'd said.

"Yes. He's called several times trying to borrow money from me. He's even called Savannah. Claims his life is in jeopardy because he owes a gambling debt. But I found out differently. Seems he has a drug problem, and he was fired from his last job a few months ago because of it."

Now it was her time to pause. Then she said, "So what are you going to do?"

He raised his brow and looked over at her. "What am I going to do?"

"Yes."

"Nothing. That man hurt my mother and because of him Jess lost hers."

Megan swallowed tightly, telling herself it wasn't any of her business, but she couldn't help interfering. "But he's your father, Rico."

"And a piss-poor one at that. I could never understand why he wasn't around for all the times that were important to me while growing up. His excuse was always that as a traveling salesman he had to be away. It never dawned on me, until later, that he really wasn't contributing to the household since we were mostly living off my mother's trust fund."

He stopped at another traffic light and said, "It was only later that we found out why he spent so much time in California. He was living another life with another family. He's never apologized for the pain he caused all of us, and he places the blame on everyone but himself. So, as far as me doing anything for him, the answer is I don't plan on doing a single thing, and I meant what I just told him. I don't want him to call me."

Megan bit down on her lips to keep from saying anything else. It seemed his mind was pretty made up.

"Megan?"

She glanced over at him. "Yes?"

"I know family means a lot to you, and, believe it or not, it means a lot to me, too. But some things you learn to do without…especially if they are no good. Jeff Claiborne is bad news."

"Sounds like he needs help, like drug rehab or something."

"Yes, but it won't be my money paying for it."

His statement sounded final, and Megan had a problem with it. It was just her luck to fall in love with a man who had serious issues with his father. What had the man done to make Rico feel this way? Should she ask him about it? She immediately decided not to. She had enough brothers and male cousins to know when to butt out of their business… until it was a safe time to bring it back up again. And she would.

CHAPTER FOURTEEN

"MR. CLAIBORNE, MS. Westmoreland," Dorothy said, reluctantly opening the door to let them in. "My daughter told me you called. We've told you everything, and I'm not sure it will be good on my grandmother to have to talk about it again."

Rico stared at her. "Just the other day you were saying you thought it would be good for her to talk about it."

"Yes, but that was before I saw what discussing it did to her," she said. "Please have a seat."

"Thanks," he said, and he and Megan sat down on the sofa. "If your grandmother isn't available then perhaps you won't mind answering a few questions for us."

"I really don't know anything other than what Gramma Fanny told me over the years," she said, taking the chair across from them. "But I'll try my best because my grandmother hasn't been herself since your visit. She had trouble sleeping last night and that's not like her. I guess breaking a vow to keep a promise is weighing heavily on her conscience."

For some reason Rico felt it went deeper than

that. "Thanks for agreeing to talk to us." He and Megan had decided that he would be the one asking the questions. "Everybody says your grandmother's memory is sharp as a tack. Is there any reason she would intentionally get certain facts confused?"

The woman seemed taken back. "What are you trying to say, Mr. Claiborne?"

Rico sighed deeply. He hadn't told Megan everything yet, especially about the recent report he'd gotten from Martin while she'd been sleeping. "Stephen Mitchelson was not the one who survived that fire, and I'd like to know why your grandmother would want us to think that he was."

The woman look surprised. "I don't know, but you seem absolutely certain my grandmother was wrong."

He wasn't absolutely certain, but he was sure enough, thanks to the information Martin had dug up on Mitchelson, especially the man's prison photo, which looked nothing like the photographs of Raphel that the Westmorelands had hanging on their wall at the main house in Denver.

He knew Megan was just as surprised by his assertion as Ms. Banks's granddaughter. But there was that gut feeling that wouldn't go away. "It could be that Clarice lied to her about everything," he suggested, although he knew that probably wasn't the case.

"Possibly."

"But that isn't the case, and you know it, don't you, Mr. Claiborne?"

Rico turned when he heard Fanny Banks's frail voice. She was standing in the doorway with her cane.

"Gramma Fanny, I thought you were still sleeping," Dorothy said, rushing over to assist her grandmother.

"I heard the doorbell."

"Well, Mr. Claiborne and Ms. Westmoreland are back to ask you more questions. They think that perhaps you were confused about a few things," Dorothy said, leading her grandmother over to a chair.

"I wasn't confused," the older woman said, settling in her chair. "Just desperate, child."

Confusion settled on Dorothy's face. "I don't understand."

Fanny Banks didn't say anything for a minute. She then looked over at Rico and Megan. "I'm glad you came back. The other day, I thought it would be easier to tell another lie, but I'm tired of lying. I want to tell the truth...no matter who it hurts."

Rico nodded. "And what is the truth, Ms. Fanny?"

"That it was me and not Clarice who went to Wyoming that year and got pregnant. And Clarice, bless her soul, wanted to help me out of my predicament. She came up with this plan. Both she and I were single women, but she had a nice aunt in the East who wanted children, so we were going to pretend to go there for a visit for six months, and I would have the baby there and give my baby to her aunt and uncle. It was the perfect plan."

She paused for a minute. "But a few weeks be-

fore we were to leave, Raphel showed up to deliver
the news that Stephen had died in a fire, and Raphel
wanted me to have the belongings that Stephen left
behind. While he was here, he saw Clarice. I could
see that they were instantly attracted to each other."

Rico glanced over at Megan. They knew firsthand
just how that instant-attraction stuff worked. "Please
go on, Ms. Fanny."

"I panicked. I could see Clarice was starting
something with Raphel, which could result in her
changing our plans about going out East. Especially
when Raphel was hired on by Clarice's father to do
odds and ends around their place. And when she
confided in me that she had fallen in love with Raphel, I knew I had to do something. So I told her that
Raphel was really my Stephen, basically the same
story I told the two of you. She believed it and was
upset with me for not telling him about the baby and
for allowing him to just walk away and start a new
life elsewhere. She had no idea I'd lied. Not telling
him what she knew, she convinced her father Raphel was not safe to have around their place. Her
father fired him."

She paused and rubbed her feeble hands together
nervously. "My selfishness cost my best friend her
happiness with Raphel. He never understood why
she began rebuffing his advances, or why she had
him fired. The day we caught the train for Virginia
is the day he left Forbes. Standing upstairs in my
bedroom packing, we watched him get in his old

truck and drive off. I denied my best friend the one happiness she could have had."

Rico drew in a deep breath when he saw the tears fall from the woman's eyes. "What about the baby? Did Clarice have a baby?"

Ms. Fanny nodded. "Yes. I didn't find out until we reached her aunt and uncle's place that Clarice had gotten pregnant."

Megan gasped. "From Raphel?"

"Yes. She thought she'd betrayed me and that we were having babies from the same man. Even then I never told her the truth. She believed her parents would accept her child out of wedlock and intended to keep it. She had returned to Texas after giving birth only to find out differently. Her parents didn't accept her, and she was returning to Virginia to make a life for her and her baby when the train derailed."

"So it's true, both her and the baby died," Megan said sadly.

"No."

"No?" Rico, Megan and Dorothy asked simultaneously.

"Clarice didn't die immediately, and her son was able to survive with minor cuts and bruises."

"Son?" Megan whispered softly.

"Yes, she'd given birth to a son, a child Raphel never knew about…because of me. The baby survived because Clarice used her body as a shield during the accident."

Fanny didn't say anything for a minute. "We got to the hospital before she died, and she told us about a woman she'd met on the train, a woman who had lost her baby a year earlier…and now the woman had lost her husband in the train wreck. He was killed immediately, although the woman was able to walk away with only a few scratches."

Dorothy passed her grandmother a tissue so she could wipe away her tears. Through those tears, she added, "Clarice, my best friend, who was always willing to make sacrifices for others, who knew she would not live to see the next day, made yet another sacrifice by giving her child to that woman." Ms. Fanny's aged voice trembled as she fought back more tears. "Because she believed my lie, she wasn't certain she could leave her baby with me to raise because I would be constantly reminded of his father's betrayal. And her aunt couldn't afford to take on another child after she'd taken on mine. So Clarice made sure she found her baby a good home before she died."

Megan wiped tears away from her own eyes, looked over at Rico and said softly, "So there might be more Westmorelands out there somewhere after all."

Rico nodded and took her hand and entwined their fingers. "Yes, and if there are, I'm sure they will be found."

Rico glanced back at Fanny, who was crying profusely, and he knew the woman had carried the guilt of what she'd done for years. Now, maybe she would be able to move on with what life she had left.

Standing, Rico extended his hand to Megan. "We have our answers, now it's time for us to go."

Megan nodded and then hugged the older woman. "Thanks for telling us the truth. I think it's time for you to forgive yourself, and my prayer is that you will."

Rico knew then that he loved Megan as deeply as any man could love a woman. Even now, through her own pain, she was able to forgive the woman who had betrayed not only her great-grandfather, but also the woman who'd given birth to his child…a child he hadn't known about.

Taking Megan's hand in his, he bid both Banks women goodbye and together he and Megan walked out the door.

RICO PULLED MEGAN into his arms the moment the hotel room door closed behind them, taking her mouth with a hunger and greed she felt in every portion of his body. The kiss was long, deep and possessive. In response, she wrapped her arms around his neck and returned the kiss with just as much vigor as he was putting into it. Never had she been kissed with so much punch, so much vitality, want and need. She couldn't do anything but melt in his arms.

"I want you, Megan." He pulled back from the kiss to whisper across her lips, his hot breath making her shudder with need.

"And I want you, too," she whispered back, then outlined his lips with the tip of her tongue. She saw the flame that had ignited in his eyes, felt his hard erection pressed against her and knew this man who had captured her heart would have her love forever.

Megan wanted to forget about Ms. Fanny's deceit, her betrayal of Clarice, a woman who would have done anything for her. She didn't want to think about the child Clarice gave up before she died, the child her great-grandfather had never known about. And she didn't want to think of her great-grandfather and how confused he must have been when the woman he had fallen in love with—at first sight—had suddenly not wanted anything to do with him.

She felt herself being lifted up in Rico's arms and carried into the bedroom, where he placed her on the bed. He leaned down and kissed her again, and she couldn't help but moan deeply. When he released her mouth, she whispered, "Let's get wild again."

They reached for each other at the same time, tearing at each other's clothes as desire, as keen as it could get, rammed through her from every direction. They kissed intermittently while undressing, and when all their clothes lay scattered, Rico lifted her in his arms. Instinctively, she wrapped her legs around him. The thickness of him pressed against her, letting her know he was willing, ready and able, and she was eager for the feel of him inside of her.

He leaned forward and took her mouth again. His tongue tasted her as if he intended to savor her until the end of time.

He continued to kiss her, to stimulate her to sensual madness as he walked with her over to the sofa. Once there, he broke off the kiss and stood her up on the sofa, facing him. Sliding his hands between her legs, he spread her thighs wide.

"You still want wild, I'm going to give you wild," he whispered against her lips. "Squat a little for me, baby. I want to make sure I can slide inside you just right."

She bent her knees as he reached out and grabbed her hips. His arousal was hard, firm and aimed right at her, as if it knew just where it should go. To prove that point, his erection unerringly slid between her wet folds.

"Mercy," he said. He inched closer, and their pelvises fused. He leaned forward, drew in a deep breath and touched his forehead to hers. "Don't move," he murmured huskily, holding her hips as he continued to ease inside of her, going deep, feeling how her inner muscles clenched him, trying to pull everything out of him. "I wish our bodies could stay locked together like this forever," he whispered.

She chuckled softly, feeling how deeply inside of her he was, how closely they were connected. "Don't know how housekeeping is going to handle it when they come in our room tomorrow to clean and find us in this position."

She felt his forehead move when he chuckled. His feet were planted firmly on the floor, and she was standing on the sofa. But their bodies were joined in a way that had tingling sensations moving all over her naked skin.

He then pulled his forehead back to look at her. "Ready?"

She nodded. "Yes, I'm ready."

"Okay, then let's rock."

With his hands holding her hips and her arms holding firm to his shoulders, they began moving, rocking their bodies together to a rhythm they both understood. Her nipples felt hard as they caressed his chest, and the way he was stroking her insides made her groan out loud.

"Feel that?" he asked, hitting her at an angle that touched her G-spot and caused all kinds of extraordinary sensations to rip through her. She released a shuddering moan.

"Yes, I feel it."

"Mmm, what about this?" he asked, tilting her hips a little to stroke her from another angle.

"Oh, yes." More sensations cascaded through her.

"And now what about this?" He tightened his hold on her hips, widened her legs even more and began thrusting hard within her. She watched his features and saw how they contorted with pleasure. His eyes glistened with a need and hunger that she intended to satisfy.

As he continued to rock into her, she continued to rock with him. He penetrated her with long, deep strokes. His mouth was busy at her breasts, sucking the nipples into his mouth, nipping them between his teeth. And then he did something below—she wasn't sure what—but he touched something inside of her that made her release a deep scream. He immediately silenced her by covering her mouth with his, still thrusting inside of her and gripping her hips tight. This was definitely wild.

She felt him. Hot molten liquid shot inside of her, and she let out another scream as she was thrown into another intense orgasm. She closed her eyes as the explosion took its toll.

"Wrap your legs around me now, baby."

She did so, and he began walking them toward the bed, where they collapsed together. He pulled her into his arms and gazed down at her. "I love you," he whispered softly.

She sucked in a deep breath and reached out to cup his jaw in her hand. "And I love you, too. I think I fell in love with you the moment you looked at me at the wedding reception."

He chuckled, pulling her closer. "Same here. Besides wanting you extremely badly, another reason I didn't want you to come to Texas with me was because I knew how much finding out about Clarice and Raphel meant to you. I didn't want to disappoint you."

"You could never disappoint me, but you will have to admit that we make a good team."

Rico leaned down and kissed her lips. "We most certainly do. I think it's time to take the Rico and Megan show on the road, don't you?"

She lifted a brow. "On the road?"

"Yes, make it permanent." When she still had a confused look on her face, he smiled and said, "You know. Marriage. That's what two people do when they discover they love each other, right?"

Joy spread through Megan, and she fought back her tears. "Yes."

"So is that a yes, that you will marry me?"

"Did you ask?"

He untangled their limbs to ease off the bed to get down on his knees. He reached out for her hand. "Megan Westmoreland, will you be my wife so I can have the right to love you forever?"

"Can we get wild anytime we want?"

"Yes, anytime we want."

"Then yes, Ricardo Claiborne, I will marry you."

"We can set a date later, but I intend to put an engagement ring on your finger before leaving Texas."

"Oh, Rico. I love you."

"And I love you, too. I'm not perfect, Megan, but I'll always try to be the man you need." He eased back in bed with a huge masculine smile on his face. "We're going to have a good life together. And one day I believe those other Westmorelands will be found. It's just so sad Fanny Banks has lived with that guilt for so many years."

"Yes, and she wasn't planning on telling us the truth until we confronted her again. Why was that?" Megan asked.

"Who knows? Maybe she was prepared to take her secret to the grave. I only regret Raphel never knew about his child. And there's still that fourth woman linked to his name. Isabelle Connors."

"Once I get back to Denver and tell the family everything, I'm sure someone will be interested in finding out about Isabelle as well as finding out what happened to Clarice and Raphel's child."

"You're anxious to find out as well, right?"

"Yes. But I've learned to let go. Finding out if there are any more Westmorelands is still important to me, but it isn't the most important thing in my life anymore. You are."

Megan sighed as she snuggled more deeply into Rico's arms. She had gotten the answers she sought, but there were more pieces to the puzzle that needed to be found. And eventually they would be. At the moment, she didn't have to be the one to find them. She felt cherished and loved.

But there were a couple of things she needed to discuss with Rico. "Rico?"

"Yes, baby?"

"Where will we live? Philly or Denver?"

He reached out and caressed the side of her face gently. "Wherever you want to live. My home, my life is with you. Modern technology makes it possible for me to work from practically anywhere."

She nodded, knowing her home and life was with him as well and she would go wherever he was. "And do you want children?"

He chuckled. "Most certainly. I intend to be a good father."

She smiled. "You'll be the best. There are good fathers and there are some who could do better... who should have done better. But they are fathers nonetheless."

She pulled back and looked up at him. "Like your father. At some point you're going to have to find it in your heart to forgive him, Rico."

"And why do you figure that?" She could tell from the tone of his voice and the expression on his face that he definitely didn't think so.

"Because," she said, leaning close and brushing a kiss across his lips. "Your father is the only grandfather our children will have."

"Not true. My mother has remarried, and he's a good man."

She could tell Rico wanted to be stubborn. "I'm sure he is, so in that case our children will have two grandfathers. And you know how important family is to me, and to you, as well. No matter what, Jeff Claiborne deserves a second chance. Will you promise me that you'll give him one?"

He held her gaze. "I'll think about it."

She knew when not to push. "Good. Because it would make me very happy. And although I've never met your dad, I believe he can't be all bad."

Rico lifted a brow. "How do you figure that?"

"Because you're from his seed, and you, Rico, are all good. I am honored to be the woman you want as your wife."

She could tell her words touched him, and he pulled her back down to him and kissed her deeply, thoroughly and passionately. "Megan Westmoreland Claiborne," Rico said huskily, finally releasing her lips. "I like the sound of that."

She smiled up at him. "I like the sound of that, as well."

Then she kissed him, deciding it was time to get wild again.

Two weeks later, New York

RICO LOOKED AROUND at the less than desirable apartment complex, knowing the only reason he was here was for closure. He might as well get it over with. The door was opened on the third knock and there stood the one man Rico had grown up loving and admiring—until he'd learned the truth.

He saw his father study Rico's features until recognition set in. Rico was glad his father recognized him because he wasn't sure if he would have recognized his father if he'd passed the old man in the street. It was obvious that drugs and alcohol had taken their toll. Jeff looked ten years older than what Rico knew his age to be. And the man who'd always taken pride in how he looked and dressed appeared as if he was all but homeless.

"Ricardo. It's been a while."

Instead of answering, Rico walked past his father to stand in the middle of the small, cramped apartment. When his father closed the door behind him, Rico decided to get to the point of his visit.

He shoved his hands into his pockets and said, "I'm getting married in a few months to a wonderful woman who believes family is important. She also believes everyone should have the ability to forgive and give others a second chance."

Rico paused a moment and then added, "I talked to Jessica and Savannah and we're willing to do that...to help you. But you have to be willing to help yourself. Together, we're prepared to get you into rehab and pay all the expenses to get you straightened out. But that's as far as our help will go. You have to be willing to get off the drugs and the alcohol. Are you?"

Jeff Claiborne dropped down in a chair that looked like it had seen better days and held his head in his hands. "I know I made a mess of things with you, Jessica and Savannah. And I know how much I hurt your mom...and when I think of what I drove Janice to do..." He drew in a deep breath. "I know what I did, and I know you don't believe me, but I loved them both—in different ways. And I lost them both."

Rico really didn't want to hear all of that, at least not now. He believed a man could and should love only one woman, anything else was just being greedy and without morals. "Are you willing to get help?"

"Are the three of you able to forgive me?"

Rico didn't say anything for a long moment and then said, "I can't speak for Jessica and Savannah, but with me it'll take time."

Jeff nodded. "Is it time you're willing to put in?"

Rico thought long and hard about his father's question. "Only if you're willing to move forward and get yourself straightened out. Calling your children and begging for money to feed your drug habit is unacceptable. Just so you know, Jess and Savannah are married to good men. Chase and Durango are protective of their wives and won't hesitate to kick your ass—father or no father—if you attempt to hurt my sisters."

"I just want to be a part of their lives. I have grandkids I haven't seen," Jeff mumbled.

"And you won't be seeing them if you don't get yourself together. So back to my earlier question, are you willing to go to rehab to get straightened out?"

Jeff Claiborne stood slowly. "Yes, I'm willing."

Rico nodded as he recalled the man his father had been once and the pitiful man he had become. "I'll be back in two days. Be packed and ready to go."

"All right, son."

Rico tried not to cringe when his father referred to him as "son," but the bottom line, which Megan had refused to let him deny, was that he was Jeff Claiborne's son.

Then the old man did something Rico didn't expect. He held his hand out. "I hope you'll be able to forgive me one day, Ricardo."

Rico paused a moment and then he took his father's hand, inhaling deeply. "I hope so, too."

EPILOGUE

"Beautiful lady, may I have this dance?"

"Of course, handsome sir."

Rico led Megan out to the dance floor and pulled her into his arms. It was their engagement party, and she was filled with so much happiness being surrounded by family and friends. It seemed no one was surprised when they returned from Texas and announced they were engaged. Rico had taken her to a jeweler in Austin to pick out her engagement ring, a three-carat solitaire.

They had decided on a June wedding and were looking forward to the day they would become man and wife. This was the first of several engagement parties for them. Another was planned in Philly and would be given by Rico's grandparents. Megan had met them a few weeks ago, and they had welcomed her to the family. They thought it was time their only grandson decided to settle down.

He pulled her closer and dropped his arms past her waist as their bodies moved in sensual sync with the music. Rico leaned in and hummed the words to the song in her ear. There was no doubt in either of

their minds that anyone seeing them could feel the
heat between them...and the love.

Rico tightened his arms around her and gazed
down at her. "Enjoying yourself?"

"Yes, what about you?"

He chuckled. "Yes." He glanced around. "There
are a lot of people here tonight."

"And they are here to celebrate the beginning of
our future." She looked over his shoulder and chuckled.

Rico lifted a brow. "What's so funny?"

"Riley. Earlier today, he and Canyon pulled straws
to see who would be in charge of Blue Ridge Man-
agement's fortieth anniversary Christmas party this
year, and I heard he got the short end and isn't happy
about it. We have close to a thousand employees at
the family's firm and making sure the holiday festivi-
ties are top-notch is important...and a lot of work. I
guess he figures doing the project will somehow in-
terfere with his playtime, if you know what I mean."

Rico laughed. "Yes, knowing Riley as I do, I have
a good idea what you mean."

The music stopped, and Rico took her hand and
led her out the French doors and onto the balcony. It
was the first week in November, and it had already
snowed twice. According to forecasters, it would be
snowing again this weekend.

They had made Denver their primary home. However, they planned to make periodic trips to Philly
to visit Rico's grandparents, mother and stepfather.
They would make occasional trips to New York as

well to check on Rico's father, who was still in rehab. Megan had met him and knew it would be a while before he recovered, but at least he was trying.

"You better have a good reason for bringing me out here," she said, shivering. "It's cold, and, as you can see, I'm not wearing much of anything."

He'd noticed. She had gorgeous legs and her dress showed them off. "I'll warm you."

He wrapped his arms around her, pulled her to him and kissed her deeply. He was right, he was warming her. Immediately, he had fired her blood. She melted a little with every stroke of his tongue, which stirred a hunger that could still astound her.

Rico slowly released her mouth and smiled down at her glistening lips. Megan was his key to happiness, and he intended to be hers. She was everything he could possibly want and then some. His goal in life was to make her happy. Always.

* * * * *

Don't miss Riley Westmoreland's story
ONE WINTER'S NIGHT
Available December 2012

Only from Harlequin Desire

YOU HAVE JUST READ A

HARLEQUIN®
Desire

BOOK

If you were taken by the strong,
powerful hero and are looking for the
ultimate destination for **provocative
and passionate romance,** be sure
to look for all six Harlequin® Desire
books every month.

REQUEST YOUR FREE BOOKS!

2 FREE NOVELS
FROM THE ROMANCE COLLECTION
PLUS 2 FREE GIFTS!

YES! Please send me 2 FREE novels from the Romance Collection and my 2 FREE gifts (gifts are worth about $10). After receiving them, if I don't wish to receive any more books, I can return the shipping statement marked "cancel." If I don't cancel, I will receive 4 brand-new novels every month and be billed just $5.99 per book in the U.S. or $6.49 per book in Canada. That's a saving of at least 25% off the cover price. It's quite a bargain! Shipping and handling is just 50¢ per book in the U.S. and 75¢ per book in Canada.* I understand that accepting the 2 free books and gifts places me under no obligation to buy anything. I can always return a shipment and cancel at any time. Even if I never buy another book, the two free books and gifts are mine to keep forever.

194/394 MDN FELQ

Name   (PLEASE PRINT)

Address   Apt. #

City   State/Prov.   Zip/Postal Code

Signature (if under 18, a parent or guardian must sign)

Mail to the **Reader Service:**
IN U.S.A.: P.O. Box 1867, Buffalo, NY 14240-1867
IN CANADA: P.O. Box 609, Fort Erie, Ontario L2A 5X3

Not valid for current subscribers to the Romance Collection
or the Romance/Suspense Collection.

Want to try two free books from another line?
Call 1-800-873-8635 or visit www.ReaderService.com.

* Terms and prices subject to change without notice. Prices do not include applicable taxes. Sales tax applicable in N.Y. Canadian residents will be charged applicable taxes. Offer not valid in Quebec. This offer is limited to one order per household. All orders subject to credit approval. Credit or debit balances in a customer's account(s) may be offset by any other outstanding balance owed by or to the customer. Please allow 4 to 6 weeks for delivery. Offer available while quantities last.

Your Privacy—The Reader Service is committed to protecting your privacy. Our Privacy Policy is available online at www.ReaderService.com or upon request from the Reader Service.

We make a portion of our mailing list available to reputable third parties that offer products we believe may interest you. If you prefer that we not exchange your name with third parties, or if you wish to clarify or modify your communication preferences, please visit us at www.ReaderService.com/consumerschoice or write to us at Reader Service Preference Service, P.O. Box 9062, Buffalo, NY 14269. Include your complete name and address.

Kick back and relax with a

HARLEQUIN®
Desire
book

Passion, wealth and drama make these books a must-have for those so-so days. The perfect combination when paired with a comfy chair and your favorite drink or on the subway with your morning coffee. Plunge into a world of **hot cowboys, sexy alpha-heroes,** secret pregnancies, family sagas and **passionate love stories.** Each book is sure to fulfill your fantasies and leave you wanting more.